Also by Robert Boswell

DANCING IN THE MOVIES
CROOKED HEARTS

The Geography of Desire

The Geography of Desire

ROBERT
BOSWELL

Alfred A. Knopf   New York

1989

This Is a Borzoi Book
Published by Alfred A. Knopf, Inc.

Copyright © 1989 by Robert Boswell

ISBN: 0-394-57690-X
LC number: 88-046181

The author wishes to thank the following for their assistance in the writing of this novel: the National Endowment
for the Arts, the Arizona Commission on the Arts, and
Northwestern University. Thanks also to friends and family who read the manuscript, and especially to Susan
Nelson, David Schweidel, Antonya Nelson,
Peter Turchi, and Julie Nelson.

Manufactured in the United States of America
FIRST EDITION

For Toni and Jade

The Geography of Desire

*T*HE SENSUAL paradise and the erotic paradise are two separate places. They are not on the same map.

Leon Green walked barefoot and two thousand miles from home along the shore of the opaque Pacific. The cuffs of his white pants were rolled to mid-calf, but the waves that rushed up the beach failed by inches to reach him. In his right hand, he carried a bottle of tequila, and with his left, he laced fingers with Pilar Rios. Her tan skirt, blown by the wind, flapped between her legs, shortening her stride. She walked ankle deep in dark water and white foam. Beyond her, in the ocean to his knees, Leon's best friend, Ramon Matamoros, waded along, keeping up with them, hands in the pockets of his brown fishing jeans—his lucky pants—which were soaked.

Pilar was speaking. "There are a hundred ways to lose the things you love." She gathered her hair, black and long, which had begun to blow in her face. A receding wave eroded the sand beneath her feet, tickling her soles. "Women lose children to adolescence. Wives lose husbands to death. Have you ever noticed how many widows there are and how few widowers?"

"I suppose," Leon said, "but I'd rather not think about it tonight. I'd prefer to get drunk." The night air, heavy with spray, pressed against his face, and he inhaled deeply, closing his eyes. He was a handsome man with blond hair and spectacular green eyes. In his face were both intelligence and a curious sort of indifference, as if the former had never proved all that useful and so he approached the world each new day as if it had been invented the night before. "Why don't we get drunk," he said, "and I'll tell you how lovely you are. I'll start with something obscure, the heels of your feet or your gums. You have the most beautiful gums." He grinned at her and drank from the bottle. Tequila lit his throat, which was what he liked about it—the sensation of being lighted from within, like a phone booth or one of the little diners he had loved when he'd lived in the States.

"She has a point." Ramon had to yell to be heard over the waves. "There have always been more women than men in La Boca. The women hardly ever die."

Pilar released her hair to take the bottle from Leon, then drank from it, the dark strands slapping her cheeks. "We have to talk about something," she told him. "The night is too dreary to do without talk."

Leon did not let on that he found it almost inconceivable to think of this night as dreary. He conceded that not everyone who imagines paradise thinks of a beach at night, the sounds of waves as they topple, a sky lit by a brilliant moon but obscured by a sea of clouds.

"Have I ever praised your voice?" he asked her, teasing once more. "What a beautiful voice you have."

Smiling, Pilar punched him in the arm, then she took his hand again, and they continued walking.

A crooked line of foam lay in front of them, glowing in the moonlight, floating on invisible water, its movement arbitrary and lifelike. Ramon thought it resembled an enormous eel, its pale and luminescent belly rocked by the tide. Pilar saw it as a long wavering lip forming impossible words against the shore. It made Leon think of the crooked turns his life had taken, but he quickly abandoned the thought. He disliked things that reminded him of the past or spoke of the future. It was the present that interested him—this walk along a moon-whitened strand that curved like an open mouth, the pink and white houses that lined the cobblestone boulevard above the shore, the scatter of trees—papayas and palms, a stray palo santo, a dying mangrove—that cast night shadows across the sand, and the silhouette of the jungle in the distance, rising darkly in the night sky.

There were also things in the landscape that he could not see. From their first steps on the beach, they had been secretly observed by two people. A young woman shut off the light in her room as soon as she spotted them, then watched from the darkened window, leaning across the sill to keep them in view. She could hear only an occasional word of their conversation, but she wore a look of complete concentration, as if studying their movements for a hidden meaning that would change her life. The other, a young man, spied on them from the ocean, treading water until he found a familiar rock on which to rest his feet. He could hear nothing but the waves and seemed nervously excited, unable to be still, looking for lighted windows, turning to gaze over the expanse of black water, singing to himself while the swells rocked him.

"The last woman who died here was my great-grandmother, nine years ago." Ramon crossed himself as he spoke. "She woke up one morning barking like a dog and by evening she was dead."

"Coughing," Leon said. "All of your stories have nonsense in them. She woke up coughing."

"It wasn't a cough. It was a bark," Ramon told him. "You weren't there."

Leon coughed loudly from deep within his throat. "Aagh, aagh. She coughed and some superstitious member of your family, probably you, decided she was barking."

"It was not that kind of a bark. She didn't sound like aagh, aagh at all."

"You two have the stupidest conversations," Pilar said.

"Errep," Ramon said. "Errep. Like that. It sounds nothing

like a cough. Barking has always been done with some delicacy in my family. I know in the United States people bark and cough and hack and gag like it was all the same thing. We make finer distinctions here."

"Pass the bottle," Leon said. "Have you ever noticed this aspect of his storytelling?" He spoke to Pilar, but loudly enough for Ramon to hear. "He hogs the liquor while he talks."

Ramon drank, then handed Pilar the tequila. "Since you demand additional proof, listen to this: She spent the entire day on her hands and knees. And—you can't repeat this—she wet the floor. Don't tell me she was coughing while she did it. She barked from sunup until the minute she died."

Leon let out a short laugh, almost a bark itself, and shook his head. Because explosive sounds carry better than speech, the woman spying from the window had heard the men barking but none of the conversation. The barks had taken on a quality of mystery. She thought they might be speaking in a secret language. She was a woman who believed in secrets.

Pilar had a funny look on her face and she spoke to Ramon. "I heard that story when I was a little girl. That couldn't have happened just nine years ago."

Ramon stepped closer to her so he would not have to yell. "It happens to all the women in my family. The day they die they behave like dogs. You probably heard about my great-great-grandmother. She had a little Chihuahua bark: reff, reff." A wave spanked his legs, and he paused to steady himself. "I don't remember you here as a child, or any Rios children. I can't understand that. I have a good memory."

"We left La Boca when I was young," Pilar told him.

Ramon pointed past her. "What *he* doesn't understand is what it's like to grow up where yesterday isn't the only day people remember—if they remember that. In California people think life is a movie: they just watch it and wait for the good parts."

"May I remind you that you've never been there?" Leon said.

"I've seen movies of California—little cars that hold two people and big yards with pink driveways. Not a place to live. But what's important is I know La Boca like you know that bottle of tequila. Most of the people in the world don't know La Boca exists. Even the people in my own country—many of them aren't sure. Me? I know."

Ramon felt the powerful urge to tell one of his stories. The sensation began in the pit of his stomach and bubbled up into his chest, a lightness that demanded his attention. He was confident that even Leon would like this one. For his part, Leon could tell a story was coming and drank to fortify himself.

"For years," Ramon said, his voice rising, the tone changing slightly, "the village of La Boca existed on the edge of the country as a dream exists in the mind of one just wakened: It was there and it was not there." He turned his hand palm up, then down. "Mapmakers included it or discounted it according to whim, superstition, or political expediency. Mail to La Boca became synonymous with Dead Letters, sometimes for as long as a year, and included, when it finally arrived, postcards to Napoleon Bonaparte and crayoned notes to Santa Claus. Priests failed to mention La Boca in their prayers. Merchants forgot to fill its orders. Teachers flunked students who wrote papers about it . . ."

"I concede," Leon told him. "Whatever we're arguing, you win."

"Centuries ago," Ramon said, "the great conquistador Esteban Matamoros led a party through the jungle to take La Boca for his king. He never returned. Legends were born—that the Indians were fiercer than any other on earth, that it was populated by women so beautiful no one would leave, that it was nothing more than an open mouth that swallowed anyone who came near." Ramon gestured with his arms in a circle over his head. "The truth"—he lowered his arms and shrugged—"pathetic under the weight of legend, was that Esteban, as much a poet as a conqueror, could never muster the energy to fight his way back through the jungle, and so he settled among the peaceful villagers who admired his clothing."

Pilar laughed, but Leon only smiled and reached for the tequila, which had settled once more in Ramon's hand. "You see?" he said, extending his arm.

Ramon looked straight ahead and pointed with the bottle. "During the nineteen-thirties La Boca had its greatest moment of national influence. General Arguello claimed one hundred thousand votes from the village, enough to win the presidency. By the time the election commission worried through the jungle to the Pacific shore, counted the few hundred men of voting age—none of whom had voted or knew the names of the candidates or the form of their government—and struggled back to the capital, the opposition party had disintegrated because of a number of unrelated suicides, and the report was never filed, causing much of the country to conclude that La Boca was a figment of political imagination."

"The bottle?" Leon said.

Ramon, startled to find it still in his hand, drank and turned to Pilar. "What was I saying?"

"I think you were trying to decide whether La Boca exists." She snatched the tequila.

"Ah," he said. "Yes. The controversy will now be laid to rest." He threw open his arms. "La Boca, with its back to the immense jungle and its face to the enormous ocean, exists where the two great bodies fail to meet, like an ellipse of darkness between sleeping lovers." He stared now at Leon. "It is an ugly little village, I will acknowledge that, crowded onto a spit of stone and sand, a tiny wart of civilization, but as real as tequila, as real as a speck of blood under a fingernail." He displayed a fingernail to provide an example. "As real as—"

"Loss," Pilar said.

"No." Ramon waved his hand. "That's not it. As real as the room where you plant your head on a feather pillow and produce the dreams of sleep."

Pilar applauded, her hair lashing her face again. "I didn't know you were political," she said.

"I'm not," Ramon told her. "Why do you say that?"

"That story," she said. "All the politics—that Fascist general falsifying the election, the politicians who recognized La Boca only when it was to their advantage, Spanish imperialism, that poke you took at the inept conquistador."

"I am a direct descendant of Esteban Matamoros," Ramon told her. "He was a great man."

"You're kidding." She turned to Leon. "He's kidding, right?"

"Have I ever told you how the whites of your eyes excite me?" Leon touched her nose. "And there's the shape of your nostrils. What erotic ovals. Look at these nostrils, Ramon."

"Yes." Ramon ducked his head under her chin. "Lovely. My great-great-grandmother had nostrils like those."

"She of the Chihuahua bark?" Leon asked.

"Yes, she had the most beautiful nostrils in all of La Boca. She, by the way, remembered Esteban Matamoros from when she was a little girl. He was a poet, a philosopher, and a stylish dresser."

"She remembered the conquistador and you remember her?" Leon asked him. "She'd have had to be four-hundred years old."

"That's not exactly what I said."

"I can't believe the way you two act together," Pilar said.

"History is passed from one generation to the next." Ramon opened one hand, then the other. "I am a part of that history because I've heard it all my life, I've seen it all my life, and I've told it all my life."

"You were boring people from the crib?"

"Men in my family have always talked early. My grandfather said 'sugar' the day he was born."

"Oh, he did not. Talk to him, will you?" Leon took Pilar by the elbow and turned her to face Ramon.

She, however, spun back and spoke in Leon's ear. "He's putting you on."

"Is that what you think?" Leon laughed bitterly. "Ramon, are you joking with us?"

Ramon shook his head. "No, it's true. He said 'sugar' his first day on the planet. My own father spoke when he was two weeks old. If you'll send the tequila this way, I'll tell you about it."

"No," Leon said.

"Very well." Ramon crossed his big arms. "I'll tell you anyway."

"What about the conquistador?" Pilar asked him. "Did he say 'genocide' the day he was born? Or 'pillage,' perhaps?"

"No." Ramon shook his head seriously. "He did not speak until he was nearly three, and then began with complete sentences. The tradition did not begin until the first birth here, in La Boca."

"Let's don't start with politics," Leon pleaded. "No history, no stories, no politics. Let's talk about this walk we're taking— not that we're making much progress with all this chatter, but let's try. I'll start. There, the moon. Doesn't it look dramatic?"

The moon, partially obscured by dark clouds, had corners— a rhombus of white light. They all stared so intently that the young man in the ocean shifted his feet on the submerged rock and looked up also, but he was in such a state of agitated anticipation that he could not imagine why they were staring.

"It looks so odd," Pilar said. "It's lovely."

Leon slipped his arm around her waist. "It's like the whites of your eyes," he said softly. They were nearing the Hotel Esperanza, which Leon managed and which had been their starting point. He was tiring and hoped Pilar was ready for bed.

"Light from the sky is an opening in the membrane that separates us from God." Ramon turned to the embracing couple. "That sentence was little Esteban Matamoros's first words. Can you believe it? And he not yet three years old. Hardly the first utterance of an inept man."

Leon lifted Pilar, a little unsteadily, into his arms. "Please continue with that story," he said to Ramon and began staggering up the beach.

Pilar giggled. "Put me down," she told him, but she didn't insist.

Leon, however, was too drunk, and they fell in the sand. "How can such a thin woman weigh so much?"

She pinched him on the shoulder. "Ramon," she called. "Your friend is mistreating me."

Ramon waved to her, staring at the sky still, in the ocean to his navel, moonlight casting his shadow over the water.

"He can't hear you out there," Leon told her.

"Maybe we should go for a swim," she said. "Do you think Ramon would mind if we took off our clothes and jumped in the water?"

Leon shook his head. "No, but there's the danger that it might stimulate a story."

"That sounds sexual."

"Yes, but even his sex stories are boring."

Ramon approached now, his pants clinging to his legs, dripping onto the beach. He stopped just before reaching them and scowled. "There didn't use to be all this noise!" He flapped his hands in the air as if to make noise visible. The gesture was too vigorous, and he tipped over, falling to his butt beside Pillar. "The summers in La Boca used to be free of the electric hum of cicadas."

"I can't hear the cicadas," Pilar told him. "We're too near the water."

"Back then, the air was as calm as arctic air. Oh, yes, next to the water was the applause of the ocean, and in the jungle there was the screeching and gumping of monkeys, but in the heart of the village, silence reigned." Ramon smiled, fell backward into the sand, and stared straight up, as if speaking to the clouds.

"When the rattle of the cicada was first heard in La Boca,

Jorge Matamoros, my great-great-grandfather, claimed the insects were living dice, and when they died the translucent wings would contract over their bodies forcing them into perfect cubes. For months, Jorge led groups of men and children to search the bark of trees for dice. Of course, they found only the hollow shells of the molting insects. Jorge, although a man of vision, was a fool, a man who would die under a wooden yoke he had bought for his ox, and the resemblance of the cicada's hum to the rattling of dice was more in his head than in his ears. But his legacy lives on: Ninety years later in La Boca the cicada's drone is still called gambling.''

When Ramon paused, the sound of the ocean rushed in and a delicate spray landed on their faces. A breeze from the south brought the odors of baked sugar and flour from the bakery. Pilar placed her hand on Leon's arm. He lay next to her with his fingers laced across his belly and his feet pointing out, but he shifted at her touch, his body turning toward her of its own accord. On her other side, Ramon sprawled in the sand. He raised his head in order to speak once again, but she reached over and touched his elbow with her free hand, which stopped him. He, too, turned at her touch.

The breeze abruptly shifted and lifted her skirt. It billowed in front of them, as if suddenly alive, then folded back, the wet hem slapping her pelvis. The wind against her bare legs was sexual and delicious, and Pilar believed she could feel an electric charge run through her arms. With a hand on each of the men, she raised her legs, lifting them as high as she could. Drops of seawater trickled down her ankles and across her calves to her thighs, where they evaporated.

For a moment, it seemed that even the sea was silent.

"There," Ramon said. "Do you hear the cicadas now?"

Pilar's legs flopped to the sand.

"The whole village used to be as quiet as the sun." Ramon sat up, looking past Pilar to Leon. "There was a thicket separating the town from the jungle, so dense nothing could pass through it, not even sound. A man from your country, a ragged bum, his skin flaking like powdered sugar, brought the cicadas to La Boca. He died on this very beach. The pockets of his coat were crusted with eggs." When he stopped speaking the buzz of the cicadas was finally audible, a new party in the conversation. "They should have burned his clothes on the spot. But they didn't. And not long afterward began the gambling."

Leon laughed and said, "That is the stupidest story I've ever heard—not one of the stupidest, but the very stupidest. Am I supposed to apologize for all of America? An old man with insect eggs—how is that an explanation?"

"It is an explanation." Ramon slapped the sand beside him for emphasis, falling to his elbow. "It's always a mystery that explains a mystery."

"You're both idiots," Pilar said, sitting up and covering her legs.

At this, Leon began laughing. He had an easy laugh, so melodic and pleasing that Ramon and then Pilar reluctantly joined him. The three of them laughed until the laughter grew a life of its own, shaking them and arching their backs. They laughed until they exhausted their lungs.

And even while they lay silent in the sand catching their breaths, one head craned from the dark window to observe them, while the solitary swimmer, almost out of patience, dipped his face in the black water and ran his fingers through his hair.

LEON WOKE in the white rectangular room in which he lived. He stared at the blank walls in a quiet panic until sleepiness fell away, and he could recall the town where he resided, the name of the hotel he managed, the face of the woman who lay next to him. Awareness came in only a few seconds, but they were the most frightening moments of his daily life. Fear of dislocation woke with him each morning and passed over his bed like the shadow of a bird.

Pilar sat beside him, knees raised, sheet gathered at her waist, a book held with both hands in the crease between her legs. Beyond her, past the open French doors, lay a sky the hazel color of morning. Cicadas whined, and waves, as if in response, whispered, "Shh, shh, shh."

Pilar was an early riser and she read constantly—the great novelists, Marxist writings, underground poets. Leon often found himself erotically attracted to Communists. He liked their seriousness. Plus, they were the best kissers he'd ever known, and any slight variation in bed surprised and delighted them, which made them enthusiastic lovers. His first wife had been a leftist from El Paso, a tall and moody woman who had once told him that even loneliness was the result of rampant capitalism.

"We've been brainwashed to shop whenever we're depressed," she had said, sorting through the colorful department-store boxes that covered their couch. "Then the material possessions fail to make us really happy."

"Shopping letdown," Leon said.

"Exactly. Which leads to further alienation from the self and results in loneliness and even greater depression. Which, in turn, leads to more shopping. You like these?" She'd raised earrings to her lobes. Tiny red peace symbols.

Pilar had been a professor at the national university until the government ordered a purge of socialists, Marxists, and other troublemakers. Unable to teach, vulnerable to disappearance, she returned to La Boca, her childhood home, and opened an unprofitable bookstore. At thirty-four, she was two years older than Leon.

He propped himself on his elbow to look at the book's title. Pilar folded the cover back at just that instant. A trace of a smile skimmed her lips. Her face was heart-shaped, like the leaves of the moonflower vine that clung to the hotel's walls.

"What are you reading?" he asked her.

She lowered the book. "You snore like a mule," she said.

He smiled. "Whenever I wake, you're always up, even if it's the middle of the night. I'm beginning to think you never sleep."

"I had a funny dream last night." She dropped her book and allowed him to pull her close. "There was a tree, not a jungle tree, but one like you see in the north, an oak or a maple. At the point where the trunk branched out into limbs, there was a fire, and you and I were cooking eggs over it."

"What were we doing in the tree?"

"We weren't in the tree—that's another thing. We had long poles with strings at the end. The eggs were out of their shells, but somehow they were tied to the strings. We were like fishermen with our poles, dangling the eggs over the fire in the tree. The eggs cooked into perfect globes, which meant they were done. Then the strings burned and the globes floated down to us."

"Strange," he said. When he tried to kiss her, she pulled away.

"Tell me your dreams."

Leon looked again at the white walls, the striped pillows on the two wood-and-lattice chairs, the cheap dresser encumbered with books and dirty clothes. A trail of sand curved like an eyebrow across the cracked tile floor.

"I don't dream," he said.

She placed her palm over his face and pushed his head into the pillow. "I don't sleep with men who don't dream."

He waited until the hand lifted. "Yes, you do," he said.

"I think you don't dream because you drink so much." She rested a leg alongside his and placed her head on his shoulder.

Leon ran his hand past the small of her back, over her bottom, to her thighs. "Dreams are so much fluff," he said. "I like to have things more concrete."

"What's more real than dreams?"

He grabbed her ass. "This," he said.

"Yes, all right." She pushed his hand away as she crawled on top of him. "A hammer is real, but so are dreams."

He laughed, then put his hands over her breasts. "Perfect globes," he said and she smiled.

Because Pilar was a persecuted Marxist, Leon had expected their sex to be good, which it rarely was. The mechanics of the act were fine, but sex created a peculiar distance between them, as if by entering her, he was sending her away. To keep her near, he kissed her passionately, then bit her earlobe.

Pilar felt differently about their lovemaking. She believed Leon failed to give himself up to the act, that he thought too much. It was as if he wanted her to think of nothing but him and his movement through her, but he also seemed to be thinking of nothing but him and his movement through her. And so her face became a mask—a soft one, but a mask nonetheless.

Once, while making love on the beach in front of the hotel, she had stared at him with an intensity that had frightened and then excited him—ultimately exciting him too much, bringing things to an early close. Another night, floating in Ramon's boat in the north estuary, they had made love slowly so as not to tip over, and both of them had responded to the rocking in the still water, the barking of the monkeys in the trees, the moonlight splintering through the palms. Leon had felt them lift together, momentarily, out of the boat and into the night air, a foot above the water—a thing he knew to be impossible. Pilar, on the other hand, had felt them fuse together, become the same person, a moment of communication that transcended sex.

More often, though, he believed she was fantasizing about another place or another man, and she believed he was thinking about his own locomotion. He wanted all of her, not just her body, or even her passion—what he wanted from her was like his waking dream of dislocation, a sort of possession, both momentary and overwhelming. And she wanted him to give up his wanting and let the moment take hold.

Their sex was seldom good, but the night on the beach, the night in the boat, and the possibilities they raised were enough for Leon to know he would never willingly give her up. As for Pilar, she had grown very fond of him, and, besides, he was the only man in the village who would make love with a Communist. Sex, after all, had long been proven a political act.

When they were through, she sat on the edge of the bed and lifted her hands high, stretching, rolling her head against her shoulders. With her arms extended and her head thrown back, she looked like a prophet hearing the voice of God for the first time—or so Leon imagined.

He closed his eyes and was assaulted immediately by memory, the unwanted companion he could not shake. He saw his second wife, Charla, in the kitchen of their little apartment, glaring at him, although it was she who had just dropped something: ice. Little cubes were strewn across the floor, a spray that ended at his feet. He spoke to her, but Leon in bed in a hotel in Central America could not make out what Leon in the kitchen of an apartment in California said. Charla's right hand was over her heart, as if she were about to pledge allegiance. There were people talking in the next room, raising their voices to be heard over a rattling noise, an enormous grating. He knelt to gather the ice.

Then there were hands at his body.

"Leon. Wake up." Pilar stood over him, shaking his arm. Her breasts swung like apples from a branch. "There's a bird in the tub. I don't like it. Please."

He sat up. "What is it?"

"Birds inside frighten me."

A finch hopped along the white rim of the tub. One wing flapped; the other remained pressed against its side. The bird bounced against the white tile wall twice before Leon trapped it in his cupped hands. Pilar followed him onto the balcony. They stepped naked to the black wrought-iron railing, and Leon heaved the bird aloft. The finch spiraled down to the beach, one wing extended.

Pilar ran back inside and to the bathroom door. "I have to hurry," she said, her back to him, a hand over her face. He could tell that she was crying.

Below, the bird opened the one wing, flapping, then hopping in the sand. The sight disturbed Leon's sense of fair play. Birds had nothing going for them if they were denied flight. He felt the same about stupid people. What advantages did humans have except intelligence? Their bodies were soft and vulnerable to the elements. They didn't run that fast or swim that well, and they certainly couldn't fly. They were prone to a vague and constant discontent that they'd manufactured thousands of words to describe, but that Leon thought of simply as loneliness. Charla had said that it was inescapable, that it lived in the last layer of skin, the layer that was always dying. He had teased her about her theory of epidermal loneliness, but at times it made as much sense to him as anything.

He picked up Pilar's book from the floor as the shower began with a thudding of pipes, then the sizzling of falling water. The book, written by a man imprisoned by Mussolini, told how he led an anti-Fascist movement from his cell, smuggling out instructions. Leon let the book drop. History didn't interest him, even his personal history, which he declined to discuss. He couldn't, however, help thinking about it. When he'd been a college student he'd found that everything he knew about himself was defined in the negative—he knew what he didn't want, whom he didn't want to emulate, what failed to make him happy. Most of his friends had felt the same, and they had consoled one another in dark bars and brightly lit diners, the dingy nightclubs and identical motels that cluttered the California coast. Only after his second marriage failed did he understand that he would have to separate himself from the mass of others to find happiness, to escape loneliness, to discover the true shape of his desire. Which was what he'd done in coming to La Boca.

The water pipes rattled again and the shower stopped. Leon removed a pair of pants from his dresser and pulled them on before Pilar stepped into the room, white hotel towels wrapped around her body and hair. She kissed him lightly on the lips and let the towel around her body fall. Whatever sadness the damaged bird had caused was gone.

"You need a mirror," Pilar said, staring at the wall over the dresser as if she could see her reflection. She was dressing quickly, and Leon became fascinated and then aroused by her movements—the way she stepped into her skirt and pulled it up her legs, then brushed away wrinkles with her flattened hand, how she fastened her bra, both hands behind her back, the angles of her elbows giving her wings. He laughed aloud at himself and his erection.

Pilar kissed his cheek, patted the bulge in his pants, and walked around the bed to pick up her book. "Come by the store," she said, heading now to the door. "Tomorrow, or the day after." She waited for him to nod. "I have to hurry." She was already in the hall.

She didn't like to be seen leaving the hotel in the mornings, believing that discretion was important, especially in a place the size of La Boca. People didn't care so much what you did as how you went about doing it. Leon, disappointed that she had left so quickly, decided to watch her walk home.

He climbed the little-used steps to the third floor of the Hotel Esperanza. None of the rooms on this level were habitable, damaged years ago by an earthquake and never repaired. He threw back the bolt to the door that cut off the ruined level from the rest of the building. Glass and plaster littered the floor. Cracks in the walls crossed and intersected like highways on a road map. During the rainy season, the windows were boarded up, but Leon let the floor air in the summer to prevent heat from accumulating, which would make the hotel impossible to cool. Cicadas buzzed loudly, and it occurred to him that the crackle of cicadas must have caused Pilar to dream of fire in trees.

He dusted off a stool he'd taken from the hotel's small bar. The view from his room was only of the ocean, so he often came to the abandoned floor to drink beer and look out over the village. A moonflower vine covered the window ledge with heart-shaped leaves.

All of La Boca was visible from the window. The two principal buildings, the hotel and the cathedral, were at opposite ends of the village, north and south, each bordering an estuary. A cobblestone street, which curved like a sickle to follow the contour of the shore, connected the two. Groceries, bakeries, restaurants, stores, and a few of the finest houses lined the road. No other street was paved, and at the edge of the village there were no streets at all, just groups of mud huts, unevenly spaced, with conical palm-thatched roofs. A dense thicket bordered the south estuary, thinning as it curved north. The jungle began where the thicket left off, surrounding the village like cupped hands.

Pilar appeared below, a rhythmic sway in her walk. Leon placed his hands on the window ledge and leaned against them, crushing the leaves. As she strode, Pilar's shoulders rocked slightly like the loosened board of an old signpost. For a moment, as Leon studied her, his hands throbbed as if the bird were still trapped within them.

BETWEEN THE decaying hotel and the ancient white bakery stretched a clothesline with several brightly colored skirts. Sea gulls also rested on the line and along the roof of the bakery.

Pilar hurried across the street. A spotted brown dog who had been sleeping in the shade of the hotel loped behind her, nails clicking against the cobblestones. "Shoo," she said and clapped her hands.

As if they had been waiting for the cue, the gulls lifted noisily into the air, swirling above the buildings. The dog, too, responded, pulling up sharply, looking along with Pilar at the birds. Next to the bakery, in an empty window on the top floor of the hotel, Leon leaned out, hands invisible in the vines, and stared at her. The sun, as it rose, shone directly on him, turning his skin golden. He was motionless and, though Pilar stared back at him, he did nothing to acknowledge her.

She began walking once more, annoyed that she was being watched but fascinated by the golden image. She resisted a desire to turn and stare at him again, until she thought of Lot's wife, and that obliged her to look, to defy a god in whom she did not believe.

Leon was still in the window and now he smiled and waved, but the sun had already risen above him, and he was, once again, an ordinary man, his figure made puny by the size of the dark window and the expanse of the white building. Even the vines, which spread from their trunks like a network of veins across the stucco walls, were larger and more significant.

In the short distance she'd traveled, the houses had declined in size and substance: red tile roofs replaced by corrugated tin, windows covered with burlap instead of glass. Hens nailed the brown earth with their beaks, flexing their wings at intervals, scattering as she approached. She turned south and the road evaporated. A path wound through adobe buildings, identical one-room huts with imbricate palm roofs. Ramon's house was the exception, stupidly large, almost entirely without windows, a ridiculous brick house.

Eventually she came to an undistinguished hut and pushed aside the cloth curtain that covered the doorway. Across the small room from her, Maria Peralta Cardenas, her grandmother, stood with her hands raised, palms out, as if she were being robbed. The hem of her red polyester dress rose two inches above her slip. "Pilar," she said, then bent down to touch her toes, although the tips of her fingers barely reached past her large fleshy knees. "Fifty," she announced and straightened, flapping her hands against her dress.

"Fifty?" Pilar said brightly. "And you're not even sweating."

Maria lifted one shoulder and tilted her head toward it. "Some mornings I do a hundred."

"You're a faker," Pilar said and laughed.

Maria, who had mastered the ability to impersonate her own feelings, cast a look of hurt that would have convinced anyone else, but Pilar knew her too well and continued laughing. Maria countered by narrowing her eyes and pursing her lips, but she quickly realized Pilar was not to be fooled, and so she smiled. "How is your North American boy?"

Pilar kissed her grandmother and sat on the unmade single bed, which still smelled of sleep. "He says he doesn't dream."

"Maybe he cast a spell on you. People who don't dream often have that power. I always look for him when I go to the bakery. Does he have a scar right here?" She traced her finger from the top of her forehead to the base of her chin.

"No, he's very pretty."

"If I could see his hands I would know whether he's worth your time." She made fists and positioned them against her hips. "Do you like what I've done with the room?"

The room, the sole one in the hut, looked no different to Pilar. Shelves, none any deeper than two inches, lined the walls from floor to ceiling, most of them crooked and all of them populated by a strange array of knickknacks—little colored jars, tiny stick dolls, peculiar jewelry, toy automobiles, plastic snakes, tins of gray powder. Her grandmother had once made her living predicting the future, and Pilar knew that many of the items were props she had used, but they were such odd props—scraps of fabric, surprises from Cracker Jacks, chips of broken glass, tabs from beer cans—silly and inconsequential things.

"I can't see that you've changed anything," Pilar told her.

Maria walked to the bed and sat beside her. "The pillow used to be at this end," she said. "I moved it up there." She pointed to the other end of the bed and the crumpled feather pillow. "Now, when I lie down, the room is completely turned around. It's like getting a new house."

Pilar laughed again. "I'll have to try it."

"The problem with North American men is that they are simple." Maria pointed to her temple. "You know? Not smart. And they stick their heads out in front of them when they walk."

"They don't do that."

"And they waddle." Maria stood and waddled across the room, her head leading her feet. "If I were you, I'd get a good dog or maybe a European. I've heard Frenchmen are very clever. The English are loyal. How is this boy with sex? I hear in the United States sex is timed so they can have something to do between television programs. They plug in, then pull out just in time to catch the opening of the next show."

"He's a good lover," Pilar said, fluffing the solitary pillow.

"You're lying, but that's a good sign, lying to protect the dignity of your lover, but it's a bad sign that you can't tell your own grandmother the truth, and, you know, I am still the only person in La Boca who owns a television." She walked to an old black-and-white Magnavox.

"You can't get any stations here," Pilar reminded her.

"Yes, but people still come to look at it." She turned the switch several times but nothing happened. "The electricity in this house comes and goes like a foolish man. Why do I bother? Did I tell you Angelica and I have a plan?"

"Let me guess," Pilar said. "You're going to start a burlesque show. She'll sing and you'll strip." Angelica Roches, Maria's oldest friend, ran the bakery with her daughter.

"No, not that. She's going to spread flour over her counter whenever she sees your boy leave the hotel. So when he comes in the bakery he'll put his hands in the flour and I'll be able to read his palm by studying the prints he leaves."

"You embarrass me," Pilar told her. "Why is this so important to you?"

"It's a good plan, or it would be if this boy weren't so lazy. Angelica's daughter has to deliver his orders, even though he's just next door. I think he has cast a spell on you." She crossed her arms as if thinking. "He admitted he never dreams? Right out in the open? Does he ever smell peculiar? Sniff him for me. Especially here." She put her finger to her wrinkled neck, just below her jaw. "If he smells like metal, leave him. If he smells like steam, marry him. If he smells like sweat, wash him." She laughed at her joke. "You didn't think that was funny?"

"Let me tell you my dream." Pilar described the fire in the tree, she and Leon like fishermen, the perfect globes floating down to them.

Maria listened, nodding and turning her head. "It's a good dream and not so good, too. You like seeing this boy and you may love him, but the fire, that's your passion, and it's up a tree. That's not so good. How about the local boys? They carry their fire in their pockets." She reached to one of the counters and removed a package of cigarettes. "All this talk of fire has made me want a smoke. You? They're American."

Pilar shook her head and stood. "I have to get to the store."

Maria sucked heavily on the cigarette, an unfiltered Camel. "Isn't today a holiday?" She coughed, leaning forward and smacking her chest with her palm, then she took another long drag and exhaled. "You open the store on holidays?"

"What holiday is it today? It's the middle of July." Pilar waited at the door for an answer.

"Perhaps it's not a holiday, but let me tell you this." She pointed the glowing Camel at her granddaughter. "There are no men in heaven. None. A couple, your grandfather and St. Augustine, came very close, but none have entered. Heaven is full of women, and this earth is crawling with lizards."

Pilar smiled and stepped through the curtain.

The sun, for a moment, made her blind. Sweat grew from her forehead and along her arms. She stepped carefully over a pile left by a mule, noticing the rim of water stain around the bottom of her skirt. Her life confused her.

A barefoot man in a straw hat waited between houses for her to pass. He was pushing a wooden wheelbarrow, and the space was too narrow for them both. She hurried ahead, nodding to him. He kept his eyes turned down, a man of fifty, she guessed, deep lines in his face, his feet as wide as books. As soon as she was out of the way, he stepped to the pile of mule dung and lifted it with his hands into the wheelbarrow. It had not dried, and the sickly sweet odor rose with it. He wiped his fingers on his pant-legs and continued on. The dung, she knew, would earn him a few cents.

It was this that made her remember, although she couldn't say exactly why, a sunny day years ago when she had been a college student. There had been a protest on campus in opposi-tion to military aid from the United States. She had painted a banner and dragged her boyfriend along. He was studying to be a chemist and failing. At twenty, he already had a tiny bald spot and had grown a patchy beard as if to make up for it. She had loved him for his sweetness, but knew, even then, that she would not marry him.

When soldiers fired into the crowd, her boyfriend did a brave and stupid thing. He lifted one of the wounded protesters and dragged her into the Humanities Building, where the student, a girl who had been studying drama, died in his arms. He had not done this to be heroic, only because it was part of his nature to act correctly. Soldiers arrested him and questioned him for three days, breaking two of his fingers and damaging his kidneys.

Pilar nursed him and, in a rush of guilt and envy, promised to marry him. They set the date a few months ahead to give him time to heal. Her anger at the government had been multiplied by his injuries, and she couldn't understand why he didn't feel the same. "I'm interested in smaller things," he told her. She thought this was a reference to chemistry, to molecules and their mixing. Later, she wished she had asked him to explain.

They never married. He found he could no longer make love with her. She suggested a doctor, but he went instead to a pros-titute, to prove what he already suspected. He could make love, but not to Pilar. She accused him of cowardice. When he didn't respond, she taunted him about his failed academic career, his reactionary stances, his growing baldness. Finally, he leaped at her and pushed her to the floor, where he twisted her arms behind her back, then forced open her mouth, and, with his fingers, pried loose one of her teeth. By the time he held it in his palm, she was screaming. Blood ran down his hand and across her cheek.

"Now you have what you want," he told her. "You've made me into the person you desire, and you, you've paid your dues."

The memory was her most excruciating, worse than any with her parents, more painful even than her flight from the university to La Boca when she heard that her name appeared on the government's list. She ran her tongue over her teeth, the bridge, remembering now that Leon had said she had lovely gums. How could she possibly be sleeping with an American?

When she'd changed her name and come to La Boca, she'd sworn to keep her politics a secret, arguing with herself that she'd done enough, that losing her career and her name were enough. But the townspeople knew by the books she stocked, and though they bought from her, none asked her to coffee or to dinner or to bed.

She had spent so much time with her grandmother and Angelica Roches that she had begun to feel like an old woman herself. Then one day a tall American with green eyes spent an afternoon in the store, tucking one paperback after another under his arm, buying, finally, a dozen different titles.

"I'll be open tomorrow," Pilar had said. "You don't have to buy them all now."

He nodded, a little embarrassed, then said straight out, "I'd like to take you to dinner, or, if you prefer, I'll meet you at a restaurant. You're a beautiful woman and you love books, and I'd like to talk with you over a meal. I've been wandering around this store an hour trying to think of something clever, but I'm not all that clever."

He had smiled then, and they had become lovers.

By the time Pilar reached her shop, a circle of sweat marked her blouse like a target. She lifted her hair off her shoulders and unlocked the back door. Upstairs, in her bedroom, she selected clean clothing, deciding at the last moment not to open the store until the afternoon. She found her bathing suit in the bottom drawer of her dresser and pulled her hair back into a ponytail. There was a hole in the center of her life and an omnivorous contradiction, but the Pacific was fresh and cool, and the waves rushed to her like friends.

THE BOOKSTORE had five regular customers: Leon, who read only fiction; Pilar's grandmother, who wanted the oddest books imaginable, often in languages she did not know; Angelica Roches, who came almost every day and bought anything Pilar recommended; Angelica's daughter, Lourdes, who liked to stay and talk about books or the university and pretend that she and Pilar were conspirators against the numbing sameness of La Boca and the prospect of becoming as old as Angelica and Maria Peralta; and Benjamin Matamoros, Ramon's son, who ordered books about rock-and-roll singers as well as any that Lourdes bought, having asked Pilar to keep a record of all the girl read.

Pilar also sold novels in English to tourists from the hotel who discovered that there were no movie theaters in La Boca and no television. As for the remainder of the townspeople, they bought books occasionally, usually as gifts. Most La Bocans preferred giving books to actually reading them.

"I must have a book by a black African," Maria Peralta said, her hands clasped at her neck. It was early afternoon, the hottest part of day, when most of the businesses closed for an hour or two. Pilar, refreshed by her morning swim, had sat behind the simple wooden counter all day without a customer, watching the ocean through the big store windows and reading a novel with a biblical title about slave owners in the United States.

Angelica Roches followed Maria into the store, smiling and nodding at Pilar, a tooth missing from her bottom row.

"Angelica, what happened? You've lost a tooth."

She laughed and waved her hand at Pilar. "You can't fool me with that one," she said. Her dress, a polyester orange, obviously a gift from Maria Peralta, had a clean square around her breasts, but flour marked the sides, outlining her missing apron. Her daughter trailed in after her. Lourdes still wore her apron, so spattered with smears of fruit and flour a stranger might have taken it for an artist's smock.

"Why, Angelica," Maria Peralta said, "I think you did lose one. Open up." Maria leaned so close, her nose actually entered Angelica's mouth. "Gone," she said. "Poof!" She threw open the fingers of one hand.

Angelica ran the tip of her index finger over her teeth, stopping at the gap. She pushed her tongue through. "When you get this old, you can't keep track of all the things falling out. Look at this." She began giggling and untied a green scarf that was knotted at her chin. "Look." She bent over.

Her crown was bald, a spot the size of a saucer.

"Mama," Lourdes said, "quit showing off. She thinks this is the funniest thing. It's not really funny."

Maria Peralta, however, was laughing. "Show her your lip."

Angelica straightened and smiled into Pilar's face, a long crinkle of aging lips and failing teeth.

"I don't see anything odd," Pilar told her.

Angelica laughed. "My mustache fell out."

"She had one there for ten years. Black as a bruise," Maria said. She and Angelica laughed so hard they had to lean on one another to stand.

Although Pilar's grandmother, Maria, had been a beauty in her youth and Angelica obese, their bodies were now nearly identical—thick through the middle, their shoulders heavy and rounded, their hips heavy and squared. They were handsome old women with clear eyes and strong jaws and noses long enough to reflect their ages. Each had a few dark strands remaining in hair otherwise as gray as rain.

"I'm never going to get that old," Lourdes said confidentially. She was a teenager—Pilar wasn't sure how old, seventeen or eighteen—but around Pilar she acted younger. She was intelligent and had worked in the bakery since she was a tiny girl, which made her immaturity harder to understand, but, as far as Pilar could determine, Lourdes was still a kid—physically grown but childish. Her features were ordinary, but her vitality made her attractive, that and a little birthmark on her cheek shaped like an elongated heart. Pilar found it hard to believe that Angelica had given birth to her, but Maria Peralta claimed it was true. Angelica must have been nearly fifty at the time. Maria Peralta was quite a bit older, close to ninety, Pilar guessed. Maria refused to confirm or deny speculation.

"Now, my book," Maria said. She and Angelica had finally stopped laughing. "It must be in its natural language and by a black African. I would prefer a woman writer, but I'll take what you have."

Pilar shook her head. "All the books here are in Spanish or English. How often have I told you that?"

"I am the customer." Maria Peralta pointed at herself. "How many times do I have to ask for a little variety?"

"I need a new book too," Angelica told her. "But I want one I can read." She wrapped her scarf around her head again.

Maria Peralta took Angelica's arm, and they looked over the same titles they had considered the day before, discussing the first few sentences of several to determine whether they had already read them.

"I finished that last book you suggested." Lourdes stepped closer and threw her elbows on the counter. "It was pretty boring, but I read it."

"I'm sorry you didn't like it," Pilar said. "It's a book I found interesting when I was your age."

"Maybe I'm smarter than you were." She laughed, but Pilar sensed she was only half joking. Lourdes continued, "It was really slanted, though, don't you think? First off, I like people from the

United States, don't you? I'd think you would." She laughed again, a self-conscious giggle. "You know about what's going on in the world is what I mean. You don't just hate foreigners like half the people here. Did you see that movie last year? They showed it on the wall over there." She flicked her hand in the direction of the cathedral. "It was made in the United States, and it was great. All these people with cars and they had a good time every night. You must have liked that movie."

"I missed it, although I admit that I enjoy American movies, but then I enjoy movies from everywhere. That's one of the hardest things about living here—no movies." She smiled because she suspected she was inept at making small talk.

"You probably miss all the men, too. There must be a thousand good-looking men at the university. Don't you ever think about going back and seeing a few?"

Pilar affected a shrug. "I miss movies more," she said, and they both laughed—as if they were schoolgirls, Pilar thought, snickering about boys. "I thought you'd find the book a good introduction to dialectical reasoning."

Lourdes screwed up her face. "I don't remember anything like that being in the book."

"No, but that is its method of argument."

"Then dialectical reasoning is boring." Her expression flattened. "I can't stand to be bored."

Angelica stepped between them. "What do you recommend, Pilar? There are too many choices."

"Don't suggest another mystery." Lourdes crossed her arms and turned her back. "She gets all worked up in the first few pages, then makes me read it and tell her what's going to happen before she will finish it."

"Shush." Angelica rapped her daughter on the shoulder. "Don't give away my secrets."

Pilar found Angelica a book about a family trying to survive on a farm. For Lourdes, she recommended a book on women's rights, but the girl wanted fiction and continued looking. Maria Peralta bought three paperbacks of identical size. "I'm going to separate these pages and mix them together. Books don't have enough confusion in them. There's no mystery, no challenge. That's why I don't like the north. It snows there, and all the confusion gets blown white."

The two old women bought their books and were ready to leave. Lourdes promised to hurry to the bakery as soon as she found something. She lingered near the window until her mother and Maria Peralta were gone.

"You have any dirty books?" Lourdes said.

Pilar was only slightly startled. "What kind do you mean?"

"Dirty, with sex, a lot of sex in it. Men and women. All that." Lourdes twisted the skirt of her apron as she spoke.

"There may be a few books that you'd find erotic."

"Yes, erotic, exactly." She continued wringing the apron, as if nervous, but nothing else in her demeanor suggested it. "I used to like this boy, but boys are boys, you know. I'd like to get a book with *men* in it."

Pilar thought Henry Miller would satisfy her but discovered that the only copy was in English.

"I could probably read it. Friends could help me." Lourdes put the book on the counter, then began meandering through the room again, pausing in the children's section. "Sometimes everything has lines like these." She held up a page from a coloring book. "Everything is distinct. I like that. Other times, it all runs together, like a big blur—I know it doesn't really do either, but I see things that way, you know?"

"I guess," Pilar said. "There are some days when I see the world differently. All the things I see every day suddenly look new."

"Yeah." Lourdes said this one word in English and looked out the window at the ocean. "I always thought I'd just take off one day. Get out of here. Go to the university. What I feel, half the time, is that I'm right on the brink of knowing what makes the world go, how it makes sense." She turned to face Pilar. "I can almost see what it is that makes you love one person and not love another, or how all the stuff that happens keeps happening. Or something like that. It's as if I understand it, but I can't talk about it."

"Books are a good way to escape," Pilar said.

"No, books just remind me how much more there is everywhere else." She stepped to the counter and bought the novel. "Just the same, I'm not leaving. Not by myself anyway. My mother was so fat when she was a girl she couldn't get married for years. That's what she told me. She got my father because he was an old man. But look at me." She stepped away from the counter and spun on one foot, the tail of the spattered apron trailing her as she twirled.

"You're a pretty girl," Pilar said.

"Yes." Lourdes grabbed her book. "I just wanted to hear you say it." She waved as she walked out the door.

Pilar added Henry Miller to her order list. The profit she made from selling books was not enough to survive on, but she had saved some money as a professor, knowing she might have to live in exile. A nice sum of money, which, in La Boca, was a fortune.

An hour later, Benjamin arrived, saying that he'd seen Lourdes with a new book.

"Tropic of Cancer," Pilar told him. "She bought it in English."

Benjamin stuck his hands in his pockets. Tall and very thin, he seemed to grow too big for his shirt as he stood there, shifting his weight, rocking his head, fretting in place. Finally he said, "I'll try English, too. My dad knows English. But maybe I should stick to Spanish. How long is it?"

"I'll order it in both languages," she said. "You can pick later."

This relaxed him and he took a deep breath. "I guess that's it then," he said, then added, "She reads a lot."

Pilar agreed, and he was gone.

Her final customer for the day was La Boca's only school-teacher, Rosa Ojeda. She came to the store once or twice a week and never talked to Pilar, not even a word, but looked over the shelves until she found the book she wanted, purchased it, and left. She refused to order books for the school through Pilar's store.

This trip was particularly quick. She bought a romance. On the cover a woman in a red blouse held a long gold necklace in her hand near her breasts. The necklace was broken, gripped in the middle, one end falling into space, the other into cleavage.

"Enjoy," Pilar said.

Rosa Ojeda pivoted like a soldier and walked out of the building, leaving Pilar alone in a room full of words.

*T*HE BUS from Santa Josefina, an ancient Dodge Powerwagon with wooden benches bolted to its rusting bed, came every Monday, usually in the morning, but often well into the afternoon, depending on the weather, the road conditions, and the number of breakdowns. The owner and driver, a tiny man with a handlebar mustache, went by his last name, Cruz, and made puns in English over the course of the long and difficult drive about "Cruz-ing through the jungle" and "Cruz Control." He smoked little cigars with plastic tips and brought Leon tourists every week.

Leon and Ramon watched them arrive from a window on the ruined third floor, Leon on the barstool drinking a beer, Ramon propped by his elbows against the window ledge and its vines, his bottle of beer, long empty, beside his shoes. Both the bottle and his shoes were speckled white with flakes of paint and tiny chips of plaster from the decaying wall.

Leon sat with his legs crossed, his hair wet but combed. He had taken a quick shower after lunch and changed into clean clothes. Dressing up for the guests' arrival was not strictly necessary but provided a small ritual in a life that was largely without routine. "Cruz is arriving late," he said. "That means there's a pretty woman aboard."

Ramon turned to look at him. "The bus breaks down more often when it carries a beautiful woman? Some machines have the same sensibility as humans."

"Cruz has visions of seducing tourists." Leon leaned over the ledge to improve his angle. "Even when they're with husbands and children."

"Step careful," Cruz said in English. He had placed a rickety and unnecessary footstool beneath the open door of the Powerwagon. Turning to the doorman, one of Leon's three employees, Cruz spoke in Spanish. "Two couples. Americans. The old ones are loaded. Check out her camera." He offered his hand to a woman wearing a camera with a telescopic lens hanging from a strap around her neck.

She smiled at Cruz and accepted his hand. Her graying hair parted in the middle and fell straight almost to her waist, a style that emphasized her age.

"She's a little old for Cruz, don't you think?" Ramon whispered.

Her husband followed, a tall man with a handsome and ironic face, who looked several years younger than his wife. As he stepped down, a young Oriental woman appeared in the doorway of the Powerwagon.

"Bingo," Leon said.

"This is it?" She spoke in English.

"She seems to be disappointed in the hotel," Ramon said softly and crossed his arms. "I can't blame her." He looked around the damaged room purposefully and started to say more, but Leon stopped him.

"Watch Cruz," he said.

Cruz offered his hand to the woman. When she took it, he threw his free arm around her waist. "Step careful," he said, his fingers at her hip.

Ramon covered his laugh with his hand, then whispered, "He's half the size of my son. And no better with women."

The final passenger was a young man in glasses who carried a green backpack so large it reminded Leon of a bundle of bananas. Cruz had called this man and the Oriental woman a couple, and they looked to be about the same age—twenty-five or so—but Leon could see that they were not together. She wore a long pink skirt and an expensive blouse, while the man was unshaven in a corduroy work shirt and worn jeans. She had three matching suitcases and an overnight bag, while he carried only the pack.

"Don't you have to register these people?" Ramon asked. "Shouldn't you see if Cruz has the liquor you ordered?"

"What's the rush?" Leon waved his bottle. "I have a beer to finish."

"They'll smell it on your breath."

"Cruz will be back next Monday. Until then, the Esperanza is their home, whether they like it or not, no?" Leon smiled at his friend. "Besides, people expect the manager of a hotel in such an out-of-the-way place to be eccentric."

"You have a point," Ramon said. "Sometimes I think I should make myself appear to be odd. They have the same expectations of a tour guide, don't you think?"

"We could shave your head. Or better, give you a Mohawk."

Ramon had never heard of the hairstyle.

"We shave all of your head except for one strip in the middle." Leon gestured with his hand from forehead to the back of his neck.

"I knew a man who did that, except his hair went the other way." Ramon ran his open hand from ear to ear. "He grew it long and used coconut milk to make it stand on end. He claimed he could predict the weather."

"How good was he?"

"It's hard to say. He predicted fifty years in advance. Every morning he would walk from the cathedral to the rocky point down that way, you know the one I mean? Near the south estuary? I'll take you there this afternoon. He walked there every morning and climbed the rocks to look out over the town You have a good view of La Boca from there. Then he'd say, 'Fifty years from today it will be partly cloudy.' Or whatever. Then he'd climb down and go home.''

"Yeah," Leon said as he rose from the stool. "Let's go downstairs."

"It isn't one of my best stories."

"At least it was short."

"But he did have that funny haircut." Ramon ran his fingers over his head again, ear to ear. "I want to meet your new guests, but I have to hurry. My son's teacher has asked for a conference."

"What is Benjamin doing in school now? In the middle of summer?"

Ramon shook his head. "He's a smart boy but he had a bad year. He needs this one class to graduate."

"What's the equivalent of apples here?" Leon stepped into the hall and began descending the stairs. "Bananas? Mangoes? How do you soften up teachers in La Boca?"

"I don't know," Ramon said. "I've been out of school too long. I could bring her a fish. What do you think? Toss a flounder on her desk?"

Leon smiled. "Try cash," he said. "Just don't tell her a story."

THE HIGH CEILING combined with the floor of white tile made the lobby of the Hotel Esperanza seem airy and light, but anyone who entered the room more than twice realized it was little more than a wide hallway and the sense of spaciousness had come as much from its barren walls and vacant walk space as from the lighted windows. A pair of dun-brown wooden doors opened to the street and never quite closed, the space between them narrow at the top but wide enough at the threshold to permit the entry of enormous beetles, iguanas, and even an occasional wayward mud hen. The registration desk was situated beneath the wooden staircase which angled down along the south wall, curving and widening at the last moment to open into the lobby. Leon spent a good deal of time behind the desk—reading, taking reservations by means of one of the few phones in all of La Boca, and doing the little figuring necessary to justify his job. His stool faced a long white wall, blank except for a handsome little arch, which led to the hotel's bar. At the far end of the lobby, a pair of French doors with sidelights of yellow glass offered a view of the beach and the enormous recalcitrant ocean.

Waiting for him at the desk were Cruz and the old couple, who, as it turned out, spoke Spanish. "We're not really that rich," the woman told Cruz.

"I didn't know you spoke the language," he said, unflustered. "We could have discussed photography." He introduced them to Leon. "American," he said in English, slapping Leon on the back, then added confidentially in Spanish, "I brought him here in my bus a few years ago." He smiled, as if proud of the accomplishment.

They were from the state of Washington, they said, Peter and Heidi Geddest. They had been all over Central America. "I photograph birds." Heidi lifted her camera slightly. "It's a hobby."

"We're retired," Peter added. They paid for two weeks in advance. Leon introduced them to Ramon, and they arranged for an excursion into the jungle sometime later in the week.

The young man was from Arizona, a college student. His Spanish wasn't as good as he thought, and Leon laughed, correcting him, but he seemed to have no sense of humor. His wire-rimmed glasses magnified his eyes, making him appear to be concentrating all the time. He bore the backpack like a cross. "I'm looking for the real towns of Central America," he said in English. "The real people. I didn't expect the hotel manager to be a gringo."

Leon pointed. "My friend there, who is a native, can show you the jungle and the town, if you like."

He shook his head. "I'm looking for the real culture. The real way of life. No tours." He waved a finger left to right in Leon's face.

"Relax," Leon said.

"No time for that," he said, then insisted on paying by the day because he didn't want to be tied down.

Cruz attempted to lead the Oriental woman by the hand to the registration desk, but his sole return passenger, an anxious Canadian, handed him a pair of suitcases and she slipped away. She was exotically beautiful, like the Tahitian women in the paintings of Gauguin. Her eyes seemed a bit sleepy, which Leon found erotic. He heard her tell Heidi that her heritage was one hundred percent Japanese. Her grandparents had come to the United States and never learned English. Her parents spoke both English and Japanese. She spoke only English.

"My husband will be meeting me next week," she said, signing the registration card.

Someone's husband, Leon thought, but not likely hers. La Boca was an ideal spot for a discreet rendezvous. She paid for a week, registering under the name of Janet Anderson. Leon liked the way she walked—fluidly, effortlessly, with just enough movement in her body to remind him of a bass string vibrating.

He rarely mingled with hotel guests, except to ask about the country he'd left behind, and even then he seemed most interested in trivial matters that had bored him when he'd lived there, such as what music was popular, how the Dodgers were doing, the fate of a few politicians.

Once, early in his stay, before he'd made any friends, Leon had slept with a woman who'd come by herself, an American movie actress seeking relief from her fans and press. There was no theater in La Boca, although an occasional film was shown on the wall of the cathedral. No one recognized her but Leon, who remembered her from one movie in particular. She had played an actress trying to get a part in an off-Broadway production, who had to compromise her integrity in several ways in order to land the role, only to have the play fail. What Leon remembered was a scene where she stood alone in her bedroom going through clothes. She held up one dress, then another, staring in the mirror.

As the scene continued, she became progressively less interested in the clothing and more in herself, until she dropped a handful of hangers and dresses and stared at her face and neck, finally pulling off the blouse and skirt she wore, and staring at her body. It had been a startling moment in an otherwise ordinary movie.

Leon had played the scene over and over in his mind: an actress who is playing an actress who is unknowingly playing the part of Narcissus. He came to believe that at the moment when the character realized she wanted to look at herself and not the clothes, there had been a second, identical discovery—however fleeting—on the part of the actress making the movie. It was this second realization that made the scene convincing.

He decided the best way to ingratiate himself with this woman was to acknowledge her as an actress and to express his admiration by recounting the scene. He reasoned that such a woman, although trying to escape the consequences of fame, would nonetheless become interested in the only person who recognized her, and he intended to make it clear that he recognized her not only as an actress, but for the character who was revealed in that scene.

All of his strategy proved unnecessary. In a foreign country with no one near who knew her, she responded to his earliest advances. It was not so much an affair as a courtesy, and though she was pretty and enthusiastic, Leon found himself disappointed.

One evening after dinner they walked to the north estuary, talking and looking at the moonlight on the calm water. During a pause in the conversation, Leon realized that she was staring at her own reflection. He said, "You truly are as beautiful as you suspect." She became suddenly nervous and, at the same time, passionate. They made love on the ground next to the water, and it was no longer a courtesy.

But she had been the exception. Normally his relations with hotel guests were strictly trivial.

.   .   .

RAMON WALKED with his arm on the shoulder of his son. The streets were empty and most of the shops closed. They would open again later in the afternoon, after the worst hours of the day had passed. People sat near open doors and windows, fanning themselves, waving or nodding to Ramon and Benjamin as they passed. Even the smell of the ocean was flattened by the heat and by the dust that rose from their shoes.

Although he knew that he should be upset, Ramon was taking pleasure in strolling through La Boca with his son. In the past year, Benjamin had entered that age when boys want less to do with their parents, and Ramon was happy for the chance to talk with him.

"What do you think Mrs. Ojeda wants?" Ramon asked. He didn't really care, as he was already convinced that Benjamin was smarter than his teacher.

Benjamin scratched his cheek, then the top of his head, distracted and annoyed. "She's probably mad about something. She gets mad a lot."

"Her husband's dead," Ramon told him. "You have to make allowances." He lifted his arm from his son's shoulder. A narrow line of sweat shone through Benjamin's shirt where the arm had lain. "She was a different person before his death. Did you know she was the first La Bocan woman to wear a two-piece bathing suit?"

"I wish you wouldn't tell me that kind of stuff," Benjamin said. "Now whenever I see her I'll imagine her in a bikini. It's disgusting."

"She was very pretty back then. A little wild, the old people thought. She's only a few years older than I am." She was ten years older, but Ramon wanted to minimize the difference. Ten years to a teenager was half a lifetime.

"I haven't done anything," Benjamin said. "One day I made an airplane and threw it across the room, but that's not so terrible, is it?"

"You did that?" Ramon said. "I could never make one of those. The wings always drooped. You could be an engineer. Have you decided what you're going to study at the university? An engineer is a good thing to be."

Benjamin wiped sweat from his forehead, then scratched his cheek again. "I'd rather be a singer."

"How do you think they get started, these singers? At college. They study history by day, play in clubs at night. You think you just open your mouth and sing? Ha ha, everyone would be a singer then." He waved to a man leaning with both hands against a cane in the doorway of a pink adobe house. The old man nodded, a former drinking companion of Ramon's father. Ramon shoved his sleeves above his elbows and returned his attention to his son. "That Beatle, the one who sings."

"They all sang," Benjamin said.

"The one your mother likes."

"McCartney."

"Yes, him. I understand he is a professor at the University of Cincinnati, teaching languages. He is a linguist and a teacher, and he sings with the Beatles in his spare time."

"The Beatles broke up a long time ago."

"There you go. He's lucky he had his degree to fall back on."

"I'll go. I'll go. I just don't know what I want to study. It's all the same."

"You didn't always have this attitude. That's probably why we have to go see your teacher now: your attitude. And don't think I don't know what it is. As soon as Lourdes graduates, Benjamin no longer cares about school."

Benjamin looked quickly over both shoulders. "This is how rumors get started, Dad. Do you want to ruin me?"

"I want you to go to the university. I've saved enough money to start a revolution, and it's all for you, for school. Do you remember what your great forefather the conquistador said?"

"The sky's a big bubble?"

"Membrane. No, not that one. He said, 'An educated man has the fingers and the fist.' "

"Great."

"Me, I have just the fist"—Ramon made a fist—"which is how I make my living, beating it out of life." He made several punches at invisible opponents. "What I want you to have is fingers."

"Uh huh." Benjamin suddenly straightened, reminding Ramon that he slumped. "Mom says I should be a doctor."

"There are worse things to be."

"I guess. Like what?"

"Lots of things. Lourdes would jump at the chance to go to school."

Benjamin looked over his shoulders again. "You don't know that," he whispered.

"It's too bad that both of you couldn't go."

Benjamin stopped and stared at his father. "She doesn't like me, Dad. Not like that. We're just friends. Let's drop it, okay?"

"Things can change," Ramon told him.

"There's Bones," Benjamin said. Rosa Ojeda sat in a chair by the front door to the small schoolhouse.

"You shouldn't call her that," Ramon said under his breath. To Rosa Ojeda, he spoke loudly. "How pleasant to see you, Rosa."

She stood so quickly, Ramon thought he felt a rush of wind. Her look had an air of intensity about it that reminded him of a snake ready to strike. Bones was an unimaginative nickname— one Benjamin must have overheard rather than created—because she was more like a bundle of twisted wires.

She ushered them into the building and through the short hallway. "I have been teaching here how long?" She spoke while she walked, her back to them. "I should know but I don't." As soon as she entered her classroom, she whirled and faced them, freezing them in the doorway. "A student like Benjamin, a fine young man, smart and doesn't get into trouble like other boys, trouble like I could never tell you, a boy like this is a treasure, and what is it I've called you about? This treasure, this boy like none of the others in his class, has suddenly become nothing more than a lump of seaweed in a shirt, as God is my witness." She raised one hand solemnly. "Ramon, we have known one another since before the sun was anything but the glowing end of a stick. And for what reason is it I call you into my schoolroom? To show you a paper written by your son on the very sort of thing in which this boy should be excelling, a paper on the tides. His father being a fisherman, and a fine one, we all know. So what does he write? A thing I cannot repeat—it turns me away like the music these children pretend to like. This paper, he's talked to you about it?"

"Let me see, now. We talk so often that it's hard to tell." Ramon put his hand to his mouth, glancing to Benjamin for help, but Benjamin stared at his shoes. "No," Ramon said, "not a word."

"It's just a paper," Benjamin said. "I heard this stuff about the tides and menstrual cycles . . ."

"These are things I want to hear? On a paper about science? No, they are not." Rosa waved the sheets of paper back and forth, as if erasing spoken words.

"I was trying to be creative," Benjamin told her.

She shoved the paper at Ramon. "To pass my class, he must write a new paper. Is there to be any discussion about it? No, there is not." She glared at Benjamin. "It must be on my desk the day you take your final examination." She turned, parted them with her hands, then marched out of the room and down the hall.

Ramon tugged on his son's elbow. "So how does a woman's period affect the tides? I don't get it."

"The other way around," Benjamin told him.

"You could be a biologist. It's very clear." They stepped cautiously into the hall. Rosa was gone. "That woman is a fine person. But she does not have the insight to recognize a future biologist."

"I hate science," Benjamin said as they walked through the narrow passage and into the sunlight.

"Of course," Ramon said. "Most men of some sensitivity do." He stopped a few steps later and stretched his arms. "Would you look at that?"

"What?" Benjamin turned.

Ramon pointed at the building they had just left. "This school building has no character at all." Whitewashed brick with a sloping roof and a pathetic arch over the doorway, the schoolhouse seemed to slump in the afternoon heat. Ramon shook his head sadly at the sight of it. "I wish there were someone here who could design a decent building or two."

"Yeah," Benjamin said in English, a habit he had picked up from Lourdes. "Sure."

"Sensitive minds are often fascinated by architecture. I bet Pilar has some books on the subject. We could go and see."

Benjamin grunted his disapproval of the idea. "I ought to go write a new paper."

Ramon shoved his hands into the back pockets of his pants, mildly deflated. It worried him that his son had lost his enthusiasm for school just when it should be at its peak. A drop of perspiration grew like a wart on the tip of his nose, and he thumbed it away. The afternoon sun was making the surfaces of things move—walls quivered, windows trembled, even the cobblestone street rippled like water. Perhaps his son's attitude was like the simple white wall before him: It appeared to waver but really it was as sturdy as ever. This thought lifted Ramon's spirits once again.

"So how did Bones's husband die?" Benjamin asked him.

"Ah," Ramon said, "that is a sad story. He and Rosa had gone to the university to see about enrolling."

"A degree hasn't done much for her," Benjamin said.

"She never got a degree. However, she is smart enough to have one, and that's why she's your teacher."

"Yeah. Okay."

"She and her husband went to see a movie. While they were watching it, a group of men in uniform came and dragged her husband out. She ran after them. They were members of the army, and they told Rosa that her husband had just been drafted. You, by the way, will not go to movies while you're at the university."

"Just like that he was drafted?" Benjamin snapped his fingers.

"Yes, and several weeks later Rosa left town and returned with his body. I helped carry the coffin myself."

"How'd he get killed?"

Ramon lifted his hands to express both ignorance and sadness, then returned them to his pockets. Benjamin also walked with his hands in his pockets. They looked very much like a father and son.

"I love La Boca," Ramon said. "It's a good place to live. A safe place. No one will draft you at the movie theater."

"There is no movie theater."

"Yes," Ramon said. "Exactly right. You could be a lawyer. Have you ever thought about the law?"

LOURDES CAME to the Hotel Esperanza at one. She was seventeen, strong through the shoulders, and vaguely pretty, although Leon recognized that much of her beauty was youth, the muscular firmness of her thighs and stomach, the spongy resiliency of her breasts. She had a scar on her cheek the exact shape and size of a melon seed, and this was how Leon had thought of her before he knew her name: the girl with the melon-seed scar. The bakery closed for two hours in the afternoons, and, when possible, Lourdes slipped away to make love with Leon, or just to lie in his bed and talk.

She stepped onto the balcony where he sat with his feet against the wrought-iron railing, reading while he waited for her to arrive. Her slate cotton blouse and brilliant yellow skirt were covered by a white apron, which, in turn, was covered with flour, splotches of fruit and jelly. She smiled at him, two conch-shaped rolls in her right hand, a ripe papaya in her left. The fruit, green and yellow with a dark tint, looked to Leon like an internal organ, and he said, "I'm not really hungry."

She squatted beside his chair, kissed his cheek. "What are you reading?"

"That book," he said, turning it for her to see.

"I thought you bought that for me." She had asked him to buy her a dirty book before she'd asked Pilar. It had been an experiment to see if Pilar would pick the same one Leon had. She hadn't, which, for Lourdes, was evidence that they were not right for each other. She pressed the papaya against his cheek.

"Please get that away from me," he said and stood. An inflamed kidney, an enlarged heart, Leon couldn't name the organ, but the fruit looked obscene.

"You like papayas." She set it with the rolls on his chair. "How much have you read?"

"I started it this morning." He covered the papaya with the novel, so he wouldn't have to look at it. "Your apron is a mess," he said, "but you look lovely."

She reached behind her neck to untie the apron strings, watching him all the while, the play of the sun on his white shirt. She never tired of studying him. It was as if he had stepped out of an American movie—clean and blond and handsome, thin in the American manner. Glamorous. "The woman at the bookstore said this novel wasn't especially good. 'Just another best-seller,' she said." The top of the apron fell forward. He didn't respond, so she lied to get a reaction. "I told her my boyfriend bought it for me."

Leon turned from her and walked into his room. Recently she'd begun mentioning Pilar—a game of sorts. He had never talked about her with Lourdes, but he hadn't denied that he saw another woman. He believed it was essential not to lie. Lourdes had been furious when she first heard, saying she'd rather die than have half of him, but she had returned to his bed after only a week. Since she'd discovered that Pilar was the other woman, she played the game of knowing and pretending not to know. Leon lay on his bed. He felt uncomfortable whenever she mentioned Pilar, but he also found a curious pleasure in it.

He could not have guessed the extent of Lourdes's fascination concerning Pilar. Daily, while she worked dough across a table, counted change, cleaned the black oven, even now while she stood on the balcony without him, Lourdes pictured Pilar as precisely as she was able, troubling herself over the smallest details—the part of her hair, the lift of her lips, the curve of her brows, the sway in her shoulders as she walked. She knew Pilar possessed a quality that made her different from others, a quality Lourdes could not name. Certainly she was pretty, but that wasn't all of it. Hadn't everyone said that she, Lourdes, was pretty too? Even Pilar admitted it. There was some additional quality, an elusive one.

From her bedroom in the rear of the bakery, Lourdes had watched Leon walk with Pilar along the edge of the water. They had held hands, conversing with Ramon, although Lourdes had been unable to hear more than an occasional word. The walk had seemed aimless, but there had been one moment Lourdes could not forget. The three of them had lain in the sand separately, each gesturing to the other, wallowing around. Then Pilar had stretched her arms from one man to the other, and at that instant, everything changed: Their moods seemed to alter, their movements became graceful, the men suddenly relaxed and turned toward Pilar, everything—even the color of the sky, the taste of the breeze off the ocean, the quality of the moonlight on the radiant shore—everything had become new. Lourdes had watched it happen, and then suddenly, as if by magic, Pilar's skirt inflated before them, and she lifted her perfect brown legs toward the sky. Lourdes had felt her heart stop.

Since witnessing that moment, she'd known that Pilar possessed knowledge she did not have, and she wanted it. Lourdes was not going to give Leon up.

The apron flew into the room from the balcony, its strings trailing like streamers. Sandals, one at a time, sailed through the slant of sunlight and bounced off the far wall.

"I believe I'll undress out here," she called.

Leon took a cigarette from the pack on the dresser. "Do you want a smoke?"

She entered unbuttoning the slate blouse with one hand, holding the novel with the other. "I like this book." She pulled on the tail of her shirt, freeing it of the yellow skirt. An old bra, straps attached by safety pins, crossed her chest like a solemn promise.

"I don't think it's all that good," he said, the cigarette in his mouth but unlit. "I should have bought you something I already knew."

Her blouse fell. She pulled the bra over her head. Her breasts, though small, were perfectly round.

Leon flicked the cigarette across the bed to the floor, sat up on his knees, and kissed those breasts while her hands moved through his hair. The latch on her skirt was tricky, but he remembered it and undid it expertly. The skirt slid down her legs. Her underwear, dirty with a hole at either hip, made him wonder at the layers of her clothing—the filthy apron, the clean blouse and skirt, her frayed bra and tattered panties. He tugged the panties down.

Making love with Lourdes was an athletic contest, and Leon sometimes imagined it as literally that—an Olympic event complete with judges who would hold up cards to indicate his score. He never felt more that he represented his country than when in bed with her. It was a battle of wills and strength, both invigorating and tiresome. In this particular match, she wrestled him beneath her, digging her nails into his wrists. He locked his right leg around her left, then rolled her onto her side. He was stronger than she, but barely. He kissed her neck, she bit his ear, and he entered her as she pitched toward him. The judges would have been pleased.

Lourdes believed sex should be furious, dramatic. Leon believed the man should please the woman. He flung himself against her, biting her nipples. She struggled against him one moment, then lifted her bottom to meet him the next. When they finished, they were both exhausted, pleased from sexual fulfillment and relieved at successful conclusion. This encounter ended with Lourdes laughing.

Leon turned to where she pointed. In a rectangle of sunlight on the floor near the terrace, a large iguana stared at them, doing push-ups. Leon lifted one of his shoes from the floor and threw it backhanded. The lizard ran to the balcony and down the wall of the Hotel Esperanza.

"I bet that was my father," Lourdes said. "I wish you'd hit him." One legend that survived in La Boca was that people who cannot gain entrance to heaven are sent back to earth as iguanas. Whenever one was conspicuously present, few people could resist speculating who might be returning.

"Did your father like to watch you fuck?" Leon reached across her to take matches and cigarettes from the dresser.

She slapped his ribs playfully but hard. "He tried himself when I was twelve. Just before he died. Mother hit him over the head with a broom."

"He died from a broom wound?"

"No, he was so old by then he didn't know what he was doing. But he still liked sex. He would sit behind the counter with his cock out. One time my mother caught him wrapping it in dough." Lourdes giggled.

"How old was your father?"

"He was a hundred and twelve when he died."

Leon snorted and stood up on the mattress. He walked across the bed, flicking ashes onto the floor. "So he was a hundred years old when you were conceived?"

She stared up at him and smiled. "My mother used to threaten him. She said that if he didn't die soon she would take him to the ruins where he would harm no one."

"The ruins? What ruins?"

"*The* ruins, but never mind. I want to read you this part of the novel."

"There aren't any ruins around here."

Lourdes giggled again, reminding Leon, as she rarely did, that she was seventeen.

"The ruins are a secret," she said and took the novel from the dresser, then rolled onto her stomach. "Let me find this part. It's sexy."

The possibility that there might be more to La Boca than he knew intrigued Leon. He wanted to ask her again but knew she would make a game of it, a secret, like her knowledge of Pilar, something she would play with for weeks. Asking Ramon would be simpler, although Ramon would have some long story. Leon genuflected, shaking the bed, and watched the gentle sway of her ass. He stepped between her legs, staring—her dark hair, which spread over her wide brown shoulders, the tight cylindrical waist that opened to her light bottom. He parted the cheeks of her ass with the side of his foot. She laughed and continued paging through the book. He lowered himself on top of her and looked over her shoulder at the novel.

"This isn't the part I was looking for but it's good," she said. "Read it."

Leon took the novel from her, but did not roll off. He had read the first thirty pages and found it boring. The story of an American missionary struggling to keep his faith. The first chapter was one long confession from a woman who had traveled with a carnival and performed sexual acts with animals. Lourdes had it opened to a later chapter.

> In the horse latitudes, there are no curtains. People live shamelessly. Native women give me mash and bread in chipped stoneware—skeptics, believing I am here to beguile them, a messenger of some other god. One woman holds a dictionary to my face. Her blackened fingernail quivers beneath the word missionary: *propagandist.* She laughs bitterly, then shows me the door.
> The sky, filled with stars, turns out the moon to pace the earth, and it's this that has caused the chill. Frost settles on the hardening ground. My breath turns to vespers. How did I lose track of the seasons? Did summer die a natural death?

"This is awful," Leon said. "I apologize for giving it to you." He put the book down and cupped her chin.

"Did you get to the sexy part?" she asked. "Keep reading. Let me hold it, so I can read it too."

"Christ," he said, wriggling against her bottom.

> A window burns with lights. It insists I look: The black woman is nude, her round body skewed across the wooden table. A man, almost as black, cracks an egg and stirs it into a bowl of dark sugar. He flattens the shell against the table with his palm, then flicks the fragments to the floor, which is littered with crushed shells.
> The man dips a shaving brush into the bowl of sugar and strokes the hips of the woman. They speak; it is a litany.
> "Am I beautiful?" she asks.
> "You are the beautiful one," he says obediently.
> "Do you love me?"
> "You are the loved one."

"Great dialogue," Leon said.

"Shush." Lourdes smacked his thigh. "Don't stop yet."

I squat by the window, open despite the cold. She licks her palm and rubs her breasts, which sparkle now with sugar. A sparkle that lights the fuse of my desire. "Dear father," I whisper, too loudly. The man and woman stare.

"Who's out there?" she demands.

The man steps to the window and grasps my shoulder, pulling me into view.

She smiles. One finger circles a nipple immaculately dark. I search through my mind for script, and what comes is this: *What man is there of you who if his son asked bread will give him stone? Or if he ask a fish will give him serpent?*

Her lips give shape to my desire. "Am I beautiful?" she asks me. She extends her arms through the window. Sugar glistens on the hand.

I lick her palm. The sweetness spreads through my chest like a swallow of boiling water.

"Am I beautiful?" she asks again.

God's words enter me. "The light of the body is the eye," I exclaim, hoping she understands. I encircle her index finger with my mouth.

"Do you love me?" she asks now.

"I love God," I whisper, too softly, betraying my God even as I defend him.

"Do you love me?" she demands.

My heart cannot expel God and cannot refuse her, and so it divides like an amoeba. "Thine is the glory," I tell her. And as I say it, I am lifted, not by the spirit of God, but by the black man, dragged through the window. They undress me, and another passage of scripture flexes through my brain, but I do not speak it. I fight it off my tongue: *Tonight the fir tree howls for the cedar has fallen. The forest of the vintage has come down.*

"What crap," Leon said.

Lourdes reached both hands behind her, arching her back, grabbing his ass. She slapped his cheeks. "It made you hard, didn't it?"

Then she whispered, "Do me in the ass." She ran her hands as far as she could reach down his legs. "Does your other woman let you fuck her in the ass?" She lifted and rocked her butt against him.

"Do it," she said. "Do me."

ROSA OJEDA had introduced summer classes as a way to give herself more work. She required the stupid and the lazy to take them. Over the years, she had tried a number of means of adding to her work requirements. Night school for adults had almost been successful, but the students didn't want to come five nights a week and they didn't want to write all the papers that she demanded. So they quit coming, and when she went to their doors and demanded excuses, they became embarrassed and forced their children to feign illness.

If they did not write the papers, then what was the point? She needed work to grade, to mark up in detail. Without it, she was forced to do art—which she hated, but which she found necessary. She did not practice or perform or work at art; she did it. The more plainly she could speak of it, the better. There was nothing grand in it. Art was merely a means of survival.

She couldn't specify the date that she began living entirely in the schoolhouse, but she would have guessed that it had been something like seven years ago. At first, she had moved a single bed to the little chamber opposite the classroom so that she could sleep there when she had to stay late marking essays. A dresser came soon afterward, and, at some point, she quit returning home and told her landlord to find another tenant.

The room originally had held the bucket and mop, the push-broom and duster. It barely had space for her narrow bed and there were no windows, but she found it adequate, and over the years, she had come to feel possessive toward it. As for the janitor, he'd quit months before she moved in, citing no reason, although she believed it was out of contempt for the job that required nothing of him, this because Rosa kept the building immaculate.

It was in this tiny room that she did art. She wrote stories, filling lined sheets from border to border, disregarding margins—a thing she lectured against in the classroom—writing in a tiny script so that between the sheer blue lines she was able to fit three rows of words, one on top of the other. She filled page after page to the point of darkness.

She did still lifes, charcoal drawings of textbooks, pencils, rulers, things that washed up on the beach, and, over time, she became adept, but the compulsion to fill in the blank spaces forced her to darken the lines and shade the shadows with increasingly darker splotches, until the pad was almost nothing but black, a few areas blacker than others—a still life in the dead of night.

Her best drawings she framed and hung on the walls of her little room. Also framed were many of the pages of her fiction, as they were largely indistinguishable from her other art.

She had grown disdainful of food and ate the same thing every day—one whole boiled chicken and almost nothing else—until, after years of this, her body had become terse and birdlike itself, the skin shrinking over the hollow bones. While she ate, she read romances, tales of beautiful women who fell for rogues while, at the same time, men of wisdom and fairness came calling, bringing orchids, lilies, roses the pink of a sunset. She wanted to write stories of this genre. But her stories, although they started out with such characters, never ended as she wanted. The men, both the bad ones and the good ones, inevitably forgot about the women or turned on them, or if they were true to the women they loved, then accidents befell them, gruesome dismemberments rendered in great detail. The lives of her characters twisted out of her control.

The only other art she did was a sort of painting which, for years, she had practiced with great regularity, and the canvases were wedged together in a row crossing the narrowest part of the room, and stacked almost to the ceiling. She did not use paint. She sat naked and motionless on the canvas and let her menstrual blood find its own shape. After an hour or two, she would rise carefully and study it for meaning, looking for resemblances. Then she would cover the canvas with a fixative, and file it with the others.

And this was her life: teaching so that she would have the money to live and the time to do art; teaching so that she would have something to do and would not have to face her art.

She was a woman of consummate fierceness.

DUSK SETTLED like smoke over La Boca. Leon sat on top of the granite formation that overlooked the ocean and the south estuary. Behind him lay the village, and just below him stood Ramon, wedged in a crevasse, taking a piss. They had grabbed a bottle of red wine recommended by Cruz and walked to the far rocks. Leon worked at the bottle with a corkscrew.

La Boca, the town itself, was something of a mystery to him. The beach was sandy, but the strand wasn't long enough to attract many tourists. Some came to dive, but the water was murky and the marine life dull. It wasn't a good fishing port. Boats larger than skiffs couldn't navigate the igneous reefs, and the estuaries were too shallow for commercial fishing. The narrow road that wound through the jungle was rough and the trip expensive because real buses couldn't drive the route. As far as Leon could tell, there was no economic reason for the village to exist.

Which was why the ruins intrigued him. He thought they could explain why the village had come into being and why it was still around. And they might provide an additional source of entertainment as well. He was sure Ramon would know all about the ruins, although they had never been a part of his many tales concerning the town—as far as Leon could remember. He hadn't always listened closely.

Ramon spat and zipped his pants. "Why is it that peeing makes you want to spit?"

Leon grunted, struggling with the stubborn cork.

"I pity women that," Ramon said. "It must be much less satisfying to spit from a sitting position."

"I don't think they get the same impulse," Leon told him. "It has to do with standing and watching it fall."

"Once I knew a woman who liked to watch me pee," Ramon said, climbing the rock. "She liked to hold my penis and feel the pee running through it." He sat beside Leon on the broad slab of granite. "She thought that was a wonderful thing."

"What happened to her?" Leon asked.

"I married her, but you keep this quiet. Celita is shy about sex."

Smiling, Leon turned from the ocean. The setting sun had begun to hurt his eyes. "I used to know a woman who liked to be blindfolded in bed."

"And what happened to her?"

"Nothing," Leon said.

"You just left her there blindfolded?"

"No, I mean that nothing ever became of us." The cork finally submitted to his pull, making a little pop as it left the bottle.

A wave crashed against the rocks, sending spray high into the air and misting their faces. The salt water stung Leon's eyes, but it made Ramon nostalgic, and he thought that the ocean's mist was somehow tied to his memory of adolescence. The cool water made his skin feel young, while the haze and refraction imitated the dreaminess of youth. "Have you ever been in love?" he asked Leon.

"Yes and no. Probably." Leon passed the bottle of wine beneath his nose. Its fragrance was darker and sharper than he had expected. "What about you?"

"I'm married," Ramon said. "Of course I've been in love. I am in love now, this very moment. I'm asking about you."

"This smells funny," Leon said and handed the bottle over. "Sometimes I think I am for a minute or two. Sometimes an hour. Sometimes even all day."

"That's love. That's what it is." Ramon drank from the bottle.

"No, it's not. I've never felt connected, had any continuity of feeling." Leon thought of the passion he had felt for Charla while he had still been married to June. Then he recalled the longing he had for June once he had divorced her and married Charla. "One moment I love a woman, but it fades and I know it was only desire or a reaction against loneliness."

"What is love then? Maybe you know something I don't."

"I'm the wrong person to ask, but I'd guess it's the way you love Celita. Day in, day out."

Ramon dismissed the idea with a wave of his hand. "I get angry with Celita. Impatient. I—"

"But you still love her," Leon insisted. "How is the wine?"

"Bitter as a bad tooth." Ramon took another drink and spat. "When you forget this woman or that, the love you felt for her still wells up inside you. Falling in love is just a direction." He pointed to the sea. "You aim your love toward one woman, then you stick to it."

"Why do you stick to it?"

"To keep the world from being totally crazy. Here." He handed Leon the wine. "Love comes and goes like the hiccups, but even when it's gone it's there."

"You sound like a teenager."

"Yes, and you sound like a dead man."

"No, I don't. I sound like a rational man." He swallowed a bit of wine and grimaced. "This is awful." He read the label again, looking for an explanation.

"Cruz-ing wine," Ramon said in English.

Leon emptied the bottle down the side of the rock, squinting against the sun. "I met a woman once at the grocery store . . ."

"In the United States?"

"Yes, she was twenty-five, a bank teller, and we made a date while we were shopping."

"A blonde?"

"Sort of, that in-between color, the color of stones."

"What color stones?"

"Dirt-colored stones. What difference does it make?"

Ramon pointed to his temple and squinted. "I'm trying to picture her—hair the color of dirt."

"Fine."

"Sandy dirt or this dirt here?"

"See that rock?" Leon stabbed his finger in the direction of the shore. "Like that rock. Exactly that color."

Ramon leaned backward to look. "That's the color of adobe."

"Fine. We made a date and we went to the movies."

"Just like that?" Ramon snapped his fingers.

Leon wagged his head, already tired of the story. "We talked. We followed each other through the aisles a while. In the vegetable section, I asked her if she'd seen this movie . . ."

"What movie?"

"I don't remember what movie. It was about divorce. The point is it was very popular, so I thought she would go."

"People popularize divorce?"

"Shut up, Ramon."

"How do people live fornicating in the vegetables, glorifying divorce? Was this woman married?"

"No and we didn't fuck in the vegetable section. We fucked in my apartment. Would you let me tell the story?"

Ramon crossed his arms, indignant. "You leave out the best parts."

"I'm trying to keep it to the bare minimum, all right? Some of us don't like to ramble on until it's pitch-dark." He glanced at the sun, which had already begun to disappear beneath the water. "The point is, I thought I loved her. We were there in bed—we'd only known each other a few hours—and I felt this thing come over me, this feeling."

"In the stomach?"

"No, it was like floating."

"Yes, that's love. One of the many ways love has of—"

"But, at the same time, I knew she was just out for fun. I was the man she'd met in the vegetable section of the grocery."

"She didn't have high morals. Neither did you, of course. That goes without saying."

Leon felt thoroughly frustrated. The damp rock was hard against his butt and marked by the stain of wine as if he'd urinated blood. The sun, only a crescent above the ocean, reflected off the water and burned his eyes. "I thought I was in love," he said. "Even though I knew that she didn't really care about me, I still felt it."

"You were in love."

"We dated a few more times." He remembered, for an instant, finding her asleep face down on his bed, the telephone receiver by her pillow, its long spiraling cord trailing down her bare back and between her bare legs. "She wouldn't see me after a while. She was engaged."

"Nevertheless, love at times is just a sound, one note." Ramon flicked his finger against the empty wine bottle that Leon still held. It made a flat tink. "But it's all part of a symphony. You may hear only one note, but it's playing all the time. I myself have heard a whole chorus without interruption."

Leon tossed the bottle over his shoulder and into the sand. "What was it playing?"

"I'm not sure. It sounded like the song my son Benjamin used to sing when he was little. Or maybe it sounded like fire."

"You always contradict yourself, Ramon," Leon said, feeling suddenly vindictive. "We've never had one conversation where you failed to contradict yourself."

"So you constantly claim. So what?" Another wave splintered against the rock and sent a new mist over them. "True, a boy's song and fire do not sound the same, but they have something in them that sounds the same, and that something sounds also like the sound of love."

"You're a lunatic. You talk like a lunatic, and you contradict yourself, and if we had any liquor, you'd hog the liquor."

"Thought and sound are very different things. But they may share some element." It was obvious that Leon was not convinced, and Ramon struggled for an example. The connection between the ocean's mist and adolescent dreaminess sprang to mind, but he decided that it would be a poor choice for Leon, who liked to pretend the past had never happened. "Let's take something more solid than sound, like this rock we're sitting on. A stone and a thought are very different things, but they may also share some element."

"Only if you think about stones." Leon sighed. He had grown tired of the conversation and wanted a drink.

"Your problem is you put limits on the world that don't exist," Ramon told him.

"Okay, and your problem is that you're a lunatic." Leon pulled his knees to his chest, then shifted his weight to his feet to relieve his aching butt. "I've thought a lot about love and happiness and sadness and all that."

"And what are your conclusions?"

"Just this. There are two basic kinds of loneliness."

"Only two?"

"Two. One is the loneliness of having no partner."

"Yes," Ramon acknowledged, "that is a big one. The second?"

"The loneliness of having one."

Ramon nodded solemnly. "How long was it you thought to come up with this revelation?"

"I'm serious," Leon said, but realized he probably didn't look it, squatting like a baseball catcher. "I've thought about this a lot, believe me. Our ideas about love and monogamy are what keep us from being happy."

"And this is why you sleep with Pilar but you don't marry her? Why you sleep with Lourdes and keep it secret?"

"I'm honest with them. I treat them with respect and kindness. I've never tried to get them together in bed with me, or anything like that. I've never asked them to see only me." He shifted to face Ramon, taking little steps. "My life has a design of my own making. How many people can say that?"

"How many would want to?"

"I'm not lonely."

"There are worse things than loneliness."

"Name one."

Ramon paused for a moment, then he too pulled his feet underneath himself and sat like Leon, not because his butt hurt, but to nurture empathy between them. They squatted on the rock, knee to knee. "Do you know that the exact population of La Boca is not known?" he said.

Leon swung his head sadly, letting his chin drop to his chest. "Oh, hell," he said.

"In 1954 the census takers became discouraged trying to follow the narrow burro path through the jungle and turned back. They developed a formula for predicting our growth based on the severity of the summer and the state of the economy. Now, even though the road is navigable to certain vehicles, certain times of the year, they still use the formula, if, in fact, they remember to include La Boca at all. This would not be the case if my great-grandfather's plan had come to fruition."

"You've convinced me," Leon said. "You can stop."

"If you stand—" Ramon stood on the rocks and pointed to the edge of town. "You have to stand, Leon. You'll like this story. Now, you can see that the thicket that once cushioned the village from the jungle has been encroached upon to the point that it exists only in the south. My great-grandfather was responsible for much of the damage."

"The bastard." Leon returned to his squat.

"Juan Matamoros, through dozens of letters he dictated to his wife, convinced the government that La Boca should not be separated from the rest of the country, that a railroad connecting it with other cities was a necessity."

Ramon too dropped back to a squat. "Juan was a great orator. Often he swayed the citizens of La Boca as easily as he had the government through his use of classical rhetoric, syllogistic reasoning, grand emotional appeals, and the Socratic method." Ramon flipped out a finger for each as he spoke, his hand just below Leon's face. "All of these he stumbled upon while speaking because he had never been educated and could not even write his own name. If La Boca had been a larger community, Juan, no doubt, would have been its mayor; however, La Boca was too small to support politicians and so he was a bum, saved from total poverty by the labor of his wife, whom he had charmed with his magnificent tongue."

"There seem to be a lot of bums in your family history," Leon said.

"That stems, in part, from our delicate constitution. Now, when the burro carrying the mail arrived with the news of the government's decision, Juan immediately staked off the whole of the thicket with little sticks he had carved from palm fronds in his spare time. He called a town meeting to claim his property. All of which was unnecessary, since no one had any interest in the thicket, and there was no official who could accept any such legal claim. The citizens of La Boca, however, enjoyed gathering to hear Juan speak regardless of the pretense, and the priest, Father Montoya, reluctantly agreed to accept Juan's piece of paper claiming deed to the thicket.

"It was the beginning of a time of chaos. Neighbors who had lived side by side for generations began hammering palm fronds in one another's yards and winding coarse string around them to stake their claims. Borders that had never existed were suddenly contested. Brothers who had lived under the same roof for sixty years argued over ownership. Women demanded rent from lazy husbands. Fences suddenly appeared. The industrious baked mud they dug out of the estuaries and made proper adobe fences. The lazy threw up ugly things of woven twigs. Overnight, La Boca became a walled city. Dozens of people were suddenly homeless, tossed out by their spouses, parents, lovers, friends. Father Montoya found himself in the middle of the first case of mass insanity in La Boca's history."

"Can we walk and do this?" Leon asked him. "I'm going to need something to drink really soon."

Ramon continued the story as they climbed down the rocks. "Meanwhile, Juan began hacking at the roots of the thorny brush that made up the thicket. Eight feet high, with dark twisting limbs and the resiliency of steel"—Ramon waved his open hands over his head to simulate branches—"the plants resisted Juan's ax. After each swing his fingers stung and the bones in his arms vibrated like marimba tines. He tried to enlist help from the many unemployed in the village, but no one wanted such hard work. However, when Juan saw what was going on, he put out flyers advertising the brush as excellent material for fence building. That afternoon a dozen men and women were at his door. For a modest fee they were permitted to chop down the brush and cart it away.

"Juan planned to clear a narrow stretch just wide enough for the laying of railroad tracks. He was sure the government would pay a great deal for the already cleared land, and the plan might have worked but for some unforeseen complications."

"Every time I talk to you there are unforeseen complications," Leon said. They were walking slowly back to the hotel. The few streetlights, bare bulbs with tin backings tacked to the trunks of palm trees, suddenly came on. Leon turned to see if the bookstore was lit, but they had already passed it.

"The fence builders swung their machetes at the fierce roots from sunup to sundown in the terrible heat, frustrated by the tenacious plants and irritated by the constant cicada gambling, but driven by their desire for fence wood and by the few dollars they had paid for this tiresome privilege. After they had cut a narrow passage fifteen yards deep, they began hearing noises. It had taken two weeks to progress those few yards and many became discouraged."

"Let me guess," Leon said. "It was another one of your relatives gabbing about bushes."

"No," Ramon said. "That wasn't it. Juan, although tired from dictating a new letter to the government, investigated the noises himself. He took a machete from one of his customers, then waved people back." Ramon waved. "He took a huge sweeping swing"—Ramon swung—"and lashed into the stem of the bush making a cut nearly a quarter of an inch deep. The vibrations ran back through the thicket in widening circles. No sooner had they begun than came a low throaty groan that grew into a growl. Led by Juan, the men and women evacuated the excavation area in haste."

"Another guess," Leon said.

"Go ahead."

"One of your women relatives, about to croak, barking her head off."

"No. A number of possible explanations were speculated on by the citizens of La Boca. Most centered around the existence of some beast, probably a jaguar. But no one could explain how it would be able to move about. Then Juan discovered the answer. He reminded them that the thicket was too dense even for the passage of sound, and so he reasoned that the noises they were hearing were jungle sounds that had been trapped in the thicket for centuries, freed now by the vibrations from the hacking at the plants. Having discovered this bit of wisdom, Juan launched into one of his finest orations, exhorting the citizens to think of the great opportunity presented them—to hear the roar of the brontosaurus, the screech of the pterodactyl, the bellow of the tyrannosaurus. The people of La Boca would be the first humans ever to hear such sounds. As you can imagine, it was an honor no citizen could resist."

"Right," Leon said.

"In an act of generosity unprecedented in the history of La Boca, Juan gave permission for the whole city to chop down the thicket without charge. The following day the streets were empty. The tiny school was closed because the educational experience of a lifetime awaited anyone with a machete or ax. Even Father Montoya, sweating and praying in his robe, took a hatchet to the thicket. Of course, the whole community could not fit into the narrow area Juan had designated and no attempt at organizing shifts of labor was successful regardless of the beauty of his reasoning. The thicket was attacked across its full breadth. Men, women, children, the aged, the ill, the mentally unstable, pregnant wives, fishermen, salesmen, widows, widowers, a battalion of La Boca's finest unemployed—all of the village went after the thicket. And do you know what happened?"

"I assume the question is rhetorical."

Ramon turned and pointed to one of the dusty streets they were passing. "By noon the sounds of mastodons trumpeted through the narrow streets. The clumping of the stegosaurus wakened the few drunks who, knowing nothing of the miracle, swore off liquor and dove into the ocean, a baptism so powerful that they remained sober, some of them, for almost a week. Near the estuaries, the squawk, flutter, and splash of the great ichthyosaurus caused a panic among the jungle birds, who filled the skies like a biblical plague, then vanished, flying north and south, many species never to be seen again in La Boca. As soon as the sky emptied, it filled again with the swoop and screech of the pterodactyl, the yodel of the brontosaurus, the gnashing cough of the theropod." Ramon impersonated the beasts as he described them. "People were overwhelmed with wonder and chopped at the thicket with unmatched ferocity."

"Doesn't this seem the least bit farfetched to you, Ramon?"

"Compared with sex in vegetable bins?"

"So what's the point?"

"Children discovered that if they dropped to their knees and screamed into the brush no one would hear until an ax shook the bushes and their voices came jumping out at them. Those men who were fascinated by their own voices stopped hacking and listened to themselves come out of the brush while others chopped. 'Do I really sound like that?' they said, then yelled into the brush again. Shy men found they could propose to their sweethearts in this manner and three marriages were set on that day. Even Juan Matamoros tried it. At the urging of others, he screamed into the thicket a full speech about the nature of right and wrong and the beauty of a woman's shoulders. Then, while his friends chopped, he sat cross-legged on the ground and heard himself as others did, the lilt and charm of his voice, rising and receding like the ocean." Ramon paused and put his hand on Leon's shoulder. "Juan moved himself to tears." Ramon wiped at his dry eyes, and they continued.

"Before long, human voices had drowned out the roars of the ancient beasts. It took a lecture on humility from Father Montoya to convince people to quit screeching into the thicket and ruining the history lesson. Most quickly agreed with the priest, embarrassed and shamed. Those who weren't entirely convinced heard his speech again when they chopped into the brush and decided he was right. The townspeople hacked in silence, waiting for the sounds of dinosaurs to return, but they were gone, replaced by new sounds—a few creaks, an odd whistle. Do you want to guess what this was?"

"Let me get some liquor first." They had reached the Hotel Esperanza and walked through the lobby to the bar. Leon requested a bottle of vodka. Outside again, at the water's edge, he uncapped the vodka and took a swig. "Okay, what were the goddamn creaks?"

"No one knew," Ramon said, and waited for the bottle. He drank. "Once again, it was Juan who deduced what had happened. He reasoned that the sounds had filtered through the thicket in varying degrees, the oldest having traveled the farthest. He calculated that now they were beyond the age of the dinosaur, into the mammal era or perhaps an ice age.

"People quickly lost enthusiasm. Neither ice nor mammals were as fascinating as dinosaurs. Everyone was ready to quit, but Juan convinced them to stay. If the sounds were jungle sounds, he told them, they should be able to work back far enough to find the sounds of people, the voices of their own grandparents and great-grandparents.

"A new wave of excitement swept over La Boca. The thought of hearing the voices of people they had lost was invigorating. The chopping resumed. For many of the townspeople, the work was silly since their ancestors had rarely stepped into the jungle, the only paths into it being rugged and narrow. Banana harvesters, hunters, fishermen, and bird merchants took the estuaries back into the jungle, but townspeople never did unless they wanted to be alone, or, more likely, wanted to be alone with someone else's wife or husband."

"Good," Leon said, "we're getting to the sex part."

"The chopping of the thicket continued into the night, and although some wanted to light torches and keep working, they were persuaded to wait until morning. This gave Juan and Father Montoya the opportunity to look into something unusual. Children near the south estuary reported odd smells. Juan and the father directed their considerable noses to the thicket and they smelled it too—the unmistakable odor of biscuits cooking.

"The priest sent the children home. He and Juan agreed they had to investigate before they resumed chopping, but how?" Ramon threw out his arms. Leon shrugged. "It was then Juan had another of his illuminations."

"That was on the tip of my tongue," Leon said.

"Because of the sudden demand for palm fronds, stacks of huge leaves littered the village. Juan and the father hurried about, collecting several of the largest. Juan also took string that marked the yard of a sleeping neighbor and borrowed a sewing needle from his wife. Father Montoya brought the ladder he climbed to ring the mission bell to the spot of the odors.

"The father, at Juan's instruction, sewed the largest leaves to the bottoms of their shoes—both Juan and Montoya wore shoes every day, not unusual for a priest, but highly pretentious for a bum. They leaned the ladder against one of the plants, and Juan climbed it barefoot. The top of the thicket was nearly level, dense, and thorny. The priest threw Juan his shoes. With them, Juan stepped out onto the thicket. The pile of palm leaves kept him from sinking into the thorny mire. The priest threw up his own shoes and joined Juan. They walked like men in shallow water, lifting their feet high." Ramon demonstrated, raising his knees to his chest and stomping in the sand. "You try it."

"Is the story over?" Leon said.

Ramon shook his head and pointed to the sky, which was now dark and sprinkled with stars. "By the light of the moon and the power of their nostrils, they traced the origin of the odor. There was a square hole in the dense growth. Smoke curled out of it, smelling of biscuits. Juan tried to look in, but the smoke was thick and hot. The father tapped his shoulder and pointed to another hole. There they saw the Roches family, one of the poorest in all of La Boca—Tico Roches, his wife, Guadalupe, and baby, Angelica." Ramon paused to drink.

"Great story, Ramon. They discover the baby who will one day be the town baker."

"I'm not finished yet. Be patient."

"Give me the vodka," Leon said, but it was too late, Ramon had already resumed.

"The Roches family had carved a small room out of the thicket. A few flat stones were the floor. An ashy circle directly beneath the hole was their stove. The only entrance—a crawl hole that led to the nearby estuary." Ramon drank and hung his head. "Both of the men standing on the thicket in their shoes of palm leaves were deeply moved. They found five more chimney holes, but did not look inside them, feeling already like a pair of peepers. They walked back to the ladder, weighted by sadness. Neither had known such poverty existed in La Boca."

Leon pried Ramon's fingers from the bottle.

"The following day people returned at dawn to begin chopping. They found two long palm fronds linked by string marking off the south end of the thicket. The priest said that the roped area was not to be attacked any further. He refused to give any explanation, which, for a man of the cloth, is often the most convincing argument. Many thought they knew the reason. They had seen a vision the night before, an image of men walking on air, visible to humans as great silhouettes in moonlight, ghosts with feet the size of anvils. They reasoned that this stretch of thicket was sacred ground. Father Montoya, when he heard this rumor, did not correct it. After all, he confided to Juan, what is more sacred than the home of a family?"

Leon plopped down in the sand, and Ramon followed.

"The remainder of the thicket went much faster. Within a matter of hours the chops of machetes were answered by human voices. At first, the voices were unintelligible, but by midmorning they heard Esteban Matamoros, the famous conquistador—my direct ancestor, you'll recall—reciting poetry about the nature of life and death and the charm of a woman's ankle. By noon, an old woman heard the voice of her grandmother. By two, La Boca was filled with ghosts.

"Juan heard his father, Jorge, leading the first ox in the history of La Boca down the burro trail and was deeply moved. He had forgotten the musical quality of his father's voice when cursing an animal. Father Montoya heard his mother and father whispering to one another and was touched so profoundly he wept. When he discovered they were preparing for lovemaking, the good priest tried to hold the branches still, as if they were the limbs of his adolescent parents, but the vibrations could not be stopped and rattled through his fingers and into his bones, the closest this man of God ever came to actual lovemaking: the trembling of his own conception."

Leon moaned and rolled over, face down in the sand.

"So it was that Father Montoya discovered that he was conceived illicitly, but, at least, his parents did eventually marry. A dozen women and men discovered they were bastards, that their fathers were not the men who had raised them. And then the worst happened."

Leon raised his head from the sand. "Some voice in the bushes started telling this story?"

"No. With only fifteen yards of thicket remaining, people began hearing their own voices, only several years younger—men with their neighbors' wives, daughters with the local delinquents. People realized that anyone who had done anything in the jungle that he wanted kept secret was in jeopardy. All who had such worries quit chopping at the thicket and took their children home with them, which, of course, was everyone. While the first day resulted in three marriage proposals, the second ended with fifty divorces."

Leon spit sand from his mouth and sat up again.

"Or so it would have been, but that night a wind off the mainland blew through what was left of the thicket and into town. It dislodged the remaining sounds, and the night streets filled with the noises of lovemaking. The townspeople, at first wary, became enthralled as the night continued and sounds of love reverberated around them. Men became excited. Women became passionate. Couples who had broken apart irrevocably in the afternoon were back together before morning, resulting in a baby boom like La Boca had never known before, or, for that matter, since."

"A happy ending," Leon said and raised the bottle. Ramon took it.

"In the light of morning only Juan was unhappy. The pathway for the train was just a few yards from completion but he could find no one interested in working regardless of what he might pay. Then one more of his insights struck him."

"Damn," Leon said.

"He called for yet another town meeting, which once again delighted the people and they gathered happily. He told them that he was going to donate part of his land for a water tower for the train. The people of La Boca were overwhelmed by the generosity of this man who only a few days earlier had let them clear his land for free. He suggested that the town take up a collection, and those too poor to donate money could volunteer their time to build the tower. His part, of course, was the donation of the land itself.

"Happy from their night of love, people were easily persuaded. The spot he donated lined up perfectly with the narrow path he had envisioned for the rails. He reasoned, quite logically, that with only a few yards of thicket to clear and a free water tower waiting, the railroad would happily choose the route he suggested. As the final touch, he took all the money he had collected from the people who paid to clear the thicket and all his wife had saved and used it to build a storefront near the water tower, facing the imaginary rails, making it large enough to live in besides."

"They lived happily ever after," Leon said.

"No. The railroad never came. Every few feet of jungle they cleared to lay the tracks would be covered overnight by new growth. Monkeys hid their tools and ate their food while they slept. Some even attacked a group of men, biting off the tip of one man's nose. Then the rains came and work stopped. By the time the rains were over, there was a new government that did not believe La Boca existed. The railroad was abandoned." Ramon drank the last of the vodka. "This was a small bottle."

"You took the last drink?"

"It was hardly a swallow, and full of saliva. I did you a favor."

For a moment they were silent, Leon flat on his back again, Ramon sitting up in the sand.

"So you're finished, right?" Leon said.

"Yes," Ramon said. "Now do you understand?"

"Do I understand? Absolutely. You don't have to add a word."

"Then you'll quit seeing Lourdes?"

Leon leaned forward. "What does that have to do with anything?"

"What you're doing isn't right." Ramon prodded him with his finger as he spoke. "We have our customs."

"I'm not hurting a soul." Leon pushed the finger away. "And how does that have anything to do with dinosaurs in the jungle?"

"The thicket. There were no dinosaurs in the jungle."

"Whatever."

"It is a story that illuminates your problem."

"I don't have a problem," Leon said.

"Sleeping with two women, two respectable women, will bring disaster. Each thinks you're planning to marry her, do you know that?"

"I've given them no reason to think that."

"You make love with them. In this country, women only see men they intend to marry. Unless they're prostitutes." Ramon held the bottle upside down over his mouth to let the last drops hit his tongue. "If you must see them both, marry one and make the other your mistress. At least, then, each will have a place in society."

Leon laughed contemptuously. "The great society of La Boca." He pivoted onto both elbows and faced Ramon. "You live in the past, buddy. You live entirely in the past."

"No. You live in a country that isn't yours. You have to understand our history and obey our customs, or you will ruin them both and yourself as well." He could see Leon was not impressed. "We come from different traditions. True, if I lived in California, I might have trouble adjusting to sleeping in a hot tub or fornicating with strangers in the middle of a city street. I might find it hard to base my life on a television program. But this is a bigger issue. Marry Pilar. She's the one for you. Let her make you a father. Don't see Lourdes. She's too young anyway."

Leon laid his head on his arms. "You're a good friend, Ramon. But shut up, all right?"

"Because I'm a good friend I'm warning you."

"So," Leon said, almost wistfully, "for the thousandth time, I'm warned."

"You really didn't get the point of the story?" Ramon asked him.

"Tell me."

"I mentioned that the brush was thorny, didn't I?"

"Yes, thorny and thick."

"And it held history in its branches—that's important. Then people yelled to erase history, you remember that part? Let's see—Juan was lonely for the rest of the world, and what about the drunks? Did I leave that out?"

"They jumped in the ocean."

"That was a good little detail, don't you think? Terrified of the dinosaurs, they leapt into the water. I do an especially good pterodactyl. My father did wonderful dinosaurs. He could do a mastodon that would turn your blood cold. I thought the mean-

ing of the story was perfectly clear, although this damn vodka
makes it difficult for me to put my finger on it at just this moment.
How much did Cruz charge you for this? Or the wine, for that
matter? Didn't you like the part about walking on the thicket?"

"Once I knew a woman who loved her own reflection," Leon
said softly.

"Yes?" Ramon waited but Leon said nothing more. "There
are many things worse than loneliness." He settled back in the
sand. "There is ignorance, for example. Not to mention hunger."
They lay side by side. The night was dark and close. "Humiliation is worse, no? Betrayal? Greed? For that matter, I've suffered
more from constipation than loneliness."

"I want to know about the ruins," Leon told him.

"The ruins? How did you hear about the ruins?" Ramon
rocked against the sand, burrowing. "The ruins are La Boca's
pride and embarrassment. But I can't tell you any more. The ruins
are only for townspeople."

"You can tell me," Leon said. "I'll get us another bottle of
vodka."

"Yes," Ramon said. "A bigger one, perhaps?"

Leon stumbled as he stood. "This may be a two-person job.
Are we drunks, Ramon?"

"Of course not," he said, standing slowly, taking Leon's elbow. "Now walk."

"Why won't you tell me about the ruins?"

"Only the people of La Boca know about the ruins."

"I pay taxes, don't I?" Leon said. "Well, actually, I don't, but
who does here? The point is, I've lived here as long as I've lived
anywhere. Not counting when I was a kid, I mean. We're not
drunks?"

"We are drunk, but we are not drunks—a fine distinction,
but significant. The same is true of your stay in La Boca. You
have to do more than just live here to become one of us—another
fine distinction but equally significant."

There were now guests in the bar and Leon seemed to sober up immediately, straightening his shoulders, correcting his stride. He nodded and smiled at them, although the lighting was too dim and his vision too blurred for him to make out who they were. He let Ramon select the bottle. As soon as they crossed under the arch back into the lobby, Leon again leaned heavily against Ramon. They stepped out the door to return to the beach.

"Look at this." Ramon pointed to his feet. Plaster from the top story littered the ground around the building. "You've made no commitment at all, not to La Boca, not to your friends—pass that vodka—not even to your work." He accepted the bottle and used it to point to the hotel. "The Esperanza is crumbling at this very moment and you make no effort to stop it. And what about me? Your best friend and you've told me nothing about why you left the United States, why you came here, what you did before. You're arrogant like all the others from your country. You assume. You assume."

"All Americans are arrogant, Ramon?" Leon refused the bottle. "You exaggerate."

"You see? Americans you call yourselves. Everyone in this continent is an American, but you give that special label to yourselves alone. Now you want to know all about this village but give nothing of yourself, not even to your best friend." He gulped vodka. "This is good," he said. "We should drink this more often." He offered it to Leon again, then capped the bottle. "If you want La Boca's secrets, first give me some of yours."

Leon felt too drunk to be having this conversation, but he was also too drunk to end it. "You're the only one who knows about Pilar and Lourdes," he offered.

"Hah," Ramon said. "That's not so much a secret as a private boast. If I hadn't warned you, you would have broadcast it on loudspeakers."

Leon reeled for a moment, stepping forward to avoid crumpling to the sand. He steadied himself. In front of him, the ocean collapsed rhythmically, while behind him, the Esperanza slowly deteriorated. He turned to face Ramon. Beneath one of the patio lights a fluttering moth shone like the eye of a cat. "All right. I'll tell you one secret, and, in turn, you show me the ruins. Tonight."

"Tonight? I have to go home once in a while. But all right, tonight, after I eat a bite."

Leon put his hand on Ramon's shoulder and whispered in his ear. "When I lived in the States—it was a while ago. Anyway, I poisoned someone."

Ramon rocked back. "You killed him?"

Leon nodded.

"Intentionally?"

"I poisoned him on purpose, yes."

"Why? Why did you kill this man?"

"Why is none of your business. I told you a secret, a big one. Now . . ."

"He was with your wife." Ramon thrust the bottle into Leon's chest. "You came home from work, suspecting nothing, of course—you hadn't been married long, and there they were. What color hair did your wife have?"

"No. Nothing like that. I have no intention of telling you why. That would be another secret, and our deal was for one."

"He cheated you in business," Ramon said. "He was your partner. You had known him since you were no larger than a turtle, and you trusted the son of a bitch, so you never suspected that it was he who was embezzling money . . ."

"The ruins. I want to see them."

"I'll guess the reason. I have a talent for such things. Eventually, I'll guess it."

"Maybe you will." The image of the man he had poisoned took shape before him, incomplete, faceless—only his hands were distinct, as white as the caps of waves that broke in the distance. "Then again, maybe you won't. When will you be back?"

Ramon looked at him for several moments as if he had forgotten what they were talking about. "Oh yes, the great ruins of

La Boca. I'll be back in about an hour. Here." He handed the vodka to Leon. "We may need this. Be sure to bring it."

Leon cradled the bottle against his shoulder.

FROM BEHIND the bookstore window, Pilar had watched Leon and Ramon as they walked down the beach that afternoon. She had not intended to wave unless Leon turned toward her, but she couldn't stop her hand. He hadn't seen her, tapping the bottle against his leg as he walked, his gaze focused alternately on the ocean and the ground beneath his feet.

"He didn't even look this way," she said.

"My God in the ground, I'm tired of hearing about that son of a bastard." Cruz sat on the bundle of books he had just delivered and lowered his head into his hands.

She stepped away from the window, pushing her hands into the pockets of her simple striped skirt. "If I didn't know better, I'd say you were jealous."

"Yes, but you know better." He spoke into his palms as he massaged his forehead with his fingertips. "It's hotter here than anywhere on earth." He ran his fingers through his hair. "I have a fool sitting out in the bus. Sweating to death, I imagine. I asked him to wait at the hotel, but he was afraid he'd miss me. The thought of another week here terrifies him. He's Canadian. I generally like Canadians, but this guy is an idiot—not that I blame him for wanting to be out of this hole."

"Does that mean you can't stay and talk with me?" Pilar cleared a spot next to her cash box, flattened her palms on the counter, and lifted herself to it.

"That idiot can rot, as far as I'm concerned. I told him to wait at the hotel. I can't be responsible for everything." Cruz touched the tips of his mustache. He breathed heavily. "It'll be dark soon anyway, and the heat will let up. You'd think I'd be used to it by now, wouldn't you? I don't think I've ever gotten used to anything. Not one thing."

"You should take a swim. I could never make it through the

summer without the ocean." She looked out the window at the water, but what struck her was the room, how, with its walls of shelves and brightly colored books, it resembled her grandmother's shack. Why hadn't she recognized that before?

"Would you like something to drink?" she asked him.

Cruz shook his head and raised one diminutive hand, opened as if to say *Halt*. "I drank a beer with your sweetheart after I deposited his guests. I admit that he's generous—with the hotel's liquor, at least." From his shirt pocket, he pulled a little cigar with a white plastic tip. "This is all I need."

"No," Pilar told him. "You can't smoke in here. You'll make the books stink."

"Most books stink already." He sighed again and stood. "Where can we talk that I am permitted a smoke?"

She led him to her kitchen, walking quickly. She had always felt uncomfortable with short men, a feeling that, in turn, made her annoyed with herself. She pulled a chair from the table for him. Sitting, he seemed taller. She took a white bowl from the cupboard. "I don't have ashtrays," she said, setting it on the table. "I loved smoking when I was a kid, especially American cigarettes. But I quit because I thought it would discolor my teeth."

Cruz lit his cigar. "Let me see them."

Pilar smiled, then opened her mouth. "I have one bridge," she said, tapping the artificial tooth with her fingernail.

"You told me. Quite a beautiful story. Politics, erotic passion, and dental handiwork woven into one tight little tale. You can tell it to me again, if you wish. It must be frustrating to know such a story and be unable to tell anyone."

She ran her tongue over the artificial tooth. "Oh, I've told a few people."

Cruz exhaled a long cord of smoke and leaned forward. "Then you're stupid. You risk enough with some of the books you sell—not that you sell all that many." He folded his arms and crossed his legs, bumping the table. "You're not one of my profitable customers. But you can't tell people about your past."

"I've only told my grandmother, who knows everything, after all. And one of her friends, the baker, who is my grandmother's confidante. She wouldn't repeat any of it."

"And Leon?"

"He knows that I used to be a professor and that I had to quit. Why are you saying this now? Do you know something?"

Cruz waved the cigar in quick glowing arcs. "Not really. From what I've heard, your name is still on the list, but they have no idea where you are. I don't think they're really looking. They expect people like you to flee to Mexico or Costa Rica. They forget about places like this. You're safe here, but I don't see how you can stand it."

She was tempted to tell him what a relief it could be to live in La Boca—to swim and read and make love with a man, to attempt to make interesting meals without spending much money, to forget that people she knew were in prison. This was not something she could tell Cruz or anyone else. The only people who could understand the relief were people who would despise her for it. Yet when she was with people who lived here, she found herself disparaging the town, the weather, the texture of her days. From the outside, she thought her life looked grand, but in truth she found herself vaguely discontented with it.

Cruz stared at her like a guard dog waiting for an abrupt movement. "We all do what we must in order to get by, don't we?" she said.

"Is that supposed to hurt me? Am I supposed to apologize for the stupid Canadian in my bus? The silly routines I play for the tourists? I'm still working—I'm not the one in hiding."

"Your name isn't on the list."

"No, and with any luck it never will be. But there *are* things you could do. Let's not pretend otherwise. What was it you taught? I've meant to ask you a dozen times. Let me speculate." He took another long drag on the cigar. She disliked his posturing and wondered if she would like him at all in other circumstances.

"I'm very good at logical deduction," he said. "First of all, you're beautiful, so you couldn't have taught any of the hard sciences. You don't lisp or whine, so it couldn't be psychology. You're a Marxist, so you could never have taught political science or sociology or history. Literature would be the obvious choice, since you run this foolish bookstore, but that would be too easy. It has no interest if it's that easy. My guess is that you taught anthropology. You studied the hairstyles of the Mayans or the food utensils of the Eskimos, something like that."

"Wrong," Pilar said. "Completely wrong."

"No?" He looked genuinely surprised. "What is there left?"

"Not all psychologists lisp and whine."

"You're saying that to throw me off." He pointed with the cigar. "If you were a psychologist, you'd have made a pass at me by now as a result of my utter indifference to your beauty. Psychologists go wild for that. No." He dismissed the idea by twitching the cigar, and Pilar wondered if it was nothing more than a prop. She felt a sudden tenderness for him, curious what a psychologist would think of a short man who used little cigars as props.

"I hope you're not an economist. I loathe economists, but you have no strong body odor, so you couldn't be. Physical education? My God in the ground, is that it?"

"Geography."

"Hah," Cruz snickered. "They still teach that? What is there to learn? Europe is here, Africa is there. Australia is too big to be an island, so it's a tiny continent. Central America is the twisted neck that connects a fucked-up head to its fucked-up body, the tortured throat of a ridiculous hourglass. There's nothing to it. You know all of that by the time you're twelve."

"Stop it." She pretended to be angry. "Geography is very important. You're always so nasty, Cruz. Why do I look forward to seeing you?"

"Because I know you, the real you: the fugitive. No matter how often Leon splays those beautiful legs of yours, he cannot know you as I do. He cannot ever understand you as well." He leaned forward once more, his elbows on the table. "Let me tell you a story. This was back when I was a college student."

"Before they had geography classes," she said.

He smiled. "Perhaps a class or two was offered in geography. I, by the way, majored in political science, a wonderful thing to study in this country—if you asked the wrong kind of question, you were subject to disappearance."

"I think you're exaggerating now. I hate exaggeration."

"Then you really should go to another country." He waved the little cigar again. "I had quite a number of girlfriends in college but there was one I particularly liked, a very lovely girl. The only problem we ever had was her height. She was a little taller than I, and, back then, I was sensitive about my height."

"You've grown out of that now—so to speak."

"Very humorous. In any case, we went together to a concert—she liked classical music, but in all other respects she was perfectly normal. We were in a gym, sitting on folding chairs, but everyone was dressed up. While we were listening, two men in front of us started arguing—it was very irritating. They pushed one another, and finally, there was a full-scale fight. One of them came tumbling back into our laps, knocking both of us over. And then something very unusual happened. My girlfriend suddenly kissed this man on the lips. She licked a trickle of blood from his cheek."

Cruz paused to smoke, wanting, Pilar could see, to add dramatic tension to his story.

"I was surprised, of course. The police were already working their way down the aisle. My girlfriend threw her sweater over this man and helped him up. She told the police that her husband had been kicked in the mouth, and he needed a doctor immediately. They let them pass.

"One man was arrested. I was almost taken with him, but the people sitting next to me said I was not one of the trouble-

makers. I didn't see my girlfriend again until the following night.
She came to my apartment and crawled into my bed—for the
first time, I might add—and she explained. Now it is your turn
to speculate."

"No," Pilar said.

"Please, I would like to hear what you think."

"He was an old lover," Pilar said, "someone who had left
her long ago."

"Just as I suspected." He covered his eyes, his mouth twisted
into a smirk. "What a predictable romantic you are." He smoked
again and tapped the ash into the bowl. "My girlfriend took off
her clothes and got into my bed and told me her story. When
the man fell against her, she discovered that he was not a man at
all but a woman dressed as one. Her breasts were wrapped tightly,
but my girlfriend felt them. So she kissed her to let her know
she would help. Can you imagine what the police would have
done with such a person?"

Pilar cringed to think of it. "Your girlfriend was brave."

"Yes, and now we have been married nine years." He leaned
back in the chair. "She is the true reason for my utter indifference
to your beauty. She is also the one who arranges to get the books
you want that can't be bought openly. She finds clothes—
disguises—for the people whom I take to places like this."

Pilar's heart suddenly fluttered. "Are there such people here?"

"Besides you?"

"I don't count. I grew up here. I would have come here
whether I met you or not."

"You count. Remember that: You count. No, there are no
others here. There have been, but the only place to stay was the
hotel, and that American you sleep with made them nervous.
Besides, most people think this place torture enough."

"You exaggerate again. There's the beach and books and
people."

"And once a week, news from your trusty book procurer

about the world you left behind, the causes that you've abandoned." He stubbed out his cigar in the bowl. "I want to bring someone here—to stay with you."

There was a sudden pounding on the door. They turned to the sound, but neither stood.

"Leon, I imagine," Cruz said, resettling in his chair. "He's finished that cooking wine I sold him, and now wants to screw his little leftist."

"I don't like the timing of it," she said. "And I don't like your idea." She jumped from her chair before he could respond and walked to the door.

A strange man stood in the fading light of dusk. Red-faced, with a peculiar smile, he looked like a clown. "Yes?" she said.

"I'm with Mr. Cruz." He spoke awkwardly and with an accent. Pilar realized he must be the Canadian. "I was getting hot in the automobile." He sounded each syllable slowly. "I am here to ask if I may sit inside the house, please."

"Come in," Pilar said in English. "Make yourself comfortable."

Cruz stood in the kitchen doorway, slightly stooped and smiling—his disguise. "Oh, comb in, comb in," he said, his English intentionally bad. "I just telling her how is almost time to go Cruz-ing."

The Canadian smiled at Cruz but spoke to Pilar. "Your English is very good. I've been surprised at how few people speak English here. It's terrible to be unable to communicate. I feel I have a million words backed up in my skull. You were at the hotel the other day, weren't you? With Mr. Green? I talked with him a couple of times. Odd gentleman."

"Would you like water?" Pilar asked. "Come into the kitchen."

Cruz sat beside his passenger. "You talk weeth *Me*-stir Green? Lots of talk, that *Me*-stir Green."

Any idiot could see that Cruz was faking, embellishing his accent ridiculously. He believed every North American was a

CIA agent. "Give them what they expect," he had said to her. "Shuffle your feet, pinch their behinds—they will never suspect someone they don't take seriously." She gave him a disapproving look for his act.

"Mr. Green told me the best way to enjoy my breakfast was to pretend I'd never had food before. He said the same about the beach, that it would become a great beach if I imagined that I'd never seen another. I like to bodysurf. For some reason there are no substantial waves." He accepted the glass of water from Pilar and thanked her.

"There are rocks and reefs just beneath the surface of the water," she said. "They break up the waves, especially near the hotel. The beach down here has larger waves."

"Rocks end reefs?" Cruz looked puzzled. "You mean rocks end rolls. I like rocks end rolls berry much. Cruz-ing music."

"No," the Canadian said. He spoke loudly and slowly. "In the ocean. Rocks in the ocean, the water." He held his glass up to Cruz's face.

"Oh," Cruz said, nodding. "Where fish go."

Pilar giggled. "Cruz," she said, shaking her head.

"We shouldn't laugh," the Canadian said seriously.

"I just telling Pilar," Cruz said. "She got lot a room ear. Take some boarders. *Me*-stir Green, he don't take care a coast-tumors too good."

"Well," the Canadian said, staring at Pilar, his face redder than ever, "you would be a charming hostess, I'm sure."

Cruz poked him with his elbow, winking several times. "Hot tamale, no?"

"Mr. Green needs to do something about the building itself. There was a crack in my room the size of my finger." He held up his little finger. "I actually put my finger in the crack to measure."

Pilar stared at her lap, angry with Cruz for continuing their conversation in front of this man but determined to have the last word. "I couldn't take in guests, I'm afraid. This place isn't really that big. There's only the one bedroom and the store. I'd have to close the store to take in guests."

The Canadian nodded. "I hate to be pushy," he said, "but I'd really like to get on the road. The drive through the jungle is so awful. It seems that we should get started."

"You obsolitely right. I have joost a few more stuff to do. Pilar end I has to see her gran-mudder. Then we go. You wait in booze, no?" Cruz smiled grandly.

"In the bus?" He looked to Pilar. "Is that what he said?"

She nodded. "We won't be long." She led him to the door, and watched as he walked to the Powerwagon before returning to the kitchen. "*Me*-stir Green? Cruz, you're terrible."

"Fuck him," Cruz said. "I studied English to understand the enemy, not to please bourgeois fools who stick their fingers in others' cracks. Come on, let's go to your grandmother's before he melts all over my floorboard."

"No one knows she is my grandmother—practically no one, anyway." It pleased her to put him in the wrong.

"That's wise." He extinguished the stub of his cigar in the bowl. "I'll be more careful."

La Boca had turned dark, but the heat hadn't broken. Windows were lit, but curtains hadn't yet been pulled. "When we return, I am going to grab your ass," Cruz said. "I don't mean anything by it, but the Canadian will expect as much."

Pilar smiled at him, but immediately became uneasy because he only reached her shoulders. She looked away. "I think you like your sleazy disguise."

"It's a difficult job, but it has its small pleasures. We can hope word will not get back to your American."

"He wouldn't care. I can do as I please. He can do as he pleases."

"Ah, modern love. How beautiful it all is. And who else is Mr. Green pleasing with his passion?"

"I have no idea. Hotel guests, I imagine. Actually, I'm glad he sees other women."

"You mean *fucks* other women." He said it savagely.

Pilar glared at him. Cruz enjoyed making her upset, but she refused to let him. "Yes, that is what I mean." She spoke slowly, without emotion. "It makes him less possessive."

"I dropped off a pretty woman today—not that you'd care. Japanese-American. A nice little waddle in her walk."

She could see that he was determined to make her uncomfortable, but he had chosen the wrong tack. "Why are we going to my grandmother's?"

"I've been seeing her for years. Your grandmother reads my palm. Not that often. Every now and then. She's not all that good any more, but I enjoy her company." He took Pilar's hand and lifted it to his face. "You have lovely hands. What has your grandmother seen here?" He ran a finger over the soft mounds of her palm.

She liked having her hand held by Cruz and was disappointed when he dropped it to light a cigar. "When I was little, she told me I'd be a teacher, which turned out to be accurate, although she said I'd teach here."

"You've returned here after being a teacher—that's close enough."

"The last time she read my palm, she said I would have a virgin birth." Pilar allowed herself a short laugh. "Her predictions have become a little screwy. I don't put much stock in them."

Cruz shrugged and smoked, wiping drops of sweat from his forehead. "I just like her company. She's a charming woman."

At this moment, Pilar stopped believing him. He was maneuvering her, trying to get her to agree to hide someone. She decided to undercut his strategy. "There aren't going to be any guests in my house. I'm not hiding anyone. Right now I need my life to be simple. I don't want any complications."

The road had evaporated. They walked on the narrow path that separated one hut from another.

"Simplicity," Cruz said, waving his hands at the simple mud

shacks. "What a wonderful thing. What a marvelous, childish joy. This is a very simple proposition, so you will like it. It has all the simplicity of life and death. There is a man I know of who is dying, a revolutionary hero, let us say, a man the government would very badly like to capture. They suspect, rightly, that he is in a certain city. As we speak, they search for him, and, needless to say, if he is found, it will mean the murder of those who hide him, a great propaganda victory for the government, and a death for our hero that denies him any dignity at all." They had reached Maria Peralta's house and they stopped. "Now, here is the simple part: You are his only hope. He is in no condition to travel through the mountains and across the border—the drive here would kill him, for that matter. We would come by boat. It would be risky, but we could do it." Cruz put his hand on the curtains to the hut. "Maria Peralta, are you decent?" he called, then whispered, "If you choose not to accept him, I will have to kill him."

"Cruz, Cruz," Maria called. "Come in, foolishness."

Pilar held him back. "You wouldn't kill him."

"Yes, I would. To protect others. To cut our losses." He pulled the curtains aside. "Simple, no?"

"Ah," Maria said, seeing Pilar. She clasped her hands. "You two are getting married. I'm so happy."

Pilar forced a smile. "Don't be crazy. How are you? What is that on your head?"

"You're not going to marry? I thought I saw it on your faces. Let me have a drag on that, my dear Cruz." Maria extended her arm to him. She wore a white towel on her head, knotted in the front. Gray branches extended from the rear and forked above her crown.

"Let me give you one of your own." Cruz produced a cigar and knelt to light it for her, smiling graciously, which made Pilar wonder how many personalities he had and which was the real Cruz.

"Now will you tell us why you have sticks in your head?"
Pilar asked her.

Maria puffed on the cigar. "People have been asking me that
all my life." She laughed. "Don't you think it's becoming? I'm a
deer tonight. That's the real reason. I'm seeing what I can learn
from the deer."

Cruz sat on the floor beside the bed. "What have you learned
so far?"

"Patience. Vulnerability." She looked to the ceiling so suddenly that Pilar and Cruz turned their heads up. "I have a craving
for poplar leaves. Do deer eat them? Where do you suppose I
could get a few?"

"Cruz is here to have his palm read," Pilar said.

"No, he's not," Maria told her. "He's here to convince you
to marry him. Do you think these antlers would help my television? I can't get a thing to come in."

"I hate to disappoint you, Maria Peralta, but I am already a
married man," Cruz said.

"Oh," she said. "And happy, too. You are a very happy man.
Of course, you're married. I remember now. You have daughters."

"Two," Cruz told her.

Pilar sat on the floor beside him. "You don't remember the
past any better than you predict the future." Maria feigned a
look of hurt, which fooled Cruz but not Pilar. "So, are you a
doe or a buck?"

Maria laughed again and pulled the cigar from her mouth.
"A doe. A buck would just want to ram things."

"I thought only bucks had antlers," Cruz said.

"Yes," Maria told him, "all men think that. I know because
I made myself a man once. It wasn't that interesting—just boom,
boom, boom—nothing like a real life. I put baseballs in my un-
dershorts and the fender from Armando Garcia's ruined car on
my shoulders. I made eye patches out of coins to block most of

my vision, and tied bags of sand to my ankles—it was just like being a man. I spent an hour humping that couch over there." She pointed at one of the walls. "Oh, I threw it out afterward. I remember feeling an overwhelming desire to say something smart. You feel it right here." She lodged her hands between and beneath her breasts. "Tits keep that from happening to women. Our blessing."

"Men are a little more complex than that, don't you think?" Cruz made little circles with his cigar.

"I try to give them the benefit of the doubt," Maria said. She puffed again on the cigar, then carefully snuffed it with her fingers. "Give me your hand, Cruz. I don't do palms much nowadays. Hooves, that would be another matter." She laughed once more. "I just love my jokes. Now, I will tell you one thing, and then I'm going back to grazing. Let's see." She moved her finger back and forth along the lines of his palm, then turned his hand over and examined the fine hairs at the base of his thumb.

"Someone is waiting for you," she said, then released his hand.

THE CANADIAN sat on the hood of the Powerwagon. From this distance, he looked handsome, Pilar thought. The red splotches on his face, from three houses away, could be mistaken for a ruddy complexion, like that of fishermen. She and Cruz paused at the corner of an aqua house. "First of all," she said, resting her hand against the wall, staring still at the Canadian, wondering at the power of distance to change perception.

"Yes?" Cruz stood beneath the branches of a scrawny avocado tree. "First of all?"

"You couldn't send him by boat. The water is too treacherous. You have to move through the reefs very carefully."

Cruz shook his head. "I already thought of that. We'll send him in a little rowboat. It's the only kind that could go unnoticed anyway. It will skim over the rocks. I will row it myself."

"You don't understand. Even a little boat will crack on the reefs. The waves will throw you right into one. You probably couldn't do it in daylight, but at night it would be impossible." She knew that as she spoke her resolve against taking in the man was faltering. Accepting him hypothetically was only a short step from accepting him physically. She had done enough, she reminded herself. Losing her career, her name . . .

"Then we have to hire someone who knows the waters here. Whom do you suggest?"

"You're not going to like this," she said, "but if we were going to do it, we'd need Ramon Matamoros."

"Good God in the ground, no. He is your American boy's best friend, and he is a terrible gossip. This has to be done discreetly." Then he took her in his arms and kissed her. "He's spotted us," he whispered. "He's coming this way." He kissed her again. "Bend down a little. I'm straining my neck. He's still coming, the idiot." He grabbed her bare thigh, then ran his hand up her leg to her ass, slipping his hand inside her panties.

"You're showing the world my butt," Pilar said. His hand felt warm and familiar, and she felt an urge to giggle. "I think you're going beyond the call of duty."

"He's turning back," Cruz said and pivoted them around the corner of the house. He removed his hand. "Can you trust Ramon or not?"

"Just like that you go from fondling my ass to political intrigue?"

"Don't flatter yourself," Cruz said. "I never changed the subject."

Pilar blushed, which further embarrassed her. "Ramon will keep quiet if you pay him enough," she said, straightening her skirt. "He wants to send his son to college."

"The eternal trap of the poor. They pay for their hope with poverty. How can a fisherman even dream of affording that?"

"He takes Leon's guests on little boat tours, walking tours."

She turned to look around the corner, half hoping that the Canadian would be approaching again. He was sitting on the hood as he had before, and she wondered whether he had really seen them or if Cruz had just pretended.

Cruz pulled a cigar from his pocket and stuck it between his lips. "If he won't take money, you can let him hold your ass. You seem eager enough for that."

Pilar jerked the cigar from his mouth and broke it in two, tossing the pieces to the ground. "Don't be a prick," she said. "Posture and pose all you want, but don't expect me to take any abuse from you."

Cruz knelt and recovered the cigar halves, taking his time. He blew dust from them and returned the pieces to his pocket before he stood again.

"I apologize, Pilar. It's traditional that men place the blame on women for their own feelings. I try not to be a traditional man, but it's a fight. Inside me, there's always a struggle." He tapped his chest, then dropped his hand and shoved it in his pants pocket. "Even with this confession, I have to fight the urge to make it something grand. I try to be a good man. But I can't always overcome the powerful force of being a man in a man's world." He turned from her. "I should cry right now. That would be perfect, wouldn't it? You see the contradictions? You see how difficult it is?"

"The truth is, I liked your hand," Pilar said shyly. "I know I shouldn't have. It seemed playful, although that sounds decadent, doesn't it?" At that moment she became aware of the evening light, which had taken on a purple tint. The air suddenly became charged—little pricks of electricity against her pores. She stood motionless, feeling a specific knowledge descend upon her: She was going to accept the dying man into her house. From that moment on, she knew any struggle would be pointless.

No sooner had she resigned herself to this than she sensed something new following it, something much bigger.

She turned quickly, as if she might see it in the slumping aqua walls of the house, or the shadow of sweat on the neck of Cruz's shirt, or among the scraggly limbs of the wind-damaged avocado tree. She touched her throat, which now failed her, making her breaths short and painful. Something powerful and large was suddenly proximate. She tried to catch her breath. Her heart, fluttering against her throat, choked her. Her eyes burned with tears, as if from smoke, and she could feel the approach of flames. She looked skyward through the tree's limbs at the scatter of stars in the immense black sky because the heat seemed to be coming from above. The sky was the same and was not the same—a mysterious change had taken place above her and now it entered her, searing her flesh.

And what she felt was passion.

She discovered in that instant that she loved Leon—she was deeply in love with Leon. The discovery caused her to tremble. How could she possibly know this? She wondered, but could not concentrate, the question too small for her consideration: Her chest was on fire.

"Are you all right?" Cruz asked her, and she had no way of answering. "You're going to let me bring you this man?" She nodded that she would. "I have to tell you exactly what you must do, and what Ramon must do, I suppose. I hate using that clown. Are you listening?"

She heard him as if from a distance, muffled by the pounding of her sudden and inexpressible love, but she heard him, and no longer wanted to argue, knowing that she would accept a stranger into her home as she had just accepted Leon into her heart.

BENJAMIN LAY on the floor, his hands locked beneath his head, and stared at the expanse of brick that led to the ceiling. Only from this angle could he imagine the house as something majestic rather than ridiculous. Even his friend Mono, who rarely had opinions about anything, thought it was a dumb house. Which

made Benjamin wonder what kind of chance he had in the world:
If you come from a bad house, you'll have a bad life. Not that
he blamed his parents or grandparents or anyone, for that matter.
But as long as he could remember he'd wished they'd lived in an
ordinary place, and he couldn't help but tie the miserable house
to his miserable problems. Thinking about it caused him to shift
on the floor. His body was helpless before his mind, and any
spark in his brain caused a response in his limbs, his movement
stirring up the musty odor that lived in the dark crack between
wall and floor.

"Catch." His mother stood over him, spoon and mixing bowl
cupped against her hip with one hand, a pillow thrust into the
air by the other. She was never happy unless doing two things
at once.

He lifted his hands too slowly, his head bumping against the
floor as the pillow hit his face.

"If you have to lie on the floor, at least put that under your
head." She waved the wooden spoon as she spoke, a short woman
with a round head and wild, flouncy hair. "You have a perfectly
good bed, but this is some sort of man thing, isn't it? If I let him,
your father would sleep on the ground every night." She tapped
the spoon against her hip and blew her hair off her forehead with
a puff of breath. "Have you finished your studying? Written that
paper Rosa wants?"

Benjamin slid the pillow beneath him and smiled at his
mother. Her busyness had the effect of making his movements
extra slow. "The paper's finished. I'm going out later to study
with Mono."

"Later? It's already later. Why do you two have to study
during the time God meant for sleep?" She raised the spoon as
if to gesture toward God, but when Benjamin looked up all he
saw was the same insanely high wall of bricks.

"I already explained all that," he said, fidgeting again on the
floor.

"I would like to hear the explanation once more. Complex problems of logic are difficult for me to hold in my head. You'll have to forgive your aging mother." She paused, then kicked one of his feet lightly. "A good son would be quick to point out how youthful his mother is."

"Mono's parents make him work late. They don't care anything about school." He crooked one arm, then the other, over his head as he spoke.

"You say that as if Mono did. Why you study with a known idiot is beyond me, especially when there are others much smarter who would probably still study with you—who used to study with you back when your grades were the best in the school."

Benjamin pulled the pillow out and put it over his head. "I can't hear you," he told her.

"Men never hear women," she said as she walked to the kitchen, whipping the batter in the mixing bowl.

His parents had long assumed that he would marry Lourdes. Benjamin knew this so well it caused him physical pain, an ache deep in his bowels. He and Lourdes had played and studied together all of their lives—until she became interested in the American. Then she had less to do with Benjamin, and once she had graduated, he almost never saw her. His grades had fallen. He had known that she was the smart one. He was brighter than the other boys, but it was Lourdes who had ideas, who figured things out, who made studying exciting.

He had purposely failed to take a required class so that he would be forced to go to school this summer, which meant he would not have to fish in the mornings with his father. This had once been his favorite part of the day: fishing in the early light, his father telling stories and guiding them expertly through the network of reefs. He could no longer bear it. His father's plans about the university distressed him. Benjamin was not at heart a good student. Lourdes was, and without her, school seemed a cruel joke.

Besides that, he knew the expense was more than his parents could possibly have saved. Tuition for one semester was more than a fisherman made in a year. His mother's rolls and cookies, her baby-sitting and house cleaning—none of it earned enough to buy even the books he'd need. He doubted that the entire town, pitching their spare money together, could afford to pay for a student's schooling.

All this thinking had caused him to roll off the pillow, face down on the floor. No sooner had he turned himself than his father burst into the house.

"What a beautiful night!" Ramon said, jubilant, his arms thrown open. Sand streaked his hair, making him look old. He stepped over Benjamin's legs, wavering a little, and dropped to his knees.

"You're going to have to warm your dinner yourself," Celita called from the other room. "I'm baking." She stuck her head in the doorway. "Where do men get this reserve of laziness?" Flour marked her hair as sand marked Ramon's. "We have chairs."

Ramon fell back against the wall and straightened his legs. He patted his son on the shoulder. "Have you ever seen such a tantalizing woman? I am sorry I missed dinner. Was it good?"

"Of course it was good," Celita said sternly.

Ramon looked to Benjamin, who nodded in confirmation.

"Have you started that essay yet?" Ramon asked him.

Benjamin had known the question was coming. His father fretted more about schoolwork than he did. "Finished it," he said.

"I knew it." Ramon stretched out across the brick floor, matching his son's position, which caused him to stare upward at the towering wall. "Have I ever mentioned that my father designed this house himself?"

"It's come up a time or two," Benjamin said.

Ramon raised himself to one elbow. "Perhaps you could tell me about it then."

"Do I have to?"

"Of course not," Ramon said. "I can tell you, if you prefer."

Benjamin sighed deeply, although he knew it would do him no good. "Grandfather didn't know anything about houses, but he built it anyway."

"Yes," Ramon said. "Ignacio Matamoros."

"Right," Benjamin said.

"And his handsome and talented son, Ramon," Ramon added.

"Him, too. So grandfather . . ."

"Ignacio."

"Ignacio had seen blueprints only one time—I don't have to tell that part, do I?"

"That is your decision, although it is a magnificent story, and you tell it beautifully."

"I don't think it's necessary."

"Very well." Ramon stared at the ceiling. "Ignacio knew nothing about building a house, but he did not let that discourage him. Go ahead."

"So the family lived in the bookstore."

"It wasn't a bookstore then, just a storefront."

"But it was a good location, so he got a lot of money for it and started drawing up designs for this big house he wanted to build."

"Like the one he'd seen the designs for."

"I'm skipping that part." Benjamin paused, running through the story in his mind to see if there were other parts he could drop. "So his plan was to have this big front room for parties and stuff, and then a bunch of other rooms and so on. He had a lot of bricks made from mud and marked off the ground where they were going to build, but this whole time he had to live with his wife's parents, and they didn't like him because he didn't have a job."

"His father-in-law was a very rude man," Ramon said.

"Why don't you tell this part?"

"To avoid the impudence of his father-in-law, Ignacio and his loyal son rose early each day before the others were awake, and walked down to the site where they were going to construct the great house. They worked quickly to complete the first big room, thinking that they could live in it while they finished the rest. However, they soon discovered that laying bricks in straight level lines was not an easy task. It's not, you know."

"Yeah. Okay." Benjamin used his favorite English words, then added in Spanish, "Tough."

"The bricks were heavy and the mortar was chunky. Ignacio discovered that his hands were about to become callused, which would make it hard for him to do the delicate work of drawing up plans. He decided to hire bricklayers to do the labor."

"Otherwise, you guys would never have gotten anywhere," Benjamin said.

Ramon poked Benjamin in the ribs. "The courteous and intelligent Ramon woke his father each day, and they marched to the site to see that all of the workers were present before finding a shady spot to rest. So determined was Ignacio not to permit his father-in-law's rudeness to interfere with his life, he slept more than usual, just to be sure none of the cross man's habits became his own. The work on the mansion went so quickly that Ignacio and even the brilliant Ramon failed to check the work as often as they had planned. But a man is capable of only so much." Ramon lifted his arms in resignation.

"Some men are capable of only so little," Celita called out from the kitchen.

Ramon and Benjamin shared a smile, then Ramon continued. "When the crew foreman went to the shady spot and woke him, Ignacio was surprised to hear that the job was finished. He took his son's hand and walked to the site."

"And it was a big mess," Benjamin said.

"The result did not quite match Ignacio's vision of the house. The workers had built it exactly as he had laid it out on paper, but the scaffolding had hidden their progress. Neither Ignacio nor Ramon was prepared for what was presented them." Ramon sat up, leaning against the wall. "The thirty-foot-square room was also thirty feet high—Ignacio believed in the value of symmetry. There was a large rectangular window facing the thicket." They both turned to look at the window. "And a tiny window . . ." They looked across the room.

"The size of a notebook," Benjamin said.

"A paperback," Celita corrected, standing now in the doorway, cleaning her fingers with a washcloth and shaking the flour from her hair.

"It was small," Ramon acknowledged, "and it faced the ocean. There were two doors, opposite one another in windowless walls. The door on the north side was wide enough for a wagon and several oxen."

"The other door was for bamboo men only," Benjamin said.

"And insects," Celita said.

"It turned out to be a little narrow," Ramon conceded, "and there were a few minor details he had omitted in his haste. There was no plumbing, no wiring for electricity, no bathroom."

Celita pointed at the south window. "And in the afternoons it was as dark as a grave, with only one tiny beam of light through the silly little window."

Ramon turned his gaze upward. "The ceiling was impossibly high." They all looked. "There was a magnificent fireplace, but no chimney."

"But Ramon built that later with the help of his brilliant son, Benjamin," Benjamin said.

"And his lovely wife, Celita," Celita added.

"Yes, and they did many other things to the house under the guidance of the gifted Ramon, but that is far in the future."

"Women's contributions always seem to get left out of your stories." Celita threw the wet cloth at him.

Ramon sighed sadly. "Such is the nature of history."

"That's because men tell it," Benjamin said.

"Did you hear that?" Ramon said. "You could be a philosopher. Have you ever considered philosophy?" He didn't wait for a reply. The washcloth had landed on his head, and he wore it like a hat. "Now, where was I?"

"The house was a big mess."

"Yes, but Ignacio was not discouraged, although when he finished paying the workers and praising their craft, the money from the sale of the storefront was gone. After all, in the larger scheme of things, this room would only be an entrance, and it would be a grand one. Besides, there were mounds of brick all around that they could use to finish the house as they wished. Ignacio moved his family to their new home."

"Now's the sad part," Benjamin said.

Ramon nodded slowly, the washcloth flopping with his hair. "Unfortunately, Ignacio did not live long enough to finish his dream house."

"He lived another twenty years," Celita said.

"Within a year he had begun a new room, but abandoned it after laying as many as ten bricks"—Ramon held up ten fingers—"when his wife pointed out that the room could not be reached from the house. So, less than six months later, he began a new room, and actually had one wall over two feet high, when a neighbor pointed out that the room would cover the big window and cut off the only source of light and heat in the house. It was then that Ignacio decided the drawing of plans was too complex for a mind as prone to artistry as was his. He decided to send his charming and exceptional son to the university to study the language of house plans—the language he had heard spoken years before when he saw the only real blueprints he was to see in his life. A very moving story, which you have decided we should not tell at this moment."

"Right," Benjamin said, rolling onto his side. "Not necessary."

"Ignacio told everyone in La Boca that his son was going to the university when he was old enough. The townspeople were very impressed, and it became clear to Ignacio that a party was required. Overcome with pride at the accomplishment his son would one day achieve, Ignacio invited everyone in town. Each brought a plate of food or a bottle of wine, and the party was a grand success. But during the party Ignacio discovered how much it cost to go to the university. He became so depressed that he found a job the next day and continued to work the rest of his life, hoping to save enough money to send his boy to the university. When Ramon's own son, the exceedingly brilliant—"

"And extremely good-looking," Benjamin said.

"And extraordinarily lazy like his father and grandfather," Celita added.

"—Benjamin began secondary school, Ignacio knew he had failed. He knew that Ramon would never go to the university. And Ignacio died of despair."

"Despair?" Celita said. "He was hit by a car."

"Yes," Ramon said. "But only a man in great despair would be so careless."

"He was drunk as three monkeys," Celita said.

Ramon nodded sadly. "Only a desperate man would drink so heavily."

Benjamin jumped to his feet. "Great story, Dad. I've got to go."

"Go?" Ramon said. "Where are you going so late? You haven't even digested this tale."

"I'm going to study at Mono's," Benjamin told him, already at the door.

"Mono can read now?" Ramon said. "Good. Just remember, you're studying for three generations."

"Yeah. Okay," Benjamin said, and he was out the door, closing it with a bang.

"I wish he wouldn't go out so late." Celita had washed the

mixing bowl and now ran a dry cloth over it. "I hope he doesn't get into any trouble."

"Studying?" Ramon removed the washcloth from his head and stood.

"Oh, Ramon. Do you really think a boy his age goes out in the middle of the night to study with a donkey who can barely count his fingers?"

"Of course I do." He kissed her forehead. "Donkeys don't have fingers, which is probably Mono's great problem." He put his arms around her. "What else could he be doing?" His smile was so large it hurt his cheeks, reminding him that he was still drunk. "I, by the way, have to go out too."

"You? Do you have studying to do as well?"

He kissed her again, remembering his conversation with Leon. How could a man refuse to understand love? Every day provided a dozen lessons in it. "I have to take Leon down the estuary."

"In the middle of the night?"

"Yes, do you want to come with us?"

Celita pushed the mixing bowl into his gut. "I am going to continue the tradition of being the only one in this family with any sense. I am going to bed." She turned and he followed her to the stove. "As soon as I finish these rolls," she said, peeking into the oven. Then she pointed to a pan. "That is your supper. You may thank me for keeping it warm."

"I knew it." He waved the mixing bowl above his head as if it were a tambourine. "That's why I volunteered to heat it myself."

She slapped his arm and spread flour across the table. Ramon took the wooden spoon which lay on the stove and began eating from the pan. "What else could he be doing?" he said.

BENJAMIN FOLDED his pants and put them with his shirt in the arms of a palm tree. His underwear he threw on top of the pile. He took three quick steps and plunged into the estuary.

His body moved through the water with a grace he could not hope to equal on land. He swam silently with little wasted motion, and he felt instantly better. The water was cooler than the night air, but just barely, and he dove, eyes closed, the world silent, his arms and legs moving him forward.

The ocean was more difficult. The currents and the waves directed and redirected him in the darkness, but he didn't have to think about it, at least it didn't seem like thought, his body automatically compensating for the push and pull, guiding him through the reefs. There were old men in town who tried to draw maps of La Boca's waters. They made their drawings in the sand with long sticks, marking the reefs and rocks with little ovals or long bars, arguing over distances and heights, making the hieroglyphics of old age again and again. Benjamin could not have drawn such a map, but in the water he never erred, angling ahead without thinking, turning without needing to measure or count strokes. He swam out and circled back, then let himself drift for a moment before curling his legs, his feet settling against a high stone, the same stone he had found three times in the past week.

He had swum past the hotel but he could see it clearly. More than once he had watched his father and Leon Green wander around the beach, drinking and, he presumed, talking, although he could hear nothing but the waves and the call of an occasional gull. Several rooms were lit in the hotel. A woman stood on one terrace; her shape, the jut of her hip, stirred something inside him, but she didn't hold his interest long.

The back room of the bakery, where Lourdes slept, was lighted, walls made yellow by the bare bulb. He stood on the rock, the ocean supporting him, and waited for her to appear.

All his life he had loved her. He dreamed of her almost every night, waking to her image, which would dissolve in sunlight. During the day, he imagined schemes to win her, but she treated him now as if he were still a little boy. Because she was older and smarter, she had always been the leader, but he had thought that age would bring them closer; instead, it had separated them.

Most nights, he saw only a blur as she walked through her room. One night he had seen her dancing and laughing with her mother, spinning in and out of his sight. She often read on her bed, which was too low for him to see; this he knew from the countless evenings he'd spent with her when they were children. He only hoped she would stand in front of the window. He wanted just to look at her as long as he desired, without worrying that someone might notice. Even her window, its rectangle of yellow light, caused a tingle of excitement in his chest and a sugary ache in his limbs.

While he waited, his thoughts wandered, settling for a moment on the image of his teacher, Mrs. Ojeda, in a bikini. It wasn't a pretty thought. How could people change so much? And if they did, how could you be expected to choose a partner for a lifetime? Then he imagined her husband sitting in a dark theater, watching a movie, wondering how it was going to turn out— maybe he had his hand on her leg—and then everything was suddenly thrown off, the whole of his life erased, their plans made to look stupid, their lives stupid. Drafted, and in a few months dead. It seemed to Benjamin that there were dangers beyond imagination.

His father claimed his grandfather had died of despair, and Benjamin wondered if that were possible, to die from losing hope. While the salt water slapped against his back and the vacant yellow window matched his stare, Benjamin decided that people must die of despair all the time. He pictured his own death, his heart refusing to nourish him if he did not give it what it wanted— which was Lourdes. She was all his heart had ever wanted.

He remembered the day of his grandfather's death. He had been eleven, Lourdes twelve. They had made special plans because school started the next day. It was their last chance to do something spectacular. Lourdes suggested they go on a hunt, but he could think of nothing all that interesting to kill. She, however, pulled him to her by the shirt and whispered in his ear, "Pterodactyls."

Ramon had told them a story about the screeches of dinosaurs being trapped in the thicket, and Lourdes had believed it. "If they heard dinosaurs," she said, "then there must have been some." Pterodactyls were the only ones that intrigued her because they could fly. She always had been fascinated by flying things. Benjamin had collected butterflies with her, watched as she pinned them to trees, their wings flapping more and more slowly, finally stopping. He had sat quietly in tree limbs to trap birds with her, seeing her leap like a cat after them, often tumbling through the branches, bird in hand, refusing to let it go even to stop her fall. Hunting pterodactyls didn't seem all that different.

They filled a paper sack with throwing rocks and Benjamin looped it around his belt, then they headed for the south estuary, where the thicket still crowded the water. There they followed the narrow path along the water's edge, imagining pterodactyls gliding through the sky above them. They walked quietly to match the silence of flight and looked for clues, examining piles of excrement, prints in the muddy bank.

Where the thicket turned to jungle, they chose a tree and began climbing. Lourdes laced her fingers together to give Benjamin a boost to the first limb, then he pulled her up. They climbed to the high branches and searched the sky for pterodactyls. And though they saw none, they did see the ocean, which was a radiant green as if the water covered an enormous source of light. They saw the whole of La Boca: the hotel at the far end, beautiful and white, its windows the yellow of the sun; the orderly houses and stores that lined the coast and nudged inward, boxes of turquoise, pink, and white; the old water tower, a monument of rust and graying wood, which would fall later that same year during the earthquake; the cross at the peak of the cathedral, its row of high windows; and closer to them, the huddle of adobe huts, roofs of sun-bleached palms, and Benjamin's own enormous cube of a house—all put at a distance from them by the thicket, its thorny top a field of purple spires.

"We should go higher," Lourdes said. "We can't see anything from here."

Facing the jungle, Benjamin could see only a confusion of limbs, a wash of green and yellow leaves, and Lourdes, who pointed to a dangerously thin limb six feet above them.

"We can see the ocean," Benjamin told her, turning his head again. "There's my house. Hey, there are people entering the bakery. I think I see a pelican way, way out."

"We have to look over the jungle," she said with scorn. "Dinosaurs don't fly over cities." She had already embraced the tree and begun shimmying up the trunk. He followed, imitating her as best he could. Monkeys barked and chattered nearby, invisible in the crush of leaves. The rough bark scraped his legs as he climbed, and the earth below him looked distant and unreal.

Halfway to the limb, he felt that he was being watched. The sensation was so powerful that he had to shift his shoulders, almost losing his balance.

"You think too much," Lourdes called from above him. She had reached the narrow branch and sat contentedly, swinging her legs.

When he finally arrived, he kept one arm around the tree trunk, Lourdes scooting out onto the limb to give him room.

They could see the crowns of many of the jungle trees, but several still towered above them. The colors of the leaves lightened as they neared the sun, turning waxy or a speckled yellow, while the lowest leaves visible, on the banks of the estuary and around the few hollows, were dark green. Several low trees along the water's bank had large leaves so white they flashed like mirrors in the sunlight. Patches of palms clumped together among the other jungle trees like families.

From this height, both the jungle and the ocean looked infinite, but Benjamin knew that his father, who trusted him in the waves of the Pacific, would have been furious if he had seen his son perched so high in the tree. This thought worried Benjamin, but also made him a little proud, a sensation that caused him to put his arm around the shoulders of Lourdes.

She struggled to get something out of her skirt pocket. A corner of paper showed. "You get it," she said. "I've got to hold on." She giggled when he stuck his fingers in her pocket. "That tickles," she said. He withdrew a page that had been ripped from a book. Lourdes flattened it against her leg. "This is what we're looking for." The drawing featured a gliding pterodactyl, thin arms extended, winged fingers spread. Clouds billowed behind it.

"How big is it?" he asked her.

"As big as its name," she told him.

They sat in the afternoon sunlight, swaying with the breeze, until the branch had worn deep grooves in their legs, but no pterodactyl showed itself.

They descended carefully, helping one another, measuring the strength of branches with a bounce of the foot. They had not dropped more than a few yards when a monkey suddenly appeared in front of them, sitting calmly on a limb, fingers to his mouth. He stared at them a moment, showed his yellow teeth, then swung through the air onto the bough of another tree and disappeared.

They headed back toward town, but Lourdes wanted to show him the opening in the thicket, the carved-out room where her mother had lived as a child. On their hands and knees, they crawled though the dark hole. The walls, a solid gnashing of limbs, had grown new arms, which protruded into the room, sleek and pointed. Benjamin and Lourdes huddled together near the entrance, listening for the beating of great wings, the high and piercing screech. While they crouched together, holding hands, the jungle became their personal possession, and Benjamin believed that he would never be happier. He was instantly proved wrong.

The sky suddenly darkened. A shadow passed over. They crawled out quickly to the estuary bank and caught a glance of something huge gliding above. Benjamin's legs trembled. Lourdes jumped straight up, screaming with happiness, and landed too close to the edge, sliding into the water. Benjamin grabbed her arms to stop her fall, but she yanked him in on top of her, and they sank beneath the surface.

Muddy and ecstatic, they ran home. The bag of rocks bounced against his legs as they ran, leaving identical purple bruises on his thighs. When they burst into his house to tell his parents they had seen a pterodactyl, his mother took him in her arms and held him close until he grew still. She whispered in his ear that his grandfather had died.

Across the stretch of water, the yellow light in the bakery turned suddenly dim. Lourdes filled the window. She leaned outside, her hair falling past her shoulders, and turned to look at the hotel. Benjamin looked as well. His angle was better than hers, but there was nothing to see—a crumbling building, dark windows, a few white lights. Lourdes rested her elbows on the windowsill for another second, then disappeared inside the room.

Gentle swells passed over him, rising to rinse the hairs on his neck. Lourdes appeared again, only for an instant, and as she did, fish began leaping out of the ocean all around him, a foot into the air, flashes of silver, then little splashes so close their mist sprayed his face.

The eruptions stopped as abruptly as they had begun. He shifted his feet against the stone, then, in response to an urge he only half understood, he turned slowly to look over the ocean's immense plane.

An apron of moonlight covered the surface of the water, broken by great stretches of darkness. Here and there, little mouths of white opened and shut. The ocean, at this moment, seemed to embody a secret, a promise so enormous as to make it impossible to keep. If he'd had the time, he might have stared until the secret made itself known, but the yellow window held a promise he could name: a glimpse of the woman he loved.

He waited another hour before despairing and beginning his swim home, following the same invisible route through the hidden barriers.

At the mouth of the estuary, a boat approached. Benjamin swam to the far bank, where he hid in the shadows. It was his father's boat. The American slouched in the front. Behind him, his father rowed, talking the whole time. As they came near, Benjamin slipped beneath the water. He felt the current of the oar but could not see it. When he surfaced, the boat was past him, his father's broad back a dark shape against the night sky.

He dried himself with his shirt, then pulled on his pants. Carrying his shoes and damp shirt, he ran home and slipped quietly into bed.

Sleep refused him. The image of his father and the American in the dark boat wouldn't leave him alone. He thought of Lourdes to free himself of it, the way her hair fell, the yellow light behind her, the sensation of falling when she, as a little girl, had pulled him into the water.

When sleep finally came, he dreamed of being on the hunt once more, alone this time, the sack of rocks looped around his belt. Once again the shadow passed over, and this time he heard her hoary screech. The jungle parted for him as he ran, his legs pumping hard. The bag of rocks wagged between his thighs, its weight increasing as he ran. Then the jungle abruptly opened, a clearing, and at the far end, a pterodactyl spread her enormous wings, opened her ancient mouth. Tired from flight, breathing heavily, she shrieked at him, then crossed her great wings, a triangle of shadow. He took a step toward her. She pointed a long winged finger, freezing him, filling him with fear.

But the weight of the hunt settled in his belly, and he lifted one rock after another from the bag, throwing them with tremendous force and accuracy, bloodying her, causing her to scream. And he continued until his sack was empty.

THOUGH WIDE at the mouth, the north estuary narrowed dramatically after the first hundred yards. Ramon sat in the rear of the boat, working an oar. Leon, in front of him, held his paddle but did not use it. The inlet backed into the jungle over a mile, crooked as memory. Trees arched over it, closing the faint light of the night sky.

"Don't you need the flashlight?" Leon asked as soon as the stars were gone.

Ramon did not speak for several seconds, his oar in and out of the water, a gurgle and a rush. "No," he said. Then, "You can help now."

Leon pulled against the water, his paddle waffling in his hands.

"Not so hard," Ramon said. "An easy approach works best. It's like sawing wood. Have you ever noticed? You find an easy rhythm and it goes much faster than muscling against it."

Leon turned to comment, but said nothing. The darkness had grown so that he could barely see Ramon—a white glow across his cheekbones, diamonds that must be his eyes. "Why don't you want to use the light?"

"Let the jungle sleep," Ramon said, then lifted the bottle of vodka to his lips. "The two things I hate most live in the jungle."

"This isn't the beginning of a story, is it?" Leon said, a reflex, and dishonest. At this moment he liked the sound of Ramon's voice and would have been happy to hear anything.

"No story," Ramon promised.

"What are the things you hate most?" Darkness, Leon thought, silence. Loneliness, death.

"Snakes and monkeys," Ramon said. "Do you want some of this?" The vodka changed hands, Ramon shaking the bottle so that Leon could find it. "Monkeys are the vilest creatures on earth. They'll stare at you as if they're human. They make me sick."

When Ramon stopped speaking, there was only the dark, the sounds of the oars in the water. And the cicadas, which must have been there all along, but Leon hadn't noticed them until now, and what he noticed was that they were fading out the farther into the jungle they rowed.

"This is about as far as I take most of the tourists," Ramon said. "Maybe I should begin night tours. Did I tell you that once when I was out here—it was one of my first tours with your guests—the young man and woman kept kissing and fondling one another, as if I weren't here. Rude children. I was at about this point, letting the boat stall in the water, and I spotted a monkey—they all want to see monkeys, but I watch for them in order to keep my distance. Do you know what the little bastard monkey started doing? Masturbating. My tourists thought I'd taught it to do that, the idiots. 'Monkey see, monkey do,' the girl said. I detested them."

"How can you know where we are? I can't see a thing. What if we plow into the bank?"

"The oar tells me everything. A fisherman learns to let the water talk to his oar."

"I'd feel a little better if my eyes could be involved. My paddle doesn't have a hell of a lot to say to me."

"It's telling you, you just don't know how to listen. The language of oars takes patience to learn, like any other language."

Suddenly, just above Leon's head, the darkness that had seemed infinite turned to tree limbs so near him he ducked. Ramon shone the light ahead, and Leon sat up, the leafy branches higher than they'd first appeared. The channel of water was so overgrown it seemed to have a ceiling, as if they were in a tunnel. The estuary reflected back the light, a shimmer of white, and beneath it, water black as oil. Trees crowded against one another, every opening filled. The grassy banks were ringed with black mud. One white trunk on the bank angled down into the estuary, roots twisting out of the earth, a single branch rising from the water, its few remaining leaves brown and curled at the edges.

"The tide is lower than I thought." Ramon took the bottle of vodka from Leon and lifted it into the light: three-quarters empty. "We'd better hope the damn Russians haven't confused my reckoning."

Leon shot a glance at him. "What would happen?"

Ramon's expression was one of amused concern. "We'd have to wade through this putrid water. The mud's soft. Every step's a nightmare. You'd best pray I'm not as drunk as I think I am." He switched the light off. "It's better in the dark, don't you think?"

"No, not at all."

Ramon prodded him in the back with the flashlight. "Suit yourself," he said.

Leon directed the light ahead, but no sooner had he done so than he saw, out of the corner of his eye, movement on the bank of the inlet. He flashed the light there. Nothing. The water lapping against the mud, waves from the progress of the boat. "Calm down," Ramon said, and Leon turned the light toward him, but he was gone. He waved the light again, and Ramon was back. His mind had begun playing tricks.

"We'll need the light soon," Ramon told him. "The tree limbs are low ahead."

In another twenty minutes they reached the point where the estuary forked. Ramon guided them to the right, down the branch, the narrow passage growing thinner. Boughs of trees Leon could not name hung even with his chest. "Watch it," Ramon said. He ducked and Leon copied him. Leaves brushed across his hair. "Snakes and monkeys," Ramon said, looking above them. "Let me have the light." He flashed it about. Ceiling of leaves. Long gray limbs. "We're getting close."

The boat grated against the bottom, floated, bumped again. Ramon edged the boat forward, pushing off against the mud with his oar. He flashed the light again. Jewels on the leaves, tiny drops of water. Bark the color of skin. They slouched low.

"Here we are," Ramon said finally. "The ruins."

The light shone on a tall white wall—a house, falling apart. The red tile roof had several holes the size of men. Vines streaked the walls. Tall grass and a single palm grew through the bricks of the veranda. As the light ran over the porch, a moth the size of a hand fluttered out from under an eave. An iguana on a window ledge stared back at them.

"Renaldo, you son of a bitch!" Ramon held the light on the lizard, which made the iguana motionless.

Just then, from a limb above them, a monkey swatted at the flashlight. "Cheet, cheet, cheet," it screamed.

"Christ." Ramon fell backward, flattening himself against the boat. The light shone directly upward and the faces of monkeys stared down, eyes and teeth. "Devils," he said and swung the oar at them. A few jumped to a higher branch, others swung at the oar and screeched.

Ramon sank his arms into the water, pushing against the muddy bottom. "Help me turn it," he yelled. Leon shoved his paddle into the mud and pushed. As they spun, a monkey dropped into the boat between them.

"No," Ramon yelled. He swung with his oar, hitting the monkey in the chest, flinging mud and water on Leon. The monkey landed on its back in the black water and disappeared.

"Cheet, cheet, cheet." The branches rattled with simian movement.

The men bent low and paddled furiously, the boat angling forward from Ramon's powerful strokes. "Switch sides," he yelled, slinging water across Leon's back as he shifted his oar. When they reached the fork, Ramon pulled in his oar. Head in his hands, he leaned forward and whispered, "Monkeys. I hate monkeys.

They'll swarm like bees. Like goddamn sharks." He rocked far-ther forward with each breath until he locked his head between his knees.

Leon sat quietly, catching his breath. "What was that place?" he asked.

Ramon stared at him a moment before forcing a laugh. He ran his mud-covered hands through his hair, then began paddling once more. In another moment, he began speaking.

"If you were expecting something ancient—an Incan tomb, an Aztec temple, maybe a Mayan pyramid—hah, there's no such thing near La Boca. Only Renaldo Peralta's ruined house. I don't suppose you want to hear this story." He lifted the flashlight from the floor of the boat and switched it off. The world went black again.

"You have a captive audience," Leon said, wanting, more than anything, human sound.

"Renaldo Peralta was the son of the banana merchant Hi-dalgo Peralta and the beautiful palm reader Maria Peralta Car-denas. Hidalgo often worked as many as five days a week scrounging through the jungle. He had his own shop where he sold bananas to those too lazy to pick them themselves. At first he had little luck, but one day Hidalgo claimed monkeys picked his bananas, selecting only the best. He stuck his thumb into a bowl of ink and then onto the peels of the bananas he sold, telling people to look for that mark or they would be eating inferior fruit." Ramon paused for Leon to make a sarcastic remark. When none came, he slowed his rowing to provide time to tell the whole story.

"Soon he could not meet the demand. At every fine restau-rant, people asked for their bananas unpeeled so that they could see the mark and be sure they were eating the best. At parties, hosts always put a bowl of bananas with Hidalgo's mark in a prominent spot. And perhaps they were better, since typically people took the easiest ones—those closest to the ground or ones that had fallen. Hidalgo, however, sent his son Renaldo into the jungle to climb the trees and hacked off the best possible bananas, those just hours from being perfectly ripe.

"Maria Peralta Cardenas, the palm reader, was also a business success because, unlike charlatans in the big cities, she always included the absolute worst, which was what people were most curious about, and, like any good mystic, she left enough mystery in her predictions to keep people from losing interest in their lives altogether. Are you following me, Leon?"

"Bananas, palm readers, business—are we getting close to town? I can't tell how fast we're moving. I can't tell how long we've been in the water."

"We have a ways to go. Just relax and listen. You'll like this story. The birth of Renaldo was peculiar because up to the very day of delivery Maria showed no sign of a child inside her. She was as thin as this oar." He lifted the oar, but it was impossible to see. "The only way anyone knew she was pregnant was that she had read her own palm months before and predicted the day she would give birth. She made an appointment six months in advance with young Angelica Roches, who was going to act as midwife. When the day came, Maria Peralta, as thin as a lie, walked across town to fetch Angelica, who had just begun to work at the bakery that would one day be hers. She was a teenager, much heavier then than she is now, who worked to support her ancient parents, having failed to find a husband to help her because of her obesity. She had never acted as midwife before, nor had anyone else in La Boca except Maria Peralta Cardenas—after all, who wouldn't want a midwife who could predict the day of delivery, saving all that worry about false labor? Angelica, the poor girl, had no idea of how to be a midwife, especially for a woman who did not look pregnant. She followed Maria Peralta through town, sweating and rubbing her hands, her face red, her gait awkward. A crowd of people gathered along the street staring at the pair with wonder, following them to Maria's house. They waited outside to see if the miracle would happen.

"Men cupped their hands together, showing the size of Maria's waist. The child would be no larger than a fist, they reasoned. As the afternoon aged, the crowd grew. Then, just before dark, a yelp came from inside. In another minute, they heard an infant cry. Hidalgo threw open the front window, and there stood Maria with a bundle in her arms, a baby boy of normal size, young Renaldo. The crowd was stunned into silence until Hidalgo walked among them passing out complimentary bananas. As for Angelica, the miraculous birth had been too much for her. She had fainted and never once spoke of it to anyone."

"I get it," Leon said. "The old switch."

"What do you mean?"

"The fat one really had the baby."

"That's absurd," Ramon told him. "To start with, Angelica wasn't married. She was only a teenager."

"It's been known to happen. How else do you explain it?"

"It was a miracle."

"Oh, sure, miracle birth." Leon sighed. "I should have known."

"Listen now," Ramon told him. "We're getting to Renaldo. Perhaps it was from living among the monkeys, perhaps it was inherited from his mother, but Renaldo Peralta moved with a grace previously unknown in La Boca. He had a way of stepping as if he were not moving at all, as if the earth itself spun to accommodate his feet. As he got older, he shared his father's profits and was the most popular young man in La Boca. Ignacio Matamoros—my father, you'll recall—was Renaldo's best friend and privy to his secrets.

"Many of the local girls tried to get Renaldo's attention, and most succeeded, but none kept it long, until one, a child by the name of Antonia, became pregnant. All of eleven years old, she had menstruated only once before taking his hand and following him into the jungle. Her father had been a fisherman, who one day rowed out into the ocean and never returned. Her mother raised goats, animals Renaldo hated. He denied being the father of the child, which created a great controversy, half the town believing Antonia—why would this little girl lie, they argued—the other half believing Renaldo, pointing to the mysterious disappearance of her father and raising their eyebrows." Ramon raised his eyebrows in the darkness. Annoyed to be without the power of his gestures, he turned on the flashlight and laid it by his feet.

"Thanks," Leon said, touching the flashlight. "Why'd they raise their eyebrows?"

"Because her father disappeared and then she turned up pregnant."

"Oh, big scandal. I get it."

"The mystery was resolved with the birth of the child, a beautiful girl, who could walk at birth. There was no question then that she must be the grandchild of the fortune-teller. Renaldo left town. His father had to hunt for his own bananas and his business began to fail. Maria Peralta Cardenas, however, became more busy than ever. People believed she must be a powerful mystic since God had punished her with a ruinous son."

Ramon opened his hand and tapped Leon's shoulder. He wiggled his fingers. "Five years passed. The girl, Antonia, and her child, who was never given a name because she had no father and was just called Baby Child or Sweet Dream or My Little Squash, helped raise goats and ran errands for the palm reader and delivered rolls to the restaurants for Angelica Roches. Then one day a stranger checked into the Hotel Esperanza, a huge black man. He posted flyers offering gold in return for labor. Ignacio Matamoros, who happened to be unemployed at the time, was one of many men who answered the ad. When he showed up for work, he discovered they were to finish the job begun years earlier by his grandfather—to clear a path through the thicket. Do you remember that story?"

"Are we going in a circle?" Leon asked him. "I'd swear that this is the same spot we passed earlier."

Ramon shut off the light. "The black man called himself

Chute and he worked the men tirelessly. Within a week the narrow passage through the thicket was complete, and he instructed them to begin hacking at the jungle—which no one wanted to do. Many quit, and some boys were hired in their place, including the young son of Ignacio, Ramon Matamoros."

"Why do you speak of yourself in the third person?"

"It is the nature of history; otherwise, it would be self-serving. So Ignacio and his hardworking son chopped and sawed at the jungle plants. The impressionable boy—"

"Ramon?"

"Yes—he was bitten by a snake. One as big around as your waist. And he would have died from the poisoning, but Chute took the wounded leg into his hands and sucked on the punctures until the leg turned translucent. He then spat out a stream of blood yellowed with poison. Ten minutes later, the brave child returned to work."

"Scared shitless of snakes," Leon said.

"Yes. Then the rains came, and no one bothered coming to work. But Chute knocked on their doors, screeching at them in an uninterpretable language, until they trudged to the site, only to find that the growth from the morning of rain had recaptured all the ground they had cleared the previous week."

"Look." Leon pointed, shaking the boat. "There's a light in the trees."

"In this country, we call that a star." Ramon shone the light overhead. Leaves and branches, gaps of sky appeared and the star disappeared. He turned off the light and everything vanished, but the star reappeared. "The men worked hard, knee-deep in mud, vines curling about their ankles, but each morning when they returned they could not tell what they had accomplished or even where they had worked. Finally, Chute sent them home and disappeared for three days. When he returned, he was accompanied by a dozen black men. They ambled out of the jungle path in a haze of rain, enormous men with hands the size of palm leaves.

Shirtless, water streaming down their chests, they seemed to fill the village just entering it, speaking a language made not so much of words as of one long rhythmic stutter.''

The overhanging limbs became more sparse. Ramon could see the surface of the water, and shapes in the distance.

''At the end of the day, when the village men were leaving work, Armon Garcia showed up in his car—the only one in town at that time—and Chute pulled enormous lights from the trunk. While he wired them to the car battery, the black men arrived and began hacking. All through the night in the pouring rain, the black men chopped ahead, while Chute spread a dark paste over the ground. The crews worked day and night. They cleared the earth, and Chute painted it black. Nothing grew through the paste.''

Ramon hesitated. He had seen movement, just ahead of them, in the estuary. He didn't mention it to Leon because he would be unable to finish the story, but he studied the water.

''Story over?'' Leon said.

''Two questions rose in the minds of the workers: One, why were they building this road out in the middle of the jungle? And, two, when did Chute sleep?''

Ramon saw more clearly now, a swimmer, moving to the shadows. He pretended not to see, maneuvering the boat away. What would a man be doing in the estuary after midnight? As the boat drew near, the head submerged. Ramon's oar told him that the body was swimming beneath and away from them. His eyes had told him something else: It was his son.

''God, I'm glad to be out of there,'' Leon said.

Ramon pulled against the oar with all his strength. His son had been in the ocean and was returning through the estuary. In the middle of the night. It made no sense. Celita had worried that Benjamin would get into trouble. Had he met someone in a boat out by the reefs? There could have been some kind of exchange. He feared his son was into something bad. Drugs—but

Benjamin had nothing to sell and no money to buy. Black market—but it did not extend to La Boca. Revolutionaries—they recruited young men. Idealistic boys who thought the impossible could happen. He rowed too hard to speak.

"Hey," Leon said. "What are you doing?"

"Paddle," Ramon commanded. "We're going into the ocean."

"What the hell for?" Leon asked, although he had lifted his paddle.

Ramon continued the story so he wouldn't have to explain, talking in spurts when he could catch his breath. "Chute, they discovered, almost never slept." Like my son, he thought. "And he rarely ate, but chewed leaves all day. And the road was leading to a great house in the jungle." Water slapped the hull, spraying them as they crossed into the ocean's waters. When they reached the break point in the reef, Ramon quickly directed the boat through the narrow gap, turning back toward the beach to avoid high rocks. He could see no one, no reason for his son to be in the water.

"Let's go in, Ramon. I'm getting seasick out here."

Water, stars, a few lights on the shore, the sky as big as mystery itself, but Ramon could see nothing out of the ordinary. He rowed slowly now, through openings in the invisible maze. He spoke easily. "When the men finally reached the estuary, they found a clearing and the skeleton of a building. For Ignacio and Ramon, the work was over, but they rowed out to the site daily to watch the construction of Renaldo's great house. Chute studied a huge book, pages the size of bed sheets, then directed his workers in that strange stuttering language. Ignacio examined this book, which was covered not with letters but with long blue stuttering lines, some thick and dark, others hardly there at all. For Ignacio, this was a revelation."

Ramon spread his feet, balanced himself, and stood. "Don't move," he told Leon. The ocean was empty and beautiful, white from the sinking moon. The hotel darkened the shore, lightless, but beside it, a window in the bakery glowed yellow and bright. He saw movement within, and let his eyes adjust. Lourdes, her back to him, pulled a white blouse over her head. She faced the window and unhooked her tattered bra. The breasts of a child. Ramon sat, embarrassed, and began turning the boat.

"What?" Leon said. "What's going on?"

"Nothing." Ramon dipped his oar against a rock to make the boat tip—just enough to distract Leon. He didn't want him to see Lourdes. Which was silly, since he slept with her, but Ramon did it nonetheless. "I just wanted to keep my captive audience captive." He laughed nervously.

"I should have guessed." Leon clutched the sides of the dinghy. "Be careful."

Ramon tried to regain enthusiasm for the story, but he found it hard to concentrate. He knew now what he had long suspected was true: His son would not complete college without Lourdes. It was as obvious as the ocean's promise of death.

"Chute told Ignacio that a man from the university had written the book." These words burned his throat, but Ramon continued. "Later Ignacio would try to send his son to the university to study this language of buildings, so that he would return, stuttering beautifully and guiding workers in the building of a magnificent cathedral or school."

Ramon felt himself begin to cry. He lowered his hand into the water and splashed his face. Somehow he would have to find the money to send Lourdes too. He would have to convince Leon to let her go. He raised his head and wiped the salt water from his brows. It trickled down his chin to his shirt.

"You falling asleep?" Leon asked him, smiling. "I thought I was the only one put to sleep by your stories."

"This may interest you." Ramon began rowing to calm himself. "One day, while his father studied the construction, the boy Ramon climbed a tree to sleep, and he was attacked from behind. I have never told anyone about this. A monkey latched onto

Ramon's shoulders and struggled to commit an act of sex against his person." He paused to let Leon laugh. "And the little beast might have succeeded, but one of the workers threw a stone at the monkey, hitting him squarely in the head—that, and the resiliency of the pants his mother had sewn, saved the boy."

Ramon guided them back into the estuary, where he let the boat stall in the water. He had not told the story well, and now he wanted only to finish it. "They built a magnificent house, then the black men vanished, but Chute stayed to distribute fliers announcing a party for everyone at the great new mansion to celebrate the return of Renaldo Peralta to the village and jungle of his youth.

"The night of the party, the house shimmered with light. Renaldo stood at the door in his tuxedo to greet his guests, but only Antonia and the nameless daughter came. They alone had forgiven him. The three of them disappeared that night, never to be seen again in La Boca." Ramon lifted his oar from the water, splashing Leon, and let the boat run aground. "I had no idea what had happened to any of them until tonight." He stood, rocking the skiff, then stepped out into the shallow water.

"What do you mean?" Leon steadied the boat before rising.

"Tonight I discovered that Renaldo is dead. That iguana was him. Poor fellow." Ramon dragged the boat into the sand. They walked along the beach toward the hotel. "My father and I rowed out that evening to watch from a distance. What a beautiful house it was that one night. But it has gone to ruin, and the road, without maintenance, returned to jungle."

"So what are people doing here, Ramon? I thought the ruins might explain it, but . . . I can't see why this town has survived. There's no reason for a town."

Ramon dropped to his knees in the sand, his hands sinking to the wrists. "Well," he said, "perhaps everyone is here for the same reason you are. Figure out why you're here and you'll be able to answer the question yourself."

Leon frowned. "I ask you a straightforward question and you give me a riddle, which I shouldn't complain about. You could have given me another endless story, and I'd get no sleep at all tonight."

"Answers can't be as straight as questions. If they were, people would give up living altogether. Children would be taught to dig their graves as soon as they were old enough to hold shovels. But I will tell you one thing straightforwardly, and then I'm going home. Quit seeing Lourdes."

"Ah, Mr. One-Note." Leon turned from him and began his short walk to the hotel. "Thanks for the ride," he called.

Ramon watched him walk away, then trudged back to the inlet for his skiff. By the time he propped the boat against his house, he had also figured the amount of money he would need—almost a third more than what he had. Otherwise, he could not hope to send Lourdes with Benjamin.

*T*HE PALE young man sat cross-legged beside a zippered green backpack on the stoop of the bookstore, half-eaten banana in his lap, open plastic bag of raisins next to him. He wiped the thick lenses of his glasses on the tail of his blue T-shirt, then held the bifocals at arm's length, looking for smudges. The banana sprouted obscenely from his crotch, flowering peels, sharply bitten fruit.

Pilar watched him as she might an animal in the jungle, remembering a dawn hike through the cloud forest with friends, coming across a quetzal, how she pointed then did not move, how beautiful that bird had been, so beautiful that she was amazed it wasn't extinct. One of her friends, a boy—they were all college students—raised his camera, a tiny rustle, and the bird flew, disappearing into the jungle. Another boy said, "What I wouldn't give for just one of those tail feathers." That was the nature of men and beauty, she had decided, they want to possess it, even if they have to destroy it in the process. It was intolerable otherwise.

The memory had returned to her again and again during the endless clammy meetings of revolutionaries and pseudo-revolutionaries, the bickering among men and boys about means and methods, no detail too small to cause acrimony because they were arguing about personal possession of a thing near inconceivable in beauty, a beauty whose liberation would be literal, physical, intellectual, psychological. How many nights had she heard the prerogatives of possession enter the voices of men who would turn against the revolution if they could not make it their own? At one point she'd thought that this was the real distinction between boys and men, the ability to understand the difference between possessing beauty and embodying it.

The fellow on her stoop was not at all beautiful, but there was something primitive and natural in him as he hunched forward, elbows on his knees, biting into his green banana, tossing raisins in the air, his mouth receiving them with a snap that reminded her of a frog catching insects. He turned at the clicking of tumblers.

She held the door open and smiled. He stared up at her for a moment, the last of the banana in his mouth. Swallowing, he dropped the peel and raisin bag into the backpack, then stepped inside the bookstore.

"I am to notice that the people sleep late here," he said cheerfully, after the banana had cleared his throat. "I am to come to look for the book that I love."

Pilar addressed him in English. "What book would that be?"

He stared at her again. A darker stare. The first one had to do with her looks. It was vain, but men stared at her and she would not deny that. This stare, however, was full of suspicion.

"You speak English," he said.

"That's correct."

He shook his head sadly and turned from her. He lifted a book from a table and replaced it. "I'd heard that this village was one of the few unspoiled places in the hemisphere, but wherever I look there's American influence taking over." He sighed heavily.

Pilar began disliking him at this moment. She stepped behind the counter and pulled her money box from its shelf. "Who told you about La Boca?"

"This guy I know. A backpacker. He said this place was

pure." He lifted another book, turning the title toward her—*The Great Gatsby* in English. "You might as well sell T-shirts."

"You are a stupid, smug fool," Pilar said, speaking quickly in Spanish and smiling. "Don't you agree?" she added in English.

"I didn't catch all of it," he said.

"Is it the fact that I'm educated and I speak English—is that what offends you?"

His hands shook as if from electric shock. "I didn't mean it that way. It's just not what I expected. The guy who runs the hotel is American."

"Yes, I know."

"See, I want to find out what's at the heart of this culture, but all I find are Americans and tour guides and books in English."

"Do you read Spanish?"

"Not really."

"Well?"

"Nothing's like I expected, that's all."

"Then perhaps you should give up your expectations. What sort of book were you looking for?"

He ran his fingers over the table and stared at his canvas boots. "I didn't mean to be rude," he told her. "I was looking for some maps. I'd like to go hiking in the jungle."

"There are no maps of the jungle."

"Really?" He brightened.

"I wouldn't advise hiking there."

"Lions and tigers and bears?"

"Mosquitoes and snakes and oblivion. If you must go, stick near the road the bus travels."

"Oblivion, I like that." He pulled a pen and a yellow pad from his shirt pocket and scribbled quickly. "I like you," he said. "I'll put you in my book."

"Well, an author." She relaxed and settled on her stool. "Have your publisher send me copies for the store."

"I will," he said, smiling. "I'm serious. Have you got a card?"
She told him no.

"I've written three hundred pages. Longhand." He started to say something more but stopped himself and put his pen and notebook away. "I've been looking for a place where there are no maps. It's not so easy to find any more."

You need a map to find one, Pilar thought, but said, "If you get lost in the jungle, you may very well die."

He nodded, barely containing a smile. "The trick is to lose yourself without getting lost."

Pilar laughed. "You seem to have all the answers already."

"Everybody does," he told her. "The trick is discovering the right questions."

He bought a postcard before leaving.

PILAR SPENT the day examining her love for Leon. It thrilled, baffled, and annoyed her. It turned in her chest like a gyroscope. When she'd taught, she'd been careful not to fall in love. The men she slept with were always in danger of disappearing. She had loved them, but it was a love grown out of commitment. They shared a passion for revolution, not for each other.

She went over the night with Cruz time after time, their talk, the Canadian, her grandmother, his hand between her legs. What was it that had opened her heart and permitted Leon such easy entrance? Had she compared him to Cruz? Felt the thrill of adultery when Cruz grabbed her, which made her think of Leon as her husband? Was she such a slow learner as to have wakened just now to what had long been alive? Did she love him because he was North American or despite it? Was it the fact that he left her alone much of the time, letting her have her own life without harassment, loving her without attempting to possess her? Or did her love for a North American become permissible once she'd committed to taking in the revolutionary?

Questions and no suitable answers, this was the nature of love, she thought, then remembered what the American boy had said. Everyone has all the answers, the trick is to find the right questions. It made an odd sort of sense to her—she was asking the wrong questions. The correct question would have the one answer which she was delighted to possess: that she was happily and hopelessly in love with Leon.

Love did not blind her to his faults. She knew that he was a philanderer and guessed that he regularly seduced North American tourists who found him handsome and mysterious. The politics of the country in which he lived didn't interest Leon, but she was happy for this narrowness in him, glad to have one part of her life separated from the revolution—as if he were an oasis from the conflict. He drank too much, he snored, he was intellectually lethargic, but these things meant only that she had that much more to give him—another cause, this one less hopeless than the first she'd dedicated her life to.

She made herself a light lunch and tried to read but couldn't concentrate. She took the one good wineglass she had from the cupboard and a bottle of cabernet sauvignon Cruz had stolen from Leon and drank, paging through a magazine without really reading.

Lourdes stepped into the store at one. She wore a tight-fitting blouse and short skirt. The dirty white apron was much longer, reaching past her knees.

"Where's your mother?" Pilar asked, smiling, putting the magazine away.

"Sleeping," Lourdes answered. "I can't stay long."

"What are you looking for?"

"What is it you know that I don't?" She stepped to the counter, propping her elbows there. "That's what I'm looking for." She stared with such earnestness that Pilar couldn't laugh. Then Lourdes added, "I guess I want to know what you got from the university."

Pilar relaxed, smiled. "I got a mediocre education. It's something like school here, I imagine, except that the issues are more complex, the assignments more difficult."

"What issues? What assignments?"

"It depends on what you study." She filled her wineglass and considered offering some to Lourdes. The conversation pleased her because she had been feeling an urge to talk, especially the desire to confess her love for Leon—even the thought of it caused a slight rush of sensation. Love made you a child, she thought.

"I feel like there must be something else." Lourdes, sullen, put her fists against her temples. "I look at you and I look at the other women in town and I can see that there's something you know that they don't, and it's more than English or psychology or chemistry. And I want to know what it is." Her fist came down against the counter.

"I don't know what you mean. I've lived in cities, while the others have only lived here, there may be . . ."

"You have to know. You're not fooling me. I'm smart. I was the smartest person in school. Every class. Ask Mrs. Ojeda. Ask anyone. And what about her? She's supposed to be smart. She's a teacher, anyway, but she doesn't know what you know."

"I'm not so special," Pilar said, feeling, as she said it, extraordinarily special: a human in love.

"Fuck you." Lourdes didn't say it so much as spit it. "Don't lie to me." She pointed. "You don't want me to get angry." She whirled away and walked to the window, where she stood, arms crossed, silent.

The pleasure Pilar had taken in the conversation left entirely. She tried to muster concern, but what she felt was irritation. "Lourdes, I don't know what you want."

"Secrets," she said softly, facing the ocean, sunlight shining through the apron that appeared beneath her skirt.

"I don't have any secrets." She had become impatient. "Not any that would mean anything to you."

Lourdes faced her once more. "How do you know? Tell me.

Let me in on your secrets. Look." She lifted the tail of her apron. "See this smashed fruit? I make the fruit tarts. My apron is always like this. You know what I used to do? I let Benjamin clean my apron, with his mouth. Suck the fruit off while I was wearing it." She put her hands over her breasts, two stains. "That's good, isn't it? As a secret? Tell me what you know. Something. There must be something that you can tell me."

Pilar felt a sudden wave of compassion for her, which, combined with her impatience, caused her to laugh nervously. "I don't know what you want."

"Don't you laugh at me." Her voice carried the flat tone of a threat.

"I'm not, I just don't have secrets like that."

"I could tell you things you wouldn't want to hear," Lourdes said.

Pilar felt a sudden tremor of fear, not that different from the sensation of love, if there were some way of being objective. But there was no reason to be afraid of this girl, she reassured herself. "I'll tell you a story. I don't know if it's what you want or not, but it's something that happened to me when I was a professor of geography. Then you go home."

"Geography?" Lourdes said, considering it. "All right. Yes." She walked to the counter, leaned against it again, but now she seemed uncomfortably close, and Pilar stepped back against the wall.

"I had a morning class and an afternoon class and nothing to do in between—oh, I had work to do. There was always work of one sort or another, but there was also time, and I got into the habit of walking across campus to the art gallery. It wasn't a wonderful gallery but the exhibitions changed often, and it gave me a break in my routine."

"Paintings?" Lourdes asked her.

"Paintings, small sculptures, sketches—it varied from week to week. One day I was there by myself and the room, the gallery

was only one room with a few dividers, the room was empty—
there were no other people, I mean—or so I thought. There was
one painting I liked very much. It was of a girl about your age,
her hair in a ponytail, holding a clear bottle of water in one hand
and a white cat in the other. It sounds sentimental, but it wasn't
at all. In fact, it was almost scary, the way she was painted. The
next painting also had this same girl, still holding the clear bottle
of water, but in this painting she was standing in a pond, waist
deep. I stepped around a divider to look at the next painting, and
there were a man and a woman making love right there in the
gallery."

"Who was on top?" Lourdes asked.

The question startled Pilar. "They were standing. The girl's
bottom was toward me and I could see . . . everything."

"You could see his cock go inside her?"

"Yes. That's what I could see. I backed around the divider,
out of sight. I would have left then, but I couldn't hear anything.
Nothing. I peeked around again, and I realized that it was a
painting—and not even life-size. In fact, it was the third in the
series of the girl."

Lourdes continued to stare. "That's the whole story?"

"Well, I've never forgotten it, and it seems important to me,
although I don't know exactly why. I suppose it has to do with
art and meaning, the power of art . . ."

"I'm tired of stories," Lourdes said. "They don't mean a
thing."

"Then what does?"

"This." Lourdes lifted the wineglass by the stem and slammed
it against the counter. Glass and wine sprayed them both. "This."
She threw what remained of the stem and base to the floor and
stomped it with her foot.

"Stop that." Pilar grabbed her wrist. Blood and red wine ran
across Pilar's fingers. "What's wrong with you?" A shard of glass
had lodged in Lourdes's wrist. "Be still." She removed the frag-

ment carefully, then led her to the kitchen sink. Lourdes neither cried nor resisted, submitting like a child while Pilar washed the wound.

"Wait here." Pilar ran up the stairs for bandages, but when she stepped from the bathroom, she found Lourdes lying on her bed, holding her wrist and staring at the ceiling. Pilar crawled onto the bed beside her. "Let me wrap your cut," she said. The wound was not deep, but blood trickled down Lourdes's wrist and left a trail of red dots across the white bedspread. "That was my last good wineglass," Pilar said.

"You shouldn't let yourself get attached to things like wineglasses," Lourdes told her softly.

"And you shouldn't get so worked up."

"Yes, I should."

Pilar knotted the bandage and they lay side by side on the bed, Lourdes on her back, Pilar on one elbow. "Now, what was that all about?" Pilar asked.

Lourdes stared at her and then past her. "I'm in love," she said.

Pilar nodded, looking at the dollops of fruit on her apron, imagining her and Benjamin in the bakery. "Be careful," she said. "There are a hundred ways to lose the things you love."

"I don't intend to lose," Lourdes said. Suddenly she leaned close to Pilar's face, so close that Pilar thought she was about to kiss her lips, but she just stared, her breath hot against Pilar's cheek.

Lourdes studied her for several seconds. Then she jumped to her feet and ran out the door and down the stairs. Pilar heard her stumble and fall near the bottom, but by the time she reached the landing, Lourdes was gone.

Only after she'd cleaned the counter and wiped the blood and glass and wine from the floor did Pilar realize that Lourdes was Leon's lover. The knowledge hit her like a fist, and she wept.

.   .   .

THE DREAM that Benjamin would go to college was as real to Ramon as seawater, as powerful as the memory of his own father, a hereditary dream that carried the weight of history, that was the product of history, that became, in Ramon's mind, indistinguishable from history.

But time was short. He would have to send Benjamin and Lourdes soon or wait for another year to pass, and too much could happen in a year. That Lourdes might not be willing to go was a possibility he was incapable of considering. The problem of money loomed larger and cast a darker shadow. The only feasible source of such money was the tourists, but he would have to do more than merely overprice his tours; he would practically have to steal their money. Somehow lie to them. Swindle them. This, in itself, did not bother him as much as he thought it should, but he would have to cheat them while showing the places that he loved, while telling the stories that he held dear. He didn't want to cheapen his stories in this way, but he could not abandon the dream.

The question spinning in his brain was this: How does a man choose among the things he loves?

The hotel rose before him, white and streaked with vines, dazzling in the bright sunlight. It did not take much for Ramon to imagine it as an oasis, but the windows on the top floor were vacant, and, as he neared, he could see gouges and long striations in the plaster. His stomach was nothing but acid, and it was impossible for him to quit feeling his shoulders—they ached, not an ache exactly, a squirreling forward, a hunching.

Here was the irony that soured his stomach and troubled his shoulders: He could make the hereditary dream come true only by making it profane.

Before entering the lobby of the Hotel Esperanza, Ramon crossed himself, swallowing gastric acid, then threw back his heavy shoulders and lifted his chin, trying to look strong and determined. He pushed the door open so hard it banged against the wall and bounced back against his arm. Leon, who sat at the registration desk copying figures into a little book, only glanced up. "He raped your sister," Ramon bellowed, smiling self-consciously, his voice louder than he'd expected.

Leon again looked up from the ledger. "What are you talking about?"

"The man you poisoned." Ramon wanted to stop the smile now but couldn't. "He beat you into unconsciousness with a baseball bat, then raped your sister while you lay in a coma."

"Give me a break," Leon said, returning to his numbers. "Your couple is in room three."

"Can't you call them for me?"

"The intercom is broken."

"You're letting this place go to hell." He started to slam his fist on the desk, but he thought that would be too much and pulled up, his hand barely grazing the surface before disappearing into his pocket.

"It's a small building. We don't really need an intercom," Leon told him. "Except for lazy gigolos like you."

Ramon laughed too hard. "I have the looks for it but not the disposition." His throat had suddenly gone dry. He swallowed again, stared at the floor, and switched the subject. "Your wife then. He caught you by surprise, tied you to the bedposts with a clothesline which he had thought to rip down from your yard . . ."

"No," Leon said.

"No?" Ramon said softly, and for a moment he calmed as a new thought entered his head. "Did he rape you, Leon?"

Leon waved him away. "I have work," he said.

Ramon nodded but paused in the lobby several seconds, scanning for a memory that would encourage him to go on. He could not find one and became agitated again.

"Something wrong?" Leon asked him.

Yes, Ramon thought, but he said nothing, merely smiled at

Leon, the same false grin as before, his shoulders a vague torment, his stomach a pit of acid, and he walked on.

Peter Geddest was surprised that he'd confused the fees. "I didn't write them down," he admitted. The look he gave Ramon was one of bewilderment and not indignation. A sweet odor of lotion rose from the pores of his freshly shaven neck. He wore a guayabera, a green so pale that it was almost white, and a pair of short pants, which made him, in Ramon's eyes, ludicrous. Men did not wear short pants, only boys, or young men on the beach. Men of the age of Peter Geddest did not wear them even to swim. The short pants made it slightly easier for Ramon to continue with his lie.

"That was the charge for one person," Ramon said, grinning and trying not to. "It's twice that for two, of course."

Heidi appeared in the doorway behind her husband. She lifted the gray hair from her shoulders and began making it into a bun. The camera hung from her neck like an amulet. "And this is a walking tour?" she asked him.

"Yes." Ramon nodded vigorously, the smile out of his control, causing his cheeks to ache. "The boat into the jungle can be arranged, too. Not today. It's too late, but tomorrow, perhaps." Then he added cautiously, "That costs more."

"We'll have to think about that." Peter took his wife's hand, but she pulled it away to finish her hair.

Ramon had been saving to send Benjamin to the university since before the boy's birth. Celita had cleaned houses, taken in children, baked rolls and cookies. He had supplied fish to every restaurant in town. But only the tours made a difference. With the help of Pilar, he had determined precisely the minimum he would need for tuition, books, a rented room. And he had made more than enough for Benjamin, but now he knew that Lourdes had to accompany Benjamin or his money would accomplish nothing. And so he was forced to lie about prices, to squeeze what money he could from these people, knowing that it was far too little. Why did this bother him so? Why did it make him feel like a criminal?

The walking tour was nothing more than a stroll around town with local narration, descriptions of the landmarks and buildings, including the names of the builders and their parents. "You've lived here all your life?" Heidi asked him as they ambled through the village.

"Yes," Ramon said. "I am one of La Boca's native sons."

"Never had the urge to go away and see the world?" Peter asked.

"Yes." Ramon nodded. "But there have always been other things to do first. My life has always been too full to leave it."

Heidi smiled and touched his arm. She spoke with a confidential and self-mocking tone. "We almost didn't come down here because the porch needed paint. Isn't that the way it is though?"

Ramon forced a chuckle. "Exactly. Yes. Just as you say."

"We've got to get that done as soon as we get back," Peter added.

"Now, here is an interesting artifact." Ramon pointed to a rusting automobile carcass overgrown with weeds. "Born in Detroit in 1932; died in the hands of Armon Garcia in 1967. This was the first car ever seen in La Boca. It is still a mystery how he got it here."

Peter and Heidi Geddest were amused and interested, but Ramon could not put his heart into it. He went on, as he knew he must, showing them a broken wooden wheel in a weed-filled lot, telling them that it was exactly where it had come to rest after dumping Eduardo Moreno and his load of bricks in 1939. He took them to the wooden yoke that Jorge Matamoros had used on the first ox ever seen in La Boca, the ox that died after it was put to plowing the impossibly rocky fields, leaving Jorge to take the yoke himself. "When Jorge died in less than a month, the yoke was discarded as bad luck, and it has lain here since."

And so he continued, the old words slipping from his mouth as they had time and time before, but desecrated now by his tongue. He thought himself a thief; worse, a prostitute.

They walked along the beach, then toward the jungle, weaving through the huts, before returning to the cobblestone boulevard at the cathedral. As they passed the bookstore, Pilar knocked on the window. She gestured for them to come in.

"What a lovely girl," Heidi said.

"La Boca's bookstore," Ramon told them. "No city this size has a finer one. There's a good selection of books in English."

The introductions were barely concluded before Pilar took Ramon aside. "I need a favor," she said, pulling him by the arm into the hall.

"You don't look well," Ramon said softly. It was obvious that she had been crying.

"I need you to pick up a relative of mine, a cousin, in your boat. He's ill, dying. He wouldn't survive the jungle drive." She spoke flatly, but her manner was full of agitation, as if what she spoke of and what caused her this grief were not the same thing. Ramon listened, but he did not entirely believe her.

"You'd have to do it at night," she added. "The heat, he wouldn't . . ."

"What is your cousin's name?"

She reached into the pocket of her dress and withdrew a tissue. She touched her eyes, and then her nose. "His name is Samuel. Cruz would meet you at the dock in Santa Josefina Sunday night. He said if I could arrange something, he'd take my cousin to the dock." She took his elbow again, squeezing it now. "I would want you to keep it quiet."

"Why is that, Pilar?"

"He is my cousin, but he's a grown man. People would talk if they knew he lived here."

"Have you told Leon of this plan?"

She looked at the floor. "Not yet."

Talking with Pilar calmed him. Judging by her disposition, her problems were greater than his. "I am not one to quibble about politics. But if your cousin's attitudes are anything like yours, I could be arrested for transporting him."

Pilar nodded earnestly. "My family is not well thought of by the law."

"Our government has some flaws and we have not always had the best of presidents—"

"Dictators, you mean."

"As you wish, but the law is the law and I obey it. I'm sorry I can't help you."

"I'd pay you," she said. "Whatever you want."

And then there were hands inside him, gripping his intestines, paralyzing him. He shook himself to be free of them, but they clung powerfully, wrenching his bowels. He leaned against the wall, the pain spiraling through his trunk, and turned from Pilar. The tourists faced the window, looking over a table of books washed with sunlight. Peter's back pocket bulged with his wallet.

"I will slip a note under your door," Ramon whispered. He didn't look at her, and wasn't sure he'd spoken loud enough to be heard. "I'll write the figure on the note."

"Couldn't you just name an amount?"

"No, I have some arithmetic to do." What he did not say was "I could not face you with a request for so much."

Ramon waited outside while Peter and Heidi bought paperbacks. Rosa Ojeda walked by, but Ramon stared at his feet, pretending not to see her, humiliated by his needs.

THE STILL LIFE Rosa Ojeda was drawing would not stay still.

She had collected shells from the beach, an odd calcified turd from the banks of the estuary, and an old shoe she'd found months earlier behind the cathedral, and she'd arranged them on her bed, adding three pencils, a broken stick of chalk, and shavings from the pencil sharpener. She positioned a desk lamp to one side, in order to control the shadows. It was a festive arrangement.

But as it took shape on her pad, it changed. The ribs of the scallop shell exaggerated themselves, a crinkle of such violence that it became, unmistakably, a mouth forcibly silenced. The clam shell betrayed her too, growth lines radiating concentrically from the gently humped beak to form a delicate pubic triangle, but one without an opening, another violent silence. The pencil shavings had been transformed into fire, and the pencils themselves became caskets disguised as pencils. The shoe, fetally curled, its sole separating, embodied birth and death simultaneously, the infant and the decrepit, the wrinkling of the newborn and the aged in a single crease along the tongue. The broken piece of chalk stayed a broken piece of chalk; the turd remained a turd. Before she realized it was happening, the white sheet of her bed had turned black on the paper, making the other dark figures bright in contrast, as if they were connected to a source of light.

Rosa's great secret surfaced in all of her art, which was why she could show it to no one. She worked against this, choosing the most banal objects she could imagine to draw, contriving stories that had nothing to do with her past, but the secret wormed its way in and found expression in the way light fell across an open book, in the actions of her heroines or the long-winded speeches of the noble men, the heartbreaking confessions of the scoundrels.

With each new drawing or story, she swore to avoid the point where her past splattered across the paper. But she was unable to keep the secret down, though she had done just that in her life. Every morning she woke with bile burning her throat from the effort. The soft tissues that separated her skin from her bones had been eaten away by her secret, her beautiful body made to resemble a brooding hen, but she told no one.

She kept it down in every way, except in her art—in the drawings, where a spoon would suddenly bulge with a secret or a chalk eraser would be transformed into a man's genitals, and in the stories, where sometimes it would be shamefully explicit, and a woman would report her living husband dead, then bury the mutilated corpse of another, while she, dressed in black, cried tears of the most sincere grief.

Rosa struggled with the still life until well into the night. When she finished with the drawing, she studied it, disappointed by her failings. She carefully tore the page from the pad, studied it again, then placed it with the others. She knelt beside her bed, moved the lamp an inch, positioned the pad against her knees, and began once more.

PILAR FLUNG OPEN the back door and took Leon's hand. "Hurry," she said, leading him through her house to the bookstore window, where she stood in white light beside a tray of novels, pointing at the moon, which was almost full and slightly misshapen, just above the water.

Leon was used to this sort of thing. Everyone in La Boca seemed to think the movement of the sun and moon called for human attention. They were always pointing and demanding his interest. He had even begun to use it himself when in a pinch. Now, he decided to appease her. "It looks like the palm of a hand," he suggested. "A hand without fingers."

"No." She shook her head. "It's a fetus, don't you think? With damaged limbs—deformed arms and legs. The result of incest, maybe, or just bad luck. A fetus." Below, cradled in the ocean, the moon's reflection, identical twin.

A boy and a girl appeared on the street in the unreal moonlight. Pilar's attention switched to the young couple, who were now holding hands, walking slowly. "Some nights," she said, "I sit in this room to read. People walk by. They can see me and I can see them, but I don't want to acknowledge them. There are so few people in this town I can tolerate . . . but I can't stop my hand from waving." She touched the sleeve of Leon's shirt. "Have you ever found yourself doing something like that?"

"I'm not sure what you mean. Like what?"

"Waving at people you don't care for, people who don't care for you—acting out of convention, just convention."

"No," Leon said. "Not any more."

Pilar shook her head. "I try not to." She stepped away from the window and retraced her steps to the hall, pointing to a spot beneath a window on the house side. "The sun shines there in the mornings. It's where I have my coffee." She turned and faced the big store window. "And there in the afternoons. It's where I read when there's no business." She pointed to the place where moonlight now shone, then looked at Leon oddly, as if trying to place him.

He was amused by her talk. It seemed typical of La Bocan silliness, but she was serious and he hid his amusement. Was that acting out of convention? He supposed that it was.

Pilar put her hand to her cheek and shook her head. "Don't pay any attention to me," she told him. "I'm in a peculiar mood."

"Perhaps it's the moon," he offered.

"That girl you've been sleeping with," Pilar said softly. "She's been coming here to talk with me."

Startled, Leon almost denied the existence of any such girl, a reflex he barely avoided. He touched the buttons of his shirt, bottom to top, during the short time it took him to recover. "She told you she was my lover?"

"We talk about books. About the university." Pilar had covered her eyes, as if she were shielding herself from the moon.

"Then what makes you think—"

"Her attitude toward me." She walked past Leon once more, to the window. "I know her mother. I imagine everyone in La Boca knows her mother." Moonlight whitened her face. "She usually comes with her mother."

"And the girl knows that you and I are lovers?" Leon asked.

"At first, she may have been uncertain. But now . . ." Pilar crossed her arms, twisted at the waist slightly, the turbulence of her emotions barely in containment. "Now she looks at me . . . she sees us as sisters."

Leon did not know what to make of the answer, but he discovered that he felt relieved. "Does she bother you?"

Pilar faced him, moonlight now in her hair and on her shoulders. When she spoke, she spoke plainly, as if announcing a fact to a classroom of students. "She loves you, Leon."

Leon did not want to, but he smiled. "And the sun shines right there? Where you're standing?"

"Yes," Pilar said, ignoring the smile, forgiving him for it, pretending she had not seen it. "Yes."

He pointed at the hall. "And here in the mornings?"

Pilar walked to him, slipping her arms around him. "She loves you very much."

"And you?"

Pilar grunted. "She doesn't love me."

He took her shoulders, pulled her closer. "Do you love me?"

"Yes, I love you." She tried to sound casual but the confession caused her to tremble. To mask her feelings, she added, "I think it's better to love you than to love no one."

He kissed her and guided her into the kitchen. She broke from him and went directly to the fireplace, remembering suddenly that she was cooking a meal they were going to eat. She turned the spit, which held a flank of goat, feeling that she had been far away. Black beans simmered on the stove, and she stirred them, grateful for the realities of food.

Leon seated himself at her narrow oak table and watched her brush a red sauce over the goat. He could not imagine Pilar and Lourdes having a conversation.

"Do you talk about me?" he asked her.

Pilar turned, brush in hand, bristles near her face. "It's just like you to think we would." She resumed basting. "We talk books. She was interested in my days as a professor—her mother told her I used to be a professor, I imagine. We never mention you." She dropped the brush into a bowl of sauce. "I had a dream last night. Do you want to hear? It was about a man with two heads. He was as broad at the shoulders as two men, but he had only one body."

"You and your dreams," Leon said. "Who did he look like?"

"I don't know. No one." She joined him at the table. "The head on the right spoke to me. It told me that the two heads acted as one. 'Unlike stupid movie versions,' it said. But while the head on the right was talking, the head on the left was struggling to speak, to disagree, I think. I realized that one head ruled the other. I felt so sorry for the head that was mute that I woke up crying."

Leon laughed, which offended her, but he continued laughing and her mood changed. She laughed with him, although she could feel pressure beginning behind her eyes. From where she sat, she could see the end of the hall, where a ray of moonlight now shone. Her mood shifted again. "You and I rarely speak in the daylight. Are you aware of that? Once I leave the hotel, we never touch until dark. You don't know anything about the way I spend my time. What I do, where I drink my coffee—I take it black. Did you know that? Monday I saw you and Ramon walking by here. You never even looked this way."

"We were going to those big rocks down past the cathedral," Leon said. "He was talking. You know how he is."

She rose from the table while he spoke and stepped to a cupboard. "It's light here too much," she said softly and removed two white plates. "My grandmother used to tell me that the moon was made of china. She had one china dish when I was little. She told me the new stars were made of bone and the old ones of ivory." She set the plates in front of Leon, then walked down the hall. The moon touched the water, its twin rippling beneath. And at the far edge of the window, a girl stood with her hands cupped around her eyes, staring in. When she saw Pilar, she spun and ran, the moonlight catching the whir of white apron.

Pilar touched the collar of her blouse, the waist of her skirt. She felt naked, and rubbed the material between her fingers as evidence that she was not. How had she let herself get into a situation where a teenage girl could humiliate her in her own house? She hurried back down the hall to Leon.

His back was to her. He stood at the stove, spooning beans onto his plate.

"Leave her," she said. "Don't see her any more."

Leon turned very slowly, staring at his food before he looked at her. "I don't think we should talk about this. Would you like me to fix you a plate?"

She ignored him, stepping to the stove. The beans bubbled, and she adjusted the burner. "I am on the government's list," she told him. "If they discover where I am, they'll send people to take me away." She faced him. "Or they'll just have me killed."

He was nodding. "I suspected as much. But you're safe here."

"I do love you, Leon," she said. "I only just discovered that."

He smiled at her. "You love me and you love this leftist stuff. I, at least, don't endanger your life. So there it is, we both have our two passions, don't we?"

She couldn't breathe, the pain at her ribs and in her stomach like the pain of hunger, and so she filled her plate and sat beside him. Every word he said turned in her mind, and she examined it for clues. Each of his movements seemed to carry hidden explanations she could not interpret. He was a mediocre lover, he offered her no commitment, but love for him had settled inside her. A pathetic love, she thought, but she could not bring herself to ask him to leave.

In bed, his breath on her shoulder, she asked, "Would you hide me, Leon? If they came for me. If the government came for me?"

"Of course," he said softly, nuzzling. "They wouldn't mess with an American."

"Yes, they would. Here, they would. That's not the answer I want anyway."

He was silent several long seconds. "Cut off my arms," he said. "Cut off my legs. I would protect you." He wrapped his limbs around her. He said, "You're mine."

They lay intertwined several moments in Pilar's soft bed. She rubbed her hand up his ribcage to the coarse hair beneath his arm. She found a little mole and examined it with her fingers. Wind chimes sounded nearby, and she felt more at peace than she had for days.

"I want you to meet my grandmother," she told him. "She's dying to see your hands."

"I didn't know you had relatives here."

"I didn't want you to know."

"Why does she want to see my hands?"

"She reads palms. Her name is Maria Peralta Cardenas, but you can't let anyone know that she's my grandmother. If they came for me, she'd be in danger."

Leon kissed her. "So you trust me."

"I love you."

"I've heard that before," he said, and this upset her, but he was referring to something else—not to her love. "That name. I think Ramon told me some story about her. She predicted a horde of dinosaurs would come out of the trees, or something like that."

Pilar laughed. "Her predictions have become a little shaky."

"Is she the one who pulled the old switch? That would be something," he said. "I can't remember, but she's in one of Ramon's stories."

"You'll like her," Pilar told him.

They passed the hours that he stayed holding one another, talking occasionally about the meal they'd eaten, the view from her window, the star-shaped birthmark on his thigh. She almost told him about the man who was coming that night to stay with her—one love replacing the next—but decided that one confession was enough, no matter how much it pleased her to tell him secrets, the thrill of surrendering to love.

IT WAS LATE when Leon left the bookstore and walked through the darkened streets to the hotel. The night air was cool, and he found himself happy and feeling self-congratulatory for having come to La Boca, for having constructed a life that suited his desires. And there was no question in his mind that it was desire that had led him away from the United States, away from friends and family, away from his past.

Sexual longing accounted for only a small part of the desire that had made him change his life. He had wanted a life where the power of erotic passion did not pass into routine, and he had needed a life that provided him with a constancy of happiness. But neither his wanting nor his needing had caused his metamorphosis, rather his fierce desire for a life that expressed his identity. He had come to La Boca in order to become his natural self, which, he hoped, would be a man of integrity and independent thought. He was capable of pointing to a single day that had transformed his life.

It had been a holiday, Thanksgiving. He and his second wife, Charla, had recently moved to Oakland, and the living room window in their second-story apartment overlooked a vacant lot, where a backhoe had begun digging a hole Wednesday morning, a prehistoric strain and creak filling their rooms. Leon had hoped it would be gone by evening, but Thanksgiving, minutes before guests were to arrive, the apartment began to shake.

"Jesus," Leon yelled from the bedroom, then charged to the kitchen doorway. "Don't they know it's Thanksgiving?"

Charla, in skirt and bra, closed the oven door and dropped the basting syringe on the counter so that she might follow him into the living room. She was twenty-four and had a slowness about her that had attracted Leon from the very beginning.

The backhoe rested so near they could have opened the window and placed a hand on the joint in the enormous arm. Mounds of black earth bordered a hole roughly the size of a car. A night of rain had collapsed one of the piles, which sloped into the muddy pit. Water puddled in the slough, a trace of gasoline giving it faint color.

Charla told Leon that the noise, the thuds and moans, the motored rumble, reminded her of the rides at the county fair, but he could not be appeased. Their first guest, Charla's best friend, arrived before Charla had finished buttoning her blouse.

"I didn't want to spoil our weekend so I came by myself." Judith laughed, her eyes flitting up to a ceiling corner. She had come from the airport by taxi and without her boyfriend. "I cashed in his ticket and bought myself gloves. It's the most I ever got out of a relationship." She had a fish mouth, and Leon speculated that this was why she talked so much, using her mouth to distract from its fishiness. Charla had told him he thought like a man, which, he gathered, was not a good thing.

Judith pulled a crumpled pack of Winstons from her purse, then crushed the cigarette she was smoking. "That digger must be driving the both of you crazy," she said, lighting up. "I used to date a man who dug wells. He'd come to bed smelling like earth and water. You know that smell?"

"Dirt and water make mud," Charla said, laughing. "I introduced you to him, don't you remember?"

"Of course I do." Judith exhaled a funnel of smoke. "I was trying to let you off the hook." Her chatter and her smoking, more than any of her confessions, had convinced Leon that loneliness could be a way of organizing one's life. She seemed both terribly lonely and perfectly happy.

Cynthia and her new boyfriend, Joe Brogan, arrived shortly after Judith. "And this is Leon," Cynthia said, extending a long and golden arm in his direction. "I was his dance instructor back when I was a graduate student."

"Intro to Country Swing," Leon said, stepping forward to shake Joe's hand. Cynthia misunderstood and took his hand in hers. She twirled once, then led him through a few steps. "This used to be popular," Leon explained, embarrassed.

Cynthia laughed and let him go. He and Joe Brogan, a balding man with a rough face, shook hands. "You've got some noise in here," Brogan said.

Leon led him to the window. The backhoe lifted soil black as rubber. Judith stepped between them. "That looks like good dirt, doesn't it? Topsoil."

"Or sewage," Joe Brogan said.

Leon lifted the window. A cold gust of air swept into the room.

"That's not sewage," Judith told them. "It smells just like I was telling you, like that no-good guy Charla forced on me." She laughed, staring at the same corner of the ceiling.

Leon cupped his hands over his mouth and leaned into the window screen, waiting for a break in the noise. "What are you digging there?" he yelled.

The man behind the controls of the backhoe leaned out from its canopy. "A hole," he called out, then threw a lever, and the shovel rose.

"It looks like one of those Disney things," Judith said as the shovel paused. "One of those mechanical dinosaurs." The head plummeted to the ground, its jagged teeth consuming the earth.

The turkey took longer than either Charla or Leon had anticipated. "Let's slice it now," Leon said, poised with a knife over the steaming bird. "Everybody's starving."

"The book says to wait twenty minutes." Charla wrapped the cookbook in her arms as she spoke. "I didn't know you took dancing lessons from Cynthia."

"Long time ago," he told her. "She was a lousy teacher. Doesn't this stuff go inside the turkey?" He pointed to a pan of stuffing.

"Not necessarily." She said this quietly. It was her first turkey. She set the book on the counter. "One of us should go out and talk to our guests."

"Judith is showing everyone how she made a turkey drawing when she was a kid." He spread his fingers and traced around them as if drawing. "Doesn't she know everybody in America did that? And talking to Joe Brogan is like conversing with a tractor. Where does Cynthia come up with these clowns?"

"Don't be mean," Charla told him.

"You're thinking the same thing, you're just too nice to say it. Cynthia likes anything in pants."

Charla slapped him. Her swing had begun with some power, but she had tried in mid-swipe to stop it. It didn't even move his chin. She laughed, as if it had been playful, but Leon was infuriated, an anger with sources deeper than he could name. He spread his fingers into the shape of a turkey and pressed his open hand into the pan of dressing. It was hot but he held his hand there while his wife winced, as if it were she who felt the pain. Then he snatched a dish towel from its hook and wiped crumbs from his palm as he left the room.

In the bathroom, he faced the mirrored door of the medicine cabinet and ran cold water over his hand, which was not badly burned. The water soothed his anger as well as the pain, but as soon as he turned off the faucet, the sound of the digging returned, and he sensed danger—real danger. Later, he would wonder if the sudden peril he'd felt had to do with his marriage and its impending demise, but at the moment it overtook him, he could only name the sensation.

The grinding noise had made the rooms of their apartment mysterious to him, and he felt an urgency to take some sort of action in order to combat it, if only to engage others in talk. Stepping into the living room, he said nervously, "I have an ugly mole in my armpit." It was the first thing that had come into his head. He raised his arm, although the mole was covered by his shirt sleeve. Seeing the confused looks of his friends, he felt immediately foolish and lowered his arm. "It's not cancer. It's nothing."

Judith bailed him out. "It's good you had it checked," she told him. "I go to the doctor every time my chest aches. It's better to be safe. I tell myself that, then the doctor makes me feel like a fool." She inhaled deeply on her cigarette, with much obvious pleasure.

Leon suggested they watch a football game on television. "It doesn't seem like Thanksgiving without a crowd screaming in the background," he said. None of the women was interested. Joe Brogan only shrugged. The backhoe clanked and rattled.

"Could they be putting in a pool?" Cynthia asked.

"Surely they'd tell us," Charla said. She touched Leon's back gently as she walked into the room from the kitchen, a gesture meant to convey her remorse for the slap, a line in their secret dialogue. Leon made no response.

"The hole's definitely too big for a grave," Cynthia told them.

"They could be about to plant a tree," Judith suggested.

"I wanted to work with trees at one time," Cynthia said. "I thought it would be a good way to live, trying to preserve the living things that live the longest."

"So why didn't you become a tree doctor?" Leon asked her.

"I don't know. Why didn't I become a people doctor or a social worker or a pilot?"

"There's something about flying I like," Judith said. "It makes me feel helpless. Smoking makes me feel the same way. There's something romantic about loving a thing that can kill you."

"It's carelessness that kills," Joe Brogan said, rocking suddenly forward on the couch. "Cigarettes, airplanes, those are the instruments of carelessness, but it's carelessness itself that kills you." He settled back as abruptly as he'd sat forward. "Oh hell, we're all going to die, why do we bother?"

Cynthia stepped quickly to him and patted his knee. "Joe's mother is having a bypass next week. He's feeling the strain."

"We can eat in a couple of minutes," Charla said. "Leon, let's carve it."

"Has it been twenty minutes already?" he asked her, his voice calm and full of malice.

Steam curled off the turkey slices. Giblet gravy waited murky in its boat. Charla had crumbled the stuffing into a bowl to obliterate Leon's handprint, and hunger prevented anyone from noticing.

"One day I'm going to get fat." Judith leaned back in her chair and lit yet another Winston, blowing the smoke away from the table. "Not that anyone would care. That turkey smells so good, this"—she waved the cigarette—"is the only thing that can keep me from being a pure swine about it." She laughed, her eyes jumping to a new corner now that she was across the room.

Halfway through the meal, the digging stopped and the room fell quiet.

"The thing I like best about holidays is watching the men do the dishes," Judith said when everyone had finished eating. "Are you boys going to entertain us now or later on?"

"We're going to throw those plates away," Leon told her, nestling in the couch between Charla and Cynthia.

Joe Brogan, however, stepped to the center of the room. "I'll help."

Leon wanted to sit and talk, but Brogan stood waiting, and then, as if in response to Leon's reticence, the digging began once more.

Joe Brogan washed; Leon dried and put things away. "How do you figure?" Leon said. "The one day we have people over— a holiday, no less—and there's a backhoe digging a pit halfway to hell."

"Hmm," Brogan said and passed him a dish to dry.

That Brogan wouldn't commiserate with him irked Leon, but the silence between them bothered him more. "How did you meet Cynthia?" he asked.

Brogan shrugged, swirling a sponge around another plate. "At a poetry reading. I was one of the readers. I write poetry."

"I wouldn't have guessed that," Leon said.

Brogan nodded, and Leon knew that the burden of small talk rested on his shoulders. "So do poets have groupies the way singers do?"

Brogan paused for a moment, considering the question. "I imagine the good ones do. I don't."

"You're no good?"

"I'm just good enough to know I'm no good," he said.

Judith stepped into the kitchen doorway. "They're doing it," she called. "There's something about watching men do the dishes that makes me almost weepy."

"Joe was telling me how he's a poet," Leon said.

"I heard," Judith said. "He's good enough to know he's not good. I know that feeling, Joe. I feel the same way myself about men. I'm good enough to attract them but I can't find a way to keep them."

"Oh, Judith, don't start," Leon said. "Sometimes I think you want to lose men. I think you organize your whole life around it."

"I've wondered about that myself," she said. "But it's not true. I really did want things to work out with Mack. He's a sweet man, but I seem to bring out the meanness in him. I meet nice men all the time, which is the biggest problem for most women. They get tired of me or something. I can't figure out what it is. What do you think?"

"You haven't met the right guy, that's all," Leon told her.

"Oh, I can't believe that's true," she said. "Joe, what do you think? I've never had a poet talk about me. What do you think, Joe? What is it about me that makes a man want to leave? I know you've just met me but sometimes that gives you just the right distance, you know what I mean? Joe?"

"You talk too much," he said and dropped the gravy boat into the water. He looked up in time to see her step into the other room. "That didn't come out the way I meant."

"She kind of begged for it," Leon said.

"My mother is probably going to die next week. I'm not usually rude to strangers. I should talk to her." He dried his hands on the dish towel Leon held but stopped at the doorway and stepped back into the kitchen. "We should finish," he said and thrust his hands back into the hot water. "I write poetry about Viet Nam. It started as therapy. Now I just like poetry. I'd prefer to write about something else, but I can't seem to do it." He offered Leon a gleaming plate.

"What did you do over there?" Leon asked him.

He grunted. "That's what I'm trying to find out, that's why I write poetry—to figure out what it was I was doing over there. If I can figure that out, then I'll write about something else. You know what I mean?"

Leon nodded, although he wasn't really sure. "One hundred and thirty-five," he said. "That was my lottery number. They only drafted to—I don't know—seventy-five."

"You're young," Brogan said. "I thought you were older. Cynthia told me you'd been married before. Guess I figured that made you older."

"It didn't last too long," Leon said. "I met Charla and left June."

Brogan nodded, staring into the suds. "Cynthia says you still sleep with the first one, June."

Leon whipped his head over his shoulder. The doorway was empty. "Keep it down, will you?"

"Says you slept with her—Cynthia, I mean—while you were married the first time." He handed Leon the gravy boat.

"You trying to get me upset, is that it?" The backhoe growled, and Leon felt it in his stomach. "My first wife lives in San Diego, all right? We moved here to be away from her."

"Take this." Joe Brogan waved the gravy boat.

"Let's talk about something else because if you're trying to get me upset . . ."

"Take this gravy trough," Joe Brogan said, handing it over. "Sometimes nothing looks so good as what you've left behind," he added.

"Hey." Judith was in the doorway again. "You two should see this."

The backhoe was halfway into the hole and tipped to one side. The operator tried to work his way out by placing the shovel against the high ground, making it lift the machine. The great arm strained against the earth. The low wheel rose until it was level with the ground. The man threw a lever, but the big back wheels only spun.

"He won't get anywhere like that," Joe Brogan told them.

"He could be crushed," Charla said. "I don't want to watch."

Cynthia took her hand and led her to the couch. "What were we talking about?" she asked. "Leon, close those curtains."

"He'll be out in another minute," Leon said and pulled the curtains shut.

Cynthia made an effort to resume their conversation. "My therapist tells me what's important is the here and now. The past is like hors d'oeuvres; the here and now is always the main course. She likes to use food talk. She says you wouldn't let lousy hors d'oeuvres spoil your dinner, would you? The here and now has to be the most important thing, always. Even if something good is on the horizon, some big event—she says you can't let a good dessert that's coming up spoil the meat that's in your mouth—or something like that."

"Is this therapist fat?" Judith asked her.

"She exercises," Cynthia said.

Joe Brogan suddenly stood. "I'm going to finish the dishes." He immediately walked out of the room, but a sudden rattle and clank caused him to run back and pull the curtain aside. "It's free," he said. The backhoe was on level ground again. The operator poured himself a cup of coffee from a red thermos.

"Thank God," Charla said.

"Look at the size of that hole," Leon said. "He must be digging a basement. They're going to put up a building."

Joe Brogan shook his head. "Not with a backhoe. You'd see some big equipment."

Steam rose from the yellow joint, and suddenly the arm

straightened, the shovel rising quickly to the window, where it opened toward them. They jumped back. Below, the operator smiled and lifted his coffee as if in a salute. Then he threw another lever, and the machine returned to work.

"Bastard," Leon said. He opened the window to yell, but the grind and whack of the digging machine slapped against his ears and rattled through the apartment like the voice of creation itself. He knew then what the man was digging. It was a mouth, immense and irresistible, and when it spoke they would all tremble, as he was trembling now.

He backed away. Judith closed the window.

Leon insisted on finishing the dishes by himself, letting the sink drain and filling it with fresh water, hotter than before. His hands and wrists turned pink. What he wanted was to leave the apartment and call June. What he wanted was to fly to San Diego, make love with her and spend the night. He tried to think through the impulse, to understand the desire, but it spoke to him as the backhoe had, a voice he could not ignore, too large to comprehend except in terms of power. He immersed his arms to the elbows. The tines of a fork pressed against his wrist. He wanted to tear apart the life he'd made and watch the pieces settle.

Stepping away from the sink, he lifted the kitchen phone, holding it in the air as if it were the source of his discomfort, then put it back in its cradle. They had champagne in the refrigerator. He had forgotten.

The price tag wrinkled against the black bottle, and he scraped it off, then removed the ice bucket from the cupboard and surrounded the bottle with silver cubes. Why had he thought this would calm him? He lifted the receiver again and dialed June's number.

As the phone rang, he listened to the voices in the other room, not the words—the backhoe was too loud—but the rhythms of it, the sense that rose from syntax. In the months and years that followed, he would remember this moment as the turning point because he heard the voices and he could have hung up before June answered.

"Hello?" Her voice, her little quick breaths. In the background, something loud and cheerful—a football game, he realized and smiled.

"Who's winning the game?" he asked her.

"Leon?" June said, then paused. "Have you figured out why you left me?"

It was a question he couldn't answer. He put the receiver down seconds before he noticed that Charla had entered the kitchen, knowing only that he didn't want to talk after all, that he needed to touch her shoulders, but talk would do him no good.

Charla stared at him, her right hand over her heart, and for the longest time neither of them moved. Finally, she grabbed the bucket, the bottle of champagne rising out of it like a missile. She yanked too hard. The handle, wet with condensation, slipped from her hand, the bottle shooting out. White cubes spewed over her feet and slid across the linoleum, spreading. The bottle stopped just short of Leon's shoes.

"I didn't say a word to her." He knew it would be foolish to deny that he'd called June. He picked up the champagne. "I said, 'Hi.' That's all." He offered the bottle to his wife. "It's plenty cold," he told her, then added, "I'll clean this up."

"Men always make a mess, don't they?" Judith had joined Charla in the doorway, and it was she who wound up with the champagne. She waved it over her head. "Look what Charla found!"

Leon did not enter until he had located the champagne glasses. Charla had slumped beside Joe Brogan on the couch. His hands rested on his legs, hands as white as ice, veins as blue as flame.

"Who wants to pop this bottle?" Judith waved it again. "It makes me edgy to do it." She offered it to Leon, but his hands were filled with glasses. "Joe?" she said.

When the cork shot into Joe Brogan's white palm, champagne bubbled onto his lap and the couch.

"Oh," Charla said. "I forgot to warn you. I dropped the bottle." Champagne foamed wildly.

"I've made a mess," he said, rising, the crotch of his pants soaked.

"It's my fault," Charla told him.

Leon could not help smiling, until he noticed Charla glaring at him. She stood abruptly, bumping Brogan. And then she kissed him on the lips, champagne erupting from the bottle, dribbling down the front of her dress. They held the kiss several seconds, before she ran to the bedroom.

"What was that all about?" Cynthia directed the question to Leon.

"You should ask him," Leon said and faced Joe Brogan.

The champagne had stopped foaming. Brogan put it to his lips and drank, leaning back, raising the bottle high. When he lowered it, it foamed again. "Her husband," he said, wiping his mouth, "is a son of a bitch. Maybe she just figured that out."

Leon pointed angrily at him. "Who do you think you are?"

"You know, I'd like to see your house," Judith told Cynthia. "I'd like to see what you've done with the place. My suitcase is in the closet. You wouldn't mind, would you?"

As the women walked past them, Brogan offered Leon the champagne bottle. "I ought to punch you," Leon said. "This is my home. You ate from my table."

Joe Brogan tapped Leon's chest with the bottle. "I should tell your wife that you still sleep with your ex. Would you like me to do that?"

"Joe," Cynthia called from the door. "We're ready."

"Tell Charla I'll call her tomorrow," Judith said. "I hope that digging lets up. It's making us all nervous wrecks, isn't it? I know that's it."

Joe Brogan accepted his coat from Cynthia. "What digging?" he said. And they left.

Leon watched the backhoe work for half an hour. The operator shut the engine down when a man arrived in a pickup. Lettering on the door advertised safes and vaults. Leon stepped into the bedroom to tell Charla.

The bed shook slightly, and he knew that she was crying. In that instant he felt both sad and strangely proud, knowing that he was responsible. This was what it meant to be married, he thought, as he stepped to the bed, to feel pride that you can hurt the other, to love and hate someone in the same instant.

"They're digging a hole for a vault," Leon said. She pulled a pillow to her face. "Don't cry," he said, recognizing, in a dark corner of his heart, his desire for her to continue.

And that desire caused him to feel horror, which made him change his life. He sought to free himself of the pettiness, the vindictive smallness, the horror that came from living a lie.

PILAR'S FEET sank into the black mud, cool against her soles, rising through the gaps between her toes. The night hid everything visible from her, and only the invisible made itself known—the wind rolling over the tops of the waves, then skimming the surface of the south estuary, tired by the time it reached her, barely lifting her hair; the stench of the dead fish and stagnant water, too shallow and swampy for fishing, good only as a breeding ground for insects and frogs; the whine of the mosquitoes and under it the larger ring of the cicadas, interrupted by an occasional frog's percussion. She swiped at invisible gnats and lowered herself to an uncomfortable crouch. Ramon had estimated that he would arrive at two thirty, and already it was quarter past three.

She'd promised him a lot of money, which she knew would have to come from her savings—a development she discovered to be to her liking. The money, the caring for a dying man, these seemed easy ways to continue her commitment, to make herself feel better about exile. It cost so little to live in La Boca, the remainder of her savings would still last a long time. And the dying man might be good company, although she doubted it. As long as he didn't demand constant nursing, she didn't mind, and even then, she could get her grandmother to help. At this point, she didn't even know his name. Her cousin Samuel, she'd told Ramon, who obviously did not believe her but knew enough not to press. Only this part, the waiting, she disliked. Once he was here, she would be able to manage.

She didn't hear the boat arrive and couldn't see it until it was within a few yards of her—Ramon's wide smile, the hull of the little boat made large by its sudden appearance. Only when she stood could she see the body prone on a stretcher. Ramon sat beside the man's legs.

"What a beautiful night," he said to her softly. "Step out here, and we will carry your cousin in."

The first step startled her. The bank dropped off sharply and she was in water to her waist, her clothing soaked.

"I should have warned you," Ramon said. "This estuary is as uneven as a face." He slid over the side of the boat and extended his hand. The muddy bottom rose and fell so abruptly that the water only covered Ramon's ankles.

Pilar took his hand, and it kept her afloat because with the second step she was in the water over her head. It lapped against her jaw as Ramon pulled her to the boat. He helped her climb to where he stood. "This may not be easy," he said.

The body on the stretcher took up the full length of the boat. He was wrapped in a blanket, a white handkerchief around his face. A wild cropping of black hair was the only distinguishing characteristic. Pilar was suddenly frightened, certain that Cruz had somehow tricked her, and this man was dangerous.

Ramon put his mouth to her ear. "Your cousin hasn't spoken a word."

"He's dying," she said. Then added, "He didn't want to die in a hospital."

"He won't have to worry about that here," Ramon said.

"Stand there." He pointed. "It's not deep." She took hold of the stretcher and they lifted him out of the boat.

He weighs nothing, Pilar thought, nothing at all.

Ramon balanced himself on one leg and, with his free foot, pushed the boat over the muddy ledge into deeper water. "Now," he said, "we can put him back in the boat and walk it to shore." He lowered his end of the stretcher, then turned the boat so that she could do the same. She bent carefully and set her end down.

"Follow me," Ramon said, walking with one hand on the bow.

She traced Ramon's steps as precisely as she could, but her foot slid down the muddy slope and plunged her into darkness. Her hands and elbows hit the muddy bottom, and her face slid against the steep slope of the dip. It did not hurt so much as frighten her—the black earth, black water. She pushed against the mud and rose, spitting salt water, staring now at the black sky.

"Are you all right?" Ramon asked her. He was whispering.

"Yes," she said. "I fell."

"I gathered that," he whispered.

She wiped mud from her cheeks and eyebrows, and then climbed the slippery bank. Her clothes were drenched and filthy, and her hair clumped about her head like seaweed. The stagnant water left her skin oily, and even on her teeth she felt a film.

They carried the stretcher down the narrow path that led to town, staying near the estuary, away from the huts and houses, but there were no lights, no one to see or hear them. La Boca slept.

Ramon helped her carry him upstairs and they lowered him to her bed.

"He's so light," she said.

Ramon put his head to the man's chest. "He's breathing. That's a good sign. I'd let him sleep through the night if I were you." He smiled briefly. "I have to be going. There's a little bag in my boat. I will bring it to you tomorrow."

"I'll pay you then," Pilar said.

Ramon stared at her so strangely that she turned, thinking the man in her bed had risen. Ramon said something.

Pilar pulled her muddy hair away from her ears. "What was that?"

"I need that money very much," Ramon whispered. He put his hand to her face and gently rubbed his thumb across her brow. He wiped the smear of mud onto his pantleg. "It has been the dream of my family for generations to send a boy to college."

"I'll pay you tomorrow," Pilar said. "For your son."

Ramon nodded slowly. "Thank you," he said. "I'll come by." He descended the steps, then called back to her. "Cruz said to tell you that he'd stop by tomorrow also, after he goes to the hotel. I hope you're paying him less than you're paying me." He said good-bye again. She listened until she heard the door open and close.

Water dripped from her skirt and hair to the wood floor. Mud ringed her ears. The man who lay motionless on her bed had transformed her room. Only a few hours earlier, it had been a place where a man and a woman made love. Now it had a funereal quality, although she knew the man was still alive— Ramon had heard him breathe.

What to do now? A bath certainly. She wanted to see his face, but there would be time enough for that. For now, he was probably more interesting as he was, unknown.

She took clean clothes from the closet, holding them away from her body to keep them dry. As she closed the door, she heard the words clearly. "Good dreams, cousin."

She threw the door open again, but he said nothing more.

*I*T WAS the sort of morning that made people look to the sky: a morning when that shade of hyacinth usually relegated to the stratosphere finds its way to earth and creates a purity of air so remarkable that people turn their eyes toward heaven.

Pilar, straightening her shelves of books, stalling the inevitable encounter with her new guest, suddenly stepped to the big front window, pressed her hands against the panes, and gazed upward at the startling blue vault speckled with cirrocumulus clouds. And it was this vision that gave her the courage to climb the stairs and face her new tenant.

Maria Peralta, too, was affected by the morning: It made her burst out laughing. The clouds looked to her like immaculate bars of soap, and so she spread a blanket across the ground, filled a tub with water, and washed her dirty laundry in the sunlight. She worked so joyously that neighbors joined her, carrying soiled blouses, stained tablecloths, grimy trousers—little emblems of their lives.

Fishing was no good on a morning such as this. Fish, with their tiny brains, feared the horizon, and, on this morning of clarity, became certain that the sky was falling and swam to depths no line could reach. Knowing the habits of marine animals, Ramon did not bother with his boat but sat outside with Celita on kitchen chairs and talked seriously about what he must do, how he would have to approach Leon, while Celita reglued the spine of a textbook, sewed patches on a shirt her son would need at the university, stomped to death thirteen red ants foolish enough to approach her person, and expressed her lack of faith in Leon and, for that matter, all other members of his sex.

Angelica Roches worked in the bakery throughout the morning and missed the miraculous sky. Lourdes delivered rolls to several restaurants, but she was preoccupied and sensual details were lost on her. And Benjamin, while his classmates stared out the window, imagined a world perfect in the fulfillment of his wishes, a landscape where every feature was wrought with meaning, each a marker of his consuming love—and so the sky evaded him, also.

Leon had planned an early swim but never reached the water. He stretched across a beach towel reading, all the while watching Janet Anderson remove her short pants with the pull of one string, flaps falling forward and back, then walk down to the water's edge in an immodest white bikini. She never ran; her movements had an exaggerated slowness to them that reminded Leon of Charla, and this contributed to a growing feeling of homesickness, although it was the morning itself that had done most of the damage, calling to mind the times he had camped on the coast near Big Sur, the crystalline quality of the cold California air.

He showered as a means of combating this nostalgia, but his head filled with the little grievances of the expatriate, who now and again misses all the things that once disgusted him: fast food, insipid movies, faddish clothing, mindless television, boisterous rock-and-roll bands. He longed for the pool hall in Berkeley where once, almost by accident, he ran the table, and then won the next game by sinking the eight ball on the break. He wanted to shoot a game of pool, and it seemed terribly unfair that this cheap pleasure was denied him.

He dressed in a white shirt and matching pants, readying himself for the new guests Cruz would bring. He had been told he looked good in white. June had insisted that he wear a white suit for their wedding. "It makes you look cool," she had said. "Besides, I love the irony." She had worn a red miniskirt. Charla had bought him white pullover shirts and white corduroy shorts, even a full-length white coat. The women in his life usually picked out his clothing. He missed that, which made him homesick all over again.

What would it cost to have a beach like this one outside your door in California? he asked himself. How many hours a week would you have to work? Would you have a heart attack or a stroke to look forward to in your declining years? When was the last time you worried about traffic or crime or pollution? Where would you find a woman more beautiful and less spoiled than Pilar? A lover more energetic than Lourdes? How could you have such a pair without lying and with so little effort anywhere else? He settled behind the registration desk and crossed his arms against sentimentality. Ramon was a good drinking buddy, he reminded himself, and the liquor was free. This was the life that every American dreamed of—every American man, anyway. He couldn't be sure what American women wanted.

By the time the Powerwagon stopped in front of the Hotel Esperanza, the La Bocan morning had returned to normal and Leon had stifled his wistfulness. No sooner had the rumble of the Dodge engine stopped than Janet Anderson came running down the stairs, her dark and silky hair a black rush of movement.

She slowed when she noticed Leon, but could not help smiling as she said good morning. The smile vanished when Cruz entered the lobby alone. "Isn't my husband with you?" she asked him, her voice coarse with anxiety.

Cruz pulled his hands from the pockets of his tan trousers as if to reach out to her, but he checked this impulse and merely shook his head.

Leon addressed him in Spanish. "You brought me nobody?"

Janet didn't wait for an answer, turning slowly and walking with deliberate casualness to the stairs, before sprinting up them.

"She's upset," Cruz said in Spanish. "I think she's been jilted."

"She's paid for three weeks," Leon told him. "He might show up next Monday."

Cruz craned his neck over the desk, which almost reached his shoulders. "I'll tell you something confidentially—I had forgotten about this." He began whispering. "When she paid for the trip, she asked if I had taken her husband out here already. I told her there had been no Andersons—then that boy with the backpack showed up and I thought he was her husband. But now I see that she is still waiting for Mr. Anderson."

"So her husband is two weeks late?"

"At least. Very unusual vacation planning, no?" he said, then whispered, "Who would abandon a woman with an ass like hers?" He touched the tips of his mustache, which were curled properly upward. "Your liquor is in the bus. Who will be returning with me today?"

"I don't know that anyone is. The boy with the backpack is camping out. He may show up this afternoon."

"The old folks?"

"They're out with Ramon, floating down the estuary. They've paid for another week."

Cruz nodded. "I'll return this afternoon and check." He leaned over the desk again. "If I were you, I'd comfort that poor Mrs. Anderson."

"I'll get someone to help you with the liquor." Leon spoke as if he were dismissing the idea, but he had already decided to take her to lunch. He was curious about her. Besides, he thought lunch with a beautiful American woman might be the perfect cure for homesickness—although if he had been completely honest with himself, he would have acknowledged that his episode of nostalgia was already a thing of the past.

. . .

IN HIS SHAME, Ramon could look only at the fine dust sifting through the sunlight and settling on his shoes as he held the door for Heidi and then Peter Geddest. Once they were in the hotel and ahead of him, he could raise his line of vision, examine the woman's swaddled arm, the crude sling that looped over her elbow, the pins that held her torn blouse in place.

Leon rushed around the desk to them, but he did not touch anyone—he just stood close, and only Ramon knew him well enough to recognize that it was a display of concern.

"What happened?" Leon asked.

Heidi began to cry, silently, though she smiled at the same time, albeit weakly, at Leon.

"Monkeys." Ramon said the word as if it were a curse. Then he added more softly, "They wanted her fruit." It had been as if they could sense that he, Ramon, was no longer a person they had to take seriously. It was as if they understood what he had become, as if they could see right through him. "They swarmed out of the trees," he told Leon. "It was like my worst nightmare."

Peter Geddest spoke, his voice calm. "My wife will be all right, but we will be cutting our stay short. Has Mr. Cruz been here?"

"He'll be back this afternoon," Leon told him. "I'm sorry this happened. I assure you Ramon is very careful."

"It wasn't his fault," Peter said, touching Ramon's arm lightly, a touch that embarrassed Ramon with its kindness. "But it was frightening," he added. Heidi covered her face at this remark and let herself be led to their room.

Ramon did not speak until they were gone. "I panicked, Leon. There must have been a dozen of them. Look at my ear. The little bastards have teeth like razors." His ear was bandaged and it was impossible for Leon to see anything. "I started screaming, and thrashing about—I almost tipped the boat over." He paused and took a deep breath. "Let Jesus be my witness: I hate monkeys."

"You want a drink?"

They sat at the Esperanza's bar. Ramon cursed monkeys for twenty minutes before beginning to relax. He shifted and settled himself on the barstool several times before pointing to the lobby. "That is a brave man, Mr. Peter Geddest. He steadied the boat, protected his wife as best he could, and, you know, he insisted on paying for the excursion nonetheless. There, while Celita bandaged his wife's arm in the next room. He refused to accept money back from me."

"Another arrogant American," Leon said.

"Arrogant, yes. But a fine man, anyway. I needed that money, Leon. I had to have it. And arrogant, your other boarder . . ."

"The woman?"

"No, the boy in glasses and dirty pants. Do you know what he asked me yesterday?"

"For a real tour?"

"He wanted to know where the whores were in La Boca. He asked me, a stranger, a respectable man . . ." Ramon faltered. "How dare he ask me to pander a woman?" He blushed and looked to the floor. The boy should not have felt he could ask such a thing of him, but it must have shown in his face that he was capable of putting a price on anything. Why was it so difficult for him to take the money of others? The Geddests were willing to pay. Pilar was willing to pay. But now he felt that he had put a price on his stories, on La Boca, on his friendship with Pilar. There were some things too precious for a price tag.

Leon was laughing at the thought of prostitutes in La Boca. "What did you tell the kid?"

"That there are no whores in La Boca. They're all dead or sleeping. That was not enough for the little turd. He wanted to know if there were any nearby. 'Where are they?' he kept asking. I told him just this side of hell. If he hadn't been staying here, I would have slapped his face."

"You're going to run off all my guests." Leon laughed again.

Ramon trembled with anger and fear and humiliation. Now, to make things worse, he had to ask a favor. "There's something else," he said.

"You've insulted the woman too?"

"No, this is important."

"Important?"

"I make very little money from fishing," Ramon said, trying to keep his voice level. He didn't want to sound like he was begging. "The market's no good. People fish for themselves. They like it as much as I do." He flattened a hand on the bar, fingers tracing the grain of the wood. "But my wife is frugal, and she brings in some money with her little jobs." Fine seams in the wood guided his fingers, evidence that the bar was drying out. "You're generous with the hotel's liquor, and we get by. Although we eat too damn much fish." He smiled briefly. "But these tours, these little trips around town, to the estuaries—I make more money from one tour than a month of fishing." He raised a single finger, then pointed it at Leon. "I owe much of that success to you. And that makes it difficult now to ask you this favor. But I'm sure you'll see it's right, that it is the right thing to do."

"Let me guess," Leon said.

"No, this is not for guessing. Not a joke." Ramon shook his head from side to side. "The money from the tours, I've saved it—all of it. It's for my son, Benjamin. You don't know the boy well, but he's intelligent. Not a brilliant student, but he's good. With some assistance and encouragement, he could complete a college education. And it's here where you can help."

At this moment, Leon's attention abruptly shifted, and Ramon saw that Janet Anderson was passing through the lobby on her way outside. Leon, he realized, had positioned himself to watch.

"What is it you want?" Leon asked, now impatient.

"Lourdes is older than my boy, but they were friends. They liked each other. She, as you might know, was the best student in her class. She and Benjamin would wander all day in the jungle, or sit and talk on the beach. Until lately. These days she seems to have thoughts of no one but you."

Now it was Leon who pointed. "That's why you've been warning me. You want Lourdes for your son."

"You're only partially correct. All of what I told you was true. What you've been doing is dangerous. But yes, I have always wanted for my boy to marry Lourdes, and now it's taken on more importance. A woman can either help a man through college or she can make him quit. I have enough money for both of them to go. Together they could make it. I'm sure of that. Benjamin would never graduate otherwise, and Lourdes could never come up with the money to go any other way. And they will love each other, also. Benjamin loves her already, and her fondness for him is unmistakable." Leon looked at his watch and began to stand, but Ramon put a hand on his shoulder.

"You can't matchmake like that," Leon said and shrugged the hand off as he stood. "Your plan is insane." He walked rapidly away.

Ramon caught up with him at the door to the street. The brightness of the sun blinded him for a moment, and the heat pressed against him like hands. "I know her mother well enough to know that she would approve. Her father is dead. You know that."

"Yes, her father is dead. Look, I'll help you get your boy to college, but I'm not dumping Lourdes just to give him a live-in tutor. If you need a loan . . ."

"Let her go, Leon. It's her chance, and his, for something better."

They walked over the cobblestones, Leon leading in his white shirt and pants, hands in his pockets, and Ramon, his arms raised toward his friend, following in his brown fishing pants, the lucky pair.

"Celita knows people who live near the university," Ramon

continued. "They've worked out the details for Benjamin, and they can do the same for Lourdes."

Down the street, children began yelling. A little girl in a yellow dress ran, pointing toward the jungle. Her mother trailed her, shielding her eyes with her hands. Leon headed for the corner to look, but first spoke to Ramon, hoping to put an end to the conversation. "I couldn't do it to her," he said, glancing into the bakery where the ancient Angelica Roches stared back at him and hurriedly dusted a counter with flour.

"But you will never marry her."

"It would break her heart." He resumed walking, stepping up his pace, but Ramon again put a hand on his shoulder.

"Break her heart?" He shook Leon roughly. "When her breasts sag and you lock her out of your bedroom, you will have broken her spirit, her body, her life. Marry Pilar or marry no one. But don't deny Lourdes and my son what I can give them. My own father died dreaming of sending me to college."

"I don't want to hear another story, Ramon." He lifted the hand from his shoulder. "You can dream whatever you want, but don't confuse that with what is real. You don't care about Lourdes. You just want some insurance for your son." He paused to calm himself. "Look, let me digest this, all right? I have some business to attend to right now."

Down the corner street, several children who had been playing soccer stood now in a crowd, their backs to Ramon and Leon. A few adults had joined them, and several others leaned out of windows and doorways to stare. Past the children, just beyond the end of the street where the village met the jungle, two vultures, taller than many of the children, fought over the carcass of a spotted dog. The huge birds, black and gray, their necks crooked and pink, jabbed first at the dog, and then at one another, raising their enormous wings to frighten one another, like men flexing their muscles.

"Jesus Christ," Leon said.

He and Ramon stood shoulder to shoulder watching the birds snap and dig their claws into the dog.

"Damn buzzards," Ramon said. "They should know better than to live where almost nothing dies."

"That dog looks dead to me," Leon told him.

"He could get up any minute," Ramon said.

A gasp rose from the onlookers as one of the birds bit into the dog's head and shook loose a divot of flesh. A scream followed, which silenced the other voices. A little girl in pigtails ran from an unpainted wooden house toward the birds calling, "Tico! Tico!" The vultures turned their heads together to stare, as if she were addressing them. A boy grabbed the little girl from behind and lifted her off the ground with one arm.

"When you've had time," Ramon said. "When you think this over, I'm sure you'll see my point. Take a few days. Think." They resumed walking.

Leon smiled weakly. "I will think about it," he said, turning to look once again at the vultures, but the crowd had grown larger and blocked his view.

"Yes, yes. Think about it. Take your time. I will talk to you again Friday. I know you'll do the right thing," Ramon said. Although they stood within arm's length of one another, he waved before walking away.

Leon had no intention of giving up Lourdes, but he didn't want to lose his friendship with Ramon either. He hated such complications. Janet Anderson was nowhere in sight. If Ramon had not brought up this line of conversation, Leon would have treated him to lunch. Now he would have to eat alone.

THEY DECIDED she would continue to call him Samuel.

Pilar sat cross-legged in a sagging armchair she had shoved beside the bed while Samuel laughed, a coarse, rhythmic wheezing. She hadn't anticipated his effect on her. Despite her wariness, she had expected to find a normal man, only thinner and paler. What lay before her hardly seemed a man at all. He was not thin but emaciated, and his skin was not pale but transparent, so much so that the glow of bone shone through at the elbows and fingers, and across his sloping forehead.

She drank coffee, blowing gently to cool it, pretending to concentrate on this task so that she would not have to look at him. His cup rested untouched in its saucer on the night table.

"The truth is Cruz sent me here because he didn't want me in *his* house," he said, and more bursts of wheezing followed, bubbles of spit lining his lips. "I'm not so much dangerous as I am inconvenient." He leaned against the headboard, hunched forward, one shoulder inches lower than the other. A loose night shirt wrinkled across his ribs, opening to a sickle-shaped scar beneath his neck. His legs lay under the white sheet, crooked and bare.

"I have an odor," he continued. "You've probably noticed." He lifted his coffee cup, elbow tucked against chest for support. "I require a bedpan. One is in the package your friend delivered from the boat. I'll need that soon, as a matter of fact." Tiny swallows, his Adam's apple disappearing beneath his jaw. He lowered the cup carefully, the hand rubbing down his chest. "I can feed myself, but I can't get out of bed to do it. Someone has to bathe me." His eyes flitted away. "I'm not typically in a lot of pain. Except after I eat. And I have pills to numb it." He shook his head slightly, pursed his lips. "The good news is that I won't live long. You should begin looking for a way to dispose of my body. Cruz suggested you take it out in the ocean. I'd prefer it just to be buried somewhere. A marker is not important."

Pilar didn't know how to respond and so drank from her cup. He had said he was in his forties, but his face looked younger, the face of a man twenty-six or -seven. Perhaps it was just his hair, dark and long, a wild bush sprouting from his head, that seemed intrinsically young. Of course, his arms didn't look young, but she tried not to look at his arms. "What can you eat?" she asked finally.

"Anything bland and easily digestible." He smiled. "I make you uncomfortable. I hope that will change. I'd like to tell you that I'm really Cruz's brother-in-law and this"—he opened his fingers at his waist to indicate the damage done to his body—"happened in a car accident. Perhaps that would make you feel more at ease. There's not much to worry about as long as you don't do anything foolish with my body. The government tends to check on burials. Just dig a hole in the jungle."

Pilar felt awkward, not afraid, but she couldn't think of a way of explaining this without talking about death, how she found it impossible to be natural in the presence of his stench or while imagining the shape of his legs, which lay beneath the sheets and looked to be a series of knobby ridges. It occurred to her that he might be more comfortable if she propped pillows beneath his shoulders, but she didn't want to presume—and didn't really want to touch him.

Samuel turned his head slowly, surveying the room, his cheeks red and pocked. With him awake in the bed, the room no longer seemed like a morgue, but it did not seem like her bedroom either. Her jewelry strewn across the dresser, the watercolor of a dancing couple, the little ears of color that sprouted from her drawers, all embarrassed her, and she understood why hospital rooms were so often bare and plain.

"I like the view from this window," he told her. "And Cruz tells me that you have a bookstore. I think spending my last days reading is as good a way to die as any."

"How did this happen to you?" She spoke softly, without looking at him.

"The government has taken to bombing our cities. Even the capital, a few neighborhoods. It's terrible, but there's a certain beauty to a thing invisible made visible, don't you think? I used to know a woman whose will, it seemed to me, was all that held her family together. When the great earthquake hit, their house—a plywood shanty—shook and creaked and should have fallen, but this woman had thrown her weight against one of the timbers. If you could have seen her physically supporting the house, you'd understand the beauty there is in our government's bombing of the cities. Contempt made tangible. It is a harsh beauty, I guess. Like the earthquake, the earth itself shaking with rage. But we could never have won the revolution without the earthquake."

"You speak as if it were already won," Pilar said.

"It has become inevitable, which is why my imminent death is personally annoying but not tragic." He smiled again, a front tooth chipped and ragged. "Maybe a little tragic."

Pilar stood, self-conscious, much the way she'd felt her first day as a teacher with all those faces watching her. "I have to open the store."

"Yes," he said, "and I need the bedpan."

As were all the restaurants in La Boca, Los Comales was small—five tables, fold-up models made in the U.S., covered with green cloths and surrounded by ladder-backed chairs with matted seats and uneven legs. A dog, sprawled in a patch of sunlight, lifted his head when Leon entered but quickly lowered it, visibly disappointed, and scratched his neck, leg thumping against the rough plank floor. The dog looked so much like the one the vultures had been fighting over, Leon was tempted to run back and check. But one dog was much the same as the next, he reasoned, and let the idea drop.

A large window, thrown open, provided a view of the ocean, a steady breeze, and the smell of salt water. Janet Anderson sat by herself, her back to the window, sipping a tall dark drink. Her shoulders were bare and tan. A ruffled white blouse circled her chest, held in place by an invisible elastic band. She sat as if she were expecting bad news, hunched over her drink, hands clasped on the table, her arms a triangle of tension.

Leon was happy to see her, although it was not surprising that she would go to the nearest place to eat. As he approached her, he wondered whether she would be considered less or more beautiful in Japan. He had discovered that he was more handsome in Central America than in the States—there were so few other men with blond hair, green eyes. In the time it took him to cross the room he contemplated a memory—a friend from college, a black sociology major who had dropped a pretty black girl to date a homely white one. Leon couldn't decide whether the attraction had to do with novelty or whether it was a form of self-hatred. Of course, it was possible that his friend had been genuinely attracted to the white girl and her race was incidental. Happily, Leon felt free to let the idea go—which led him to think that he had become a master of letting things go. This idea pleased him during the short period that he entertained it.

He seated himself nonchalantly, directly across from Janet, smiling but saying nothing, as if he were an expected friend. She looked up from her drink, still sipping through the straw. The waiter arrived, a heavyset man in a rumpled white shirt. Leon ordered a beer. The waiter, Ernesto, bowed slightly and hurried off.

Janet slid her glass forward an inch and began to say something, her mouth and eyebrows set on a word, but she stopped herself and leaned back in her chair, folding her arms.

Leon said, "Your husband isn't coming, is he?" He had spoken in Spanish, out of habit, and had to repeat it in English.

Her arms unfolded and fell to her lap. Her delicate eyebrows flattened. She looked at her hands and then his, which rested on the edge of the table. "I don't know," she said softly and turned away from him, toward the window. A pelican skimmed the surface of the ocean, which, in the afternoon light, was the blue of sapphire. A solitary gull trailed the pelican. Her face tightened, cords appeared in her neck. The knowledge that she'd been abandoned filtered through her, as if hearing Leon say it aloud were enough to make it true. The pelican, then the gull flew beyond the scope of her vision. She shook her head slowly and faced him again. "No, I don't think he's coming." Her voice carried the monotone of undisguised grief.

"What are you going to do?" he asked her.

She lifted her chin at the question, then rolled her head back and forth, her tan neck and the pale underside of her chin as erotic as the white of breasts. She would be beautiful anywhere, he decided.

She took another short drink through the straw. Then she said, "How long have you lived here?"

"A few years," Leon replied.

"You're happy?" Janet asked.

"I like it here. It's a sort of paradise. How much longer are you going to stay?"

She had watched his hands move as he spoke, his little gestures. He had beautiful hands, she decided. The hands of a musician or a carpenter. She said, "What did you do before you came here?"

"This and that. Nothing of any interest."

"Tell me. I'm interested."

"It might interest you, but it doesn't interest me."

"Don't you feel the least bit obligated to be charming?" she asked him.

His smile grew broad. "This little town is charming enough. I find it's better to provide a contrast."

This remark pleased and distracted her, so that when Ernesto came to take their orders, she had to look again at the menu to be reminded of what she wanted.

"Did you notice the sky this morning?" she asked and turned once more to the window.

"The clouds were like little white pillows," Leon said.

She frowned at him. "Are you joking?"

Leon shrugged. "Maybe I've been here too long. People here talk about the moon and the clouds all the time. Anything in the sky."

"I guess that's to be expected in a place like this." She rested her chin on her fists. "I've never been to a town where there's no television or newspapers. How can you live without the front page or the funnies? I miss Ann Landers. I miss the news at eleven. There isn't even radio."

He smiled. "I was feeling homesick myself this morning. We should have ordered hamburgers. I showed Ernesto how to make them just like this little joint I knew in Ocean Beach."

"I'm not really all that homesick yet," she said. Then she added, "Do you think it's better to be in a bad relationship or none at all?"

This time it was Leon who gave her a funny look. She laughed and mussed her hair. "Well, that's the big question of our time, isn't it?"

Leon nodded slightly. "I think it's most important to be in control of your own life. People make themselves choose between being miserable together and being miserable apart. They don't see alternatives."

"Such as?"

"Such as recognizing the truth, that people are happiest when they're close but not too close." He let out a short laugh. "Or something like that."

She put the straw to her mouth, but the glass was empty. "Are you trying to pick me up?" she asked him.

"I'm not sure."

"Oh."

"I'm curious," Leon said. "At least that."

"I know I don't look it," she said, "but I'm very nervous. My plans don't seem to be working out, and I'm nervous about it." She closed her eyes and bowed her head. "I may stay another two weeks. A month. More. I can't say."

When she opened her eyes and met his, he said, "You can't go back, can you?" He half-smiled, pleased with himself for figuring it out. "That's it, isn't it?"

She responded with a stare, which he returned, remembering

the game he'd played as a kid, where the first person to look away or blink lost. The recollection amused him, but gradually the amusement turned on itself, and he felt a part of himself, a part he couldn't name, begin to empty into the space between them with a sweet rush of blood.

By the time the fish dinners were set on the table, they seemed as incongruous as naked men. "Just the way you like it," Ernesto said to him.

Leon smiled and touched his fork, knife. Janet had already begun to eat, and he couldn't tell whether she knew that he was shaken. The white fish was delicious.

"This is good," he said.

"Yes," she told him. "I like you too."

They left the restaurant together and walked around town. The streets were quiet. The white houses and adobe huts seemed to lean together, defeated by the heat.

"This is the worst time to be out," he said and rolled his sleeves, but she was unaffected, hands in the pockets of her skirt.

A flock of gulls had scattered across the otherwise empty beach. They walked aimlessly in the sand or settled close to one another in the shade of a palm tree. Leon steered Janet away from the main street so that they would not pass the bookstore— a needless complication, he reasoned. But there was a sour smell along the dirt road he chose, and so he directed her toward the jungle again, past a clapboard house with a roof of tar paper and three slumping adobe boxes, each with a rowboat leaning against a wall, one with a second, a double-ended skiff, upside down on bricks, half painted.

"There's not much to this place," he said. "But there's enough. More than enough."

"Enough? What do you mean, enough?"

"Enough complication. Enough to do. Boredom is always the biggest problem in paradise." He led her to the south end of town, where they returned, finally, to the ocean—the granite formation where he and Ramon had sat a week earlier. The tide was high and the water broke hard against the rock four times in succession, then the waves stopped, although the water still churned, flowing and ebbing through the big stones. In one eddy, white water caught in the center twisted and separated.

Leon said, "If you want to become part of the local color, you have to say this white water looks like a ghost or the face of Christ or something out of the sky."

"It reminds me of my dishwasher," Janet said. "Mine has a see-through panel so you can watch." The water churned again.

"Won't do," he said.

"It kind of looks like TV static," she said. "How's that?"

Leon shook his head. "You've got a lot to learn."

Another wave came, followed by three perfectly spaced counterparts. The next to last was the strongest, tossing itself against the rocks with real violence, throwing spray against their faces.

Janet touched his ribs with her fingertips, then licked the misty drops from his cheek. "Salty," she said and turned quickly back to the waves. A pair of crabs moved across the steep face of one big rock, hesitating, then disappearing into a crevice in the stone. Leon pointed at the crabs. "I'm going to give you a second chance."

She said the crabs looked like people on their hands and knees.

"Praying?" Leon asked her.

"No," she said. "Searching for something. Something small. Like a contact lens."

They stood on their toes and leaned forward to see into the crevice but the angle was too severe. Leon kissed her, and the kiss rang through him like a burst of noise.

"I fell in love with this man," Janet said, and they began walking again. "We worked for a marketing company in L.A. I had my own division—it was the smallest in the company. Still, it was mine. Anthony was an executive vice-president, but they had a dozen of those. He'd married the boss's daughter when he was twenty-five." She stopped walking and kissed Leon, and again it surged through him. "I want to tell someone this," she said, "but you might not want to hear it."

He took her elbow, guiding her again away from the main boulevard and the bookstore. "I'm interested."

"Anthony and I had an affair, and it became something else. We fell in love."

"That's usually what spoils things."

"Oh," she said. "I wouldn't go that far. Anyway, he couldn't leave his wife without losing his job—I'd have lost mine too, for that matter. So we began embezzling money." She stopped, staring at the ground. Leon took her hand and led her on. "You probably think I'm awful," she said.

He didn't reply at first because he didn't understand to what she was referring. The embezzling, he realized. She was a criminal. "A bit of theft," he said vaguely.

"We wanted to escape and it was so easy, and we were so happy. What's more important than being happy?" She looked up at his face but continued before he could reply. "He was responsible for the money my division received, so he shorted me each month and I made my books match his. We knew we wouldn't be caught until the summer accounting, which is going on now. The last month, we kept it all."

They walked silently for nearly a block, weaving now among the huts near the jungle. She touched a sheet of corrugated tin, part of a roof. Her hand jerked away. "It's hot," she said, then, "People live in these?"

"Poor side of town," Leon said.

"There's poverty in paradise?"

"This isn't paradise for them. It's paradise for us."

"What is it for them?"

Leon leaned close, whispered in her ear. "Home."

His breath made her giggle. "I get it," she said.

After another dozen steps, she spoke again. "Seven hundred and fifty thousand dollars. Plus his legitimate savings and mine.

We left the country separately, and by different routes, agreeing to meet here. He said it was a place where we could disappear for a while." She gathered her hair into a ponytail and lifted it off her neck. "And here I am. He was supposed to get here before me." The roof of the hotel appeared above and beyond the shacks. They turned toward it. "I still can't believe he would run out on me."

"His wife probably thought the same," Leon said.

For a moment, she closed her eyes.

The lobby was empty, but Leon was worried that Lourdes might be waiting for him in his room, so he followed Janet to hers.

She dug through her suitcase until she found the passport that her lover had had fabricated, which said she was married and named Janet Anderson. "It looks perfect, doesn't it?" She held it up for him to see.

Leon pushed it aside and kissed her. She put her arms around him. "I've been so lonely," she said and kissed him again. "I want you to tell me something, though. I want you to tell me why you're really here."

Leon shook his head sadly. Hadn't he explained that this was paradise? "I came here to change my life," he said. "I didn't like the person I used to be. It wasn't me."

Janet nodded. "I felt that way about stealing money. I mean, that's not me. I'm not that kind of person."

"And now you've been abandoned," he told her. She was still nodding and didn't seem to be listening to him. "Luckily, you've been abandoned in paradise," he added.

She put her lips to his ear and whispered, "What am I going to do?"

"You're going to change your plans," he said, and he began undressing her.

"HE SURVIVED the trip?" Cruz asked Pilar and handed her a small bundle of books. A second, larger bundle, he slid behind the counter. "A few clothes. Some of his personal possessions. How did you handle Ramon?"

"I paid him a great deal of money." She crossed her arms over the package of books and leaned against a table.

"Ah, the virtue of having intellectuals on our side—they often have money. Well, now you're poor like the people you hope to liberate." His smile, exaggerated and smug, annoyed her. "I like Ramon. We had supper before he took off with your cousin. His stories tend to run a little long, but he's a friendly oaf, the sort of fellow who should be helping us out of a sense of decency or outrage or patriotism or pure fear. Instead, he helps out his pocketbook."

"He wants his son to go to college."

"Which is their game." Cruz wiped sweat from his nose. "He feels lucky to spend his life savings in order to put his son through college. His son should be carrying a rifle, not geography books." Then he laughed at himself. "Easy for me to say. I spent half a dozen years at the university."

"The point is that education should be free." Pilar slipped the bundle of new books to the floor. "Let me get you some water."

Cruz waved his hand. "No, I don't want any." He rested against the counter. "Maybe Ramon's boy really will study geography. Make up for your absence."

"What about my cousin up there?" She gestured toward the ceiling. "Is he a college graduate?"

"I think he's a dropout. I suppose that makes him the black sheep?" Cruz ran his hand through his hair, which was soaked with sweat. He touched his drooping mustache. "I wasn't even perspiring when I arrived today." He shook his head in resignation to the heat. "As long as he's staying here, I won't be able to talk with you at any length. It could be dangerous."

"You're not going to see him?"

"It wouldn't be wise," he told her. "You should feel good. You're doing your part again." He tried to remold his mustache into handlebars, but it would not cooperate. "If everyone would do their part, we could get this over with."

"Oh? Is this my part? Nursemaid?" She said it defiantly, but looked immediately to the floor. Once she'd wanted and had a larger role; now this seemed adequate. Something to appease her conscience.

"I'm going to leave. Have lunch. Perhaps I'll take a swim." He turned to the window and the ocean. "My God in the ground, I'm tired," he said softly. He took Pilar's elbow but didn't look at her. "My oldest daughter peed in her bed last night. She's eight. The little one, who's three, claimed it was her fault. They're very close."

"That was sweet of her," Pilar said.

"They're afraid I won't come back from one of these trips. They're afraid because their mother is afraid. Hell, I'm afraid. We're all afraid." Cruz released her elbow and crossed his arms. He whispered, "I don't want to end up like your cousin."

"He says the revolution is all but won. That it's inevitable."

Cruz nodded. "All dying men believe that." He pointed to the ocean. "A swim will help, no? Isn't that your advice?"

"Be careful," she said.

He kissed his fingertips and touched them to her cheek.

THE BEDPAN held excrement, urine, and blood. Samuel had pretended to be asleep when she'd come for it. When she returned, setting the clean bedpan on the night table, he pretended to wake.

"Cruz left a package for you," she said.

"How good of him." He sat up with such difficulty that she turned away, touching the items on her dresser—a comb, mirror, paperback—until the headboard groaned as he leaned against it. She would be a lousy nurse, that much was clear to her.

"Do you know how Cruz describes you?" Samuel was almost out of breath, his pocked face flushed.

"A Marxist dilettante?"

He smiled, shook his head. "He told me that you were the most beautiful woman on earth."

Pilar laughed, although she was flattered. "Was he trying to sell you on coming here?"

"He didn't have to sell me. It was my only option. Let me ask you something." His face turned serious. One arm lay across his body, and the hand, enormous and white, twitched against his thigh.

Pilar settled in the armchair. "Go ahead."

"Do you believe in God?" he asked her.

"No."

He pushed himself up higher on the headboard, which caused him obvious pain and made his face flush once more. "Why don't you?"

"All the usual reasons."

"So bore me."

Her answer sounded more like a lecture than a reply, although she tried to keep it short—religion as a means of legitimizing oppression, a way to make the poor and disenfranchised satisfied with their place because their reward is coming in the hereafter, or in the rationalization that suffering is all part of God's plan.

"You know," she said, sighing, "He works in mysterious ways, and so on. You must be familiar with these arguments. Why are you asking?"

Samuel shook his head slowly, rolling it back and forth against the headboard—which looked so uncomfortable that Pilar made herself get up and press a pillow between his head and the board.

"You told me why you oppose the belief in God," he said, adjusting the pillow, a note of bitterness in his voice, "which I understand completely. What you believe spiritually is another issue entirely."

"No, it's not," she said. "I see God as a political idea, one that encourages rule by the elite."

"Yes, you don't need to lecture me in elementary political

science. But I'm talking about you as an individual who recognizes the evil done in God's name and the awful mediocrity and mendacity that pervades all organized religion, you as an intelligent person who sees all of that and despises it but nonetheless must wonder about the nature of life and death, the startling complexity of nature . . .''

"I don't believe in God," Pilar snapped. "I have no need for a god. Life is quite enough."

"What about when it no longer is enough?" He placed one of his big hands over his eyes. "I'm facing death—why lie about it? And I have two great fears. The first is that I, who, like you, have been an atheist since I was old enough to think for myself, could be wrong. I'm afraid that my political beliefs may have kept me from looking for the spiritual—that's not it exactly. I fear that my hatred of the goddamn pope, who sanctions our murderous government, that my hatred of organized religion has made me deny God, who, if He exists, must hate the pope too."

"In that case, He'll look favorably on you."

Samuel hissed a laugh, the hand and spindly arm falling away.

"What is the other fear?" Pilar asked him.

He looked into her face for several seconds, as if trying to remember. "My other fear is that on my deathbed, I'll turn my back on my life and embrace God, making a travesty of myself."

Pilar shook her head with contempt. "Forget God. That's their game." She remembered Cruz saying the same about college and stopped herself. "Where's the evidence?" she said.

"Many of the priests here are on our side, you know. They hate this government and what it does to people. The new government will have its share of priests."

The door to the bookstore creaked open and Pilar stood. "I'd better attend to my store." She touched his arm before she left. It did not feel like bone as she had expected, but warm and soft.

The idea of a god did not hold much power for her. No more than her grandmother's notions of reincarnated lizards. Pilar paused in the doorway that opened to the bookstore. There, behind her counter, stood Lourdes. Sweat pimpled her forehead and her red cheeks. She had been running. The bottom of her apron carried a film of sand.

"Who's back there?" Lourdes demanded. "Were you with someone?"

"I was in the bathroom," Pilar said, "not that that's any of your business. What are you doing behind my counter?"

She shook her head once, and walked across the store. "I don't know." She crossed her arms violently. "I thought I was looking for someone. Or something. Let me buy a novel. Show me one to buy. I'll read. Maybe I can read."

Pilar walked past her to a shelf, wanting to find a book quickly to get her out, one she had two copies of so she wouldn't have to disappoint the pitiful Benjamin. She ran her finger over a number of titles before hearing someone on her stairs. For an instant, she imagined Samuel tumbling down the steps. She spun and lurched toward the hall, realizing as she ran that Lourdes was gone.

"You wait!" she yelled. Above her, Lourdes leaped the last two steps. Pilar ran after. She caught up with her in the doorway to the bedroom, where Lourdes stood, staring.

"Welcome," Samuel said and coughed, but Lourdes backed away, bumping into Pilar.

"Who is he?" she whispered, and Pilar slapped her.

Lourdes raised her fist, held it suspended in the air, then, slowly, lowered it. She spun to face Samuel. "My name is Lourdes," she told him. "I'm a friend."

Samuel raised an elbow to the middle of his chest, then extended his arm. The hand bloomed from the thin arm like a flower from a stem, and Lourdes stepped forward hesitantly, taking his hand between her thumb and forefinger delicately and for only a second. When she released it, it fell to his lap.

"I am your friend's cousin Samuel," he said, lifting one finger to indicate Pilar. "I've come to your town to try to recuperate from a car wreck."

Lourdes stepped away from the bed, her head down. "You should get some sun," she muttered, then stepped around Pilar and ran down the stairs.

"What was that all about?" Samuel asked after they heard the door below close.

Pilar stepped to the window. "That girl was looking for her boyfriend, who must be missing." Lourdes appeared in the street, running on the cobblestones, her apron trailing like a tail.

Samuel laughed. "She thought you might have stolen him? I'm sorry I disappointed her."

Pilar, humiliated by her love for Leon, looked away from him.

"Pardon me," he said. "Is there such a shortage of men here that two of you must share one? I only wish I'd known of this town a little earlier in my life."

She smiled, but could not look at him. "I love this man."

"I'd say that girl does too."

She nodded and raised one knee, which she rested on the arm-chair. "It's a ludicrous situation for a grown woman to be in."

"I've found that very little in life is ludicrous."

"Oh?" she said. "This man is a North American, a drunk—or practically a drunk. He runs the hotel and does nothing else. He has no commitment to anything. Or anyone."

"The human heart is a vicious organ, isn't it?" Samuel smiled, his teeth a filmy red. His gums had begun to bleed. "I knew a man of fifty, a man of great intelligence, who fell in love with a twelve-year-old girl. He gave up his wife, his children, his job. He abandoned his political commitment, and finally he had to leave the country. He lives with this girl in Uruguay. She must be close to twenty by now."

"And you don't think that ludicrous?"

"No." He attempted to gesture with his arms, but they answered the impulse with pain. He shook his head instead. "I think men typically see women as little treasures, and when there comes a woman who transcends that, who changes who they are in a way so fundamental that they are new creatures, then the man will do anything, become anything to be with her."

"What a romantic you are," she said, facing him finally.

"Women are more flexible and, yes, less romantic than men. Change is a natural part of life as far as they are concerned, so they're more likely to really love rather than treasure men, which is why their love is more stable and why extraordinary women often wind up with ordinary men."

Pilar believed that she was being flattered. "Your generalizations are awfully large, aren't they?"

He smiled. "Yes, and here's another predictable thing." He extended his arm. "Take my hand, please." She sat on the edge of the bed and held his hand gingerly. "I hope you understand that I must ask this. You see, though I am quite damaged in dozens of ways, I can still function sexually, and I'd like very much to make love to you."

"No," she said and dropped his hand. "That's not something I'm willing to do."

"Good for you," he told her. "You shouldn't feel pity for the dying. It makes us feel already dead. Although, if you have a change of heart . . ." He laughed, wheezing spurts.

She smiled, knowing she should return to her store but unwilling to leave just yet. "There is something about him," she said, speaking of Leon, "a gentleness. And the way he laughs, he . . ." She shook her head. "I don't know why I love him."

"That girl has a funny birthmark on her cheek," Samuel said. "It looks like a skull, doesn't it?"

"At least your imagination is healthy," Pilar said. "It looks nothing like a skull."

He showed his ragged smile, and they were silent for several seconds. Samuel began talking again just as Pilar was about to go. "Listen, if Cruz told you I was a hero, he lied. Not in life, and certainly not in death. I'm terrified of death. I am forty-four years old. I had a chance to be a professional baseball player. My fastball rose, my curve shimmied. A separated shoulder ended all that when I was seventeen. I fell off my bicycle while watching a woman take a pebble from her shoe. What legs she had!" He laughed again and wiped his nose. "I also tried my hand at the fine arts. I wrote a play about men and women trapped in a swimming pool, which illustrated human duality by having the story of the people played against the submerged drama of their feet and legs. However, it proved impossible to produce."

Pilar laughed now. "You're making that up."

"Exaggerating a little."

"I hate exaggeration."

"I really did write a play set in a swimming pool," he said. "Quite a stinker. Even my friends wouldn't put it on."

"I used to write poetry," she admitted. "And a story or two."

"Life is so embarrassing," he said. "How I love it."

LEON CLIMBED out of Janet's bed and dressed again in his white clothes in order to see Peter and Heidi Geddest before they left. He owed them money.

He dressed silently so as not to wake Janet, who had fallen asleep after making love as easily as she'd fallen into bed. Leon felt that she should have cried or been unable to sleep, disturbed by the sex, an admission that her lover had abandoned her. But she had only kissed him softly on the cheek, then fallen immediately asleep. As Leon saw it, that meant that she still held on to a hope that her lover would come.

Leon did not want her to leave. She alone would be able to understand his view of La Boca as paradise. He hadn't fully realized the number of things that he could not really talk about with the people in the village until he wandered the streets with someone from his own country. And beyond all of that, a great churning in his chest told him he must make her stay. She was a complication, but one that he welcomed.

He wanted to wake her, talk to her about his favorite beaches along the California coast, ones that she would surely know, and the best bars near them—the Elbow Room in San Diego, the Blue Serpent just north of L.A.—but he had to deal first with the departing Geddests.

Peter and Heidi held hands as they walked through the lobby. Heidi's damaged arm was pressed snugly against her chest in a white sling. Peter smiled at Leon and nodded slightly as he passed the registration desk on his way out the door. He had the kind of face that inspired confidence, Leon thought, but what had his life come to, what good had it done him?

Heidi separated from her husband and stepped to the desk. She rested her healthy arm on it. "I want you to know we enjoyed ourselves here." Her head wobbled defiantly as she spoke, her long gray hair rocking against her shoulders. "Except for the incident, of course."

"I'm sorry your vacation was ruined," Leon said, pulling out the ledger.

"Oh, we're not on vacation. I thought we'd told you. We're retired. I'm a birdwatcher. You have magnificent birds here. We came here for the birds—and the beach, the water. We travel a great deal."

Leon smiled and nodded, not really listening. "According to my books, I owe you a refund. You paid in advance."

"Normally we wouldn't expect to get a refund, but considering the situation . . ."

"Yes." He had the money ready, but counted it out as if he'd only just tabulated what he owed them. "Perhaps you'll come again."

"Perhaps." She put the money in her shoulder bag without looking at it. "Some people think we're silly to go all over just to look for birds. My friends tell me to go to an aviary." She grinned at him, the kind of smile that asks for reciprocity, and Leon obliged her. He thought she would leave then, but she gazed at the door, reluctant to pass through it. "The truth is I'm the one who loves birds. Peter . . . Peter just loves me. And travel. There's nothing about retirement to be loyal to. What I'm trying to say is that home can be a hard place to be when you have nothing to do." She smiled again and touched her sling. When she next spoke, the tone of her voice had changed, as if she were requesting a favor. "My husband and I were wondering about something. If we're prying just tell me so."

"What is that?"

"You're obviously from the U.S."

Leon nodded.

"What we were wondering . . ." The index finger of her good hand touched Leon's arm softly, a little peck, a bit of punctuation. "How was it you came to live here?"

"There's no mystery," Leon told her. "I drifted here, took this job. The Esperanza has become a sort of anchor for me."

She stared at him another second or two, waiting, then said, "Very well. We didn't mean to pry." Her voice was flat now, deflated. "Give our regards to the guide, Ramon. Assure him that we don't hold him responsible."

Leon touched her hand as a way of saying good-bye.

Halfway out the door, she paused. "Do you like birds?"

He only smiled.

When the Powerwagon had thundered off, Leon began thinking again of Janet and the moment in the restaurant when he'd lost himself in her eyes. He refused to believe what Ramon insisted, that such feelings were single notes in the great symphony of love. It was absurd to think that he was in love with a woman he hardly knew. "I've only slept with her once," he said, the thought such powerful evidence that he had to speak it aloud. Besides, he didn't care what label could be applied to the feeling, it was the raw feeling itself that mattered.

If he loved anyone, and he suspected that he might, it was Pilar, which made her the most dangerous to his way of life and, he had to admit, the most important. But what good would it do him to love her to the exclusion of others? As long as he was honest, he was above reproach.

He would take Janet to dinner, he decided, and convince her

to stay. *My guess is that you're living on the savings you had,* he would say, imagining the tone he would use as well as the words. *From what I've seen, you don't speak much Spanish.* He would carefully point out that the alternatives to La Boca were debasement and jail on the one hand, and being lost in a strange country and language on the other. *You gave up everything for a man and he abandoned you.* He would not promise her love, which would be dishonest, but he could promise her a beautiful beach, good food, plentiful liquor, companionship, and passion. *This is the life you stole for*—more or less, he thought, then conceded that it was less—a minor paradise, but paradise nonetheless.

He thought of the actress, how little it had taken, only to recognize her and let her know that he saw her for who she was. And then he thought of Charla in the kitchen doorway of their old apartment, the ice that sprayed across the floor, the hand that covered her heart. "I want you to tell me why you're here," Janet had said, and even Heidi Geddest had wanted to know what he was doing in La Boca. *I am here to mold a life that does not make loneliness requisite. I am here to become a good man.*

It was only a matter of months after the spoiled Thanksgiving that Leon and Charla separated and filed for a divorce. Leon quit the job his father-in-law had arranged and found another—supervising the day shift at a restaurant on the pier. The income held him over while he decided what to do with his life.

It was not an easy decision. From the moment he recognized the pleasure he took in Charla's pain and for the first time looked at love and marriage in light of what he knew from experience rather than from what he had taken on faith, he was horrified not so much by the conventions that led men and women to commit themselves to unhappy lives as by his own unquestioning acceptance of them. He knew of no married couple who remained happy beyond the early years, yet he had married June during the same year that he'd met her—only to find himself growing restless and petty before the next year was out, overtaken time and again by a rage whose source was deep and unnamable. And how had he battled this unhappy situation? By marrying another woman as quickly as the law would allow. He had never thought to question the premise of a monogamous lifelong commitment to one person, a leap of faith so large as to be grand but also, as he saw it, grandly foolish.

The loneliness of having no partner was fully recognized in every society, just as the loneliness of having one was overtly denied. "Your mother is a good woman," his father would begin before naming the ways that she made him miserable. "I don't know how I'd survive without him," a friend would say, then describe such a life with so much obvious longing that she would blush.

Leon could not believe that there was no middle ground, a life that embraced the joy of having a partner without denying the misery of having one, a life that made love and freedom compatible, a life that redefined relations between partners.

He had decided to start anew. He would remake himself in his own image. Which would mean divorcing not only his wife but his history, giving up the conventional vision and the ties that bound him to unhappiness. It would mean that love would no longer have dominion. What good was it to love someone if doing so made you both unhappy?

He was that sort of man who, when suddenly faced with a resounding truth about himself, approached it with such a sense of wonder that it was impossible for him ever to grasp it completely, which made it all the more powerful. If there was a missing piece to this puzzle, he could neither name it nor sense its shape, although there were times he felt its blunt edge rub against him. But all he had to do to combat these qualms was to examine the plight of his friends, all of whom either were in relationships that no longer made them happy or were living by themselves, hoping to find lovers who would transform their lives. Leon became increasingly convinced of the existence of an alternative. The problem was in finding it—how did you give up your day-to-day life long enough to find the answer? There were bills to be paid, divorce proceedings to manage, friends who wanted to have him to dinner, the responsibilities of his job at the restaurant—where two dishwashers had quit within the week, a waitress had made an obscene pass at him in front of customers, and the faulty refrigerator that had spoiled the clams last week had ruined this week's mussels—and, on top of all of that, he possessed an empty bed that waited for him each night. Sharing the bed with the waitress or with other women would mean enmeshing them in a life he wanted to leave behind, making it that much more complicated to abandon, trading one kind of loneliness for another. He needed to step out of his life in order to change it.

Tired of living a lie, Leon dedicated himself to honesty. If he could discover his natural self and live accordingly, he would harm no one, and loneliness would no longer sleep with him, wake with him, pursue him through the day.

And so it was that Leon would find himself questioning the value of love one moment and questioning a cook about bad mussels the next. He would intellectually distance himself from his life, examining each aspect as if he were a scientist, and then his concentration would be interrupted by the waitress rubbing her thumbnail against the tight spots of his jeans—collapsing the distance in more ways than he could count. This was his state of mind the day he saw Joe Brogan enter the restaurant.

He wore a dowdy brown suit, several years out of fashion, and his thin hair lifted and fell with the wind that rushed in at the opening of the door. He walked with the clumsy distractedness of one lost in thought or in love. The sight of him operated as the woman's thumbnail had, making it impossible for Leon to examine his life, forcing him finally to admit that he would have to escape his old life physically as well as intellectually.

Joe Brogan took a seat before he could be directed to one. While waiting for someone to take his order, he produced a tiny spiral notebook and began writing.

"Trying to get in a quick poem?" Leon asked him.

Brogan covered the pad with his big pale hand and angled his face upward. He winced as if he were looking into the sun. "I wondered what had become of you."

"I'm leaving the country," Leon told him. The words became true as he spoke them. Until Brogan walked through the door, he had been undecided. "I have a job in Central America. I'm leaving as soon as the divorce is final."

Joe Brogan nodded, then stared at the table. A waiter approached, but Leon waved him away. "I'll take care of this gentleman," he said.

"Is this special service?" Joe Brogan cocked his head up again.

"They were digging a vault," Leon said. "A little drive-through bank."

"Charla told me," he said, looking away, scanning the room. "Cynthia and I have been seeing a lot of her."

"I figured as much. How is she?"

Joe Brogan continued to look around the room, resigning himself to the conversation. He folded his little notebook and returned it to his coat pocket. "She'll be all right."

"That's good." Leon took a deep breath and sat across the short table from him. "I'm going to run a hotel, a resort on the beach."

Joe Brogan put his elbows up and laced his fingers together. "How'd you get into that, Mr. Green?"

"I went to school with a guy from down there. His father is in the government. Some high post. I don't remember."

"And he sends his son up here for school?" Brogan feigned surprise. "Doesn't set much of an example, does he?"

At this, Leon's loathing of the man loomed before him, almost visible. "You ever lonely, Joe Brogan?"

"Yeah," he said, sighing. "What kind of question is that? Of course."

"You ever wondered if there wasn't some way to make your life over? To make it better?"

Brogan leaned forward but did not look at Leon. He stared into his lap. "What are you getting at?"

"This is who I am." Leon spread his arms. "I've been a fool to try to be someone else."

"Well," he said, "you've been a fool. I'll agree to that much."

Leon shook his head. He felt he should be grateful to Brogan for helping him realize that he should leave the country, but Leon could not muster any gratitude. He started to stand, but Joe Brogan began speaking.

"One day in the jungle—this was a long time ago—my outfit was doing nothing but fucking off, clowning, you know? And this one fellow, a big guy from Augusta, Maine, not a bad guy, he started this game of hide-and-seek, only nobody could move. You had to hide by becoming some other thing, like a tree or a tent— did I mention that we were high as kites?" His voice was friendly, but Joe Brogan wasn't smiling. "So we stood around, pretending to be *things* while this guy acts like he's looking for us."

He stopped, and Leon thought he might be finished. "This is what you write poetry about?"

"You're goddamned right it is. You listen. I was the river. I had lain on my belly and curved a little because all the rivers in the jungle twist around like intestines. And this guy from Augusta, Maine, goes around guessing who's what. He comes up to me and says, 'Ain't nobody here. I thought I seen Joe Brogan, but what we've got here is one dead motherfucker.' He leaned over and lifted one of my legs, and sure enough my foot flapped back and forth. 'Recent killing,' he said. 'We musta all just watched him pass.' And then the others, these United States soldiers, they started crying because I was dead. They just broke down. I wanted to cry too. Only I couldn't. I was dead." He knitted his fingers together again. "You go to Central America. People here will be a lot better off. You pretend to be whatever you want. But don't expect to change your life."

Leon stood and pushed the chair back to the table. The story had no effect on him. After months without direction, he felt finally in control of his destiny. He would turn in his resignation, let Charla have whatever she wanted in the settlement. And then the perfect farewell gesture came to mind.

He said, "You like mussels, Joe?"

For an instant, Brogan's face clouded, then he realized what Leon had asked. "They're all right. I was planning to order shrimp."

"Mussels are on the house," Leon said.

"If it's important to you."

As he filled the plate, Leon thought of excuses to give to the cook or one of the waiters because they had been told not to serve them. No one took notice. Joe Brogan grunted a thanks when he set the plate in front of him, covering the little pad once more with his hand.

That night, while swimming in the cold Pacific, Joe Brogan, probably more than a little drunk, disappeared. As far as Leon knew, his body was never found. Leon assumed that the mussels had poisoned him, had wrung his stomach and made him drown. He had wanted Joe Brogan to feel the same ache in his intestines that he had felt when Charla left. He hadn't meant to kill him.

Within a few weeks, Leon was in Cruz's Powerwagon with his insides rattling loose as the bus bounced over the cruel road. During that time, he had given up the past, refuted memory, denied history. In the Powerwagon, sweat dripping from his brows to his eyes, his ass aching from the bench, he gave birth to the new Leon Green. An honest man who would pursue his desires honestly. He would not pretend to be monogamous, which would free him of pettiness and possessive worry. He would deny the condition of loneliness as the natural state of humankind, a man absolved of the obligations of normalcy.

A good man.

"I'll stay with you," Janet said and pushed her plate of chicken to the side. "At least for now."

Once again they were the only customers in Los Comales. Even the dog was gone. The sky was dark and Ernesto swept the uneven floor, humming a cheerful tune.

"I don't know if I like it here," she said. "I like you, but this place. It sounded so mysterious, exotic, but there's nothing to it. A hot, dusty nothing."

He reached across the table and cupped his hand around her neck. He pulled her toward him and said, "If you live here long enough, the rest of the world becomes mysterious." He kissed her cheek, let her go. "Think what a gift that is."

"Like being a kid again," she said, and this thought made her smile. She pushed the plates and utensils out of her way.

He looked into her eyes and thought he might get lost in them as he had before, but his anticipation of it spoiled any chance he had.

"Look at this," she said and turned her head, lifting her hair from her neck. "Can you see it?"

Leon saw nothing until she gestured with her thumb, running over a long, almost invisible scar down her neck. "How did you do that?" he asked her.

"I fell asleep at the wheel. In Anthony's car, this old Volvo. He was asleep too." She released her hair and faced him. "We were lucky. We could have been really hurt, and then we'd have been discovered. Anthony said it was an unconscious act of love."

"I don't understand," Leon told her.

"He said we wanted to be caught so we'd be forced to announce our love." She shrugged. "It's just a little story." She took his hand. "I like you pretty much."

"But you have no scars to prove it."

"Give it a little time."

They walked by way of the beach back to the Esperanza. The warmth of the evening inspired a swim. They took off their clothes and strolled into the water, which was also unusually warm. The tide was low and he led her far out into the ocean. The sparse, scattered lights of La Boca made him think of the scatter of rocks that made up the reef, as if the irregular pattern of the rocks was reflected on shore by the lit windows and scant streetlights. They went past the breaking point of the waves, moving in slow motion through the water, which became too deep for Janet to stand. She wrapped her legs around his waist and looked back at the town from over his shoulder. In the salt water, she felt as light as the white foam of the surf, and Leon felt they had walked into a dream.

"What's your real name?" he whispered in her ear.

"What makes you think it isn't Janet Anderson?"

"You wouldn't be so stupid as to make a fake passport with your real name."

She laughed. "It's Veronica, but I don't want you to call me that."

"To be safe," Leon said.

"Yes," she said. "To be safe." Then she added, "It is beautiful here. I don't know if it's Eden, but the sun, the ocean, the beach—it's nice."

"Are you happy right now?"

A rise in the water lifted them at that moment, a little jump, Leon's feet leaving the sandy bottom, a rush of water between them.

"It's hard for me to believe, but I'm happy right now. I won't be tonight, when I think what Anthony has done to me . . ."

"But just this second," Leon said.

She kissed his cheek, whispered in his ear. "I'm happy."

"That's all you can ask for," he told her.

He kissed her on the lips, which provided a momentary distraction for the boy whose feet rested on a stone a dozen yards beyond them, a boy who had been there for more than an hour, who waited impatiently in the warm water for them to leave, who waited for the sacred yellow rectangle to offer him a glimpse of the woman he loved.

*F*RIDAY MORNING, Pilar sat on the edge of her bed, facing Samuel. For the fifth night in a row she had slept badly on the cushions she'd laid across her kitchen floor, and today she'd wakened angry with Leon for having a building full of beds. Samuel looked refreshed, his fingers locked behind his head on her only good pillow, a smile stretching his cheeks.

"Today," he said, "I feel that I could live to be a hundred. Well, fifty, anyway."

Pilar crossed her legs, jostling the bed. His good mood only increased her aggravation. "Do you want breakfast?" she asked sharply.

He shook his head. "I'd like this strength to last as long as I can make it. Eating ends in pain, which turns to weakness. I'll put that off for a while. You should eat, though. You look ill."

She shrugged and peered out the window. A sunny morning, which would mean another stifling afternoon. "I didn't sleep well." In the face of his pain, her complaints seemed petty but she had enough character to acknowledge them.

"Bad dreams?"

"Odd. I dreamed I rode a horse along a beach, a big red horse. And then I became the horse, and when I looked back to see who was riding me, I became the rider again."

"That is an odd one. I rarely recall my dreams."

"There was more to it, but I can't remember it all." She remembered—she could always recall her dreams—but didn't want to tell. It had been a sex dream, she and Leon in the bed where Samuel lay, and then as horses on the beach. Even thinking of it embarrassed her. Becoming a horse was bad enough, but having sex as a horse with an American horse was absurd. She would tell Maria Peralta. It was her grandmother's kind of dream.

"You know what amazes me?" he said. "That the revolution, the fighting, none of it has touched this place. It's as if nothing were going on." He lowered his arms, as they had already begun to go numb. "Two days before I was injured I was out with my brother fishing this little pond we've fished all our lives. The first bombing run had taken place that morning. No one had believed they would bomb the capital. The city was in shambles. We tried to help people who had been hurt, but we were liabilities—our faces were known, especially his. My brother is a real hero. If I live long enough, he will come visit. You will probably fall in love with him."

"Oh?" Pilar laughed bitterly. "Spare me, then. I don't need any more complications in my life."

"In that case, we can introduce him to Lourdes. She'll fall for my brother and leave the American to you."

Pilar looked at the floor, embarrassed and angry with him.

"That was in poor taste," he said. "I'm sorry. I forget the power of romantic love. I forget so many things." As he said this, it occurred to him that, perhaps, his death was nothing more than a forgetting. A losing of his life by increments until he wouldn't know what it was he had lost.

"Tell me about the pond," Pilar said, softening. "You and your brother were fishing."

"We were catching nothing, although we didn't really care that much. We were pretending to be someplace like here, some-place where the fighting and dying didn't exist. My brother is no

fisherman. I'm not one either, but he is especially incompetent."
Samuel let out the short burst of wheezing that was his laughter.
"We were talking and, for the fifth or sixth time, he got his line
caught. He tugged several times and finally it came loose. We
examined his hook—there was a knot of human hair."

"No," Pilar said.

"We took off our clothes and swam to the bottom. We could
see nothing in the dirty water. I had my hand extended like this."
He raised his arm and stretched it forward, his hand open. "I
kicked to make myself sink. My fingers touched the muddy bottom, and I patted around against the mud with both my hands
until I had to surface. I dove again. My hand touched the body,
not as cold as the mud, softer. I can't tell you how it felt. I patted
the body with both hands, trying to find something to hold on
to so that I could pull it up. I couldn't tell what part of the body
I was touching until I touched her face, the bridge of her little
nose."

"Stop." Pilar stood and turned away from him. "I don't want
to hear any more of this."

"It's not a pleasant story. I'm a rude guest."

"No, I just don't . . ." The grisly details weren't what made
her recoil. She had heard too many stories, seen too many dead
and dying people. But this story sounded like an accusation, as if
she should feel guilty for living so far from the killing. "Did you
know her?" she asked him finally. "The drowned woman?"

"A girl, and she hadn't drowned. She was dead before she
was dumped into the pond. Her arms had been hacked off at the
shoulders." He stared at Pilar purposefully. "But, no, I didn't
know her. She had been tied to the engine of a car."

"I don't understand."

"To keep the bodies submerged. We found four and cut them
loose. I don't know if they were ever identified. Do you see what
I'm getting at? There we were fishing where we'd fished all our
lives, and even there we encountered death, murder, mutilation.

But here? This place is Disneyland. You don't even hear the bombs out here. If you didn't know better, you'd know nothing."

Pilar sat again on the bed. "We had one body appear a year or so ago. It washed in on the tide, up near the hotel."

Leon had spotted it and called her out of bed. "I'm reading," she had said, and he, "Someone's drowned." He stood at the balcony door. She remembered the look on his face, and it seemed to her in memory, as it had then, to be a look of terror. He was bare-chested and in white pants. They had made love when he'd wakened and she was about to rise, shower, and leave. She pulled the sheet from the bed and wrapped herself in it, then stepped to the French door.

Rain fell into the Pacific. She saw nothing until he pointed. It looked like a barrel, almost as gray as the water, but a wave slapped it against the reef and an arm flew in an arc, then disappeared. Leon sat on the bed, his head in his hands. "I know who it is," he said, walking to the balcony again. "It's impossible, but I know who it is." He faced her. "It can't be, but it is."

It was afternoon before Ramon could find the body among the rocks. The rain had not let up, and when he lifted it from his boat, Ramon looked as drenched and lifeless as the corpse. Pilar had waited with a dozen others in the lobby. There had been two American tourists, young men who flirted with her, trying to get her to guess who it might be. "My money says Jimmy Hoffa," one said. The other shook his head. "Weldon Kees."

Bloated with seawater and battered by the waves, the body looked familiar to no one. There were bullet wounds in the chest. When Leon, who had refused to look, heard of the wounds, he began to cry. "Thank God," he said, wiping his eyes and hurrying to the hotel bar for a drink. Later, he told her that he had been afraid that it was a hotel customer who had drowned while swimming; the wounds proved it couldn't have been. She hadn't believed him.

Pilar told Samuel about the body but not about Leon. His

crying had been a moment of weakness that had baffled her when it happened, but now she felt protective of him, and the thought of his tears for a stranger created a warm spot in her chest.

"One body," he said. "Well, two, really."

"What do you mean?" Pilar asked him, still distracted by her feelings for Leon. He only smiled, revealing the ragged front tooth. "You're not dead yet," she told him.

He pointed at her. "You are a stickler for details."

THE SUN shone brilliantly through the open French doors of Leon's room, and the ocean repeated its lush promises in a steady rhythm. Even the whir of the cicadas sounded celebratory. Leon was in a good mood.

He waited for Lourdes, eager to see her because he thought he would soon cut it off—as soon as he was sure Janet would not be rescued—and so his afternoons with Lourdes became special because they were about to end. Another two weeks, he estimated, and he would turn her over to Ramon.

Then this ugly thought occurred to him: He was a villain.

Lourdes loved him, but he didn't return her love. Pilar also loved him—she'd said as much. And, for that matter, there were his ex-wives to consider: Why had he desired Charla when married to June, then wanted June when married to Charla?

Part of the answer had to do with the very nature of desire— a two-headed beast, one wanting a wife and home and the promise of constant love, while the other needed the whore's breasts, the stranger's wicked lips, a neighbor on her knees. But if desire was evil, he thought, then love was a greater evil—it made promises that no humans could keep, it destroyed people. The momentary thrill of love denied the future discontent, the inevitable boredom and pettiness. As long as he was honest, he was behaving properly. He hadn't been capable of honesty with June and Charla, and so he'd changed his life.

He felt an urge to run up the stairs to the ruined third floor and look beyond the village to the jungle, the crush of trees, a green that was the very color of life. But at that moment the door to his room swung open and Lourdes entered wearing only her apron.

"Where are your clothes?" he demanded.

"Don't you like my outfit?" She rocked her head, cocky or nervous—he couldn't tell which—and spread her apron with her hands as if to curtsy.

Her clothes made a pile in the hall just beyond his door. Leon gathered them in his arms, worried that Janet might have seen her come in, and tossed them onto his dresser—skirt, blouse, bra, panties, sandals. A safety pin bounced across the dresser and fell onto the floor. He locked the door. Glancing out at the beach, he spotted Janet under an umbrella in a one-piece bathing suit, which relieved him but also made him aware that he could not easily juggle three women—nor did he want to. He pulled the curtains closed.

Lourdes crawled onto the bed and lay on her back, straightening her apron, her breasts peeking out each side. Now he allowed himself to be aroused—her dark hair against the white pillowcase, the dirty apron, brown skin. She reached behind her neck and untied the apron strings. "I've got a surprise for you," she said.

"Another surprise? Arriving naked isn't surprise enough?" He grabbed the bottom of the apron and yanked it away.

She bent her knees and lifted her bottom off the bed. "Watch me," she commanded, and began raising and lowering her butt, an undulation of thighs, pelvis, stomach. "Watch my cunt," she said and widened the V of her legs. The pink lips of her vagina parted and a button of blackness appeared—growing now, coming out of her, black and pointed like the nose of a dog, emerging from her.

Leon reached for the wall behind him, but it wasn't there, and he stumbled backward until he found it.

The black stump grew and yellowed—a banana—and as she raised and lowered her pelvis, the banana slowly came out, curving up.

Leon laughed—a nervous laugh, he realized—and what he felt was a sort of panic and fascination. The banana continued to grow from her vagina, inching out, wet and dark. Finally the stem appeared, and the banana fell to the mattress, bouncing to the floor. Lourdes smiled, her bottom still raised, but Leon no longer felt aroused. When it fell from her, it made him think of shit.

"Get dressed," he said and left the room before she could reply.

THE IMAGE of the banana haunted Leon throughout the long afternoon, changing in his mind to a lizard emerging open-mouthed, a billy club, a raven, the tail of a monkey. He saw it as if it really were the nose of a dog, followed by a dog's head and floppy ears, a full-grown retriever clawing its way out of her.

He should have said something. She had embarrassed him and herself, and he should have comforted her, but with Lourdes, that would have meant sex, and he had been in no mood to replace the banana. He sat in a corner of the bar until he saw her rush out the door—fully clothed, he'd been relieved to see.

He took his place behind the registration desk, but the images kept coming, transforming themselves into something more horrible each time. By the time the phone rang, he had decided to visit Pilar, to let her quell this uneasiness.

"Does anybody there speak my language?" The voice was deep and masculine, a strong American accent.

"You've reached the Hotel Esperanza," Leon told him. "This is the manager."

"English," the voice on the phone said, followed by a heavy sigh. "You don't know how wonderful it is to hear English. I'm looking for my wife," he said, and Leon felt his heart fall. "Her name is Janet Anderson. Could you put her on the line?" Leon experienced disappointment the full length of his body, and he became suddenly angry—with Janet, and, oddly, with Lourdes. "Or you can give her a message." There began a ticking in Leon's chest, a trembling inside himself, a vacillation of his will. "I'd like to talk with her if it's possible," the man said. "But a message would do if she's not available right now." Temptation lived not in Leon's head, but in his chest, the soft tissues in his legs. He felt the ability to fall. He knew what was right and what was wrong—there was a decision to be made—but what he felt was the pull of gravity, and the trembling in his chest was the same a diver feels when he steps to the edge of the cliff and stares down into the tumultuous waves. "Are you there?"

"I'm sorry," Leon mumbled. "Mrs. Anderson, you said?"

He put the receiver on the desk and stared at it, knowing that he could still do either thing—the right thing, the wrong thing. And then he saw the black receiver growing slowly from Lourdes's vagina and falling out, its spiral cord trailing it down. The tension in his chest died, and so it was that he began the descent.

When he lifted the receiver to his mouth, he could smell cunt. "Mrs. Anderson checked out yesterday," he said.

"Oh my God." The man's voice was a rasp. Leon could hear age and liquor in it. And fear.

"Is there anything else I can do for you?" Leon asked him. His voice was calm water, still air, the pause between acts.

"Where was she going?" He was barely audible, and Leon heard him swallow. "Did she leave a message for me? Did she say anything? Anything at all?"

"She didn't say much, Mr. Anderson, the whole time she was here."

"Any indication?" His voice cracked. "How did she leave?"

Leon took a deep breath, exhaling slowly. "She didn't seem eager for people to know where she was going."

"Are you sure we're talking about the same—"

"Oriental. Very pretty." And he couldn't help thinking of how she made love, couldn't help wanting to tell him about the lift of her bottom, the soft wrap of her legs.

"Yes," the man said. "My God."

The phone went silent, and Leon suddenly knew exactly what else to say. "Perhaps I shouldn't tell you this," he said.

"What? Anything. What is it?"

"You're not the first to phone. Another American asked for her. He called her by a different name, but he described her perfectly. It was a rather mechanical description—height, weight, and so on. I think women should be described more poetically, don't you?"

There was a long silence, then Leon heard him exhale. "What name did he call her by?"

"I should have made a note of it. You never know what's going to be important." He listened to the man's strenuous breathing. "If my memory is right, he called her Veronica— Veronica something or other. I can't quite place it."

"I see." His voice was just above a whisper. "Did he say why he wanted her?"

Leon paused a long while. "It sounded official. I shouldn't be telling you this. I certainly shouldn't have told your wife about the call. She left almost immediately afterward. Now, this is the last thing I'm going to tell you—I shouldn't even say this, but it's common knowledge. There are three ways in and out of La Boca. There is a mule path, a difficult route through the jungle that leads eventually to Santa Josefina, a town where there's a train station and bus depot. There's also a long, gutted road that winds to Santa Josefina. She took that coming here, by bus. That's how all the tourists come."

"Yes, I know," he said. "And the third?"

"There are a few locals who, for a fee, will take you by boat to Santa Josefina. If you want to leave La Boca, you have to go to Santa Josefina. From there, you can go anywhere. She's not here, I'm sure of that. I doubt that she's still there. My guess is that she's long gone."

"When she left," the man said, "was she okay? All right, I mean?"

Leon thought for a moment. "I wish I could tell you yes, but I've never seen a person quite so lost."

There was another long sigh. "You've been helpful," he said, his voice weak, nothing more than a rasp.

"Good luck," Leon told him and he hung up.

RAMON WAS HAUNTED by a story he had not told. His life had become confused, and he found himself depressed. He had lost his enthusiasm for stories after lying to the American couple in order to take their money. Then he had charged Pilar, a friend, for something he would have done for free—charged her an amount so large that his face turned hot at the thought of it. These facts weighed on him like his forefather's oxen yoke. And still he had to hope Leon would give up Lourdes, or, what was even less likely, he would have to persuade Lourdes to drop Leon. And now, as if that were not enough, he had become afflicted by a story he longed and dreaded to tell, one that had come to him suddenly, one his mother had told him, not his father, and so one he had never made a point of memorizing, refining, and passing on to Benjamin—it had been his father who had taught him the art of telling stories. The story rested on his tongue like a wafer. He was surprised that he remembered it at all and baffled as to why it had come to him now.

He finally decided he must tell it to his son, and so he sat on the ground, his back against the wall of the schoolhouse, and waited for Benjamin's class to end. Sunlight blistered the white-washed walls. There seemed to be no shade, as if the sun were precisely centered over the pitiful building.

When he had rowed to Santa Josefina to pick up Pilar's

cousin, he'd had a meal with Cruz while they waited for Samuel to arrive. He'd told one of his favorite stories, about the conquistador's son who became the first in a long line of fishermen in the family, and who had prospered by learning how to communicate with fish. It was a good story, but he had lost his energy after only twenty minutes and finally abandoned his ancestor at sea, conversing with a barricuda. Cruz had been polite, but Ramon could tell the story had lost its charm.

He had felt like a foreigner in Santa Josefina. The restaurant where he usually dined the few times he had reason to be in the city was gone, burned to the ground by the army. "Razed," Cruz had said. "The patrons executed at their tables and buried with the building." Ramon had wanted to know why, which made Cruz laugh. "The owner was thought to be sympathetic." He paused. "Sympathetic, Ramon. To the revolution."

"But the customers?"

"They ate at a place owned by a man thought to be sympathetic to the revolution," Cruz explained.

"*I* have eaten there," Ramon said.

"You should be careful where you eat. And what you say. This little boat trip, this act of mercy for your bookseller friend— even something as innocent as this could be taken the wrong way. I wouldn't mention it to anyone. Even friends."

Cruz took him down the dark pier to an even darker café. "How do you know this place is safe?" Ramon asked him.

Cruz pointed to another table. Two men, sleeves rolled to their elbows, ties slung over their shoulders, toasted their waitress, a pretty girl, maybe fifteen. "Look for North Americans. Stay only as long as they stay."

As it turned out, Cruz had been exaggerating. The North Americans left long before they were finished with their meal; however, Ramon had been shaken. Without the stories to fall back on, he felt he had nothing, that he was as much a foreigner as the men with the ties, that he had become an impostor in his own country. His stories had been made profane by unfair profits, and his country—he didn't know what had gone wrong. He knew the arguments of the revolutionaries and the counterarguments of the men in power, but the truth? How could a fisherman know?

"Pop." Benjamin, the first student out of the building, stood above him, invisible in the enormous light, the black sunspot just one more contradiction in a country that held little else. Benjamin's friend Mono joined them, a gangly boy with short hair and eyes like flat stones.

Ramon grabbed his son's hand and pulled himself up. He put on a smile. "How was class, boys? You're late."

"We had our final exam," Benjamin said. "School's over."

"Of course," Ramon said. "It's Friday. I almost forgot. We should celebrate. I'll take you both to lunch. How do you think you did on the test?"

"It was easy," Benjamin told him.

"It was?" Mono said. "That's good to know. What'd you put for number three, the difference between arguments and comparisons?"

"That sounds like philosophy," Ramon said. "School is much more sophisticated than when I was a boy."

Benjamin shook his head, then waved at a group of boys just leaving the building. "Kinds of essays. You know, argumentative ones, comparison-contrast." He looked at Mono. "She wanted that organizational stuff. The way you order your supports."

"Right," Mono said. He nodded severely. "I think I missed that one. What'd you put for number two?"

"Two was about grammar?"

"Not that one." Mono put his hands on his hips and stood with one foot on the other, the heel of the first on the toe of the second. "I know I missed that one. The one about the ocean."

"Mono, that was the easiest one."

"The ocean?" Ramon said.

Benjamin shook his head. "Bones gave us this lecture about how the ocean is like an essay."

"Both are all wet," Mono said. "Both can cause you a bunch of grief."

"She said that you see the surface of the ocean and the beauty of the waves, but none of it would look good if it didn't have depth. Shallow water doesn't have waves. Stuff like that."

"Oh yeah," Mono said. "I think I missed that one. Are we going to eat or go to the bookstore?"

"Are you short of reading material, Mono?" Ramon asked.

"No, sir, Mr. Matamoros. Your son, he doesn't see the craziness in buying books now when school is out. He could at least wait a day or two, don't you think? Just to show some respect." The sun glinted off his plaintive face.

"I ordered a book a while ago," Benjamin said and began to walk in the direction of the store.

Ramon put his hand on Benjamin's shoulder. "I bet I know the book. That one on architecture we talked about."

"What book was that?" Benjamin asked.

"Well, we weren't specific, but we discussed architecture, remember? And biology. Law."

"It's a novel, I bet," Mono said. "She likes stories."

"She?" Ramon asked.

"Never mind," Benjamin said.

"The love of stories is embedded in our family," Ramon said, uplifted by this thought. "I was just thinking of a story."

"My dad told me a story once," Mono said. "It was about eating soup with a knife."

"There you go," Ramon said, then spoke to his son. "What is the name of this book?"

"Tropic of Cancer."

"Geography," Ramon said. "A much overlooked subject."

"You ever tried it?" Mono said.

"Geography?" Ramon asked.

"Eating soup with a knife." Mono shook his head. "Hard."

"I can imagine," Ramon told him.

"Is that Miss Rios really a Communist?" Mono asked. "She's

good-looking. I want to have a good-looking wife. But it couldn't be a Communist, of course. But I thought they were all ugly, didn't you? I used to think that all dogs were boys, all cats were girls, and all Communists were big and ugly. That's why I can't believe Miss Rios is a Communist."

"That's stupid," Benjamin said.

"I wouldn't marry a Communist because she'd try to brain-wash me," Mono continued.

"I doubt anyone would attempt that," Ramon said.

Mono shrugged. "My dad told me that Communists trade their kids around with other Communists and nobody knows who their real mom and dad are. That and they have a plan to kill God."

"To kill God?" Ramon said.

Mono nodded. "Has to do with poisoning your head—everybody's heads, which pisses God off and He tosses down a bunch of plagues. Then when nothing changes, He gets sick and dies. Something like that."

"Broken-hearted God," Ramon said. "Interesting."

"Stupid," Benjamin said. "Just don't say anything stupid in the store."

"It's not stupid. My dad told me. What did you put on that long one?"

They had reached the bookstore. Benjamin stopped and faced Mono. "Just some stuff," he said.

Mono looked to Ramon. "I know I got this one right. It was 'When did you realize you were an adult and no longer a child?' "

Benjamin shook his head. "Essay question—you don't get it right or wrong, it's how you write it."

"What did you write?" Ramon asked Benjamin, but Mono answered.

"It was this day I got into my dad's stuff and I found an old watch," he said.

"That made you an adult?" Ramon asked him.

"It's hot out here," Benjamin said. "Let's get the book."

"I sold it," Mono said, "and my dad slugged me right in the face."

"Oh," Ramon said.

"When I was a boy, he'd just spank me."

Pilar smiled grandly at them as they entered. She called them gentlemen. "I bet you want your book," she said to Benjamin, who nodded.

Mono picked up a paperback and waved it at Ramon. "I happen to know they've made a movie out of this one, so what's the point? Why keep the book when there's already a movie?"

Benjamin turned abruptly from Pilar and hissed, "Shut up, Mono," then he wheeled back.

"I've seen four movies," Mono said to Ramon. "Benjamin tell you?"

Ramon shook his head, then caught Pilar's attention. He nodded at the ceiling and raised his eyebrows. "How is everything?" he asked her.

"Everything is as well as can be expected," she told him.

"Good," he said. The urge to tell the story had been building in his chest and was now almost irresistible, but the door to the bookstore opened, and Rosa Ojeda entered.

She spoke to Benjamin. "I thought you would be in the ocean by now. Instead, I find you where? In a room of books. Hello, Ramon. Your son passed the class." She did not look at Pilar.

"What about me, Mrs. Ojeda?" Mono said.

"You?" she said. "I thought you would be in the jungle by now."

He nodded. "I thought about it."

Ramon seized the opportunity. "Did you know that people used to live in the jungle?"

"In the ruins," Benjamin said, "just one night, then they split. Uh, it was built by a bunch of black guys. Okay?"

"I'm not talking about the ruins," Ramon said.

"The thicket. They cut out places in the thicket like a cave or an igloo or something." Benjamin grabbed his book. "Well, I've got to go."

"Not in the thicket," Ramon said.

"The jungle people," Rosa said. "An old village myth."

Pilar walked around the counter, then lifted herself up to sit on it. "Go ahead, Ramon. Let's hear the story."

"It's quite a good one," he promised.

"I thought we were going to eat," Mono said.

"More than one hundred years ago," Ramon began, "two families lived in the jungle, or so people claimed. No one ever actually saw them until one day a little girl—whose name I've forgotten—saw a strange group of people swimming naked in the ocean in the middle of the night. They were very odd-looking people who had white skin, not peach-colored or pale, but white like paper, and they were out in the middle of the night splashing each other and laughing. When they saw the little girl, they called for her to join them, and she ran away."

"They could film that easy enough," Mono said.

"The townspeople were amazed to hear that the legend was true, although everyone confirmed that whenever they were in the jungle they had this odd feeling that someone was watching them. Unfortunately, no one ever saw the paper-white families again, but two things happened. First, the little girl's father went fishing with his best friend and they landed a big fish—again, I don't know what kind, but a very big one. They were happy to have caught it and drank a great deal in celebration. When they came to, they discovered that the fish, which they had sold to a restaurant, had set a record for the biggest ever caught in the waters around La Boca. For the record, the restaurant owner wanted to know which man actually caught it.

"The little girl's father stepped forward. 'I caught the fish, but my good friend helped me by clubbing its head once I pulled it into the boat.' His friend disagreed. 'Actually,' he said, 'I was the one who caught the fish, although my good friend helped me by rowing out into the deep water where the biggest fish live.' They could not agree on a story and began to argue. Within a few hours, the families were feuding."

"I know," Mono said. "One caught one, then the other caught one, but the one swallowed the other one, so they both thought they caught it, right?"

"No," Ramon said.

"Stupid," Benjamin muttered.

"The second thing that happened," Ramon continued, "was that the little girl's mother wondered what her daughter was doing out at the beach in the middle of the night. She asked the little girl, who replied, 'I went out to see who was calling my name.' Her mother was suspicious. 'How could these paper-white jungle people know your name?' The little girl shook her head. 'It wasn't one of them. I heard this from my window, a person calling my name.' Of course, the mother wanted to know who was calling her little girl in the middle of the night. The girl said, 'It was Jesus Christ.' Her mother fainted."

"I get it . . ."

"Mono!" Rosa Ojeda jabbed a finger in his direction. "Do we want these interruptions? No, we do not."

"A priest was called in—I think we're safe in assuming that this was Father Montoya—and he took the little girl to the cathedral and sat her on the floor and told her to confess her sins. She replied, 'I don't have any sins.'

" 'What about hearing Jesus?' Father Montoya asked her.

" 'Is that a sin?' she said.

" 'Tell me about it,' he replied.

" 'He called out my name several times and I got up and put on my yellow dress, which is the one I always wear to church, and he was still calling so I pulled my curtain back and said to hold on a minute.'

" 'And how did you know he was Jesus Christ?' the priest wanted to know.

" 'I thought he was God at first because he had a God kind

of voice, but I discovered he was Jesus when I looked out the window because he had little bloody holes in his palms and a big cut right here.' She touched her ribs." Ramon touched his.

"Father Montoya wanted to know exactly what happened. The girl told him, 'He took my hand and led me to the water where the people who were all white were playing. They called for us to come join them, and Jesus took off his robe and swam out to them, but I didn't want to and I went home.' "

"No, no, no," Mono said.

"Mono, do not ever open your mouth again," Rosa said.

"Jesus would've just walked out there," Mono said. "Who's going to swim if he can walk on water?"

"Why don't you wait and see what happens?" Pilar suggested.

Mono shook his head. "Something's not right with this."

"Well," Ramon said, "that would be the end of the story except that the restaurant owner who had purchased the great fish had both the little girl's father and his friend arrested—or he tried to, but there were no policemen and no jail, so really he just yelled at them in front of other people. He was angry because he had cut up the great fish and served it to many customers and all of them had become sick, and his dog, who had eaten the head and tail, had almost died. The little girl's father said, 'I don't know why you're angry with me.' He pointed at the man who used to be his friend. 'He caught the ugly beast. All I did was row the fool out to sea.' The other man was astonished. 'Me?' he said. 'I just hit the thing with a club before it tipped our boat over.' "

"One of them's lying," Mono said.

"That night the priest had a vision so powerful that he leaped from bed and ran in his underwear to the beach, the spot where the paper-white jungle people had been seen, but he found only the ocean, a bit of seaweed, a few shiny stones, and an acre of moonlight. Nonetheless, he reported his vision to the town: Jesus had come to him in a dream to say that he had led the girl to the beach and then swum out to the jungle people, and while he was in the water he had turned into an enormous fish, and all of those in town who had eaten from the fish had taken of his body and drunk of his blood. They were not sick, they were filled with the power of Christ.

"This excited the townspeople, and the next Sunday there were three times as many people as usual at mass. However, a few days later, the little girl and her mother came to the cathedral to talk with the priest. 'She made it all up,' the mother said. 'She was telling stories.' Father Montoya did not want to believe that his miracle was false—he had already drafted a letter to the bishop. He asked the little girl to tell the whole story, and she did, convincing him finally that she had gone to the beach because she couldn't sleep. She had made up the part about Jesus. 'It just popped into my head,' she explained, 'so I let it out.' But she still claimed that she really saw the paper-white jungle people."

"I knew it," Mono said. "Jesus wouldn't swim."

Rosa whirled and grabbed Mono by the ear. "You failed the class," she told him. "Now keep your mouth closed."

Ramon put his arm around Mono's shoulder, which now visibly slumped. "Father Montoya decided he had to inform his congregation, but he couldn't decide how to do it without disappointing them. At least the legend of the jungle people had been confirmed. No sooner had he thought this than a villager came in and asked for him to hear a confession. 'Forgive me, father,' he said. 'A few nights back I went with my wife and her sister and her husband and we swam naked in the water in the middle of the night. I knew the girl saw us, but I didn't want to come forward. We had been a little tipsy and we needed a swim.'

"The priest said, 'The girl claimed that you were all white.'

" 'There was a bright moon,' the man replied. 'We must have looked white.' And the priest knew then that there had been no miracle at all. He was very depressed because he thought God had made his little town special, but none of it turned out to be true. Then, that same night, he had another vision, and he ran to the same spot of beach, and he saw something amazing. Do you know what he saw?" Ramon looked at his son. "He saw the ocean, a bit of seaweed, a few shiny stones, and an acre of moonlight." Ramon threw open his arms to indicate the breadth of an acre.

"That's a lovely story," Pilar said.

"I don't remember that one," Benjamin said.

"I don't get it," Mono said. "Who caught the shark?"

"There wasn't any shark," Benjamin said.

Mono nodded emphatically. "He said a big fish. I like sharks. My dad says they can eat you with one bite."

"Your father is an imbecile," Rosa said. Her eyes were filled with tears. "My mother told me that story on my wedding's eve," she said. Pilar touched her shoulder. Rosa whipped her head around to look first at the hand and then at Pilar. "My husband was killed in prison. He hated the army and would not do what they wanted of him—what that was, I can only imagine. And what did they do to him? I don't have to guess about that. They imprisoned him, they beat him, they shot him through the heart." She slapped Pilar's hand away. "People like you think you invented justice. My husband is dead. What has his death brought us?" She stepped around Ramon, yanked open the door, and hurried out into the harsh light.

"She doesn't know what she's saying," Ramon told Pilar as he took her hand and helped her down from the counter. "She blames everyone for her husband's death except the person who pulled the trigger."

"Another body," Pilar said softly.

"Are you a Communist?" Mono asked her.

She smiled at him. "Do you know what the term means?"

"Sure," he said. "Sort of. I mean, I know enough."

"Good," Ramon said. "Then I think it's time we go." He

herded Mono and his son out the door, pausing before he left. "I hope you're not upset."

"I'm all right," she said. "It was a good story."

"My mother told me that one," he said. "I had never told it before. There are a few rough edges."

"Stories should be a little rough," she said.

He waved to her and was gone.

A few paces down the road, Benjamin announced that he and Mono were going swimming. "We can celebrate later," he said.

"Not me," Mono said. "She flunked me. Why do you think Bones is so mean?"

Ramon shook his head. "There's no accounting for some things," he said, which brought a smile from his son. "By the way," he spoke to Benjamin now, "you never told me what your essay was on—what moment it was when you knew you were a man."

"Yeah," Benjamin said. "It was when I knew I could swim the reefs."

"You could be a navigator," Ramon said. "Or, if you studied really hard, in time you might be able to become a fisherman."

"A long shot," Benjamin said.

"They got schools for that?" Mono said.

Ramon watched the boys walk away from him to the water's edge, knowing that whatever it took to get his son to the university, he would do.

"HE BETRAYED YOU, the bastard!" Ramon's voice boomed across the lobby. "You had known him since childhood and never suspected what a lizard he was. Until one day, in confidence, you told him of your business plans—perhaps you'd been drinking a little rum. Perhaps a lot of rum. He slaps you on the back, the snake, then suddenly has to go, and he makes his fortune off your idea. So, of course, you, who can prove nothing, poison the rascal."

"No," Leon said, turning his book upside down. "Come into the bar. We need to talk."

Ramon followed. "Not business? Not matters of the heart? What's left? Why else would you poison a man?"

Leon took two beers from behind the bar and directed Ramon to a table in the corner. "Forget about that stuff," he said and sat. "I've thought about your suggestion—your plan for Benjamin and Lourdes. And, after some consideration, I've decided that you're right. I'm going to give Lourdes up."

"I knew it!" Ramon said. He felt almost weightless. He threw his arms around Leon. "Ha ha! I knew when you had time to think about it, you'd do the right thing." He raised his beer. "To the future!"

Leon clinked bottles with him but did not drink. "Now, how are we going to do this? I don't know what to tell her."

Ramon was almost too happy to speak. "All you have to do is tell her that it's for the best." He drank again. The sweetest beer he'd ever tasted. "You'll think of a better way than I could offer. I don't have the knack with women that you do. Ernesto tells me that you can just walk into a restaurant and look at a woman and she will leave with you."

"Ernesto exaggerates."

"Yes, of course he does. What is that woman doing here by herself anyway?" Ramon took another powerful swallow of beer.

"She had circumstances she had to leave behind."

"So, she's like you, running from the law."

"What makes you think I'm running from the law?"

Ramon laughed. "I have a modest talent for filling in the blank spots in a story. You poison a man, and then you show up in La Boca where no one is ever found—I fill in the rest."

Leon shook his head. "The authorities thought he just drowned."

This news startled Ramon. "No one knows?"

"You and I."

"Then I don't understand. Why did you come here? Why are you here?"

"I'm getting sick of people asking me that. I like it here, all right? Look, if Lourdes comes by tomorrow, I'll talk with her. I'll tell her that I can't see her any more but that things will work out—you take it from there." He stood to signify the end of the conversation.

Ramon downed what remained of his beer and stood beside Leon. "Yes. You're a good friend." He hugged Leon again. "It has been a dream in my family to send a child to the university. And now . . ."

Leon held up a hand. "Later," he said.

Ramon nodded and started out, but he paused at the door. "You must talk to her soon, no later than tomorrow, so by Monday she will be over her disappointment and ready to go. This has to be done quickly. The new school year will begin."

Leon nodded, and Ramon ran home to tell his wife the good news.

"WHAT I CAN no longer imagine is nothing. How can there be nothing?" Samuel rested on his pillow, hair flattened against his head on one side, standing and stiff on the other.

"Let's talk about something else," Pilar said. Though she had wakened in an ill temper, she was now in a good mood, and she didn't want to lose it.

"Like what? What would it please you to talk to a dying man about? The weather? What hot goddamned weather we've been having, Pilar, my dear. I don't give a fuck about the weather. I want to know what's going to happen to me."

Although his voice was desperate, she would not patronize him. "You're going to die," she said, shifting on the chair. "I'm going to die."

"Only someone who knows she is going to live can speak like that." A bead of sweat appeared at the top of his forehead and trickled across the bridge of his nose, down his cheek, and to the bottom of his chin. "I want to know what is waiting."

"Nothing is waiting. It's just over."

"How? How can you just not be?" His stare was angry, full of the envy the dying have for the living.

Pilar snapped her fingers. "Like that."

"You are a bitch."

"Do you want to believe in God or in life?"

"I don't believe in God, but I can't deny God through simple, stupid rhetoric. That's as much a lie as anything. I don't have time for lies." He gripped her skirt. "Life is so goddamned difficult," he said. "The difference between a decent person and an evil one is next to nothing."

"I don't believe that," Pilar said.

"What *do* you believe? Is there anything worthy of your consideration?"

"There are plenty of things I believe in." She thought of the ignorant boy who'd come to the store with Benjamin. "Are you a Communist?" he'd asked, as if he were asking, "Are you a witch?"

"I want to know what you believe." He pointed at her, but the finger, knobby and broken, crooked away, pointing at her dresser. For a moment, she looked there, as if her beliefs were stored in its drawers.

"I believe this," she said. "There is a great wasteland of mindless emotion and an equally great expanse of heartless intellect, and to be fully human is to try to live in the tiny gap that separates them, knowing you'll stray into one at times and the other at times, but struggling to stay in the center." She stood, crossing her arms, turning her back to him, looking at the white doily centered on her dresser, a gift from her grandmother. "God is part of the mindlessness, the base fears. My mother chose to love my father, and then she quit choosing—no matter what he did. That is not admirable." She faced him again. "That is cowardice. My father was the opposite. He never quit choosing, designing, toying—lives were matters of abstract fascination for him." She sat again, on the bed now, catching his knee, and he jumped in pain. "Sorry," she said.

He shook his head. "It's my fault for being so goddamned sensitive. So pitifully weak." He took a deep breath. "Why haven't you mentioned your parents before?"

"They're dead." She sighed. "I'm probably too hard on them."

"I wish I had met you before this happened to me," he told her, touching her arm. "We could have been friends."

"We are friends," she said.

WHEN LEON walked into the bookstore, Pilar thought her heart might burst from gratitude. She had been dusting the bookshelves, not because they needed it but in order to have something to do with her hands while her head filled with pictures of Leon, *the man she loved,* and when she thought of him with those words her stomach flipped. She passed the feather duster over a neat row of paperbacks, raising no dust at all, then turned the feathers to her nose. It did not even smell of dust, but the pointed tips tickled and she laughed out loud, happy for no obvious reason. Her nerves were like muscles that had been overworked and now alternately ached and tingled. The aches were the product of doubt and disbelief; the tingling, from the spiral of pure emotion that made her unable to concentrate on reading or talking with Samuel or thinking of any sort. And so when Leon walked into the store, before he could say a word, she took him into her arms.

"Is something wrong?" he asked her.

She shook her head, still holding him. "I've been lonely for you."

As she said it, Leon realized that he, too, had been lonely for her. Since lying on the phone, he had begun to feel that the world he'd constructed might fall apart, and he'd wanted to see Pilar. He put his arms around her and though he did not wish it, his mind turned to the first weeks of his first marriage, how he'd held June after being away only the few hours of a working day, how he'd felt the warm glow and smug happiness of love. And from there, his mind offered him the first days of his second marriage, the smiling face of Charla in the morning making coffee, how her eyes would light the room and how when she kissed him his heart pressed against his ribs, growing like a balloon, as if she were inflating it herself with her impossibly soft lips.

He broke the embrace with Pilar, and made himself think of the day he left June, the last Thanksgiving with Charla. He had lied to Janet's lover, but he had to be honest with himself. Otherwise, he would fall into the old trap. In Pilar's arms, he had wavered, but he had not fallen. Love might eventually spoil what they had. Such was the nature of love. He would delay it as long as possible. She tugged his elbow and he turned to her but moved his hands from her shoulders to her ass and lifted her against him.

"Close the store for a while," he said.

Pilar wanted to make love with him, and in her happy delirium, she almost led him to her bed. The knowledge that Samuel lay there, that the sheets held his stench, pained her. "Let's go to the hotel," she said. "My room's a mess."

"I'd like to see that," he said. "I didn't know you were capable of messes."

"You don't get to see."

He kissed her, and she opened her eyes to see him, and everything—the color in his cheek, the movement of his eyes beneath their lids—confirmed to her what she wanted to believe, that he, too, had fallen in love.

"What do I have to do to see your mess?" he asked her when he pulled his mouth from hers.

"Live with me," she said.

He waited for her to laugh, but she didn't, her gaze intent and serious and loving. Again, he felt himself waver. He could simply say yes to her. He could let it happen. "You're in a funny mood," he told her.

"No, I'm not," she said and smiled softly.

He let her go. "We can't go to the hotel."

"You don't want Lourdes to see me, is that it?" How quickly the doubts rose in her, how powerfully they erased everything.

Leon looked at her sadly and shook his head. Not Lourdes, he thought. But he had no intention of telling her about Janet now, although he knew that not telling her was a lie of sorts. Another lie, he reminded himself. He shoved his hands in his pockets and stared at his sandals. He would be happy when Lourdes had gone to college and things were simple again.

"I just don't want to go to the hotel," he said. "I've got too much waiting for me there. Things to do. I couldn't. I don't care if your room's a mess. Christ, I . . ." He paused then stepped toward her again. "Let's make love here," he said. "Lock the door."

"People can see in here," she said, trying to maintain her equilibrium, and feeling it fall away already. It was too much, the flying and falling and flying again.

"The kitchen." He took her hand. "Come on. Don't be an old woman."

Pilar followed him. As she walked behind, she became rational and wondered again what it was that made her love him, but he yanked her into his arms, and the turning in her stomach, the thrill that wobbled through her limbs made her helpless to answer.

His hands moved beneath her skirt and beneath her underwear as Cruz's had, but while Cruz had made her feel the thrill of the forbidden, Leon filled her with the remote and powerful stirring of love.

"Run and lock the door," he said.

"I don't take orders," she said and kissed him. He twisted his fingers around her panties and rubbed his fist against her. And then they heard the door to the bookstore open.

"Shit," Leon whispered.

Pilar pulled away from him and peeked into the store. Maria

Peralta stood at the door, disentangling the pocket of her skirt from the doorknob. Pilar jumped out of the doorway and turned to Leon. "I know this old woman," she said. "I'll tell her to come back later."

Maria Peralta, freed of the doorknob, spoke, and they heard her clearly. "Oh, death has entered this house! Who is here?"

Leon laughed under his breath, covering his mouth with his hand.

Pilar panicked for a moment. To protect Samuel, she rolled her eyes, although it pained her to betray her grandmother. She ran into the bookstore.

"Who is here?" Maria Peralta demanded of Pilar. "It isn't just you here? Tell me it isn't."

Pilar put her finger to her lips. "Could you come back another time, Maria Peralta Cardenas? I am busy with inventory."

"No," she said. "I can't leave you like this."

Pilar put her finger to her lips again. "Shush," she said.

Maria hunched her shoulders and nodded. She whispered, "Death is in this house. I can smell it. I'm not leaving you alone."

"I can explain," Pilar said, "if you come back later."

"I'm not leaving," Maria said, no longer whispering.

Pilar guided her to the far corner to explain, but she heard the back door open and close. "Oh," she said, turning, hurrying to her kitchen. Leon was gone. She ran to the door, flung it open, and called his name—or meant to. She called out, "Love!"

"What is going on here?" Maria stepped into the kitchen and leaned with both hands against the table.

Pilar closed the door and took a breath to calm herself. "You just ran off my boyfriend," she said. "We were about to make love."

"Your American? You must not see him. As soon as I stepped into this house, I smelled death. I forbid you to see him."

"There's a dying man upstairs."

Maria covered her heart. "Thank God," she said. "You had me worried. Who is this man you murdered?"

"I haven't murdered anyone." She heard irritation in her voice and tried to modulate it. "He's someone who has come here to die in peace."

"What a silly thing to do," Maria said. "Is he one of your revolutionary friends? They're such bores."

"He's a playwright. He wrote a play about people in a swimming pool."

"Oh, I must meet him. How dead is he?"

"He's dying, not dead." Pilar sighed. "You really spoiled a nice moment for me."

Maria put both her hands against the kitchen table once more and pushed. The table wobbled. "You'd both have broken your necks," she said. "I probably saved your lives. The last time I had sex was on a table. Did I ever tell you?"

"No, and don't tell me now. I don't want to hear about my grandmother's sex life."

"Not a big table like this but a little round thing." She made a little circle with her hands.

"We weren't going to do it on the table," Pilar said. "I suppose we would have stood."

"This fellow was drunk and just sat there. I had to do all the work." She shook her head at the memory of the lazy man. "Are you going to introduce me to this dead man of yours or not?"

"PERHAPS a week or two. Maybe a month. But I could go tonight," Samuel said.

"That's a very rude question," Pilar told her grandmother.

Maria Peralta shrugged. "You can't beat around the bush with a dying man."

Samuel laughed and his eyes watered with pain. This was the first sign Pilar had noticed. His condition was worsening. "Should we let you rest?" she asked him.

He shook his head, then spoke to Maria Peralta. "Pilar tells me that you predict the future."

"It's not as interesting as it used to be," Maria said.

"I don't need you to tell my future," he said. "It's all too obvious."

"You want to know whether you're going to enter heaven," Maria told him.

Samuel laughed again, the wheeze now a cough, and he cut it short. "Something like that," he said. "I want to know what happens when you die—when I die."

"He's obsessed with this," Pilar said. "Please tell him something that will make him talk about other subjects. He's become tedious."

Maria flattened one hand against the bed and leaned over Samuel. She placed her other hand inside his shirt and slid it slowly down his chest, pausing at the end of his ribcage. "You need a bath," she said. Her hand reached his belly button. She put her thumb in, then each finger. As she withdrew her hand she touched a long scar that wriggled across him like a snake.

"You will return to earth as a lizard," she said and sat again in the chair. "Come see me. I put out scraps for lizards."

PILAR WALKED Maria to the door, then locked it. Once the irritation had left her, she'd felt elated, believing that she and Leon would one day live together. His reluctance had convinced her by its shallowness. She would not let herself be impatient. There was time for him to have his fling with Lourdes, time for Samuel to die in safety.

Pilar's mother had never slept with any man but her father, a slick and superficial man who seduced her when she was only a child and then denied any responsibility for years. Pilar wondered if her mother hadn't loved her father for his superficiality because she believed now that she loved Leon, in part, because he was North American and shallow about politics, childish about responsibility. A man with such obvious faults was easier to forgive than someone like Samuel or even Cruz, men committed to the same ideals as she, men with more complicated beliefs. And so she couldn't forgive Samuel, even though he lay dying, and, perhaps, because he lay dying, for his vacillation, his pathetic grapple with the idea of a God. He should know better. He should be better. Leon was easier to forgive, and forgiveness, she knew, was one of the greatest regions of love. And so she would love Leon for his sweetness and for his meanness, for the simple and enormous flaws that he could not even see.

Two MONTHS after her husband was kidnapped in a movie theater and made a soldier, Rosa prepared to visit him to say that she missed him and loved him, to say that she would endure his imprisonment in the awful uniform, to say that her period was two months late and he would soon become a father. Her husband, Rudy, was to be free for two days and one night. She packed her prettiest dress and a nightgown that one of her girlfriends had given her, and rode in the bus with strangers across the dreadful road that led to Santa Josefina. Rudy had completed his training and would soon be permanently attached to a unit somewhere in the country. It was unlikely that she would be able to go to the university until he was free of the military, but she was willing to wait.

In Santa Josefina, she caught a bus inland, choosing to sit next to a woman more pregnant than she. "Almost seven months," the woman said, and though Rosa had intended to talk about pregnancy and giving birth, they had wound up talking about their husbands. Neither had been married long, and they passed the time amicably.

Rudy met her in the lobby of the hotel. His uniform was the first thing that made her uncomfortable—he wore it so well. A pistol gleamed in a tiny black holster, a nightstick thumped against his thigh.

In bed, she opened to him. Once the uniform was off, he was again her husband. Even the short cut of his hair reminded her of him as a little boy. He had lived only fifty yards away from her in an unlucky house, where he saw his mother and father and finally his uncle die, each from a different ailment. He had been fifteen when the last of his relatives was gone, and he had moved in with Rosa's family. She was the same age, and they had already been lovers for a year. He sold all of his parents' possessions so that she could go to the university.

Rudy was rough with her in the hotel bed, but she did not mind because this, too, reminded her of the boy he had been, the furious love they'd made in her own bed. Afterward, they sat cross-legged on pillows and drank from a bottle of wine she had purchased in town. She waited for the right moment to tell him that she was pregnant, enjoying the excitement that was building in her chest.

But she would never tell him.

He began recounting the training he had been through, the number of hours spent daily on each chore, the amazing list of things he had learned. As he went on, she became anxious because he seemed to be leading to something, which turned out to be true.

He had decided on a career in the army.

She had been too startled to cry and said nothing, but she covered her breasts with one arm and looked around the drab room, knowing that she would remember it for the remainder of her life.

His first real assignment had taken place just two weeks before. A strike at a bottling plant was threatening to shut down the company. "We were sent to restore order," he told her, then described the strikers, the rock-throwing supporters. He never said exactly what happened. All he said was "We showed them."

She clothed herself then, going into the bathroom and staying there until she found words to express her disbelief. She tried to be rational, although her distress showed in every syllable.

Rudy had not dressed, and, while she spoke, he slid to the edge of the bed and pulled on his underwear. She reminded him of their plans, and he walked around the room touching the wooden knobs of the dresser, opening the shades and closing them, snapping the elastic band of his shorts. She recalled their plans in great detail, as if he had never heard them before.

When at last she finished, he said, "Those were the objectives of children." Then he told her of the world as he newly understood it. "La Boca is a joke," he began. "We didn't know anything." Much of what he said had the tone of someone else's voice, things he had heard and now repeated. She interrupted him so often that he became angry and cursed her, which made her cry.

Her tears had a powerful effect on him, and he took her into his arms and told her again and again how much he loved her. When she calmed, his voice changed tone once more as he said words he had heard and had not, as yet, repeated often enough to have made his own. "There are only two kinds of people in this world, Rosa. Those who are masters of their destiny, and those who are slaves." He explained how the army would permit him to become his own master. By the time he was finished, he stood before her, still clad only in his underwear. While talking, he had become aroused.

"No," she said when he lay on her, and she struggled to throw him off.

"You'll see," he said softly as he trapped her arms. "You'll come around," he whispered, and he raised the skirt of her dress.

The two days proved almost unbearable. Rosa lay awake all night composing in her head the letter that she would send him, and she continued this mental composition through the next day.

She let him make love to her, which was all he wanted to do, as if he were proving something. The worst moment came in the morning when he stepped out of the bathroom with lather on his face. He smiled at her while he fumbled through his bag for a razor, and she had seen that he was still her Rudy—this monster was also the man she loved.

As soon as the taxi took him away that afternoon, she returned to the room and attempted to write the letter she had composed in her head. In it, she detailed the reasons that she had loved him, retelling several of their adventures together, reiterating the plans they had made. At the end of the letter, she made it clear that she never wanted to see him again. That he was never to return to La Boca. That she was no longer his wife. That she would send him a check for all of their savings if he agreed to vanish from her life.

She struggled with the letter for hours, but it was impossible to say all that had to be said. She spent another sleepless night in the hotel.

In the morning, she went to the local hospital, whose basement had become a warehouse for unclaimed bodies. The one she selected had no hands, no legs beneath the knees, no features on its bloodied and burned face. She claimed to identify the body by a scar along the man's ribs. A priest told her sadly that this husband of hers had died in an air raid and had not been given last rites. It was all she could do not to spit in his face.

The letter she mailed to her husband was not the one she had spent hours composing, but a simpler message. She put a promissory note in the envelope for all the money that had come from the selling of his parents' possessions. She added to that only a short note: "Rosa is among the slaves."

The body was transported to La Boca, where it was given a proper burial. During the long and rough ride through the sweltering jungle, while Rosa breathed in the decay of the mutilated body, she made plans as to how she would manage her new life. The baby, she decided, would be named after either her mother or her father. She and her child would create a bond greater than the one she'd had with Rudy, one that neither the army nor the revolutionaries could tear apart.

When the bus finally rocked to a stop in front of her little house, she discovered that she had stained her dress and the

wooden bench with her blood, and though the red splotch humiliated her, she could not help staring at it, for the blood that
had soaked into the dry plank bench had followed the contours
of her thighs and round turns of her bottom and taken on a
recognizable shape—a hen, with uplifted wings and long, ragged
claws. And somewhere, she knew, in that red-and-brown stain,
either on the bench or on her skirt or drenched underwear, was
the minuscule bit of life that would have become her child.

Rosa was inconsolable, and had the bus driver not been a
kind man and carried her to bed and seen to it that she was cared
for, she would have slashed open her arms and been buried forever
beside the anonymous, armless, faceless man who was not her
husband.

SAMUEL WOKE in a sweat, unsure whether he had been sleeping.
The bedroom door flew open. It was his brother, Armando. Samuel raised his head and his twisted chest to greet him, but the
door was not really open. He collapsed against the bed. No position eased his suffering, and all of him ached—his head, his
shoulders, arms, fingers. There was a feverish pain in his ears, a
throbbing in his chest, even his useless legs were inflamed. He
was dying. Seconds ticked in his head, a question attached: Is this
my last moment? Is this?

The door again swung open. Again, Armando, his arms
loaded with fruit—oranges, lemons, papayas, pears. What sweet
odors they carried! Armando was smiling, the fruit stacked so
high that he had to trap a pear with his chin to keep it from
falling. Samuel lifted his head, pushed with his elbows to raise
himself. "Brother," he said, tears in his eyes, a string of mucus
connecting his lips, but the door was closed. His head sank into
the pillow. Hallucinations. He would not let himself be fooled
again.

A lizard climbed the rail of the headboard; a tongue of blue
filament stretched from its lips. Samuel swatted at it with his

hand, banging the rail, the lizard gone. Pain reverberated through his fingers. Pilar rushed into the room, hair dancing about her head. "Delirium," he told her, raising his hand to her cheek, but the cheek vanished. Laughter. A record badly scratched.

Madness, Samuel thought. How do you combat madness? There was a specific stinging in his arm, a tenderness in his fingertips that made anything he touched the source of pain, even the sheets, which became as coarse as burlap—and then the door shattered, men in uniform, weapons drawn. "She didn't know!" Samuel called out, believing they had Pilar. They fired and vaporized, the ring of his execution sounding in his ears. "It's hair," his brother said, holding the fishing line, his voice incredulous and sad. Samuel shook his head. "Please, no," he said, suddenly in the bed again. His chest ached. Is this his last breath?

The door vanished in an explosion of pure light. A voice deeper than sound spoke his name, his real name, and it shook his bowels. "What are your questions?" the voice asked. "Here are your answers." Stars descended on him, spiraling like springs. His hands gripped cool earth, pulling grass by the roots. Sunlight warmed his crotch. A violin entered him and he was made to make music, and he was beautiful.

Then the door stretched toward him, becoming a platform. His wife, her arms golden, opening to him. Her blouse fell away. Bullet wounds. Blue holes through her chest. She called his name, but it was not his name. "Samuel," she said and the ice of heaven touched his head. "Samuel." Pilar's leg touched his arm. She was on the bed, a cold rag across his head. The room was dark. He had pissed in the sheets and was ashamed, but his hands felt nothing there.

"You're burning up." It was Pilar's voice. "You're on fire."

*L*OURDES POUNDED a slab of dough, flour rising like steam from the table. She worked furiously, as if she could cut through time by sheer energy, making dawn turn into afternoon. She needed to see Leon, to erase the look he'd given her, a look that had caused her stomach to twist, had inhabited her waking hours and haunted her dreams, a look that had caused the most profound humiliation of her short life. She had to see him, and the hours that lay between now and then were cruel beyond reason. Sweat trickled down her neck as the temperature inside the big oven slowly rose. She punched the bread dough. It oozed between her fingers, cool and damp at the center. She wished she could wrap herself in it to stop the burning in her chest.

Her mother entered the room, arms loaded with wood, laughing. "You'll never guess what just happened to me," Angelica said, dropping the wood with a long clatter against the blackened tile. She clapped her hands and smiled. Another tooth had disappeared from the lower row.

"What, Mama?" Lourdes kneaded with her fists, trying to make her voice calm, the same voice she would use with Leon—as if nothing had happened, as if she had not lain in his bed and caused his disgust.

"I just had a memory that was so clear, I thought I was in it.

I thought I was back there." Angelica laughed again, lifting a knotted limb from the pile of wood and banging it against the black stove handle. "You were there too. A tiny girl. What a smile you had—a little lopsided." The stove handle turned and the door swung open, heat rushing into her mother's face, lifting the fine gray hairs about her temples. Angelica threw the wood, piece by piece, into the flames.

"The dough's ready," Lourdes said, folding it into a bundle.

Angelica shut the stove door, kicking the handle down, then stepped to the table. "It's beautiful. Dough like this can save a life." She began tearing the big lump into smaller pieces. "Smell it." She shoved a handful under Lourdes's nose.

"Don't." Lourdes caught her wrist, but the faintly sweet smell cooled her lungs and calmed her. She leaned against the table. "What were we doing in your memory?"

Angelica continued pulling off clumps of dough. "You were on my shoulders," she said, "and it was raining."

Lourdes flattened the first clump with the heel of her palm. "But what were we doing?"

Angelica lifted rolling pins from a shelf beneath the table, handing one to her daughter. She spread an arc of flour across the table. "We weren't doing anything," she said. "We were very happy."

Lourdes let the rolling soothe her. She flattened the dough and lay the strips into a cross, then twisted them over one another. They were making rolls. "I wish it would rain right now," she said and wiped her forehead with the tail of her apron, leaving a white mark.

"The rainy season always comes," Angelica told her. "One year, I think it lasted only an hour, but it always comes."

"You've lost another tooth, Mama."

Angelica ran her tongue across her teeth until she found the gap. She smiled and shook her head. "The next thing I'm going to lose is my mind. What a trick that will be. I can't wait."

"You're talking crazy," Lourdes said, then, "Don't you ever get sick of this? Making rolls and bread and pastries? Don't you ever just hate it?"

"Why should I hate it?"

"It's the same old thing every day."

Angelica paused long enough to look at her daughter. "Exactly. Why should I hate it?"

"Don't you ever wish you could do something else for a while?"

Angelica resumed rolling. "Life is difficult enough without all this wanting, wanting, wanting, don't you think?"

Lourdes did not reply, her agitation increasing again.

In a few minutes, the front door opened and closed, and Maria Peralta came running into the back room. "I had a vision," she said. "Just now, on the way over here."

"Good," Angelica said, dusting the table again with flour. "What are you doing up so early?"

Maria, who had run into the room with her arms raised, lowered them now. Her blouse was green with bright yellow polka dots, like little suns. "I've been up all night writing my memoirs. I'm almost finished."

"You wrote it all in one night?" Angelica waved the rolling pin to express her disbelief.

"It's only twelve pages long. I've cut out all the unnecessary parts."

Maria's entrance had filled Lourdes with relief—new help to make the time pass. "Mama, aren't you even going to ask her what her vision was?"

"Oh, yes. What was it?"

Maria picked up a clump of dough and began patting it flat. "On the walk from my place to here, three birds spoke to me."

"Can you call that a vision, if you only heard them? Don't you have to see something for it to be a vision?" Angelica asked her seriously. "What are the rules for that?"

Maria pressed the dough between her palms. "Perhaps this was just an omen, then."

"What did they say?" Lourdes asked.

"The first one said, 'Want a kiss?' "

Angelica laughed. "A sassy bird."

"That's just Mono's parrot," Lourdes told them. "It says that to everyone."

"Yes," Maria Peralta said, "that's the one."

"How is that a vision?" Lourdes asked her.

"Omen," her mother corrected.

"You should always listen to animals when they direct their conversation to you." Maria had begun to mold her clump of dough into a shape. "They know things we don't."

Angelica nodded. "Remember old Mr. Ears, that dog I used to have?"

"You had a dog?" Lourdes said.

"Before you were born," Angelica told her. "He used to eat the furniture."

"He was not an intelligent dog," Maria agreed.

"But once he snapped at me and wouldn't let me near a pile of bricks. This was back when Ramon and his father were building their house. Remember that pile of bricks?" Angelica raised her head to Maria.

"I love that house," Maria said. "They don't build them like that any more."

"Mr. Ears wouldn't let me near the bricks, and he had good reason, as it turned out."

"What was the reason?" Lourdes said.

"I can't remember. Was it a snake?"

Maria shook her head. "You guessed that it was a snake. You couldn't get close enough to see."

"Oh, yes." Angelica nodded. "So, there is the proof."

"What did the second bird say?" Lourdes folded another cross of dough.

"The second one was a big dark bird that flew right over my head. It said, 'What?' "

"Both birds asked you questions?" Angelica said.

Maria smiled and nodded. "You lost another tooth, didn't you?"

"Are you sure the bird didn't just squawk?" Lourdes said. "I don't think you had a vision at all."

"Omen," Angelica said.

"The third bird was out by the jungle. Did you know there's a dead dog out there?"

Angelica flattened the final clump of dough. "I hate it when people waste a good dog."

"You wouldn't know a good dog if he bit you," Maria said. "You thought Mr. Ears was a good dog. He never learned his own name."

"That was my fault. I shouldn't have made it two words. It confused him. I should have just called him Ears."

"What did the third bird say?" Lourdes asked, exasperated with them both. She pulled the big flat pan from under the table.

"There was a vulture there, picking at the dog," Maria began. "The vulture looked right at me and spoke. It said, 'This dog is stale, but I am hungry. All the time I am hungry. Die for me, old woman. Let me pick at your tendons.' "

Angelica gasped and threw her hand against her throat. "He was a very articulate vulture."

"I'm not finished. He asked me a question."

"Three birds ask you questions in one day?" Angelica shook her head sadly. "In my whole life, a bird never asked me one thing."

"You have to let them know you're interested."

"What was the question?" Lourdes had oiled the pan and filled it now with the folded crosses.

Maria used a fingernail to give her dough sculptured ridges. "The bird asked me how it felt to be mortal. They think they live forever. That's the difference between birds and humans. We know we die. We know *they* die."

Angelica folded the last strips, then passed the cross to her daughter. "Did you explain this?"

Maria shook her head. "It's no use arguing with a hungry vulture. No, I said that it felt very good to be mortal. You know what I wish I'd said? I wish I'd said, 'It feels like being a little girl and having a coin in your pocket for ice cream.' " She laughed.

"Isn't that the way?" Angelica said. "You don't think of the best answer until it's too late."

Maria sighed. "I may never see that vulture again."

"How is that an omen?" Lourdes asked Maria Peralta.

"It means that the vulture is going to die," Maria said. "That much is definite. And possibly our lives will be changed by its death. It's hard to say. I used to be very good at the future—now I'm just glad to know that the world is still strange. That's what makes me happy."

"Are you through with that?" Lourdes pointed to the dough in Maria's hands.

"Not quite," she said.

Lourdes sighed. "Mama claims doing the same thing every day makes her happy."

"Did I say that?"

"Yes. And that you can't wait until you lose your mind."

"She's always been impatient," Maria said.

"I want things," Lourdes said flatly. "And I'm going to get them."

Maria slowed her sculpting of the dough. "The last person who said that to me was my son," she said. "Little Renaldo."

"He was such a beautiful baby," Angelica said, stopping her work suddenly. "So beautiful."

"What happened to him?" Lourdes asked.

Maria pressed into the dough with her thumb. "He was ruined by his good fortune."

"That doesn't make any sense," Lourdes said.

"Sometimes it does," Angelica said, "and sometimes it doesn't."

"That's what I should have said to the vulture," Maria said. " 'How does it feel to be mortal?' the bird asks. Maria Peralta Cardenas smiles and says, 'Sometimes it does and sometimes it doesn't.' " Maria laughed heartily. "I'm going to add that to my memoirs. Here, cook this." She handed Lourdes her dough, a knobby clump with little marks around the edges from fingernails.

"Is this supposed to be something?" Lourdes asked her.

"Let me see." Angelica stared over her daughter's shoulder. "Why, that's one of those sea animals—what do you call them? They latch on to rocks and eat little fish?"

"It's not that," Maria said. "What do you think?" She put her hand on Lourdes's shoulder.

It looked like an important but obscure part of the body, Lourdes thought—some gland that you couldn't do without. "I don't know," she said.

"It's what my heart would look like after that vulture got his beak into it." Maria laughed and Angelica joined her. Lourdes tossed it onto the pan with the rest.

THE LITTLE WINDOWS in the French doors that opened onto Leon's balcony had just been washed. His bed was freshly made, clean sheets and pillowcases. The clutter of clothes and books had disappeared, shoved into drawers or taken away to be laundered. Leon paced the floor, which was still damp from the mop, early afternoon sunlight angling across his thighs. His hands wanted a cigarette, but he didn't want the smoke or the ash. His shirt already was spoiled, moons of sweat beneath his arms, but he left the balcony doors closed and flipped the switch on the fan instead. It vibrated against the floor, and he had to lift and reposition it several times before it spun quietly.

The prospect of telling Lourdes he would not see her again filled him with a queasy excitement, one which, after several minutes of pacing, he remembered from the times he'd proposed to his wives. As he had back then, he'd practiced lines to say. He wanted to dismiss her without sounding cruel, but nothing seemed adequate. He couldn't imagine himself speaking the words to her, no matter the number of times he said them to himself. He slipped out of his sandals and walked away from the spot of sun, the cool floor delicious to his feet.

She came early, which he'd expected, removing her apron as she stepped into the room. She kissed him shyly, smiling, then turning away. He thought she might be embarrassed. The apron spread itself across the immaculate floor, one white string landing on his foot.

"You look funny today," she said and shut the curtains. "Do you have a hangover? I don't think I've ever seen you with one." She kissed him again. "My mother has been a tyrant. Make me feel better." She giggled self-consciously. "You look so funny."

She turned away and bent over to unbuckle her sandals, knees locked, her skirt riding up her thighs to reveal a dimple of muscle. He knew this was a deliberate show, but it worked on him nonetheless. She remained bent over, fiddling with her shoes, and his resolve faltered.

Louder than reason, desire spoke to him, a voice more persuasive than fairness, a voice so close to his own he couldn't have distinguished one from the other. It rattled in his chest and surged through his limbs, and Leon was powerless before it. He decided he would make love to her one final time.

He raised her skirt and let it fall inside out, down her back almost to the nape of her neck. She did not straighten, but reached between her legs and took his wrist, pulling his hand to her panties. He slid them down to her knees, then let them fall to her ankles.

LOURDES DRESSED herself on the edge of the bed. Leon, sitting up against the headboard, ran through the practiced lines again. While he had been inside Lourdes, he found himself thinking of

Pilar. It had been pleasant enough, the surge of blood passing through him in rhythmic waves, but it left him feeling unresolved, still churning, still seeing Pilar, her heart-shaped face, her black and intelligent eyes. He shook his head to free himself of her, then pulled on his pants, a clean shirt from his closet. Lourdes had her skirt and blouse on and was slipping on a sandal. She faced the door.

"We can't sleep together again," he said.

Her legs folded. She dropped to the floor, crying into her skirt. There had not been even a second for her to comprehend the words. Her crying was heavy, rough.

"An opportunity will be presented to you. A chance to leave La Boca, to go to the university. You should take it," he said, saddened by the sight of her pain, but darkly proud.

She lifted her head but did not turn to face him, staring at the door. She wiped her eyes. "Is it geography?" she asked him, her voice breaking.

Leon thought he must have misunderstood.

"If it's geography," she said, "I've been studying. I have." She put her hands to her face, and turned her head slightly as if to look at him, but not quite far enough to see him. "Would you like to hear about the parallels of latitude? The longitudinal lines?" She was trembling. "I've studied the arrangement of the continents, the prevailing winds, the ocean currents. Would you like to hear about North Pacific Drift? Equatorial Counter Currents?" She dared now to look at him, her face red and swollen, but hopeful. "I can name you the layers of the sky," she said solemnly.

This isn't going well, Leon thought, and the stare that he returned to her was too cold and blank for Lourdes to bear. She rose to her feet, sobbing again, and ran out the door.

PILAR RELEASED the buttons from their holes, careful not to let her arm weigh on Samuel's chest. The shirt stuck to his skin. She lifted the material gently. His fever had finally broken. She eased his arms out of the sleeves, then peeled the shirt from his back and lifted it over his head. A scar, pink and white, scrawled across his chest, a signature she could not resist touching.

"Is this tender?" she asked him, brushing across the thickened skin lightly.

"The opposite," he said, his voice rough, tired. "I can't feel your fingers. I feel the pressure, but not the touch."

She ran a wet cloth beneath his chin, up and down his neck, across his shoulders. "I should have been doing this every day." She lifted his head to clean the back of his neck. "I've been too shy." She washed the scar, his belly, then folded back the sheet. Samuel closed his eyes and turned his head away. His genitals lay in a puddle of excrement. Delicately, she lifted his penis and scrotum, then wiped away as much of the puddle as she could. She lay the sheet over him again. "I'll be right back," she said and went to clean the washcloth and run water in the tub. He weighed almost nothing, but lifting him was awkward. She scooted him to the edge of the bed. He placed his arms around her shoulders. "I'm going to pick you up now," she told him.

"Yes." He spoke softly into her ear.

She squatted and raised him from the bed. He settled against her as she stood, pressing against her chest. He was so light, she imagined that she carried a naked boy, but his size made movement difficult, his useless legs knocking against her hip. She took small steps, turning to face the door.

Her blouse was made damp by his thighs, and excrement trickled across her palm and over her wrist, down her arm to the elbow, where brown drops formed. She approached the door cautiously, watching his head and feet, turning sideways, walking crablike and with care.

His back scraped against the jamb, but lightly, as she carried him across the threshold. Paused in the narrow hall, she heard the door below rattle, the sound followed by frenzied pounding.

Samuel lifted his head slightly and he laughed, his body trembling in her arms. "This always happens, doesn't it?" he said, wistful. "At the worst moment, someone comes calling or the telephone rings. I'm becoming nostalgic for life in advance of my death." He coughed out another laugh, a dark line of spit running down his chin and against her blouse.

The pounding continued. A shrill voice called Pilar's name. The caller sounded desperate but Pilar couldn't help but laugh with Samuel.

"You're going to drop me," he said, his laughter a wheeze again.

She leaned against the doorjamb and reshifted her arms, still laughing, her knees almost folding. Her sleeve and arm were streaked with shit and urine and blood. She knew she would have to hate Samuel or to love him. She could not paint herself with his excrement and not have strong feelings. And so while they laughed together, he entered her heart, the expansion noticeable even to the man pressed against her chest.

She turned in the hall and crossed it easily, then aimed his feet at the opening to the bathroom. The voice below screamed, "Open up," then something more. Pilar couldn't concentrate on it. The bathroom was tiny, and the doorknob pressed against the small of her back as they entered. He had begun to grow heavy. Her fingers slid against his slick skin, the voice yelled her name, but she couldn't hurry.

He began to slip from her hands, and she had to crouch to catch him, then go to her knees to hold him. His feet banged against the tub. She lifted them into it, walking forward on her knees, then raised his butt over the porcelain rim, lowering him slowly until her arms were wet to the shoulders, water lapping against her breasts. At the last moment, as she pulled her arm free, her chin bobbed into the warm water, and the pounding below stopped.

"I'm going to see who is down there," she told him.

He nodded, but when she released his arm, he slid beneath

the surface of the water and she had to fish him out. "Can you hold on?" she asked him.

He spat water, blinking. "Go ahead." He draped an arm over the tub, fingers almost reaching the floor. She stepped away cautiously. "Go," he said.

By the time she reached the front door, there was no one. She pressed her face against the glass, looking south, then north. A woman ran up the street, already a hundred yards away. So far away, Pilar would not have known who it was, except for the flapping apron.

And Pilar guessed that Leon had let Lourdes go. Her heart grew again.

As she climbed the stairs, she pulled her blouse over her head. Using it, she wiped the dark streaks from her arms and belly and breasts. The blouse she selected from her dresser was one Leon had given her, beige and plain. It felt wonderful against her skin.

Samuel had straightened himself, although his elbow still rested against the rim. The water was already murky. She knelt beside the tub, dipping her hands into the water, and lathered them with soap. She worked her fingers through his long, dark hair. "We'll start here," she said, massaging his scalp. He tried to smile, but he was crying. "What is it?" she asked him.

"This feels so good," he said.

She washed and rinsed his hair, cleaned his neck, his ears, his forehead, across his face. She washed his chin and jaw and beneath his arms. She worked slowly and tired quickly, knowing she would have to carry him again to her bed. She ran the cloth along his forearms and elbows, between his fingers and across his chest. Wrapping an arm around his back, she lifted him slightly in the tub, then washed between his legs and between the cheeks of his butt. She cleaned his thighs, behind his shattered knees, his shins, his twisted feet, his toes.

While the tub drained, she changed the sheets on her bed, scrubbing the spots on the mattress as best she could, then returned to the bathroom. "Are you ready for me?" she asked.

He had dried himself, pressing the towel wherever he could reach. "I believe I am," he said, nearly exhausted.

She went to her knees. He put his arms around her again, and she scooped him up into her arms. Standing was difficult—she bruised her legs against the tub's rim—but the short walk was easier than before, and when she lowered him into bed, she felt strong again.

BENJAMIN FOLLOWED Lourdes into the jungle. She had come into his house without knocking, simply marched in, out of breath, and pointed at him. "Hurry up," she commanded, and he followed her down the bank of the estuary, too surprised and confused to ask questions. She ran, apron fluttering, and he ran after.

Where the jungle began, the bank became narrow, treacherous with roots and vines, leaves and branches. She had to stop running, but ducked under and stepped over limbs so quickly that it was all he could do to keep up. His shirt pocket caught on a branch and tore. By the time he'd pulled himself loose, she was thirty yards ahead, leaping off the bank into the shallow water, running again.

"Wait," he called. "It drops off. It gets deep."

She ignored him, and he couldn't catch up, becoming afraid that he might lose her altogether. She stopped suddenly, knee-deep in water, whirled, and faced him. "We should have taken the trail," she said fiercely, as if it were his fault. She began sprinting again.

Benjamin pulled off his shoes and shirt, noting the place where he left them. He dove into the estuary. Swimming, he calmed; his mind began to operate again, immediately curious. What could she be up to and where were they going? He lifted his head to call out, in time to see her tumble into the water.

He swam to her, but by the time he reached her, she'd already pulled herself onto the bank. "You're swimming," she said grimly and yanked down her skirt. She pulled off the apron and her muddy blouse, then flung them against a tree, the blouse snagging on a root, the apron landing in the water, where it took shape again, flexing and shifting on the water's surface like a puddle of oil. Her mud-streaked panties rode lopsided on her hips. Water beaded on her bra.

Before he could ask what she was doing, she dove ahead, kicking furiously, slapping the water with her fists. He easily caught up with her, swimming without a splash, moving beautifully in the water alongside her as he had in his fantasies.

One of her fists came down on his jaw. He didn't think it could be an accident, but he couldn't believe it was intentional. She had begun grunting, then she dipped beneath the surface and emerged by the bank. As she pulled herself out of the water, her panties slid down her legs. She gripped them with one hand and jerked twice before they tore off. She began pulling at her bra. "Shit," she screamed. A safety pin had scratched her breast, leaving a trickle of blood. She pulled the bra over her head and faced him, slashes of mud from her shoulders to her thighs, a tiny arc of blood above one nipple, her hair matted against her head.

"Well?" she demanded.

Benjamin fluttered his arms beneath the water to stay in one place, kicking slowly to keep himself afloat. "You're beautiful," he said.

"Hurry up." Turning, she entered the jungle, fighting her way through, flailing at vines, whipping limbs out of her way. She couldn't move quickly, but she progressed faster than Benjamin, who lost track of her twice, although she was never more than a few yards ahead. He called out, but she would not respond. Twigs scraped his face. Tendrils entered his ears. He ducked under a bough and stepped into a clearing, a spot no larger than his father's boat. Lourdes knelt there, her butt in the air, her head on her arms, and turned to look at him, her back and sides red with scratches, many of them bleeding, her bottom streaked as if she'd been paddled. A bruise had already begun to yellow on her ribs.

"Tell me," she said, raising her ass. "Say it again."

Benjamin abruptly and inexplicably began to cry. The sensation so startled and shamed him that he almost ran away. Instead he turned and threw his arms around the trunk of a tree, sobbing and trying to stop. Then his head and body slammed into the trunk, the wind knocked out of him. Lourdes threw herself against him again and he crumpled to his knees. She hammered his head against the trunk. "Tell me." She tugged at his soaked pants, which would not give.

"What?" he said. "What do you want?"

"Tell me I'm beautiful."

He stood on his knees and put his arms around her waist, weeping against her grimy belly. "I love you," he said, gripping her slick skin. "You're beautiful."

Immediately she began to squirm away, pulling him by the hair until he stood, then she tugged open his pants. "You're not even hard," she said and dropped to her knees and took his muddy cock into her mouth.

Benjamin tumbled forward, knocking her over. He tried to hold her, pressing a hand against her shoulder, his legs across her chest. "What are you doing?" he asked her. "What's wrong?"

"I'm fucking you," she said. "Now do it."

Frightened, his ribs aching with sadness, Benjamin wiped his eyes and tried to make her be still. A trail of blood from his nose fell across his mouth, his exhalation lifting a tiny red mist into the humid air.

"Fuck me," she demanded, then tried to wrestle him off her.

"Wait," he said. "What is it? What has happened?"

She put her hand in his face, clutching at his eyes. Wrapping her leg around his, she turned him. She was stronger than he was, and it took both of his hands to keep her from clawing his eyes. She threw herself back against his cock, but it would not enter her. She grabbed it, letting go of his face. When he lifted his hands to stop her, she punched him in the jaw, then guided him inside her and worked him and worked him until he came, crying and bleeding, calling her name.

LOURDES SAW the trees as legs, humans so large as to be recognizable only by their parts. She wove through them, naked, branches lashing her, little sprigs tearing at her skin, Benjamin already gone, the sound of her name as he yelled it gone. She knew that no one but Pilar could have made it possible for her to go to college. No one but Pilar could have made Leon give her up. But how?

In her frenzied rush, she flung herself against a tree, knocking herself down, among roots, where she struggled to catch her breath, her fingers sinking into mulch. Little leaves, the size and shape of puzzle pieces, pressed against her eyes, lips, nose.

Then she was moving, running again, as if she'd missed something, several moments left out, the jungle growing dark, limbs swooping down to slap her, enormous boughs, leaves the size of lungs, and then laughter, which stopped her, made her realize she was naked. Laughter in the middle of the jungle, her legs weakening, suddenly tired. She leaned against a tree.

Not laughter at all. Howling monkeys. Branches high above her rattled with their movement. Her legs tingled with fatigue. She rested her arms against her knees. Ants, on her legs. She screamed, rubbing her thighs, stepping high. She didn't know what she was doing in the jungle, couldn't remember, couldn't imagine.

Then she was already gone, running, time throwing her ahead, the ants gone, her legs speckled pink and with long red slashes. Her feet struck mud, a depression, surrounded by a wall of trunks, rough black bark, smooth white bark. She pushed through a narrow gap into a network of limbs and vines, leaves scratching her stomach, pressing against her face, entering her mouth as she breathed, a green flush of hands, binding her, suffocating her, holding her up when she tripped, stopping her.

She crumpled, a vine catching her chin, throwing her head

against a tree, its knobby roots bruising her butt when she finally hit the earth. She turned back, angling through the gap in the trunks, pulling against the limbs that held her calves and the branch that was a bar across her stomach. When she finally escaped, on her knees, she heard someone, once again, calling her name.

If she'd run in a circle it was Benjamin, or perhaps he'd tried to follow. But it was not Benjamin, and it was not her name that was called. She heard it clearly. English. Someone calling for help. She worked her way forward, toward the voice. Pilar had made Leon stop loving her, made him give her up—the voice suddenly closer, and she spotted him, in another tiny opening, on a fallen tree, a man in glasses, arm resting on a green backpack. "Somebody," he yelled. Then he removed his glasses, wiped them on the tail of his shirt.

When she stepped into the clearing, he started, almost falling off the trunk, the backpack tumbling onto the ground. She glared at him, her hair spangled with leaves, breasts muddy and bleeding, mulch and mud trailing down her stomach, pubic hair sparkling with diamonds of sweat, her bruised and scraped legs carpeted with muck.

The man stood slowly, backing away. He pulled his backpack between his legs. He started to speak but his voice had no timbre, like a splash of water. He cleared his throat. "I have some medicine," he said, pointing not quite at her. "Your cuts." She did nothing, and he backed away another half step, leaned against the fallen tree. He spoke now in Spanish. "Medicine," he said, then in English, "Don't hurt me."

And Lourdes collapsed.

SHE DIDN'T THINK she'd lost consciousness, but when she opened her eyes it was as dark as death. Her legs and breasts stung. She touched her chest, realizing she had been washed. Then there was light.

A flashlight shone directly on her, blinding and solitary. He had cleaned her, treated her wounds. The light lifted. He struck a match and twisted a knob on a tiny green lantern. She lay on an open sleeping bag, which she pulled over herself and zipped. although it was much too hot. Then she pretended to sleep while he adjusted the lamp.

"Hey," he said. "I've been waiting for you to wake up." She kept her eyes closed, although she could sense the light dim, and peeked to see him adjusting the lantern. He saw her watching. "What are you doing out here?" he asked her, then added, "You have to share the bag."

She spat, though not at him. He dropped to one knee, lay on top of the bag, just to the side of her. "I'm not lying on the ground," he said. She shrugged him off, but he pressed against her again, a leg over her.

"Are you lost, too?" he asked her. "Do you know the way out?"

HE TOLD HER it was the afternoon, or she wouldn't have known that it wasn't morning. He had ruined her dream, a dream in which she had been led by monkeys to the ocean, where Leon waited for her, hands in the pockets of his white pants, silver birds circling over his head, a dozen dogs sleeping near him, curled on the beach, and beneath their paws, fish flopped in the sand, scales flashing in the sunlight. Leon had lifted her into his arms and carried her to a kitchen, white and clean, a stove that sparkled with chrome, but then he left the room and hands pressed against her head, the hands of a monkey, a monkey who had crawled through the kitchen window, a monkey whose red cock was now thrust in and out of her ear, across her eyes, her mouth, her ear again. A dog began lapping at her thighs.

She woke to find his hand on her chest, his tongue rimming her ear. She pushed him away and crawled out of the bag, covering her breasts with her arm. He poured coffee from a silver pot into a tiny tin cup. Lukewarm, but she drank it and ate the raisins he offered, and when he touched her breasts again, she moved his hand to her cunt and began unbuttoning his shirt, then tugged on his belt. He quickly removed his shirt, while she unzipped his pants.

"Do you know how to get out of here?" he asked in English as he stepped out of his jeans.

She only grunted.

When he was naked, she directed him to lie down, then knelt over his face. He tried to kiss her, but she raised herself slightly, as if to tease, then she adjusted her position, her knees over his arms, and she lowered herself onto his neck.

She punched him hard in the face. His glasses cracked and cut him. He screamed. She hit him again, and then again. She beat him until he was unconscious.

His clothes were strewn around the clearing. His shirt stank, and she rummaged through his backpack, finding a red T-shirt with white lettering above a snow-capped mountain. DISCOVER AMERICA, it said. She slipped it on, then pulled his plaid shirt over it to protect her arms from the jungle. Knotting her hair in one fist, she lifted it off her neck and held it there with his cap, blue with a single star and the word COWBOYS. She rolled up the pantlegs and, with his pocket knife, made a new hole in his belt, cinching it tight. She slipped the knife into her pocket. His shoes were much too big, but he had several pairs of socks and she put them all on, cleanest pair first.

He made a noise, his head lifted slightly, a streak of blood running down his face. Then he was still again, breathing evenly, his legs as white as ash.

She set out through the jungle, in search of the mule trail. In a fit of generosity, she decided to mark the way so that he could follow when he came to, but after a few dozen yards she forgot about him. Since waking she had been aware of the startling clarity of her vision, the remarkable purity of her thought. She had wakened knowing that Pilar was pregnant, and knowing too that she, Lourdes, would stop the pregnancy if it meant she had to reach into Pilar's womb with her bare hand.

"NOT GOOD," Samuel said, his head trembling with fever. "Talk to me while I can still concentrate. What did Ramon want?"

Pilar stood in the doorway, the last strong rays of light reflecting off her white dress. "Lourdes has disappeared," she said, crossing her arms and uncrossing them. "Apparently, she spent the night in the jungle." She slipped her hands into the pockets of the dress—a coin in one pocket, a scrap of paper in the other. "She went out there with Ramon's son—who is in love with her." She walked slowly to the armchair. Unfolded, the scrap of paper held a few dark numbers—the price Ramon had asked for transporting Samuel. "It's terrible that I feel this way because she is missing—I suppose she could be in trouble—but the truth is, I'm happy." She sat in the chair and permitted herself a tiny smile.

"Your American has made a decision, perhaps?" He returned her smile, and even this gesture caused him discomfort. "A decision Lourdes doesn't like."

"Ramon told me as much. He was worried, but her mother—who doesn't know that she was sleeping with Leon—isn't concerned. Lourdes has always thrown little fits, I guess. My grandmother says the jungle should be more afraid of her than she of the jungle. I can't bring myself to worry." She refolded the piece of paper and put it back in her pocket. "Ramon said she played in the jungle all her life."

"Are you going to marry this American?"

"His name is Leon." Saying his name forced her to smile again. "Marriage, I don't know. But I'd like to live in the same house, sleep in the same bed."

"This one will be vacant soon, I'm afraid." A shiver ran through him.

She took his hand—hot and damp, beads of sweat in the dark hairs above the knuckles. "You may live longer than you think," she said, but she could not make her voice convincing.

"No, I won't. Listen, about my body." He squeezed her hand and the pressure he exerted doubled back in pain up his arm. "Throw it in a hole. If the government hears I'm being buried, they will find you. Torture you."

"Shallow grave," she said. "No marker."

"Good. Or you could cut me up and feed stray dogs."

"Your sense of humor is awful." She laughed, then placed his hand on the bed, picked a piece of lint from the dress, her favorite dress.

"The room has begun to tilt." His voice was low, just above a whisper, a guttural edge.

She kissed his forehead. "Your fever is rising. Let me get you a wet cloth."

"Shouldn't you be running your store?" His eyes widened. He grew suddenly nervous. "Won't people get suspicious?" A drop of perspiration ran from the dark beginning of his hair down his forehead and into an eyebrow.

"It's Sunday."

"How late is it?"

"Dusk," she said, running her fingers across his brow.

He seemed to calm. "How fitting." He sighed. "If I die now, I will at least have the pleasure of knowing that I did not betray myself. I don't believe in God."

"Good for you," she said.

"On the other hand, if I die slowly, anything can happen. I'm beginning to think it would take a saint not to give in and believe in God." He smiled and inhaled. "A saint of a new order, of course."

Pilar lay her hand across his forehead. "How am I going to know?"

"Perhaps I'll make my last words a pronouncement of my beliefs about the deity. I've begun trying to think of good last words." The pain had subsided, although his skin felt tender and he knew the respite would be brief. "Do you have any ideas? How do you put a cap on a life?"

Pilar shook her head. Her eyes had begun to tear but she blinked the tears away.

He wheezed a short laugh. "When I was a boy, I knew exactly what I wanted on my tombstone. Did you ever play that game? What three words would you want on your grave marker?"

"That's easy for me. My real names."

He laughed once more, his head jumping forward, a band beginning to tighten around his skull. "Of course," he said softly. "By the time you die, the revolution will be won, and you will be able to do that without endangering anyone."

"What were your three words?"

"Ha Ha Ha."

Pilar smiled, then thrust her hands in the pockets of her dress again. "So that's the kind of kid you were, the one who had to have the last laugh."

"And now I hope to laugh at God." His voice was coarse and he was no longer joking. The fever was mounting another attack. A steam of perspiration wandered across his cheek.

"If there is a God, He's been laughing at the people in this country for generations," Pilar told him.

"Yes," he agreed. "If there is a God, He lives in Beverly Hills and has people, probably people from this country, who do His laundry and make His meals and wipe His ass. Is that a real noise? What is that noise?" His chest had begun to shake.

"Someone is downstairs at my door," she told him.

He nodded. "Go ahead."

"Are you sure?"

"I'll be alive when you come back. I'm positive. You can take your time. Wait. You know what I just realized?"

She was already at the door. "What, cousin?"

"I have it all right here, don't I? Just like God. A person who does my laundry and makes my meals and wipes my ass. A beautiful woman, besides. The most beautiful woman on earth, according to our mutual friend." He smiled, open-mouthed, his head quivering, bubbles of sweat erupting across his forehead.

"I'm going to see who's at the door," she said.

"Perhaps I'm God," he said, "or perhaps each of us is God, or we all have it as good as God." His eyes were closed; his breathing, shallow gasps. "Oh, are you still there?" The light, dim as it had become, burned his retina. "You said it. Before."

He thought he heard a reply. "Yes, exactly. I'm on fire. I'm nothing but flame."

The room turned white with heat.

THE MAN in the doorway, an American—she could tell by the clothes—hammered against the door, head down. Pilar unlocked it but opened it only a crack. "The store will be open tomorrow," she said. The man shoved his way inside, striding past her. Only then did she see the hair poking out from the blue cap, the rolled pantlegs. "Where did you get those clothes?" she demanded.

Lourdes glanced over her shoulder, a dark look, which caused Pilar to shudder. Lourdes laid her hand on the counter, paused, then walked into the hall, disappearing.

"People are worried about you," Pilar called, afraid Lourdes was going to run up her stairs again. When Pilar stepped into the hall, Lourdes punched her fiercely in the stomach. Pilar's knees gave. She let out a tiny yelp as she fell. Lourdes dropped her knee into Pilar's groin, throwing her weight against her. The cap fell off, hair tumbling down, a shower of twigs and leaves.

SAMUEL GAVE HIMSELF up to the flames burning through his chest, traversing his spinal cord. Coals in his lungs. Capillaries of fire.

His mother appeared, on her knees over him; she extinguished the flames, her wrinkled breasts smothering them, but her breasts were burned black, her gray hair singed and crinkled. She held hands with a man, a general, medals across his chest, colorful trinkets. "Let me die," Samuel said and the two spoke in unison: "I'd kill you first."

He kicked to submerge himself, his arm extended, his lungs already aching for breath—cool mud, his hands patting the spongy earth—an ankle, the obscene toes, so tiny, this little girl, his lungs searing, her thin legs, little belly. He tried to surface, lungs in flame, his breath nothing but black bubbles in the pond, but still he had to touch her ribs, feel the little bones, the gristle, the tiny nostrils.

Pilar kissed him, her tongue loosening his teeth. He inhaled deeply through his nose. No fire. She pulled the scar from his chest, dangling it in front of him: a leech. She licked his face. "You lying cunt," she said, and he thought, She is angry, but she kissed him again and they were making love. Cruz was watching them, his tiny hand exploring Pilar's body—no, Samuel's body. "I get you two confused," Cruz confessed. Then Pilar's tongue locked the passages of his throat and he could not breathe, the fire in his chest beginning again.

"You're no saint"—a man's voice, and even in his delirium Samuel knew that it was a voice from inside him, a voice without sound. "Saints of the new order"—the voice now his brother's, but Armando was not here, he knew that, although he saw him, medals across his chest, the same uniform as the general's. "The saints of the new order eat the women with the bitter cunts," he said.

The room. Pilar had gone downstairs. Walls carried the rumble of a struggle. He had to help her; they were killing her. "It's me you want," he called out, but the sound barely left his dry lips. He rolled to the edge of the bed, raising his legs, but they did not rise. Lightning entered the room, ricocheting wall to wall. "It's me," he said. "I'm the one you want." He tumbled from the bed, jaw clubbing the chair, head bouncing to the floor. His legs were still tangled in the sheet, and he thought they were no longer connected to him, but as he crawled, they tugged him back, until they fell, clattering to the floor like bricks. And the clattering continued, a jackhammer, and his brother again, "The saints breathe the noise of the jackhammer into their lungs and call it the spirit of God." His lungs turned, once more, to flame.

He crawled on his belly to the door, now a lizard, now a man, the burning denying him breath, turning the world dark.

PILAR BLACKED OUT an instant, woke to Lourdes slapping her cheek, the knee still pressing against her.

"There's not going to be a baby," Lourdes told her.

Pilar shook her head but she couldn't catch her breath to speak.

"If you deny it, I'll kill you." Lourdes loomed above her, too large to be human.

"Get off me," Pilar said, a shallow whisper, but Lourdes obeyed, standing over her. Pilar held her stomach and curled her knees. "You're mistaken." She sounded calm, even to herself. "I'm not pregnant. There's no baby."

"Lying cunt. You fixed it for me to go to the university, then let yourself get pregnant." She leaned over Pilar again, ridiculous and menacing, tugging at the plaid shirt, pulling it off.

"I don't know what you're talking about," Pilar said, raising herself now on one hand, high enough to see the knife come out of the pocket, the blade flip out of the knife.

*R*AMON ROSE just after dawn. Although the sun had been up only minutes, the morning was already brilliant. Celita had roused him when she left for the bakery to deliver her pastries, but he had returned to sleep for a few minutes, tired from a restless night. He had wakened several times, thinking, each instance, that someone was trying to enter their house. Finally, he had climbed out of bed at three in the morning and walked outside to see for himself that no one was there. He circled the house in the dark, stubbing his toe on an ancient mound of bricks. As far as he could tell, nothing was unusual, and he dismissed the noises as imagined.

By the time he was fully awake and dressed, his wife had returned with news.

"Lourdes is still not back," Celita told him. "I'm going to return to the bakery and help Angelica. I just wanted you to know—Lourdes is still in the jungle."

Before his wife had finished speaking, Ramon was on his way to his son's room. If it had been Lourdes who had wakened him during the night, Benjamin would be gone.

His son lay in bed, wrapped in a sheet, his back to the door. Ramon did not want to disturb him. The afternoon before, he had come home shirtless and barefoot, bleeding, bruised, and exhausted. "Lourdes is in the jungle," the boy had said and then claimed that he'd fallen, that the bruises and cuts were from jungle limbs. "I was trying to keep up with her," he explained. "She was acting crazy." His eyes filled with tears, and Ramon did not press him for more."

"She hit him," Celita said, after they put Benjamin to bed. "Or someone did."

"She did." Ramon had no doubt. "Who else would he lie to protect?"

"I'll talk to Angelica," Celita had told him. "You tell Pilar. She should know."

Ramon had walked to the bookstore that afternoon, full of excitement and apprehension. He had been happy that Leon had told Lourdes, and though she was upset, he had been confident that she would recover.

Now, only twelve hours later, he felt less sure. He had thought she would be home by this time, ready to take the bus with Benjamin that evening. Suddenly his plan seemed faulty, stupid, full of holes. At that moment, Benjamin, still asleep, rolled onto his back, his face black and yellow with bruises, swollen and soft. And Ramon knew that his plans were those of a fool.

He shut the bedroom door silently, settled into a crouch, and rested his head against his clasped hands. He did not want a woman who could do this to his son to become his son's bride.

"It's good for him to sleep." Celita had washed her hands and dried them now on a kitchen towel, preparing to return to the bakery.

"I was afraid he might be gone," Ramon said, rising.

She nodded. "I checked this morning before I left."

Ramon rested his hands on her hips and kissed her lightly on the forehead. "You're always one step ahead of me."

"Angelica thinks Lourdes just has too much energy." Celita folded the towel while she spoke. "But I'm worried. You should let Pilar know."

"I told her yesterday that Lourdes had run off," Ramon reminded her.

"And you should tell her once more today. Lourdes is still missing, and she should know. Every day that Lourdes is missing, Pilar should be told."

"I will go to the bookstore again." He smiled but could take no pleasure in it. "And then what do we do?" he asked.

Celita answered him simply and flatly, as if she were reading the instructions of a recipe or naming the presidents from memory. "I help Angelica with her work and tend to our son's wounds. You talk to Pilar, and then go and find Lourdes."

Ramon nodded but did not move. "I'm not sure I want her with Benjamin," he told her. "Have you looked at his face?"

"She has a wild heart," Celita said. She tossed the towel onto the kitchen table, pausing with her arm extended to watch it fall. "But we cannot abandon her. We cannot even consider that. We've known Angelica all of our lives. Benjamin has known Lourdes all his. We cannot turn our backs. I am going to help at the bakery. You talk to Pilar."

Ramon obeyed, leaving for the bookstore, hopeful once again. It was he who found the body.

ALTHOUGH men's clothes were strewn across the bloody hall, Ramon had only to think of his son's face to be sure that it was Lourdes who had murdered Pilar. The body was nude. There was only a single wound, a gash in her slender throat. Pilar's underwear lay at her feet; the panties had been shredded with a knife. Ramon covered her with the plaid shirt, the red T-shirt, and he wept into his hands, hands that had brushed across the body and were marked with blood.

Samuel he found on the floor at the top of the stairs, his feet tangled in bedsheets which he had dragged along. He had dirtied himself, and Ramon cleaned him before lifting him onto the bed.

"Did they kill her?" Samuel whispered as Ramon lowered him to the mattress.

"They? Who?" Ramon found himself unreasonably elated, thinking that perhaps he had been wrong, that Lourdes was not the murderer.

"Why didn't they come after me?" Samuel asked, staring at Ramon and then past him, unable to focus. "I'm the one they want," he said.

Samuel was deluded with fever. Ramon's elation passed, leaving a residue of shame. "You rest," he said.

"She's dead, isn't she?"

"Yes," Ramon said, and he knew then that he would do what he did best—create stories. A simple one to tell the townspeople, and a different one for Leon. He covered Samuel with a blanket and set a glass of water by his bed. Ramon then knelt like a child and rested his forehead on the dead woman's bed.

"Are you praying?" Samuel asked him.

"Yes," Ramon said.

"Let me know if it does any good," Samuel said.

Ramon prayed for his children: Benjamin and Lourdes. Lourdes, who had beaten his son and murdered his friend, was now his daughter as surely as she would soon become his daughter-in-law. He would not abandon her. She and his son would marry, and Ramon would have to lie to make it happen. He would have to turn his back on the law. He would have to smuggle Lourdes and Benjamin away from La Boca as if they were criminals, which is what they would be. He would have to do all this because it was the only honorable thing to do. He would have to do it because Lourdes was now a creation of his making.

He finished his prayers, then rose and looked through Pilar's closets until he found a clean sheet, which he used to cover her body. The mound she made seemed too small. Far too small.

Sadness found his legs, weighting them, filling them with seawater, legs too heavy to be of any use. He floundered on them. The walk across town became difficult and long. His son loved Lourdes but didn't know that she was a murderer. Was it fair to let Benjamin marry Lourdes in order to atone for Ramon's sins? The weight of Ramon's sadness, which was exactly equal to the weight of history, said yes.

He stopped at the bakery and called for his wife.

THE POUNDING on the door woke Janet, and she shook Leon until he sat up in bed, momentarily panicked, unsure where he was, who the woman with him was. Then the shadow passed.

"What is it?" he yelled.

"It's Ramon. There's trouble."

Groggy and annoyed, he pulled on his pants and a shirt, pausing to admire Janet's firm back, the line of vertebrae and sacral dimples, then he cracked open the door.

Ramon shoved his arms through and yanked him into the hall. He pressed his face to Leon's and hissed into his ear. "Lourdes has killed Pilar."

Leon's knees gave. Only Ramon's strong hands kept him on his feet. But he regained his balance quickly and shut the door to his room. His hands became fists, and it was all he could do to keep from punching Ramon. "How could this happen?" he said, then added, "Where is Lourdes?"

"She hasn't been found," Ramon told him. "My guess is that she's in the jungle somewhere. Or the thicket. I suppose she could have taken sanctuary at the cathedral. I think we should try the jungle."

Leon held his head in his hands. "Let me finish dressing," he said. "Wait here."

Janet sat up in bed, holding the sheet to her neck. "What's going on?" she asked him.

Leon picked up shoes and clean socks. "I can't talk about it now," he said. "Go back to sleep." Bending over to put on his socks, he thought he might faint. The floor reeled up and the bed spun away. He clung to the mattress until the feeling passed. Janet's hands touched his back tenderly, and he turned to her.

She whispered, "Is this about Anthony?"

Leon, in his despair, had no idea who this Anthony was, and, for a brief moment, believed that Janet was insane.

"SHE'LL WANT us to find her," Leon said as he followed Ramon into the familiar street, which had been made foreign by death and was blurred by his tears. "She'll be someplace she'd expect us to look."

Ramon knew they should begin by talking to Benjamin, but he was reluctant. He explained to Leon, "I wish we didn't have to get him into this just yet."

As it turned out, speaking to Benjamin was unnecessary. Ramon's boat was not where he left it every morning, propped against the north wall of his house. He searched his memory but couldn't recall whether it had been there when he'd circled the house that night. By the markings in the dirt, he could tell the obvious—someone had dragged it to the estuary. At a neighbor's house, he and Leon took an identical skiff and rowed into the jungle. Only when the green of the trees entirely eclipsed the sky did they resume speaking.

"What will happen to Lourdes?" Leon asked softly. He sat in front and had to lift his oar from the water in order to turn and face Ramon.

"That depends on you." Ramon continued rowing steadily, shadows and sunlight washing over his face.

"How do you mean?"

"During the argument, before Lourdes attacked her, she called Pilar your fiancée. Your name was mentioned several times. Neighbors heard it clearly." Ramon spoke with such calmness and confidence that he almost convinced himself that he was telling the truth. "You will be considered the next of kin, since she had no other relations here."

"Pilar was not my fiancée."

"It doesn't matter. You're the closest thing to a relative she had. Pilar's politics make it difficult to pursue her killer with much energy. If Lourdes doesn't return to La Boca and you don't push the matter, no one will try to find her. It might be different if Pilar had relatives, or if we had police and judges here, but there's just the constable, who is a grocer, and he always does what's easiest."

"There's a grandmother," Leon said, turning, beginning to row again. "No one is supposed to know."

"Oh." Ramon paused only a moment. "We will respect those wishes—no one will know. Her politics make it dangerous for anyone to be related to her. But you're North American. You're safe. You are the next of kin."

Above them, invisible among the sunlit leaves and branches, a monkey screeched once. It sounded like laughter, and Ramon felt himself redden with embarrassment, as if even creatures who lived in trees could see that he was lying. He lost his confidence. "Stupid monkeys," he said, paddling them farther along, down the inlet. "I hate them, Leon. I see them in my sleep. Do you have monkeys?"

"Everybody has monkeys," Leon told him.

They continued, morning light illuminating the throat of space. The oars in the water made a soft *plish*, broken by a whistle of wind through leaves and the rhythms of the men breathing. Leon and Ramon felt what generations of men and women had felt entering the jungle, that they were being watched, that life itself was observing and making judgments.

At the fork of the estuary, the living shroud of limbs and leaves hunkered lower, and the inlet shone green and black in the filtered light. A dark rim of earth revealed the diminished level of the stagnant water.

"We won't be able to go much farther," Ramon said, guiding the skiff into the narrow passage. In another few minutes he pointed at the bank, his arm trembling over the water. A second skiff rested beneath a tree limb, visible as a patch of gray.

"That's my boat," he said. "She's here."

They dug their oars into the soft bottom mud and pushed themselves ahead.

Leon could not help that his mind continued to function. Despite his grief over Pilar, he thought of what was to become of his life. Without Pilar, without Lourdes, he would likely fall back into the old trap. Janet, after all, would be living in the same building, sleeping in the same bed. It was wrong for him to consider this now, but if he didn't, Lourdes would be gone before he could act to keep her.

"What if I let Lourdes stay with me?" he asked, almost a whisper.

Ramon glared at him. "You want to marry her? Now? Now, you want to marry her?"

"She could stay at the hotel." He felt a wash of embarrassment as he said it, but he continued. "I would give her a room."

Ramon slapped the water with his oar. "Wipe those ideas from your mind. She has to leave. She has killed someone, Leon."

Leon pushed against the mud with his oar. His body filled with contradictory emotions; they bounced around in his chest, tingling his legs, numbing his fingers. He shoved again, and the oar stuck in the muddy bottom. He had to work it back and forth several times before freeing it.

"From here we walk," Ramon told him.

They removed their shoes and eased themselves into the estuary.

Leon's feet sank in the bottom sludge to his ankles. The turgid water reached just past his knees. Mud clung powerfully to his feet, making his steps difficult. Ahead Ramon ducked under a limb slung low across the inlet. Bending down so that his chest brushed against the water's surface, Ramon plodded through. Leon tried to imitate him, but had to lift his feet too high to be free of the mud, and his head bumped the limb. A gray snake hit the water and skirted across the still surface between the men.

"Be careful, goddamn you." Ramon shook with fear and anger, but he continued his awkward walk and Leon followed.

Too large to be blanketed by limbs and leaves, the ruined house looked majestic in the light. The sun shone directly on its crumbling white walls, the gaps in the roof, the vacant windows. On the steps of the house lay another snake, shiny green and as thick as a man's arm at the biceps. It lay oddly, its head draped limp over the steps. Both men stopped in the shallow water.

"It's dead." Lourdes stared out at them through an empty window, a slash of mud across her brow, her hair in clumps about her neck. "You may as well come in," she said flatly, and then disappeared inside the house.

The wide porch was carpeted with grass. One small palm grew from a crack in the brick floor. Leon and Ramon climbed the stairs to the porch together, carefully lifting their feet over the snake. The heavy wooden door, scaled with old paint, had no handle, but when Leon pushed, it swung open easily.

In the great front room, whose wooden beams led to a ceiling more than two stories high, thirty monkeys lay curled on the wooden floor. The door caused a few to scurry, but they settled again, lethargic, content to watch. Most were sleeping. They lay singly, spaced several feet apart. A few lifted their heads to stare at the intruders, their sleepy eyes slits of indifference.

Lourdes leaned against the wall near the window. Her legs, pillars of mud, disappeared beneath the torn hem of Pilar's white dress. Wet and muddy, spotted with blood, the dress fell unevenly across her shoulders, wrinkling against her breasts and stomach. The waist of the skirt hung crooked on her hips.

Ramon could not look away from the monkeys—a tail of one lifting and falling with a thump against the floor, another's head cocking to one side as it scrutinized them with lightless eyes, tiny fingers of a third exploring its own furry belly.

"I can't go in there," Ramon whispered, standing motionless in the doorway.

Leon stepped forward cautiously, edging between the wall and a sleeping monkey, unsure what he would do when he reached Lourdes. He watched his bare feet, the wet prints they left. The monkey Leon had thought asleep suddenly grabbed his pantleg and sank his teeth into the muddy cuff. Leon stopped. The monkey did not move.

"She denied being pregnant," Lourdes said.

Leon looked up at her and then back down at the monkey attached to his leg.

"I beat her stomach to kill the child," she continued. "That's why I went there. I was sure she'd gotten pregnant to take you away from me. She denied it, and denied fixing it so I could go to the university to be rid of me. She denied everything."

Two monkeys rose simultaneously, eyeing Leon, leaning against their knuckles and striding slowly toward him. Leon inched his foot forward; the monkey attached to his pants slid along the floor.

"Watch the goddamn monkeys!" Ramon whispered.

The two darted ahead of Leon, then circled behind him. One tugged at Leon's shirttail, then jumped back. A third joined them, rubbing his eyes as if still sleepy. Leon stepped forward with his free leg, then dragged the other, the clinging monkey turning on its back as it slid like a playful cat.

"She denied it all, Leon. I lost my mind." As Lourdes spoke, her eyes reddened. "I couldn't stand her lies."

Close enough to touch her, Leon hesitated, and the monkey on his cuff tugged sharply. Another extended a long arm, jerked at his pants pocket, and leaped away, circling again. More had approached, stopping a few feet distant, crowded together like a jury.

Lourdes opened her arms and threw herself at Leon, but only to hold him. She began to cry, pressing wet and cold against his chest. At the same time, she kicked the monkey at his leg in the bowels, sending him scooting across the floor. The others backed rapidly away.

"I did it for us," Lourdes told him. "I cut her for us."

"Now there's two you've poisoned," Ramon said, too quietly for anyone to hear, because as he said it, a screech sounded in the back of the room, and the house came suddenly alive.

Monkeys screamed, chattered; they jumped on each other and tumbled off. One leaped to tug the filthy hair of Lourdes, another yanked Leon's shirt sleeve. Tiny fingers tore the muddy dress. A monkey jumped onto her back, cuffing her throat, then sprang quickly off.

Leon and Lourdes tried to crawl out the window, tumbling over one another, simian hands in their hair, at Leon's throat, his ears, around his belt. They grabbed the skirt hem, hung from the back of the dress. A pair of arms wrapped around her bare leg. The house of monkeys thundered with howls.

"Devils!" Ramon screamed, flailing at them with his big arms, retreating to the porch steps as the monkeys poured out of the ruins.

Lourdes dropped from the window across the floor of the porch, scraping her cheek, and the monkey at her legs crawled under her wet skirt. Little fingers. Another thrust himself at her face, hands in her hair. Leon fell across her feet, monkey humping his thigh, monkey tearing his shirt. Lourdes screamed and rolled across the bricks, kicking at her attackers. The dead snake was icy against her cheek. She hurled it at them. They jumped back from it, then began churning around the corpse.

Ramon had already sprinted down the steps and now dove into the water, but the estuary was too shallow, and he landed with a smack. He rose and ran through it, mud and water streaming from him. He fell and rose again.

Leon pulled Lourdes off the porch, but she could not run, stumbling forward, her face pallid, fearful. She raised her skirt, and Leon saw the monkey still there, arms around her bare waist, wrapped like a lover.

Leon grabbed the monkey by the throat, wrenching its neck, but could pull loose only its arms; its legs and tail wrapped around her thighs. Until Lourdes punched its face and gouged its eyes, the monkey clung to her.

They ran, holding hands, swiping at the low limbs, tumbling into the water together, surfacing and wading on.

They retrieved the boat she'd hidden, which the jungle had already begun to claim, tendrils gripping at the wood. Tearing it loose, they climbed in, then pushed against the bottom of the inlet until they floated freely.

Behind them, the noise of the monkeys echoed through the great house, screeches and howls, the thudding of bodies against the floor and walls, a frightening caterwaul. The sounds of chaos.

Ahead of them, Ramon, in the other boat, rowed seriously. "We can talk out there," he called, without looking back, pointing somewhere into the distance.

SUNLIGHT THROUGH the dense foliage dappled their bodies and the surface of the water as the two boats drifted to a stop just beyond the fork of the estuary. Ramon took off his wet shirt and wiped mud from his chest and belly and arms. Then he grabbed the hull of the other boat and pulled it next to his.

"I would let Leon explain," Ramon told Lourdes, "but there's not enough time." His breathing was heavy and his face flushed. "We're playing with the good nature of the tides as it is."

Ramon's voice was full of the awful realities of her life, and Lourdes pulled Leon close to her as if to ward them off.

"What you've done"—Ramon stared at her and shook his head sadly—"we can't undo. But Leon has a plan to help you. It's desperate, but it may work."

"Wait a minute," Leon said, putting his arm around her as he spoke, but Ramon dismissed him with a wave of his big hand.

"Let me say this," he demanded, then looked again at Lourdes, who pressed her head against Leon's chest but peeked out at Ramon. "Leon will go to La Boca and wake my son. You will wait here with me. Leon has given Benjamin a large sum of money, money he embezzled from the hotel, money he stole so that you could go to the university."

Lourdes gripped Leon's shirt with both hands and the material tore. She threw her arms around him.

Leon stared directly at Ramon. "Don't do this," he said.

"You are too modest, my friend. I suggest you keep quiet." He spoke calmly but he thrust his finger at Leon with malice. "My son will return here and meet us, Lourdes. Lourdes, look at me. I'll take you and Benjamin out of here, through the reefs, and south to Santa Josefina. From there you'll catch a bus. You'll go to live with friends of my wife. In a couple of months, after all of this has cooled down a bit, Celita and I will come to visit, and you and Benjamin will marry."

"I'd rather die," she said softly, nuzzling against Leon again.

"Did you hear that?" Leon asked him. "Did that get through to you?"

"Listen to me, Lourdes," Ramon said. "Leon has stolen enough money for both you and Benjamin to go to school." He grabbed the hull of their boat and rocked it to get her attention. "This is Leon's gift of love to you."

She had begun to cry, clutching Leon's shoulders. He continued to stare at Ramon, who said, "I'll explain the details while we wait for Benjamin, but it is important for Leon to leave now. Crawl over to my boat."

She clung to Leon, staring at him so intensely he finally looked away from Ramon to her.

"Everything is ruined," he told her.

"Come with me," she said. She pressed her hands to his neck and searched his eyes. "We can go together."

"No," Ramon said. "Then he would be an accomplice to Pilar's murder. I would have to turn him in myself."

"You would do that?" Leon said.

"A man has obligations," Ramon told him. "I would do whatever was necessary in order to keep my obligations." Then he spoke to Lourdes: "Climb into my boat now."

Lourdes rose to her knees and kissed Leon, her arms around his neck. The white dress was bunched around her waist and stuck to her muddied back. The kiss was fierce and desperate, and Leon broke their embrace.

Lourdes solemnly pressed her cheek against his chest. "Do you want me to go?" she asked him.

"We have no choice," he told her.

"You have to tell me to do it," she said.

He paused only a second. "Go," he said.

She kissed him again, then climbed into the boat with Ramon, where she hid her face with her arms.

"You must not tell Benjamin the money is from Leon," Ramon said to her, patting her muddied hair gently. "I told him I saved it. Otherwise, he would never accept such charity." He glared at Leon. "You hurry."

CELITA SAT on a wooden stool in the shade of her huge and hugely ugly house, her hands in her lap. For more than an hour she had done nothing but sit, and now she listened without expression while Leon explained where Ramon was waiting and why.

"My boy is to row himself out there?" she asked him.

Leon nodded. "I left the boat on the bank of the inlet."

She stood calmly and cracked open the door to the unsightly house. "Benjamin," she called. "Your father wants you." She turned back to Leon. "You men," she said. "There are just enough of you to ruin every woman's life." Then she sat again and stared past him into the late morning glare.

Exhausted, Leon walked with exaggerated slowness down the dusty street. The life he'd designed had turned on him so quickly that he felt breathless and confused, filled with sorrow. He leaned against a scrawny tree to find his breath, but when he stopped walking, his mind began to operate again. Pilar is dead, it said, as if to remind him. Pilar is dead. He pushed himself away from the tree's spindly trunk and resumed his slow pace.

Salt water stung his skin as it evaporated, and dust irritated his nostrils. He stepped on a sharp stone, which bruised his foot, and every new step found the bruise. In the morning light, the hotel looked decrepit, and the dark windows of the damaged floor reminded Leon of the ruins. He would no longer be able to think of this place as paradise.

Heat rose in little waves from the hood of the Powerwagon, parked, as usual, at the hotel door. In his soaked clothes, Leon was in no shape to greet new guests, but he didn't have the energy or the disposition to worry about impressions. He tried to run his fingers through his hair, but it was too tangled and muddy. And the voice inside him repeated, Pilar is dead. Pilar is dead.

Beside the bus, on the cobblestone drive, sat three matching yellow suitcases. Leon recognized them as Janet's, and he stumbled, falling to his knees.

A TALL MAN, a wave of gray in his dark hair, rested against the registration desk smoking a cigarette and counting the bills in his wallet. His nose was faintly purple, and alcohol showed in his eyes, but he was clearly a man who had once been very handsome. At his feet was Janet's overnight bag. He had begun to reach for its handle when he spotted Leon and straightened.

"You're him, aren't you?" he said, his voice high and angry. "You lied to me." He spoke in English and gestured angrily with the hand that held the wallet.

"Christ," Leon said and leaned against the desk.

"Why did you lie to me?" the man demanded, then waved his finger at Leon's filthy clothes. "What the hell happened to you?"

"Where's Janet?" Leon asked him.

"You told me she had left." His lips quivered, and Leon thought he might cry. "You didn't think I'd come, did you? You thought you could trap her here. That's what you thought. I didn't get to be who I am by giving up easily."

"You got there by embezzling," Leon said and straightened,

readying himself for a punch, but the man only closed his wallet and shoved it in his pocket. "Where is Veronica?" Leon asked him.

The man froze for an instant, then took a deep breath. "What made her think she could trust the likes of you?" he asked softly, then added, "She's coming." He picked up the overnight bag and stared squarely at Leon. "You took advantage," he said and walked to the door and outside.

Leon had just reached the stairs when Janet began descending them in her slow and fluid gait. She was smiling.

"You look terrible," she said.

"A friend has died," he told her, and his voice cracked.

Janet paused, two steps above him. "I'm sorry."

He nodded. "You're leaving."

"I want to believe that you lied to me, and to Anthony, because you love me and didn't want me to leave. I want to believe that, and because it doesn't matter now, I'm going to." She descended the final stairs and touched his shirt with her fingertips. "Don't say anything that would change my opinion."

Leon put his arm around her and let his head rest against her shoulder.

"You're getting me dirty," she said, but she didn't pull away.

Leon breathed in her cologne and let more of his weight fall against her. He thought he needed to talk but could find nothing but the obvious to say: Pilar is dead.

"Anthony risked everything by coming here. Hoping to find clues to where I'd gone. He loves me," she said. "He would have been here before, but he was almost caught. He'd been hiding, too." She shook him. "We can't just stand here." Then she whispered, "Who was it who died?"

Leon only rocked his head against her shoulder, and they stood silently on the lobby floor for more than a minute before she took his hand and led him up the stairs to his room, where she left him.

· · ·

LEON SHOWERED and sat on his balcony, wrapped only in a towel. He looked for Ramon's boat, wanting to see the three of them escaping, but all he saw were whitecaps in blue water, white gulls in a cloudless blue sky, pelicans the gray of winter. The boat could have passed by while he was in the shower, or perhaps they hadn't even left yet. He watched the ocean, unsure why he wanted to see them, except that it was a way to avoid thinking about Janet sitting in a restaurant somewhere in La Boca with her lover, or Pilar's body beneath a white sheet.

He did not know how to grieve. He wished there were a dance of grief, a thrashing sort of jig with ritualistic steps and sequences. He needed something specific to do, a means of expression. Having none, he sat on the balcony in the sun, white hotel towel across his waist, and stared at the water.

When he dressed and went downstairs to call June, he found an envelope bearing his name on the registration desk. He did not touch it. Calling required operators in the capital city and in the United States. The number he had for his ex-wife connected him with someone else, a stranger, a woman who sold cosmetics in a large drugstore. She had just graduated from college and liked the idea that he was trying to find a lost love. They talked for twenty minutes. The number he had for Charla resulted in a recording from the phone company. He felt unbearably alone.

He took the envelope upstairs before opening it. A short letter asked him, as next of kin, to officially identify Pilar's body and sign the death certificate required by the government.

In the dark suit that Charla had given him as a Valentine's gift and the thin black tie that June had stolen from her father's closet, Leon walked across town to the cathedral, where the body had been taken. The sun was high and the village seemed leveled by the heat—the shops closed, streets empty. Even the dogs had taken refuge inside friendly houses or on the muddy banks of the estuaries. Birds had abandoned the sky, and Leon might not have seen a single living thing along the way if it had not been for the lizard that scuttled across the road in front of him, and Cruz, who sat on the steps of the bookstore, his head buried in his arms.

No one responded to his knocking at the great cathedral door. He pushed it open, sweating in his dark suit, dreading the sight of the sheeted body. Light entered from high windows on either side of the long building, yellow shafts falling on the rough wooden pews. The gray tile floor had long jagged cracks, which had been filled with cement.

"Is anyone here?" he called and waited, but there was no response. He walked down the aisle, touching the high-backed pews, one by one, apprehension growing in his stomach. He climbed three steps to a simple wooden pulpit. Above him hung a life-size crucifix, the ornate cross made of wrought iron and painted white. The Christ figure looked to be a stuffed man, like a scarecrow or someone hanged in effigy.

"Is there anyone here?" he said again. On either side of the pulpit were black doors. He tried the one to his right first. Inside the dark room, a priest in a white robe sat at a table, his fist against his forehead. He looked to be a thousand years old and raised his frail head so slowly that Leon could have left him without being seen.

"Yes?" the priest said, touching his clerical collar, a clear note of irritation in his voice, his thinning silver hair parted from the rear and combed forward.

"I am here to identify the body," Leon told him.

The old man nodded, then let his head rest against his fist once again. "You must wait with the rest of us."

"Wait for what?" Leon asked.

"For Christ to rise again." The last words came out hoarse, and he bent forward, touching the brocade piping of his cloak, raising it to his eyes for inspection.

"I am here to identify the body of Pilar Rios," Leon said.

"Do you want confession?"

Leon waved his hand to say no. "I'm not Catholic."

The priest's head wobbled. "Irrelevant," he said.

"I have to identify the body of my fiancée," Leon told him. "Please."

The priest nodded. "The Communist." He extended a thin arm. "The other door." Then he turned his finger and bent it, beckoning Leon. "Come here one moment."

Leon took only a half step toward him.

The priest whispered, "Whose side are you on?"

"I don't know what you mean," Leon said. "I'm only here to identify someone who has died."

"Are you on the side of God?" With much deliberateness, the priest stood and pointed up, the sleeve of his cloak collapsing against his shoulder, revealing a thin, age-freckled arm. "God," he said loudly, then coughed forward, wiping his mouth. He lowered his arm and spoke quietly. "God sides with the state." He covered his face with his hands. "It is so hot here." He sat once more. "I've never liked coming here." He coughed again. "Well? Is there something else?"

Leon stepped out and crossed the chancel to the opposite room. The light in the cathedral had changed and he felt disoriented. The Christ figure, he saw, was not a stuffed man, but a crude wooden carving, which had been painted and given a loincloth. Leon pushed open the remaining black door.

Pilar's body lay on a long wooden table. Naked and chalky white, the body cast a faint shadow that spilled over the table and onto the floor. One of the legs would not lie flat, a dark bruise beneath the knee. Leon's heart grew weak. His eyes teared. Until now, some part of him had refused to believe she was dead.

Two old women stood by the table, one near Pilar's head, the other near her feet. They dipped cloths into bowls of water and carefully cleaned the body, oblivious to his entry.

As he watched the women bathe her body, the knowledge that he had not loved Pilar descended upon Leon, and little bul-

lets of sweat appeared across his forehead. He'd had the opportunity to love her and let it pass.

It was this loss that undid him. He began to choke on his
sorrow, coughing and crying.

The woman who washed Pilar's face lifted her head at the
noise. Leon tried to speak to her but could not control himself.
She wore a blue polyester dress. He had seen her before but did
not know her name. The woman who washed Pilar's feet turned
to face him. It was Lourdes's mother.

The sight of her startled him so, his throat cleared and his
crying stopped. "What are you doing here?" he asked her, but
they both responded.

"I am her grandmother," one said.

"I am her grandmother," the other said.

Leon backed out of the room, pulling at the jacket of his suit
because he was suddenly burning up. He lay down in a pew and
waited for the world to settle, clutching the seat, terrified by all
he did not know.

All the while, in the next room, the old women continued
their work, one dutifully washing the chin and cheeks, the soft
lids, the ridge of mouth; the other rubbing the cloth across a calf,
a shin, an ankle, and down the ride of delicate bones to the toes.

RAMON LET the boat lie in the soft sand, too tired to drag it to
his house. Then he remembered that his boat was floating in the
estuary. Benjamin had rowed out to them in it and crawled into
the other skiff. This boat was the one he and Leon had taken
from a neighbor.

He tipped it up on one side, then knelt, turning so that he
could slip his arms under the plank seats and lift the boat onto
his back. Standing caused him to stagger, but he found his balance
and carried the boat across the sandy bank and onto the narrow
street.

Bearing the boat as it had borne him, Ramon felt strong, his shoulders as wide as three men, carrying it as his ancestor had the oxen yoke, but after he knelt to deposit the boat at the spot where he'd stolen it, he became weak once more.

His house was dark. A short note from Celita instructed him to come to the bookstore. Another distance to travel, he thought, stoic in his disappointment. He drank water, ate a banana in three bites, then washed his face, rinsed his arms. He changed into clean clothes, but nothing he did revived his body.

He had made Benjamin row to Santa Josefina in order to give the boy something to do. One of his son's eyes had swollen shut, but he knew the waters as well as Ramon and could have rowed them free of the reefs even if he'd been blinded. Lourdes had been so quiet while they waited in the estuary that Ramon had thought she was sleeping, but she became inconsolable once they entered the ocean, crying into the folds of her bloodstained dress, thrashing out when he tried to comfort her. The ocean, too, was rough, tossing the little boat from side to side, nearly capsizing it time and again.

Benjamin had suggested that Ramon tell a story, and he had quickly agreed. He told of the conquistador's peaceful journey across the ocean, followed by the ungodly trip through the jungle. Which led him to tell about the son of the conquistador, a fisherman who had learned how to converse with sea animals, and the grandson, a musician so talented that his wife had stirred during her own wake in order to listen to him play, and so handsome that one look from him sent her back to the underworld.

The stories had rolled smoothly out of Ramon's mouth, one after another, every phrase in place. By the time he worked his way to the story of his great-grandfather, Juan Matamoros, walking on soles of palm leaves across the top of the thicket, Lourdes had quit crying and rested peacefully on the plank seat, Benjamin had found a rhythm in his rowing to match the cadence of the sentences, and even the ocean had quieted so that the stories could be carried across the expanse of water and the boat could find its way to a safe port.

Ramon told all of the stories he knew, finishing just as the lights of Santa Josefina became visible. He directed Benjamin to let the boat stall while Lourdes slipped out of the soiled dress and dropped into the black water. She disappeared under the surface, and rose with a squeal, the salt water stinging her raw arms and legs. She rinsed the layer of mud off her body and cleaned her hair as best she could. Climbing back into the skiff, she clothed herself in the plain blouse and skirt that Celita had sent with Benjamin. It did not fit her well, and when they were on the wharf, Ramon wished the skirt reached her heels because even in the dim light her chafed and scratched legs shone an eerie pink. This worried him, as did Benjamin's bruised face, because he knew it would be best if they could move among people anonymously.

He took them to a restaurant, passing by a number on the wharf until he came to one with North Americans—a family of redheads. Moments after they'd ordered, a group of soldiers entered, but they sat across the room, near the front window. Ramon watched them throughout the meal, but they did nothing to make him worry. Nonetheless, he waited until they departed before standing and directing Lourdes and his son to the door.

The bus station was not far, and he sat with Benjamin and Lourdes on a hard bench, attempting conversation, but they were all too nervous. Only after they were safely on the bus did Ramon begin his walk back to the pier.

Rowing home through the dark water, he expended his anger and his grief, working the oars harder than necessary, as if he were grappling with something larger than wave and tide, larger even than the vast black ocean. He imagined himself as seen from above—the tiny boat and tinier man; the action of his arms and legs; the light wood of the oars striking the water, disappearing, rising, only to fall again; the movement of the boat forward, rocked and lifted by swells; the silent water all around, ready to envelop boat, envelop man.

It was during this long passage that Ramon was struck by an

illumination, the gift and curse that was passed from generation to generation in his family as surely as were cleft chins and webbed toes in another. The knowledge that so suddenly arrived was this: His stories were lost to him. In order to help his son, he had first priced them and then cast them out to the sea, and they would not return.

One cannot lament the knowledge that comes from an illumination, no more than one can insult any gift once it has been received. In accepting it, Ramon was able to see by its light, which permitted him to view clearly what had previously been obscured. His life lay before him like a patient ready for surgery, and he examined it closely. This is what was revealed: Ramon Matamoros loved his wife. He loved his son. He loved La Boca. He was unduly fond of fishing. He had been given a gift and had misused it. There would be a hole in his life without the stories, but something would come along to take its place.

And quite by accident he cast the light from the illumination on Leon, and Ramon came to understand his secrets.

This insight, returning to him while he changed his clothes, accomplished what food and bathing had not. His body revived and lent him the strength to walk to the hotel before he went to the bookstore, to run his fingers through the sandy beach in search of stones large enough to throw.

Standing beneath Leon's window, Ramon launched the first rock and it found its target, breaking one of the little windows in the French door. "Leon," he called and hurled another, this one bouncing off the wrought-iron railing. "Leon!" he yelled. "Show yourself."

The door to the balcony opened and Leon appeared. "Ramon? What are you doing?" He was dressed in a white shirt and dark pants, although there had been no light in his room, and there was none still. Ramon hesitated, realizing that Leon was suffering. Some of his energy faded, enough for him to realize again the extent of his fatigue.

Leon leaned over the railing, a badge of sweat in the center of his chest. "Why don't you come in, and we'll have a drink?"

Ramon shook his head. "The children are on their way, Leon. But I had to come by and tell you something."

"Come in and tell me," he said. "We could talk. A drink. Please."

"No," he said. "No drink." He shook his head again and stared briefly at the ocean. "It came to me while I was rowing home," he said and pointed up at the balcony. "I know why you poisoned that man." He let his arm drop as even that gesture required too much of him.

Leon suddenly made himself more erect. He touched his collar, then sank his hands into the pockets of his pants. "All right," he said. "Tell me."

"Because he *knew* you," Ramon called.

Leon stared down at him and said nothing. A wind off the water lifted his hair.

THE DOOR to the bookstore was not locked. Ramon entered quietly. The books in their places on the shelves, unchanged by all that had happened, angered him, but it was a shallow feeling, designed to mask his sorrow, and it passed. He heard his wife speaking in the next room, although he couldn't make out precisely what she was saying. Maria Peralta Cardenas and Angelica Roches waited with her. It shamed him that he'd stopped to torment Leon before going to comfort his wife and the others. But it was done, and he would not waste time regretting it.

The three women sat at the kitchen table identically, elbows just off the edge, arms extended toward the middle, shoulders rounded by sadness.

"They are on their way," he told them.

They turned to him only briefly, weariness in their eyes. He pulled an empty chair to the table, looking for the bloodstain. A phantom of it remained, but the walls and floor had been scrubbed. He admired that about women, the ability to attend to important details during a tragedy of any sort.

"Life is hard," Angelica Roches said, addressing no one in particular. "Don't you think?"

Celita patted her hand.

"This one is," Maria said. Then she spoke to Ramon. "What story are you going to tell the others? How are you going to protect Lourdes?"

"No story," he said. "We will simply say that the government killed Pilar. No one will question that or dare to cause trouble."

Maria Peralta nodded, drearily. "One lie is as good as another."

"Are you hungry?" Celita asked him. "I made black beans and rice."

Ramon shook his head. He smelled the beans then, as if the aroma had not existed until his wife spoke.

"What will become of us now?" Angelica asked. She turned to her friend. "What is there left for our future?" she asked Maria.

"I can't see any future," Maria said angrily. "I can't remember the past, and right now, I can't bear to look at the present."

"How has her cousin taken this?" Ramon asked her.

"Who?" Maria asked.

Ramon pointed to the ceiling. "Samuel."

"Oh," Maria said. "Her revolutionary. He is sad. We all are sad, Ramon." She stood then. "I think I will eat something." She looked at the stove, but took no steps, as if held in place by a powerful force.

Celita stepped to her side and placed her hands on Maria's shoulders, guiding her back into the chair. "Let me fill you a plate," she said, hurrying across the room. "We should all eat, don't you think?"

"I was afraid the shock might kill him," Ramon said, pointing up again.

Maria looked up at the cracks in the ceiling, then down at the bowl of rice and beans placed before her.

"We must take him home," Celita said as she put bowls in front of Angelica and Ramon. She sat beside her husband. "Benjamin is gone. We have the room."

"Of course," Ramon said, pleased because he imagined that caring for the dying man would fill the gap left by the loss of the stories.

"My child is gone, too," Angelica reminded them.

"Mine too," Maria said. "My little squash."

"Then you'll help us," Celita said.

In the center of the table, they all touched hands.

THE BUS that carried Benjamin and Lourdes was stopped six miles short of its destination by members of the army. Lourdes had been sleeping on Benjamin's shoulder, her scoured legs sticking out into the aisle. Twice during the long ride she had kissed him on the cheek, then returned immediately to sleep, leaving him to wonder.

A soldier in fatigues and a camouflage helmet climbed into the bus and talked in hushed tones with the driver for several minutes. He accepted a cup of coffee from a silver thermos and drank it in one gulp, raising his black combat boot and resting it on the seat beside the driver's leg. A rifle hung at his side, the butt end rattling against the vibrating gearshift. From the moment he entered, the bus had become quiet except for the squeals of piglets from a cardboard box.

A second soldier, an officer, boarded the bus and immediately instructed the driver to kill the idling engine, which made the silence louder. He shone a blinding flashlight into the aisle, then interrogated a number of passengers, asking vague questions in a loud voice about where they were going and what they had been doing the night before, moving to a new person before an answer was complete. He worked his way to the rear of the bus and then returned to the front.

He asked nothing of Benjamin or Lourdes, but before leaving he walked back down the aisle, tapping the shoulders of three young men, who were then taken outside. Benjamin, near the back of the bus, watched him approach with mounting terror.

The officer looked Benjamin in the eyes and squatted in the aisle, a man in his fifties with sun-darkened skin and deep lines about his eyes. He leaned across Lourdes and touched the bruises on Benjamin's face, prodding gently and then harder. Benjamin squeezed her hand so tightly that Lourdes jumped, causing the officer to notice her raw arms and legs. He moved his hand from Benjamin's face to touch her legs, but before he reached them, she said, "It's contagious." He withdrew his hand and stepped away from them.

And so Benjamin was not drafted.

In the darkness of Pilar's room, Ramon embraced Samuel and lifted him from the bed. He weighed no more than paper, but he was hot against Ramon's chest and his thighs were damp with sweat. Carrying Samuel, Ramon felt his own strength return.

"You'll be living with me and my wife," he said.

Samuel's voice returned distant and low. "You must be careful."

Ramon agreed. "I am aware of that."

"You should start thinking of ways to dispose of my body now."

"And Pilar's body?"

Samuel shook his head feebly. "There can be no marker. That's how people are caught. Do not fill out any papers."

"Cruz will destroy the death certificate," Ramon said and paused. "As it turns out, I knew Pilar when she was a tiny girl. She hadn't been given a name because her father wouldn't recognize her. I only just discovered that. And there's more. She had two paternal grandmothers."

"That sounds like an interesting story," Samuel said.

"Yes, but I am not the one to tell it." Ramon looked down the flight of stairs. "I don't know Pilar's real name even now."

"Or mine," Samuel said.

"Or yours." He turned and angled them through the door and into the hall. Light from the kitchen cut a harsh angle across the steps. "Perhaps I should learn them."

Samuel's head bounced as they descended the stairs as if he were nodding in agreement, the sharp bristles of his unshaven chin rubbing against Ramon's chest.

*I*N THE END, Ramon was unable to tell the story. His gift had truly abandoned him.

"A little over a month after a local murder, the government sent planes to bomb the city of La Boca," he began, but then he backtracked to the day Leon had arrived, and then back further, to the birth of Renaldo Peralta, the ruse carried out by Maria Peralta and Angelica Roches, the building of the great house in the jungle—and Ramon was never able to return to his original purpose.

He altered the beginning and tried again.

"On a dark night when even the monkeys were quiet, pilots directed their planes toward La Boca with the intention of destroying the village." No sooner had he said this than he started describing the landscape, including the thicket and how it had been eroded during the time of Juan Matamoros and Father Montoya because of the noise of extinct animals and the railroad that never came, and, once again, Ramon lost the thread with which he had begun.

"There are a hundred ways to lose the things you love," Ramon began the final time, then hesitated, a look of grief crossing his face, and this was all he said.

Ultimately, years after the events had settled into memory, the story was told by another mouth.

"Following the murder of the most beautiful woman in the world, the skies of La Boca filled with bombs," Benjamin said, and saying it led him to the sentence that followed, and then the next, until the story was complete.

MINUTES before noon on a sweltering day roughly a month after Pilar's death, a stranger appeared at Ramon's door. A middle-aged man with dark skin and short hair, he possessed a blandness that made him look official and menacing. Little bulges beneath his eyes caused them to droop, which gave him an air of sadness as well as foreboding.

Without any introduction, he said, "I would like to buy you lunch, Mr. Matamoros. I have questions."

"You are interested in a tour of La Boca?" Ramon asked, although he was already sure this person was some sort of policeman.

"No," the man replied sadly. "I arrived by bus only just now, and I intend to leave on the same bus this evening. I'm known for my efficiency." He ran his fingers across his eyebrows to squeeze out drops of perspiration. Across one arm, he draped an expensive green jacket that matched his pants, and now he shifted the jacket from one arm to the other, staring at his shoes, which were black and anonymous. He gave the impression of being a man resigned to a task he did not relish. "In my line of work, efficiency is a very important commodity," he said, one sad eye twitching slightly.

"A commodity? You sell efficiency?" Ramon smiled, but a dark look settled on the man's face, and Ramon saw that it was a mistake to joke. "I would be delighted to have lunch with you," he said, fear making his voice as thin as wire.

The stranger walked casually, but he took long strides— efficient strides, Ramon thought. He wondered whether this policeman had come about Pilar or Samuel or—he did not want to think it possible—about Benjamin or Lourdes.

Samuel had lived with them almost two weeks before dying one night in his sleep. Maria Peralta and Angelica Roches had helped with his care, but Ramon and Celita had borne the majority of the load, one that had increased as he neared death. Ramon could not say that he had liked Samuel, although he had mourned his death. His feelings had not been confused but contradictory.

There had been nothing pretty about him. The misshapen mound his body made beneath the sheets had filled Ramon with revulsion. His breath had smelled like turpentine, and he was disagreeable, wanting Ramon to question every little thing, saying daily, "I do not believe in God." But each morning when Ramon peeked into his room, he was relieved to see the battered chest rise and fall and to hear his tortured breathing, or to find him awake and exchange a smile—Samuel's smile was an ugly thing, but it was pleasing to see. He had been buried alongside Pilar in the jungle, two unmarked mounds in a tiny clearing.

As death entered Ramon's thoughts, so did it seem to join them as they strolled across town, a third presence, an extra shadow. And Ramon wondered whether he would survive the afternoon.

"I don't like this town," the man said. "My country wants to make use of my special knowledge of this place and so I have come, but I do not like it here and I intend to leave in just a few hours. That is why I have come to see you, Mr. Matamoros. I have reason to believe that you will be able to answer all my questions."

"I am a fisherman," Ramon said nervously, "and a tour guide."

"And something of a local historian, are you not?"

"Well, yes." Ramon brightened despite himself. "I could tell you a little about the history of La Boca, if that is what you're after."

"That is precisely what I am after. Some recent history." They had reached Restaurante Los Comales, and he held open the door for Ramon to enter. "I want the answers to a specific bit of recent history."

Los Comales was empty and something in the echo of their feet on the wood floor made Ramon believe that it had been abandoned. They seated themselves at a table near the window. The way the man laid his jacket across the table made Ramon think they would not be eating, and Ernesto did not come out of the kitchen, despite Ramon's silent prayers.

"We are going to lunch without the distraction of food and drink," the stranger said. "Do you find that agreeable?"

Ramon nodded and clasped his hands together on the table, certain now that he would be killed.

"A man has disappeared, Mr. Matamoros." He spoke into his lap, his elbows on the table and bent so that he held his forehead with his fingertips. "A boy from the United States of America. It seems that his parents had advised him against coming to our country, but he came anyway." He glanced up and winced a smile, which made him look familiar, and Ramon searched his memory, thinking he might save himself if he could recognize the man. There was little logic in this assumption, but a man in Ramon's situation wants to act, and trying to remember was the only thing he could do.

"When this young man failed to return in time for the school semester, his parents made an appeal to a United States senator, who, in turn, contacted us. As you have guessed, I work for the government. An investigation was begun. Let me tell you something about investigations like these—we don't like them." He scowled and shook his head. "The Communists are waging a war against us, but we have to baby-sit American hippies." He bent over, his head dipping beneath the table, then rising. "You will pardon me." He lowered his head again and removed his shoes and thin black socks, which he placed on the table beside his jacket. "Wouldn't you like to remove your shoes?"

"No," Ramon said immediately, then added, "They're just sandals. . . . I'm used to the heat."

The man nodded vaguely. "You think I'm going to kill you."

Ramon said nothing, racing through his memory—tourists he had met, people who had moved away.

"We had to conduct an investigation, Mr. Matamoros—I say 'we,' but I was not involved at the time. Anyway, we didn't have a guess as to where this boy was and a quick inquiry turned up nothing but to confirm that he had entered the country and disappeared. A letter was sent to the senator saying what is said in such situations, that it was rumored the boy had been kidnapped and killed by leftist guerrillas. With more military aid, we added, such tragedies could be avoided." He smiled again, the same familiar smile. "You see, we try to turn these petty irritations into something positive." He suddenly bent over the table, his face close to the shoes. "These smell," he said and swept them away with his arm. The shoes clattered to the floor.

"Two weeks after we filed this report, the senator wired again with new information. A postcard had arrived from the boy after spending weeks in the mail. It had been mailed from La Boca. Would you like to see it?" From the breast pocket of the jacket, he extracted a picture postcard. It featured a burro and a cart beneath the pink leaves of a jacaranda. On the opposite side was a brief letter.

> Dear Mom and Dad,
> La Boca is a letdown, but the girl at the bookstore wants to carry my book. I'll probably beat this card back to the States. Nothing much to report. My Spanish is getting better. May ask bookstore girl for date.
> Love,
> Stuart

"Of all the kinds of people that I dislike, the two that anger me most are writers and hippies. This man was both." He sighed and shook his head. "But the United States is our closest ally. You are aware of that?"

"Of course." Ramon had grown calmer. This man was a government agent, but he wanted to know what happened to the boy with the green backpack and the dirty pants. He wasn't searching for Samuel or investigating Pilar's death. Ramon began to believe that he might live through the day after all.

"My job is to return to the capital with a suitable story. The truth, well, that might be rewarding, but it might just be a bother. You see, one of my superiors looked into our records on this boy and found only the letter filed two weeks earlier, which said he probably had been kidnapped and killed by terrorists. So I have been sent to La Boca to search for terrorists, even though I know the report was a piece of fiction. Do you see how it is?" he asked, seeming to grow angry as he spoke. "Do you see the kind of shit we have to put up with?"

"Terrorists in La Boca?" Ramon dared a tiny smile. "Let me set your mind at ease . . ."

"I am investigating the disappearance of a piece of trash in a town that I despise because of a self-generated rumor and a post-card featuring an ass. Is it possible to imagine a greater travesty? But I am a servant of our government, and I want to help in any manner that I can. I am sure that you feel the same." He stared pointedly.

"What is it that you'd like me to do?" Ramon asked, his throat dry, but the panic had left him.

"This United States senator wants only an acceptable story for the parents—he is sympathetic to our plight here." He sighed again, as if bored. "Have I made my position clear, Mr. Mata-moros? I was given this assignment because of my special knowl-edge of La Boca, and so I am making use of that knowledge and coming to you. I am quite sure that you can give me the infor-mation I need—details that are required to satisfy everyone. Something that sounds like the truth. Otherwise, well, I will have to walk these hot streets and interrogate people."

"I still don't understand what it is that you—"

"Tell me a story, Ramon. One that will save me the work of investigating in this shithole, only to have to fabricate a story of my own anyway."

Ramon was positive now that he knew the man. "Your special knowledge of La Boca—you used to live here?"

"That is not a question you ask a man of my position." He whispered this. "I imagine you know that the bus driver is virtually an idiot, but hotel manager confirmed that the boy had been a guest."

"The boy with the backpack."

"His name is Stuart Rice, and I would like you to tell me what has become of him. As long as it is convincing, my superiors will be satisfied and the United States government will make excuses to his parents." He withdrew a small notebook from the jacket. "I have a typewriter at the hotel. Before I leave, you will sign the report."

"Let me think for a moment." Ramon did not want an investigation, which was sure to reveal Pilar's murder, and so he looked for a way to begin a story, but since the evening of his illumination, he had not even attempted to create a story.

"The boy wore a backpack wherever he went," Ramon began, lifting the tone of his voice, but this led him nowhere. "His glasses were as thick as my little finger." He displayed the finger to the agent, who merely stared at him, ballpoint pen suspended over the lined sheets of the notebook as if he were a student. It was this image that woke Ramon's memory. "Oh, my God," he said. "We all thought you were dead."

"Don't digress," the man said angrily.

"Have you seen Rosa?" Ramon asked him.

"No." The man tapped the table with his pen. "Would she be able to answer my questions?" His eyebrows arched and sweat trickled from them. "Do you have a story for me, Mr. Matamoros?"

No longer fearful, Ramon had to speak his disbelief. "Rosa returned with your body. I helped carry it to the grave."

"She did that?" He straightened. "She buried someone and said it was me?" He almost smiled, then his face grew dark again. "Who did the bitch marry?"

"No one, Rudy," Ramon said. "She hasn't seen a man in all these years—that I know of."

"Really?" He seemed to consider this for a moment. "And you would know, wouldn't you? That's why I want help with this, Ramon. There is nothing that happens in La Boca that you do not know. I want you to concentrate on my mission. Surely you understand why it is hard for me to be here. All I need are a few details of his disappearance. You've been telling stories since you were a boy. We couldn't get you to shut up." Rudy Ojeda said this without any humor. "Save us all some trouble."

"All right, yes." Ramon waited for the story to present itself as it had in the past. He knew enough, a few facts—all he had to do was fill in what he didn't know. But his gift had left him, and he could relate only the little that he remembered. "The boy asked me to get him a prostitute. He wanted to know where the whores were." Again, he was stuck. "Stuart Rice appeared in La Boca one day—he took the bus through the jungle, a long and rough ride. He wore a big green backpack and dirty pants—he never changed his pants. His glasses were there, thick eyeglasses. He didn't want a tour. This old couple came with him, on the same bus, and the woman got bit by a monkey—it wasn't my fault, exactly, but they were with me on a tour. And the woman, the pretty Oriental woman. She came on the same bus . . ."

"What happened to this boy, Ramon?"

"It won't come to me," he said.

"Why do you make this difficult?"

"He went hiking in the jungle and he died."

"That is not a story. I cannot use that. We'd have to find evidence of the body. I want a truth that I can use. Something convincing. Concentrate."

Ramon tried several times, but he did not know what had happened to Stuart Rice, and his speculations were feeble.

"I find your answers distressing." Rudy Ojeda closed his notebook.

"Just a minute, Rudy." Ramon covered his face with his hands. "He hiked into the jungle. . . . He thought that he could write a book about . . . this hike . . . he was stupid, wasn't he?"

Rudy Ojeda slipped on his shoes and socks.

"Give me a moment," Ramon said. "You don't need to conduct an investigation. I have been telling stories all my life—boring people from the cradle. Now this Stuart Rice. He checked into the hotel—you know that—he got a room and he thought he would eat . . . something."

Rudy Ojeda rose from the table and headed toward the door.

"I will sign your report," Ramon called. "Let us say that he died of thirst. The body was never found—no, he drowned. He was swimming. I will take you to the spot. Now wait, I was one of your pallbearers, Rudy. You wait a moment."

But Rudy Ojeda had already stepped into the street and begun asking questions of pedestrians. Cruz was forced to delay his return drive for three days, and when Rudy Ojeda left La Boca, he took with him the exhumed bodies of Samuel and Pilar.

ROSA'S REACTION upon seeing her lost husband was nothing like she'd anticipated in any of her stories. She did not charge at him in rage. She did not faint from shame. She did not call him an assassin and attempt to strangle him. Instead, she thought, What a fine-looking man he turned out to be. And then she laughed at herself and dismissed her students. She couldn't remember the last time she had laughed so.

Rudy Ojeda had entered the schoolhouse under the pretense of interrogating her. He had bathed after lunch, shaved for the second time that day, and cleaned his suitcoat with a sponge before walking to the school. Yet upon entering the little building, he pretended not to recognize his wife. Rosa, however, didn't permit this act.

"You're more handsome than I would have guessed," she said,

her voice softer than it had been in years. From the changes that passed over his face, she imagined that he was struggling with the urge to tell her how bad she looked, how ugly she had turned.

When he finally spoke, he said, "Rosa, you shouldn't have left me." And there were tears in the assassin's eyes.

They talked for more than an hour, but only this one moment touched Rosa's heart. Neither could muster the rage that each had expected. They spoke of Rosa's parents, how long they had lived, the details of their deaths. Rudy asked about no one else in town; there was no one else he cared about. "La Boca hasn't changed," he said. "Still too hot to breathe here. The hotel is in ruin, but otherwise . . ." He paused and looked out the window. "You never remarried."

She told him no.

He ended with business. He knew already of the Communist's death, but wanted to know where he could find the body.

"Bodies are sacred things," Rosa told him, and shortly afterward, he left.

In the days that followed, Rosa did her art. She wrote a romantic story about a heroine who wavers between two men before deciding to take neither, setting out on her own to remake her world. Throughout the writing of the story, Rosa remained in control, and, for once, her past did not enter the tale. Then Rosa designed a new still life, including a mimosa bloom along with her regular objects—the chalk eraser, the old shoe, a few shells, sharpened pencils. The flower rose gracefully from the shoe's opening. The eraser and pencils took perfect shape. Even the shells remained shells. And Rosa was happy.

After two days of this success, she took an afternoon off, making herself a picnic supper—something she had not done for a decade—and eating it on the beach. That evening she reread her new stories and reexamined her new drawings, and she saw that they were terrible—sentimental and false or drab and without mystery.

She dug out some of her old work, the novel she liked best,

the still life that included the calcified turd. They too were terrible—overwrought and senselessly dark.

Rosa stayed up through the night burning everything that she had ever written, all of the drawings, and the menstrual paintings, whose power now escaped her. She canceled classes, and by noon of the following day the only evidence of her art was a circle of ashes near the thicket. After lunch, she moved her desk beneath a window and set a stack of fresh paper in the center of it, then began to write the story that would become her life's work, a fiction that would embody the truth of her being, although she would not appear in the story and there would be no character who resembled her. The protagonist, she decided, would be a man. The gothic settings and romantic characters of her past stories she abandoned; all the events would take place on recognizably human ground. She would write about an unlucky man, by which she meant a man whose desires did not suit him—not that they were intrinsically bad, but they were wrong for him.

Rosa took a pen from the desk drawer, arranged the paper to her liking, and set her hands to the work.

ANGRY WITH GOD, Maria Peralta had begun undertaking tasks that would displease Him.

Her first act had been to forgo mass, but she suspected that He might not notice, as she had been irregular in her attendance for years. So she became slovenly, wearing the same dress for days without bathing, but the polyester never wrinkled and the dirt didn't show. She cared for the ill Communist until his death, walking across town to wash his chest and change his sheets, taking him soup and herbal tea, but she couldn't convince herself that God was so small-minded as to have any interest in politics. She spat on a hen's egg, then ate it raw. This was a pagan ritual, and she knew that God would be angered, but she recalled that it was a plea to the deity of fertility to prevent pregnancy, and

God would probably think she was joking. In her prayers, she chastised Him for being cowardly and cruel and petty.

She wanted to enrage God but could find no act sufficiently wicked—none, at least, that she had the heart to perform. She began going to the south estuary in the middle of the day and strolling along the muddy bank. Shallow, stagnant, and malodorous, the inlet was useless to humans and animals, and so Maria imagined it to be a repository of baseness, although she knew it was really just a lousy pit of seawater. Caught between her deep respect for all things living and spiritual, and her outrage at the loss of her granddaughter, she found herself acting out of opposing impulses, which made her behavior seem ridiculous even to herself, even as she acted.

One morning as she walked beside the dark water swatting at gnats, she heard a wet flutter and splash, and followed the sound down the bank. An enormous bird had crashed into the inlet and now struggled to get out, raising its great wings, clawing the water. This bird frightened her and Maria Peralta approached it cautiously. She thought it might be a messenger from God sent to scold her.

As she neared, she saw that it was a vulture and that it was dying. The water streaming from its bill was colored with blood. By the time the bird had climbed out of the estuary, it was exhausted and collapsed against the black earth. Maria examined it from a short distance, and the bird seemed to look her over, too.

"Are you the buzzard I spoke with a few weeks ago?" she asked.

The vulture lifted its head and one wing, then its pink neck gave out and its head bounced against the ground. The wing rose and fell another few times. The great bird writhed in pain.

Certain that it was the same vulture she had conversed with over the nature of life and death, Maria laid her head near the bird's to hear its last words and see if it recognized its mortality at last. The bird snapped at her once, blood flying from the nostrils of its beak. Its long neck held an enormous bulge, and Maria suspected that this was causing its death.

Within a few minutes, the vulture died. Maria took the bird's own claws and ripped open its throat. What she found was solid and smooth and covered with blood. She rinsed it in the estuary. It was the cracked lens from a pair of eyeglasses.

Maria placed the lens on one of her narrow shelves. For reasons that were mysterious to her, the discovery of this bit of glass permitted her to forgive God.

LEON NO LONGER felt the panic of dislocation when he woke each morning but felt the anguish of being absolutely located, down to the precise placement of his body in his wide bed. Worse, he had begun to remember his dreams, and Pilar inhabited them all. Dreams of strolling through a snowfall. Dreams of lying together on a couch, legs intertwined, listening to the rhythms of a distant band. Dreams that broke his heart. The dreams were what made his waking knowledge of place intolerable.

On this particular morning, his bed was made unbearable by a dream of standing beside Pilar at a kitchen sink, sunlight falling across their faces from an open window, a light breeze cooling their cheeks, while their hands swirled in warm soapy water and emerged with shimmering white china. They placed the dishes on countertops made luminescent by the sunshine, jazz playing all the while on the radio, a black woman singing of her devotion to a man who drank and fooled around and did not love her.

Leon sat up in his bed and stared at his white rectangular room—the smell of Pilar's sun-warmed skin still in his nostrils—and he was in agony.

Later the same day he received an important telephone call. "You've compromised me." It was his friend from college whose father was in the national cabinet and had arranged this job for him. "But I'm going to save you anyway."

"What are you talking about?" Leon asked him.

Rudy Ojeda had filed a report saying that Leon had been consorting with Communists. "What did you think you were doing?" his friend said. "Don't you understand what kind of position this puts me in?"

"Pilar?" Leon said. "This is about Pilar?"

"Is that what she called herself?" The phone went quiet, although Leon could hear a muffled exchange of voices. Then his friend returned, his voice almost a whisper. "You're lucky that when she turned up, she turned up dead."

Leon could not reply to this.

"Now, listen. There's going to be some shit coming down, and it's coming down soon." He ranted about violence and order for a few moments before telling Leon to be dead sure that he and his guests were inside before dark that evening.

"What is going to happen?" Leon asked.

"You just stay inside. The hotel will be safe." And then he lowered his voice. "We don't know how many revolutionaries there are in La Boca, but we're going to take care of them all." He ended by speaking a warning. "If you tell anybody about this call, I'm not responsible for what could happen."

"La Boca will be bombed?" Leon said.

"You didn't ask that," his friend told him.

Leon climbed the stairs to the ruined floor where he could look over the village. He sat on the barstool and leaned with his elbows against the windowsill, his arms in the moonflower vines. He rested his head on his hands and closed his eyes.

The weeks that followed Pilar's murder had been a time of mourning and resignation for Leon, as well as one of indecision. Twice he had packed his canvas suitcases in order to leave with Cruz and return to the United States, and twice he had decided against it, having forced himself to recall the grind of a nine-to-five job, the vacuous life of adult dating, nightly television, and popular music. He had made himself think through a typical day in the States: the dread of a workday morning, the false routines with business associates, the drink with lunch. . . . He never reached day's end before unpacking. Nevertheless, the desire that had led him to leave his country and seek La Boca had vanished upon seeing Pilar's body in the cathedral, and nothing had filled its void. Had one of the villagers taken Leon to mass during that long month, he would have let faith fill the vacancy. Had Cruz brought him a dying revolutionary, he would have let idealism occupy his heart and the hard work of nursing take up his time. Had a new woman entered his life, Leon would have loved her.

He could not bear his own incompleteness, and so it was that while he laid his head among the cordate leaves of the moon-flower vine desire returned to him, the desire for resurrection.

It seemed to him that he had paused at the window a long while, so long that he jerked up his head to be sure that it was still afternoon, but he had taken less than an hour to decide what to do.

He found his doorman mopping the lobby floor. Leon handed him a sealed envelope and asked him to deliver it immediately to Ramon Matamoros.

BLANKETS AND mattresses were dragged to the hotel. Restaurant owners brought food, and several men carried wash barrels filled with drinking water into the lobby, which, by the time they arrived, had already become crowded with people, as had the bar and all the rooms, the hallways, the stairs, and even the ruined top floor.

Angelica Roches was one of several people who had decided not to take shelter in the Esperanza. When the afternoon grew late, she folded her apron and placed it beneath the bakery counter, then packed a paper bag full of rolls and pastries. Maria Peralta had agreed with her friend that the hotel should not be their sanctuary, and she was in the back of the bakery filling another paper bag with Angelica's clothing.

Together, they walked through every room one final time,

Maria carrying the paper bags in her arms as if they were about to go out for a picnic.

"Why are we leaving on the lights?" Angelica asked.

"It is our obligation to combat darkness," Maria told her, "and this night may be La Boca's darkest."

While Maria looked through Angelica's jewelry for any trinkets she might want to save, Angelica returned to the front counter, just in time to see Leon step into view. Out of habit, she dusted the bakery counter with flour.

Leon wore a tie and a serious expression as he crossed her threshold and stepped toward her. In a soft voice and with much formality, he asked if she would be his guest at the hotel for the duration of this awful night. As he spoke, he placed an open hand on the countertop.

This offer, delivered personally, touched Angelica, but she politely told him no. When he left, she called Maria Peralta into the room. "He was here," she said. "He left his print."

Maria Peralta leaned over the counter to study the palm and spread fingers. "My," she said, "what big hands he has." She counted the creases beneath his little finger, measured the lengths of his heartline and lifeline, comparing the size of his thumb against her own. Finally, she raised her head. "He sincerely wants to be good," she told her friend. Then she added, "That is often the most dangerous kind of person."

"You can see all of that from this print?" Angelica asked her.

"I'm guessing," Maria said. "All I see here is the child's outline of a buzzard."

Angelica bent over the tracing of his hand, puffed her cheeks, and blew. A fine spray of powder lifted into the air, and the hand vanished.

ANGELICA AND Maria Peralta arrived at the Matamoros house an hour before dark. Ramon and Celita were ready to go. They too had packed a bag with food, and Ramon had filled a canteen with water.

"I hope we will all fit," Angelica said as she led them across town and to the south estuary, where they followed the narrow path that ran alongside the inlet. They walked single file and in silence. A branch protruding from the thicket tore one of Angelica's paper bags, and a roll fell out and tumbled into the water. They paused to watch it float away before continuing down the path.

"This was my home," Angelica told them when they reached the opening in the thicket wall. On their hands and knees, they crawled into the hollowed-out room. Limbs crisscrossed above them and they had to remain crouched. "It used to be bigger," she said.

"Time shrinks everything," Maria replied.

Because the thicket was so dense as to prevent the passage of sound, Angelica had hoped it would prevent the movement of time as well. Secretly, she desired to feel like a child, so that the world, which had become hopelessly ugly, would seem new again. Instead, when she sat in the dirt next to Ramon, she suddenly felt like an adolescent on the verge of discovering the joys of sexual love. This confused her, but Maria's explanation helped.

"You're finally losing your mind," she said. "Enjoy it."

Angelica smiled, the gaps in her smile now taking up more space than her teeth.

As night grew near, Maria positioned herself in the narrow passage to the outside, her head emerging from the aperture like a turtle's from its shell. She wanted to hear the planes approach, hoped to catch a glimpse of them. On her stomach, her hands cradling her chin, she waited.

Ramon and Celita sat together quietly. They did not desire to see the planes. Ramon wished that he could tell a story, something to calm himself and the others, but he was no longer capable. Although it was La Boca that was threatened, he worried for his son, who was far away. "What do you think Benjamin is doing right now?" he asked his wife.

Celita, who had taken a malfunctioning flashlight with her, was trying to repair it by the light of a single candle. "It's too late for classes," she said.

"Do you think he's in the library?" Ramon said. "Do you think he and Lourdes might be studying together at this very moment?"

"They're probably eating," Celita told him, and as she spoke, she pulled their sack of food near her and began considering their meal.

"Do you think they're eating out?" Ramon asked softly. "Or are they home?"

Celita put the broken flashlight beside the sack of food, and she kissed Ramon softly on the cheek.

"I think they're eating at home," he whispered to her, as if it were a matter of great importance.

Seconds later, Maria called into the room. She could hear the planes. Neither Ramon nor Celita moved, except to hold hands, but Angelica wriggled forward on her side to join Maria in the opening. The sky was dark and spotted with clouds.

"There's one," Maria said and pointed above, a black shape moving purposefully across the background of cloud.

Angelica stuck her head out to gaze into the gathering darkness, but what she saw coursing the sky was not an airplane carrying bombs to destroy a tiny village, but the long narrow head and the great winged arms of the pterodactyl.

"It's beautiful," she said.

LEON WAITED for the bombs in his room, stepping out onto the balcony at regular intervals to check the skies. By eight that evening, nine people were sitting on his bed and another twelve on the floor, the crush of humanity flowing into every available space. By ten after eight, he was too nervous to be sober in a crowded room and he made his way to the bar, stepping over the children who slept in the darkened hall, the old men and women who sat on the stairs smoking, the families who huddled together on blankets spead over the lobby's tiles, the embracing couples, the adults on their knees praying, the adolescent pairs sharing blankets and trying to hide smiles born of excitement and dread. A few of the children who lay curled on the floor lifted their heads to stare at Leon as he picked his way across the lobby. One touched the leg of his pants with her fingers.

At the bar, he took two beers and a fifth of tequila, then instructed his bartender to give free drinks to anyone who asked. Tucking the bottle of tequila under his arm, he tried to find Ramon among the crowd. He asked several people if they had seen him. He was about to start up the stairs, but the drone of an airplane stopped him. The quiet room became utterly silent.

At the back door, where the noise of the ocean almost drowned out the sound of the approaching planes, he stepped outside and turned his eyes to the sky. He could hear the planes but he could not see them. Their steady note grew nearer. He waited.

"It would be tidy to say that the bombing marked the end of La Boca," Benjamin would say, years later, "but it was a village that had survived for a thousand years, and the bombing only encouraged industry among the survivors, who, as it turned out, included everyone." At this point in his story, he would usually shrug. "Perhaps the bombardiers were novices, or maybe they held the mission in such contempt they did not care about its success. It is possible, of course, that they were drunk. Or it could be that the sleepy little town looked too much like paradise to be destroyed.

"A dozen windows were broken, the south estuary was enlarged, segments of the cobblestone street were damaged, but mainly the bombs just shook the earth." Here, he would rattle his arms until his jowls shook. "Like certain seizure victims who collapse only if there is a couch nearby or a patch of soft grass, the bombs seemed to hunt out safe places to fall."

. . .

THE FIRST BLAST was a direct hit on the rock formation at the far end of town, and the percussion caused a shower of dust and plaster to fall from the hotel's walls. Leon ran from his post near the door and across the sand to the water's edge. A great slab had fallen from one corner of the Esperanza, and furrows riddled the walls.

Leon knew then what was going to happen. The bombs would not strike the hotel, but the decaying building, terribly over-crowded, was going to fall.

With the second detonation, windows exploded and the hotel swayed dangerously. A tide of people came rushing out of the doors, leaping off the balconies, crashing through the few remaining windows. They hurried across the beach, many of them holding hands—dragging along their children and the others they loved. Frightened and howling, they ran from the building.

Leon ran alone and dove into the water, seconds ahead of the others. He swam out to the reefs, where he discovered a smooth rock on which to rest his feet. It was from there that he watched cracks rip across the surface of the hotel's white stucco and the great vines shake loose and fall like nets over the fleeing people. The Hotel Esperanza endured just long enough to avoid becoming an agent of death, then it shuddered, rumbled, and collapsed. Its walls tumbled into the cobblestone street, across the moonlit beach, and onto the roof of the neighboring bakery, decimating the little building, extinguishing the light of the yellow window.

It was with the destruction of the lighted window that Benjamin would end his story of the bombing of La Boca.

Leon's story, however, had not yet reached its conclusion.

His strength had crumbled along with the edifice, and the explosion that followed shook him from his perch and sent him tumbling through the water, which was now crowded with people. Beneath the waves and the fluttering legs of swimmers, Leon struggled to surface, but struck his head against the very stone on which he had stood, and then, rising a second time, was kicked unknowingly by a swimmer and sank once more. His lungs ached, his limbs grew weary—he feared that he would drown. And then the white and bloated body of Joe Brogan appeared before him. Across the ghastly face stretched the lurid smile of death. Brogan's arms embraced Leon, squeezing the air from his lungs, pulling him down into darkness.

Leon thrust against the ocean floor a final time, and in an instant he was above water and breathing. The tide had been pushing him toward the shore all along, and the water now barely covered his head. He swam a few yards until his feet touched bottom, and he rested, panting and coughing, his open mouth just above the ocean's surface.

The bombing raid had ended. Already people began to appear on the beach. More swam past Leon or waded slowly forward. Names were being called and responses were shouted back. "Over here," yelled one man. "I'm all right," a woman called. The rubble of the hotel made a dark and jagged mound, which lent to it an air of the ancient, and momentarily Leon saw the shore as the explorers had labeled it: the New World. As he watched the exhausted men and women crawl out of the water, he felt connected to people of long ago, those who had experienced a wobble in their legs as the earth they knew to be flat became suddenly round, and then a lurch in their stomachs as the world began to spin.

Then someone called his name. "I'm all right," he yelled back, and he swam through the dark waters to the sandy slope, where he emerged from the sea—a good man.

A Note About the Author

Robert Boswell was born in Sikeston, Missouri, and educated at the University of Arizona in Tucson. His previous work includes a novel, *Crooked Hearts,* and a collection of stories, *Dancing in the Movies.* He has taught creative writing at the University of Arizona and Northwestern University. At present, he is an assistant professor of English at New Mexico State University and teaches in the Warren Wilson MFA Program for Writers. He lives with his wife, Antonya Nelson, and their daughter, Jade, in Las Cruces.

A Note on the Type

This book was set in Janson, a typeface long thought to
have been made by the Dutchman Anton Janson, who was
a practicing type founder in Leipzig during the years 1668–
1687. However, it has been conclusively demonstrated that
these types are actually the work of Nicholas Kis (1650–
1702), a Hungarian, who most probably learned his trade
from the master Dutch type founder Dirk Voskens. The
type is an excellent example of the influential and sturdy
Dutch types that prevailed in England up to the time Wil-
liam Caslon (1692–1766) developed his own
incomparable designs from them.

Composed by Creative Graphics, Inc., Allentown, Penn-
sylvania. Printed and bound by R. R. Donnelley & Sons,
Harrisonburg, Virginia. Designed by Peter A. Andersen.